Green Spirit Project

At EDGE Science Fiction and Fantasy Publishing, our carbon footprint is higher than we want it to be and we plan to do something about it. For every tree EDGE uses in printing our books, we are helping to plant new trees to reduce our carbon footprint so that the next generation can breathe clean air, keeping our planet and its inhabitants healthy.

Of Wind and Sand

by
Sylvie Bérard

Translated by
Sheryl Curtis

EDGE SCIENCE FICTION AND FANTASY PUBLISHING

AN IMPRINT OF HADES PUBLICATIONS, INC.

CALGARY

Of Wind and Sand
Copyright © 2009

Edge Science Fiction and Fantasy Publishing
An Imprint of Hades Publications Inc.
P.O. Box 1714, Calgary, Alberta, T2P 2L7, Canada

In house editing by Richard Janzen
Interior design by Brian Hades
Cover Concept by Justyn Perry
ISBN: 978-1-894063-19-7

EDGE Science Fiction and Fantasy Publishing and Hades Publications, Inc.
acknowledges the ongoing support of the Alberta Foundation for the Arts and
the Australian Council for the Arts for our publishing programme.

Library and Archives Canada Cataloguing in Publication

Bérard, Sylvie, 1965-
[Terre des autres. English]
    Of wind and sand / by Sylvie Bérard ; translated by Sheryl Curtis.

Translation of: Terre des autres.
ISBN: 978-1-894063-19-7

    I. Curtis, Sheryl, 1953- II. Title.

PS8553.E6225T4713 2008   C843'.54   C2008-904909-8

FIRST EDITION
(r-20080318)
Printed in Canada
www.edgewebsite.com

PROLOGUE

I 'm an old woman now. My memory isn't what it used to be. Images are jumbled in my head. The memories are piled up like file folders accidently dropped, then hastily recovered — the contents mixed into random folders. To all outward appearances everything is in order but, in reality, it's only an illusion created from chaos.

I've lived too long for one single human being.

Everything I know about how and when we arrived on this planet is a result of what I've been told. I was still a frozen embryo when the crew landed here — waiting to be thawed.

Mars II wasn't the crew's planned destination. It was just where they landed! And to mark the occasion they decided my birth was to be an appropriate symbolic gesture marking their arrival — like popping a bottle of champagne to celebrate a happy occasion, or, more to the point, like wolves marking their territory. Or something like that.

Although my test tube spent all of its time in liquid nitrogen, I do not recall ever feeling cold. As I grew up, I noted that the adults around me treated the 'cold' with a great deal of respect, like some sort of fallen, long-gone god. In the desert that is Mars II we must endure the heat of day in protective suits and, at night, suffer the lack of enough ventilation to dry our damp sheets.

We view the sun as our enemy and we treat it with the respect it deserves.

But I've digressed. Nine months after the mother ship landed on this planet, which the natives called Siexlth, I was the 'born' — the first of a clutch of fifty new babies — all screaming their lungs out, surrounded by a molten, hostile desert. Born in a world made for darztls!

Obviously, I have no recollection of the festivities that accompanied my birth!

I do know that there's always been sand in my life. Sand in the depths of the mother ship where my family lived, sand that clogged gears, scratched at throats, settled beneath eye lids.... As a child, when I was sent out to play in the desert, at dawn or dusk, I could place my toys on the ground and watch them grow into sand castles all on their own, shapes tortured by the scorching wind.

I saw my first darztl when I was five. My parents were part of the mother ship elite and, as such, among the first families to mingle with the natives in everyday affairs. They never took me with them. But when they came home, I'd hear them talking about everything they'd seen, about the monstrous creatures that looked like large lizards standing on their hind legs. I'd listen to them in silence. When they knew I was there, they'd talk about how everyone loved their neighbors. When I spied on them in secret, I'd hear them make less flattering comments about the native darztls, describing the fear and disgust they inspired. Occasionally I overheard them talking about assimilation and extermination. None-the-less, regardless of what people said about them — good or bad — these creatures fasci-nated me. And as soon as I got a chance, I browsed through the databanks, learning about reptiles, with or without feet, ovi-, vivi- or ovoviviparous, water-dwelling, desert-dwell-ing, venomous or not, the words sounding like so many magic formulas to my child's ears.

Then, one day my parents told me we would be moving near the darztls. A few days earlier, my father and mother had discussed the possibility of bringing me with them, and my mother had laid down the law. As long as I had to grow up on this inhospitable planet, I should be taught the lay of the land as quickly as possible. The lay of the land... I knew that my parents and their group hoped to learn *that* through contact with extraterrestrials, making the most of our stay to find out everything they could about the indigenous species.

It was obviously clear to the ship's leaders that our temporary stay on this planet, presumably to repair our equipment, might turn into a permanent settlement. In their wisdom, they thought it best to get to know those they already thought of as the enemy. I understood all this, as a child does, not conceptually but as a result of the conspiratorial tone my parents used when talking.

On the first evening of a cultural exchange, which was to last three local months, I slipped into the reception room where all of the dignitaries, human and non-human, had gathered. I threaded my way through the crowd to the head table where the hosts and their guests sat and studied my first native. It took my breath away.

I must have been thinking out loud because as soon as I thought, *he's beautiful,* the adults in my immediate vicinity started to laugh. The darztls wanted to know the reason for the sponteaneous outbreak and my father, who was sitting at the head table with my mother, simply remarked 'baby talk'! His translator repeated the phrase using a similar idiom from the local language. I didn't understand why my father hadn't repeated what I'd said word for word.

I wasn't scolded for sneaking into the reception room. However, the next morning, my father said, "Don't ever do that again, Chloé. Such affairs are for grown-ups."

We didn't stay with the natives long. My father complained about the heat and my mother couldn't bear to be either too far from humans or too close to those who were not. A long time passed before I saw my next living darztl. But that doesn't mean I didn't regularly visit with them in my dreams.

THE HUMAN PROBLEM

Report from Sielxthblootrd Lmasklz
Special envoy to the humans

The humans are animals. They have no sense of dignity. They live all crammed together, in filthy boxes they call 'houses.' They cling to one another; they travel in herds; they never have a minute to themselves. It's as if they're afraid to be alone. Honestly, this envoy doesn't see how darztls could associate with them. The humans have no manners; they're not civilized. They make an effort to speak our beautiful language using a sophisticated device incapable even of forming sentences. They know nothing of diplomacy and speak with our emissaries as if humans and darztls had raised haavls together.

Human envoys bring us hideous objects and attempt to pass them off as precious gifts. They do not appreciate that Darztl foundries were making beautiful jewelry even before the Human's ancestors crawled out of their oceans. Humans have no sense of decorum. They hide their bodies under motley overalls like those our miners wear. They have no sense of pageantry. Everything is functional and ugly.

Their flesh is frail; they mask their bodies from the slightest ray of liirzt. The day star is hazardous to them, and makes their skin turn red and blister as if it had been burned by acid. They are soft and weak and can be hurt by the smallest of objects. Their flesh does not regenerate. Their bodies could kill them at any time. They are powerless.

If they have a culture, this envoy has seen little sign of it — especially when the humans welcomed him with a ceremony of atrocious singing, which lasted for far too many hours, punctuated by grotesque limb movements, which they call danse, and followed by an interminable speechifying they pass off as theatre. Humans are only interested in small, trite distractions — much like the celebrations our ancestors performed when hunting was good. As for their scribbling...

Humans are parasites. They live off other species. When they first landed on this planet, the darztls helped them — showing them where it was cooler, where there was water. These creatures need so much water, it's no surprise that a nauseating liquid pours off them when they're hot. These Darztls helped them find food. The humans can't tell edible food from that which is poisonous. They would have died but for darztls. Everything possible was done to help them survive their stay on Sielxth. And, of course, they took advantage of the situation to settle, scattering their metallic boxes everywhere on the sand. Humans are vermin. They're invasive, spreading out all over Remldarztl, nibbling away at this world.

Humans are liars. They must not be believed. They are not passing through. Their claims of staying only as long as it might take to repair their flying machine are false. They are still here. Obviously they never intended to leave Sielxth. Either that, or they changed their minds after seeing our beautiful world.

The time this envoy spent with humans has at least served one purpose: to teach darztls that they should never trust this disgusting species. They're a perverted, hypocritical lot. One day they say one thing; the next day, when they think no one is watching, they do the opposite.

For this darztl it is abundantly clear: if we don't stop them soon, the humans will be here to stay. They'll infiltrate everywhere, them and their dirty, noisy offspring. These humans will settle in, taking up more and more room, corrupting the space and the culture here.

For this reason, after lengthy investigation and consideration, this envoy has arrived at the following terrible, but unavoidable, conclusion: the humans must be forced to leave. This is no time to cordially welcome a stranger, no time for mutual assistance among species. All contact with these creatures must be cut off. They must be isolated, allowed to starve in an oasis. They will not last long. They will give up and leave.

These humans, however, are slow to understand. Their thinking processes are limited, ideas flow slowly in their minds. And to make matters worse, they're stubborn.

This darztl proposes that, while burning their bridges, we take the opportunity to seize human property and individuals. This will serve as a guarantee in case others refuse to listen to reason. And, as additional insurance, this envoy suggests that the captured humans be put to work. They can help manufacture the weapons we will use against those who must now be considered enemies. It's not a matter of being cruel — just practical. It would not be wise to make the human hostages work in the foundries. It would be kinder to them and certainly more judicious to send them to the mines, those icy holes where the humans have been authorized to extract this planet's metal, supposedly for their space vehicle. Humans like the cold and they will be more comfortable and useful there. In this way, it will be easier to control the captives and they will be put to work for the benefit of Remldarztl.

Should any free humans refuse to listen to reason, it will be easy to turn the captives against their own kind.

But this envoy is convinced that they will never go to such an extreme.

If darztls are a little less accommodating than they have been to date, they will show these strangers that the hospitality of Remldarztl has limits that should not be transgressed.

And the humans will either go back where they came from or travel on to where they claimed to be heading.

A TIME FOR WAR

The wars they will
be fought again
The holy dove
be caught again
bought and sold
and bought again
the dove is never free.
Leonard Cohen, "Anthem"

First I found the silver bracelet, then farther along, behind a rock, the darztl. He was sprawled across a rocky path. His black blood formed a viscous puddle between the stones, the liquid flowing from a wicked gash in his crest, which had been partially scalped down to the nape of his neck. His skin hung in folds under his scales, which possibly meant that he was chilled to the bone despite the desert heat. I must say that it was a particularly cloudy day, a rare event in that region, and his species was used to wallowing under a blazing sun. Moreover, it was obvious that he'd tried to climb the small hill, in an effort to draw closer to the rays of the sun, but hypothermia had probably drained the last of his strength.

A few yards away, more resilient than his rider had been, an equusaur rooted out a few rare shoots that straggled between pebbles. It looked at me with its strange pivoting pupils and I clapped my hands several times while noisily scraping the ground with my foot. The animal fled, in-as-much as on can ascribe 'fleeing' to an equusaur's lumbering gait. Although a frightened equusaur could easily tear apart a human with its enormous claws, they are also incredibly craven. Doubtless this one would either die or wander alone for the rest of its days, rejected by all the equusaur herds it would come across, smelling a little too domesticated for them. But I was hardly going to burden myself with a dangerous animal that wasn't even edible!

I turned back to the darztl. He hadn't budged. His skin was so thick there was no way to tell if his heart was beating beneath it. Even if I were to examine him, I would have had trouble finding his pulse — and there was no way I was going to touch him, at least not without preparing.

I hadn't seen the usual hunting trophies, which those of his species took such pride in, hanging from his mount. He wore no breastplate or honorific jewelry on his naked body. But I couldn't rely on that. Maybe someone had stripped him. Maybe he had fallen into disgrace and they'd been taken back from him — that would have explained why he was so far from his kind. Perhaps he'd long since lost those he'd once owned — he did seem very old, his crest almost completely worn down by the sand-laden desert wind, and his body no longer seemed to be bothered with regenerating its youthful beauty.

For my own safety, I cut off his arms and legs. Blood spewed, then quickly slowed to a trickle.

Snce their vital organs regenerate, unless you chop them up into tiny bits, the only easily inflicted mortal wounds are those delivered to their crests. That's why they never turn their backs to us.

Mutilations do cause them pain, of course — and just because they're our enemies I'm not going to believe those fables that describe them as demons that feel no pain — but everything *grows back.*

I would have cut off his tail as well, but someone had beaten me to it. Either that or he'd done it himself in a desperate effort to survive. It had already started to grow out into a brownish stump that would doubtless never recover its previous splendor.

Our dissection and vivisection of darztls during our first days on the planet revealed that their regenerative abilities diminish as they age. Since then, we've given up trying to borrow this extraordinary biological ability from them, after observing that, while we share the same amino acids, their genetic code is far too different from ours.

This one failed to move as I cut him or react when I slipped a burlap bag over his head and wrapped a chain around him. After that, I painfully dragged the darztl over the rugged soil and dumped him into the back of my jeep. In the solar stillness of the trailer, the oldest of the fruit I had gathered in recent days had finally fermented in the torrid heat — for me, if not for the darztl, it was very hot. I poured a cupful of the syrupy liquid into the vehicle's tank. The jeep gave a series of alcoholic belches, which seldom bothered me anymore, and started.

I headed off for my home, carefully avoiding the areas where I noted patrols, as if it were a day just like any other and normal for me to cart off a darztl rather than chop its repugnant body into little pieces and spread them around the boiling desert.

§ § §

For me, since I knew where I had decided to make my home, the site seemed obvious and I was always surprised that I hadn't been flushed out yet. I had to admit that the area was not particularly appealing and people rarely visited me. Off in the distance, I saw the pierced rock and the numerous furrows that led to it. I constantly changed the route I took so as not to make the road to my grotto too obvious. As for the jeep, its dusty carcass blended in well with the dozens of piles of debris strewn about the makeshift scrap metal yard at the edge of the green zone, and I walked the rest of the way on foot. I'd improved the motor with various parts I'd scavenged, but I'd taken pains not to touch the exterior, not wanting to make it too attractive to others. Since the mines — located in darztl territory — had closed, we recovered everything we could, but we'd never managed to make a profit from recycling rusted metal. No one ever came here to stock up anymore.

I hauled the darztl up to the entrance, then pulled him even higher, to the top of the rocky plateau, using a chain and lever. If he'd been conscious, such treatment would have squeezed colorful grimaces from him — or at least chromatic variations on his skin that I could have considered as such. Suddenly, I was afraid I'd made a mistake and only captured a dead darztl. And what use was the cadaver of an old bipedal lizard to me? Others wouldn't have been as fussy as I was and would have taken the opportunity to replenish their larders. But I always felt my bile rise at the thought of eating a creature with the same IQ as mine, even though his civilization had done its best to annihilate mine.

Once I reached the top of the plateau, I lowered the creature into a natural well that had dried up long ago. I knew it ended at the same level as the cave I lived in. From inside, I could reach the darztl to administer first aid, threading my way through hallways that were too narrow and hollowed out of rock that was too hard for him to ever hope to follow me — either to attack me or flee. For a good part of the day the pit, which was relatively wide, was bathed in sun and a cold-blooded creature wouldn't be too uncomfortable there. The rest of the time, I'd make a fire for him, or he could make one for himself once his stumps were functional again.

I climbed back down outside. When I reached my quarters, I undid my suit. I was drenched, as much from my recent exertions as from the naturally suffocating climate of the region. My suit protected me against the strength of the sun, but certainly not against heatstroke.

By the time I reached the bottom of the pit, the darztl still hadn't moved. Attaching the chain that was wrapped tightly around him to a rock arch — even in this condition, he could still crush me under his weight — I removed the burlap bag that covered his head and stretched him out as gently as possible on the rock, leaving part of his body in the shade. The cavern reeked of decomposing reptile. The corpse of the previous occupant had rotted there for four days. In a last-ditch effort to escape from the pit, my earlier prisoner had attempted to climb the too-high, too-steep walls. Handicapped by his stumps, which I had never allowed to grow very long, he had crashed to the floor. Most likely, he could have survived such a fall if a

pointy rock hadn't gashed his crest deeply. I'd discovered
him in that state. The poor beast had died in vain, namely,
before he was of any use at all to me. I wanted to make
sure that didn't happen again.

For his crest, I made a makeshift bandage soaked with
a sort of indigenous aloe that helped heal human wounds.
Would the plant have the same effect on this reptile? I had
no idea.

When evening fell, I lit a fire in the pit and watched over
the darztl. He still hadn't moved, but he had started
moaning in his sleep. I prepared a small amount of broth
and poured a few drops into his maw. He didn't respond,
but I thought I saw the color of his wattle change slightly.

§ § §

My darztl was doing better. His eyes remained shut,
but his mouth would open spontaneously when I fed him.
I prepared broth for him, as well as small, uncooked animals
that I chopped into digestible pieces. The most disgusting part of his presence was the sanitary aspect, but I had
placed him near a narrow crevasse so deep that I never
heard his feces hit bottom. And moreover, they were rather
infrequent since the darztl metabolism, which is incredibly
efficient, recovers almost everything. That was one of the
reasons why their species had survived so long on this
inhospitable planet. His limbs were not growing back
quickly, a sure sign that he was in a bad way, but his major
wound was gradually closing. Often, in his sleep, he would
mutter things, things I obviously didn't understand. Once
or twice, however, I thought I could make out a few words,
but I told myself it was just my imagination.

One evening he finally opened his eyes. It must have
been a good ten days since he'd been at the bottom of his
pit, ten days I'd been watching over him, that I'd been
cosseting him, instead of finishing him off. I was busy
sorting through the small objects I harvested in the
surrounding areas and sold at the base camp, so I didn't
immediately feel his eyes on me. When I looked up, I
jumped imperceptibly, but I forced myself to remain
impassive and go back to my work. I'd choose my own

time. A few minutes later, when I looked up again, he seemed to have gone back to sleep.

Over the course of the following days, he spent more and more time awake, but I never showed any interest in his presence, apart from caring for his vital needs — sun, heat, food, drink... elimination.

"The human is an idiot," were his first words. I shook my head, astonished, convinced I'd misunderstood, but he looked up at me and added, "You're a female, aren't you? Female human, you're an idiot!"

With a single leap, I was on him, my foot crushing one of his mutilated paws. His wattle lost its color. "If anyone here is entitled to insult the other," I said in my fiercest voice, "it's certainly not you, darztl. Get it?"

He shook his head and that too, in addition to the language he had just used, was something he should not have known. Darztls have no need for such a code of communication; as a result of their chameleon-like skin, they're open books to one another. They only communicate among themselves to transmit the most basic data. In a voice filled with pain, he nevertheless found the strength to add, "So if you're not an idiot, you know that a cold-blooded creature doesn't need to keep a heat it doesn't possess. Remove the blanket that forms a screen between my skin and the comfort of the fire."

I brutally tore off the blanket I'd wrapped him in and spun around without even looking at him. That evening, I didn't take him any food or check to see if the fire needed to be rekindled.

The next day, I left very early to sell my stock of darztl knickknacks and bits of metal to the base camp. The base camp was turning into an actual town, with its hodge-podge of stalls, small cafés and dwellings built both on the ground and under it. You could find everything there; you could sell everything there. I traded what I'd picked up in recent weeks, except for the bracelet, jiggling at the bottom of my pocket. I returned to my camp with a small treasure of perishable goods, and spare parts for my jeep and excavating equipment.

§ § §

My darztl had dragged himself over to the last ray of sun left in the cave and, now that the sky had turned dark, he huddled in a corner at the end of the chain that was still wrapped around his body. He must have been frozen and famished. Suddenly, I felt sorry for him and hated myself for being so cruel. When all that is left of us is a tinge of humanity, we either let our enemies live or we kill them, but we don't torture them for no good reason.

I made a fire and prepared the meal for my prisoner and myself. I helped him sit up and leaned him back against the rocky wall. He was ice cold. I took advantage of the opportunity to check the condition of his crest; the gash looked as if it would open up again at any time. He held the bowl between his two upper stubs — they had started to heal and he could use them a little — and if they pained him, his color, which had turned uniformly dull as a result of his poor condition, gave me no indication. I sat down at the other end of the grotto and started to eat in silence, staring at him. He kept his eyes down.

"How did you learn our language?" I finally asked, after swallowing my last mouthful.

He emptied his bowl painfully — I believed that pain must have been shooting through his crest with each mouthful — and looked up "I... I learned it from one of your kind," he finally replied. He spoke rather well.

"Yes, I can see that," I replied impatiently. "What else?"

"From a particular human. One whom I... who spent several yanz... several months with... me."

"You mean one you captured?"

He looked at me again and I could have sworn that a glint of impotence passed through his reptilian gaze.

"If you want. But with her, it was different. She... changed something."

"She made you a better darztl?" I asked, my voice dripping with sarcasm.

"More like a different darztl. It's a bit because of her that the darztl before you became... a traitor to himself and his kind. But, deep down, she really had nothing to do with it. It all came from... from me. I imagine I'd reached that point in my life... Listen, human, I have a story to tell. But I don't know if you have enough grlithz to hear it."

There was a glint of defiance in his wattle. I almost struck him for his insolence and came close to telling him that, as a prisoner, he'd better keep his nasty comments to himself. But I had always found it hard to be mean two days in a row. And since I had him at my mercy, I could afford to be magnanimous.

I settled for sighing and feigning indifference. In actual fact, I was feeling blue and I wanted to hear his tales for reasons too many to list here.

Rliebkl liked his work at the border; it made him feel as if he were free. Like his ancestors had been. Like in the time before. All he had to do was ride under the burning sun, then go back to his warm den, away from everyone. Occasionally he'd make a detour into town, carefully avoiding the mining region, but most of the time he stayed here, in the middle of nowhere, contemplating infinite space and watching the osfts — what the humans called sand squirrels — leap.

Sometimes, he'd capture living humans. That was easy — the pale bipeds were much smaller and significantly slower than he was, even when he was on foot, and far more so when he rode his mount. And when they'd escaped from the mines — which was almost always the case — they ran even slower, of course. He would terrorize them a little, chasing them every which way, then force them towards the closest rocky peak and throw a net over them. After that, it was routine. He'd climb down from his haavl, walk over to his prey, throw it in a bag, recover his precious net and tie his booty to his saddle. The mine provided him with a cage where he could store his prisoner if he didn't want to make the trip to trade it the same day but, most often, in order to unload his burden as quickly as possible, he'd turn the human over to the mine immediately, even if he had to travel by night, shivering in the cold. He didn't want to know what happened to his captive after that. All that mattered was earning enough to live easily, without having to hunt for weeks, even months, if he was frugal.

Then he'd set off again, hunting for his quota of humans. His captives were almost always females. The males, for the most part, had been eliminated as soon as they were captured at the outset. Larger and stronger than the females — in the case of the darztls, the females were the more imposing — they would have been a more effective labor force. However, they seemed to be more naturally inclined to rebellion and escape, which meant that darztls preferred to use females in the mines. In any case, darztl studies had shown that only a few males would be needed to maintain the labor pool, now that they had given up on razzias.

Rliebkl never asked too many questions about the humans he captured. As far as he was concerned it was just a job, like installing solar panels or gathering insects. Their strident screams pained his ears and he was glad for the bag to muffle their unpleasant sounds. He understood nothing of their babbling. Some said that humans had a language, bur personally he'd never managed to make out a single word in all the hackneyed vowels.

One day, during one of his tours of the region, which usually lasted several days, he spotted a human female. In actual fact, it was the trace of her presence that he detected; she must have lit a fire the previous night to cook food. Darztls never ate anything that wasn't raw, but they could easily detect the scent of roasted meat, possibly because it was so foreign to their environment. And taking a closer look, he discovered a trail, footsteps here and there among the pebbles, and a little blood on the stones. Once he detected the presence of a fugitive he had to act quickly; some barely survived the first few days of their flight and collapsed in the desert, dehydrated, injured, or famished. They were worthless to him dead.

He found that one between two rocks. She thought she was carefully hidden but, in fact, she had cut off all means of escape. He wouldn't even have to track her; she was already trapped against the foot of the cliff. But then some-

thing strange happened. Instead of pointlessly trying to flee, she stood right in front of him, a look of challenge in her eyes. At least, given the lack of indicators for human emotions, that's how he interpreted her expression. He cast his net automatically and she didn't try to avoid it or get out from under it — although her efforts would have been in vain since no fugitive had ever gotten away from him. He slipped the bag over the human's head and retrieved his net as he shoved her into the bag, but she didn't fight. He hoisted her up onto his mount, feeling oddly uncomfortable and, rather than setting off for the mine office, he returned to his home, a sort of stone dome where he could bask in the sun on the roof by day and warm himself inside by the fire at night. Once there, he placed the bag directly in the cage and went to sleep in an effort to escape the fugitive's glance, hoping that he would recover his senses the next morning and take her directly to the mine.

The next day, he dragged the bag outside and opened it. He wanted to see what his prey looked like one last time. The human emerged, coughing, glistening with sweat. She stood still, staring at him. As a precautionary measure, he placed a halter around her neck. Apart from the fact that he'd always found them atrociously ugly, he also felt that human beings smelled bad. But this one, after 12 hours in the bag, outdid them all. He threw a few handfuls of sand at her to clean her up, and she started coughing even more. Afterwards, telling himself that she must be hungry, he tied her to a tree and threw a few pieces of fruit at her, which she did not touch. Yet when he came back, the fruit had disappeared. Without admitting it, he had already secretly decided to keep her. He knew that some of his kind kept them at home, but that practice had never really been encouraged. Moreover, this one didn't belong to him; she'd escaped from the mine and that mine employed him as a tracker. He was required to take her back. He would only keep her a few days, to relieve his boredom. His species was a rather solitary one, yet his kind occasionally experienced a curious need for closeness. Generally, though, they sought the company of other darztls.

The days turned into weeks and the weeks into months, months during which a strange bond developed between Rliebkl and the human.

He spoke our language rather well, all in all, but he had problems with our vowels. That, and he inserted words from his own language in his tale, leaving me clueless as to their meaning. The story ended there that evening. My prisoner was still very weak and my recent treatment of him had done nothing to help him regain his strength. Apparently his lengthy tirade had exhausted him, since he fell asleep while talking to me. Yet I felt that he had plunged into a sleep that was more peaceful than any he'd had in recent days. I chased that thought away. I was cruel only out of need and gentle only because it was easier to learn the truth.

§ § §

The next day I rushed through my chores and went back to see my darztl, who was dozing in the sun. He opened one eye and I would have bet that he gave me the same amused glance as Scheherazade who had just baited her sultan! I smiled at him briefly.

"I find your story very distracting, darztl. And since I don't have much to do, I've come to hear the rest."

"Well, we got to the part where Rliebkl found himself, without quite knowing how it happened, stuck with one of your kind," he said in a voice that sounded more assured than it had the night before.

I'd heard fables about some of our kind being kidnapped and kept captive, giving the darztls biddable servants, but I'd never believed them. I preferred to think that our enemies killed their prisoners after torturing them to find out our plans. I mentioned this to my prisoner.

"We need them too much for the mines," he objected.

"But they say you reproduce very quickly and in large numbers. Why burden yourselves with humans — who are always anxious to escape — when there are so many of you? Unless there aren't as many of you as it seems?"

I hadn't been very subtle. He scented the trap. If I were to force him to admit something that would harm his kind, I could trade that information, far more valuable than the metal I scavenged, for essential goods.

"It's not a question of numbers — although our lives are shorter than human lives — it's a matter of comfort. We don't survive for long in the mines — it's too cold there — unless we use heated suits, but that's too complicated. That's why the Remldarztl — which is our name for our people — have never made much use of metals. We left what you call the stone age behind us a long time ago, and yet we're basically satisfied. But you left fully operational mines behind you, along with workers we find it easy to keep captive, so we make the most of it."

He stopped, then started again. "You can go and sell that information to anyone you want. I don't care."

I didn't want to get into politics. It was the rest of his story that interested me, even though I found the story-teller extremely irritating.

"And that girl who escaped from the mines... she never tried to get away after she was captured?"

"No, but I think it's because Rliebkl rarely gave her the opportunity and because, the rest of the time, she was intelligent enough to know that she wouldn't get far. At least, not at the beginning."

First, he treated her foot, or rather the bloody wound that had once been her foot. In the mine, they start by cutting off the right foot of every captive, to prevent them from escaping or, at the very least, to slow them down. Walking on her stump had worn the flesh down to the bone. Rliebkl wrapped the stump in leaves that were supposed to have medicinal properties. Soon, bright pink flesh replaced the scabs. She expressed her needs, first using the few words she knew in his language and gradually translating into her own. Soon they were speaking a strange sort of creole composed of the labials and clicks of his language and the sing-song intonations of hers.

The hardest part was having to go back out hunt-
ing since he couldn't be sure she wouldn't try to escape.
When he started to tie her up in the cage, in the very
back of his dwelling, she looked at him the same way she
had the first day. He also had to leave her enough to
survive on for one day, two days, a week — it was crazy
how much water she needed. He didn't muzzle her. She
could have shouted herself hoarse, there wasn't much
risk anyone could hear her in the middle of the desert,
through the thick walls. He had no choice — he couldn't
very well take her with him. He couldn't carry her in
a bag tied to his mount any more than he could let her
sit astride the saddle in front of him. Moreover, anyone
he met, on seeing him accompanied by a human female,
would have had their suspicions aroused — even if he
dragged her behind him on a rope, like a prisoner of war.
In any case, she would have held him up — in a chore
that he did less and less willingly and found disgusting,
needless to say.

"You've just condemned another," she said as soon
as he returned. With an exasperated wave, Rliebkl in-
structed her to shut up and, after releasing her, he sent
her out to pick roots for their supper. She had always
come back.

"Still, you can't imagine that she was satisfied being
your little pet, that she was happy with her lot?"

"Do you think I'm happy right now?"

"I only do to you what you've done to my kind. You're
only alive because I need to hear your story..."

I stopped talking too late. The darztl's wattle turned
emerald green. I didn't want to look like someone who
was interested. If he realized the power he held over me,
he'd want to bargain, to trade his fantasies for his freedom, or a little more comfort.

"Fine, I've got things to do," I added hastily. "It's not
like I'm bored, but while I'm listening to your stories,
I'm falling behind with my chores. I'll come back later
to bring you some food and light a fire." And I walked
out of the cave.

That evening I did as I said I would. I took care of my guest's vital needs, without saying more than two or three words to him. I kept this up for a few days. The darztl knew enough not to insist.

§ § §

"She told Rliebkl a story in which neither my people nor yours played a good role," he said after a few days. He must have spent the entire time looking for an opening to make me an attentive audience once again.

"Oh, yeah?" I said distractedly, checking his bandage, which I had already inspected a minute earlier. I also examined his mutilated limbs, which I'd have to cut off again as soon as they posed a new threat to me.

"She wasn't born in the mines, of course, she wasn't that young, and she hadn't been a victim of the razzias, the raids. She'd been taken there by force."

"You mean, instead going there of her own free will?" I laughed nastily. But I didn't want to set off on that tangent again. I wanted him to tell his tale until the end. I sighed. "Fine, tell me."

"You must realize that, in the past, several years before the story I'm telling you, contact had been established between darztls and humans. Our two species didn't trust one another, but they weren't at war like they are now. We suffered patiently, waiting for you to leave. Both sides lived in a sort of precarious peace, one in the desert and the other in the temperate zone, trying to avoid confrontation. At least that's what my kind thought."

"That's what we humans thought, too. But I don't feel like hearing you talk politics, darztl, so just stick to the facts. Your story is fine and dandy, but what I want to know, above all, is why you're so close to the temperate zone."

"I'm getting to it, I'm getting to it."

"Tell me where you come from," Rliebkl asked his captive for the umpteenth time, using the lingo they'd developed.

That evening, she was sitting at his feet, near the hearth, as he often demanded her to do. Occasionally, he had the impression that she obeyed his every whim because she had abandoned her own free will the day he had captured her. Other times, he felt as if she were testing him, challenging him to go further, to debase himself in the filth of another creature. Most often he told himself she was only looking for the right time to stab him in the back and escape. The human's body was a mystery to him, although he gradually found it less repugnant — not enough to touch unless it was absolutely necessary, but enough to tolerate her presence on a daily basis.

Most of the time, she avoided his questions when they were too personal, or she responded evasively, providing just enough information to keep Rliebkl from losing his temper. But that time, she'd been more voluble.

"I wasn't always a prisoner in the mines, of course. I was once a free woman and I was once important to my people. At least, that's what I thought."

"If you were important, they would have done everything possible to get you back, wouldn't they?"

"Do you think so? You picked me up and I don't think I'm all that important in your eyes."

He whipped her with his tail, but not very forcefully. He simply wanted to remind her that she had no right to speak to him like that. She continued as if nothing had happened.

"The day the darztls went to war against the humans, I was in your territory. Fool that I was, I believed our small group of emissaries could postpone the confrontation, even prevent it. I had thrown myself into the lion's den along with my small band of idealists since I hoped, as the others did, that we'd get out of it soon, peaceful and triumphant. Instead, dozens of darztls entered our quarters by force one beautiful morning and threw us into the mines with the mining company employees who were left behind. The rest of the colony retreated. No one ever came looking for us. The only new human faces we saw after that were the new consignments of captives brought in to build up the human labor force."

The female stopped talking, as if out of breath following her lengthy tirade. It was the first time she had spoken

*so long since Rliebkl had captured her. Most of the time
she settled for saying a few words about her daily chores.
The darztl had found it somewhat hard to understand her
speech in a language he still spoke poorly, but he believed
he understood the essentials. Later, he would have an
opportunity to put the pieces into place and understand
what he had not caught the first time. In any case, the story
was not unknown to him, although this was the first time
he considered it from the human point of view.*

*"People tried to stop us from setting out on our mission.
I think that, among those who insisted the most, some knew
how the story would end. But no one said anything to us;
no one made us realize that, in the fire of our ardor, we
would go down as the worst of all traitors — spies."*

*"When we arrived at the mine, escorted by armed
darztls, we discovered a slaughterhouse. Lifeless bodies
were strewn about, lacerated, shredded, torn apart. The
mine was in darztl territory, but humans had been given
permission to operate it, when we told you that we needed
raw materials to rebuild our spacecraft. That day, you
parked us in the mine and sealed the entrance. We all
thought that you were leaving us there to die of asphyxi-
ation or starvation. But a few days later the mine was
opened up again. We were too weak to revolt in any convincing manner. You told us that the darztls were no longer
satisfied with serving humans, that the roles had been
reversed and that the humans had lost the war. After a
while, when darztls noticed that fear was no longer enough
to keep us in our place, you started mutilating us to keep
us from escaping."*

*"Darztls welcomed you to our world and you humans
betrayed us. It is said that, at the beginning, you were
like the flowers, decked out in their most beautiful colors
and perfumes, waiting for the fly. But it was a carnivorous
flower and the fly is eaten if it allows itself to be lured in.
You soon showed us your real colors: carnivores that
wanted to gobble up our planet. You never intended to
leave. That's why we did everything we could to chase you
off."*

"By keeping us prisoner? That's a little ironic isn't it?" she started to laugh.

Suddenly, Rliebkl had had enough. His captive had never spoken to him in this tone before and she wasn't about to start today. He got up without a word and threw her into her cage. "But you're the one who wanted to talk," she protested. He made as if to slap her and she fell silent. He then went to lie down quietly by the fire, closing the membrane of his ears in case she dared to start speaking again.

We humans tell another version of the story, but I kept that to myself. People said that the darztls only let us approach so they could get the upper hand and enslave us. They wanted to reduce us to slavery, but we fought back courageously. The history books the tutors use say that we came unarmed, in friendship, and that our hosts took advantage of our trust.

"It's my story against yours, darztl. I'll believe whichever one I want. For now, we're in my home."

"What do you intend to do with me?" he asked suddenly.

"I don't know yet. Once you're no longer of any interest to me, I might kill you. Or I might just abandon you in the desert and leave you to your fate. Or I might hand you over to my kind, so they can extract State secrets from you. I haven't decided."

"If I asked you to take me to my home, would you?"

§ § §

That night I tossed and turned in my bed, in the heat of my dwelling, two feet away from a mutilated darztl, but sleep didn't come. I went over and over my prisoner's question and I was unable to find a good role for me in the story. I was astounded by his insolence, but I had to admit that he had hit the bull's eye. I'd never venture into darztl territory, not with what I knew, not after what had happened! People I loved had fallen into darztl hands, starting with my sister, and no one had ever seen any of them again. Their razzias had carried off some of the best members of our colony. All that remained were the bloody, decomposing feet that our enemies came to jettison by the hundreds at the edge of our territory, as if to add to the fear they inspired in us.

The next day, as I combed through the desert looking for forgotten debris, I imagined myself crossing over the rocky plain, heading for darztl territory. I could stand before them, hands open, consenting, filled with good will and abnegation; they'd just throw me to the ground with a single blow of a powerful tail, cut off my foot and then pitch me into the mines before I could say a single word. That's what they had done to our emissaries ten years earlier, and to the mine employees who had been there under an agreement between our two races. And as for us, now we'd do the same thing, I had to admit it, to the first darztl to show his nose in our territory, even if he came crawling to us. Wasn't that what I'd done to my captive, before even asking what his intentions were?

"You know, darztl," I said to him one evening as we were eating, each in a corner of our cave, "with all your propaganda, you avoided my question. How did you come to be in the vicinity?"

"Oh," he said in a disinterested tone, a perfect replica of the one I used to address him, "I agreed to take her to her home."

That shocked me. He was insulting me, but I decided not to have noticed.

"Oh really?" I said, voice dripping with sarcasm. "Yet you were alone when I found you."

He looked away and remained silent for a moment. His body slouched and his wattle turned brownish. He started to tell me about it, as if each word pained him.

One day, Rliebkl put his human back in the cage once she had completed her chores. Because he needed a little solitude. He took refuge, as usual, on the roof of his dwelling, where he warmed himself in the sun. Lost in thought, he wondered what would happen to him and his captive, fully aware that the situation could not last forever and that he had to either set her free or risk sentencing her to death. If he treated her harsher and harsher, it was because he was trying to stifle the opposite emotion. He felt friendship for her, a bond that went beyond that of a darztl and a pet — such as a haavl or drotz. Once again, yesterday, he had struck her cruelly, using some clumsiness on her part as an excuse, but it was simply because her increasingly tender gaze was starting to move him. He didn't want to be loved by her — he wanted to be feared. That would be better for everyone concerned. Obviously that was why his kind kept the humans at a distance, keeping contact with them to a minimum, hitting them to make them work better and feeding them so they wouldn't die too quickly. When they mutilated the humans, they kept them from being able to run too far away, of course, but they were also reminding themselves each day that humans were not their kind, that they were weak, that they were unable to regenerate.

He didn't see Arhbkl, another mercenary who lived in the region, arrive. The last time she had dropped by, he had barely had time to throw his captive into her cage. Arhbkl absolutely couldn't be allowed to see his prisoner moving freely about the house. Fortunately this time, the human was properly locked up, yet if he'd seen the other approach, he would have locked himself inside as well, pretending to be gone. But it was too late; she was there greeting him with a ripple of her crest. All he could do was respond politely, climb down from his roof and offer her the customary hospitality. Darztls dealt with solitude well, but they were required to welcome their kind when they knocked at the door. Even for a female, Arhbkl was immense. She had to stoop a little to enter Rliebkl's home.

"Rliebkl is fortunate. Arhbkl is just coming back from the mine where she traded an escapee for infinite riches." She opened her bag, showing off everything she had received for her most recent prey.

As he was pouring a generous glass of hiilslt, a wine made from an indigenous cactus, she walked over to the cage to look at the human, whose eyes were wide in fear. She surely realized that each intrusion into their private life threatened the balance of their existence. If someone were to discover that Rliebkl was secretly housing a human, he would have to return her to her original owners. He could always bargain to keep her, but he could never settle for that because it would completely discredit him as a tracker.

"It's amazing how all humans look alike, isn't it Rliebkl? This one, for example, looks like the one Arhbkl just caught. Same color, same texture. And Arhbkl would swear it's the same one she saw here the other day!"

Rliebkl made an effort to control the chromatic surge of his wattle. Arhbkl was a busybody, poking her tongue in everywhere, tasting all your little secrets, destroying your reputation in the blink of an eye.

"Ah yes? That's what Arhbkl thought? To be perfectly honest, Rliebkl had barely looked. He had better things to do than waste his time looking at a human."

His words bordered on the impolite, but Arhbkl took it without comment. And without losing her cool.

"If Rliebkl wants, Arhbkl can take charge of the human. Arhbkl has just traded one for a very good price. She can take the worker back to the mine and pay Rliebkl handsomely right now."

He declined the offer, arguing that he preferred to take his own merchandise to the mine counter. He was relieved when the other had not insisted. A heavy weight lifted from his shoulders when he saw that she wouldn't be staying long. Already she was picking up her belongings, claiming that she had work to do. But as he was seeing her out, when they were out of the female's hearing, she added, "Does Rliebkl want some advice? He shouldn't keep humans too long. It's not healthy. And he shouldn't keep them in his house. They stink."

Then she jumped into her saddle and rode off on her haavl, her tail beating against the animal's flank.

Rliebkl had a horrific premonition. Arhbkl was nothing but trouble. If she went to the mine counter, she'd find out that he hadn't brought any prisoners in for weeks. Worse yet, if she waited, she'd see that he wasn't taking in the human she had seen at his place. When he went back inside, he saw that his captive, in the back of her cage, shared his concerns — he had gradually learned to decipher the expressions on her face, which barely changed color, but hollowed or swelled with her emotions.

Rliebkl felt feverish and devastated. He paced back and forth, looking for a solution. "She'll denounce us, the mining company will want you back. And I can't allow that. You've escaped before. Needless to say, they'll cut off your leg if they don't kill you, in order to punish you for being outside so long. On the other hand, I can't very well keep you where everyone can find you. I'd be too afraid. We have to leave."

She grimaced. "You know, as far as I'm concerned, being held prisoner here or at the mining company is all the same to me. In any case, I have no future. In the underground corridors of the mine, extracting ore for the enemy, I'll see the sun less often, that's for sure. But at least I'd be with my own kind and I wouldn't feel like some household pet." Her voice had taken on a tone of defiance. He looked at her, dumbfounded. What was wrong with him, tearing himself apart over the fate of a foreigner who belonged to a species that had nothing in common with his own? After all he'd done for her, after all the risks he'd taken, this was how she thanked him?

Rliebkl walked away from the cage because right then he would have struck her hard enough to kill her. That evening, he threw her a plate and they ate in silence, each in their own corner. She didn't come to curl up in a ball at his feet near the fire, and they went to bed without exchanging a single word. During the night, he heard her murmuring, like humans sometimes did when they were sad, but he closed his membranes, hardening himself against his captive's pain.

*At dawn the next day, he grabbed the human and
shoved her into a bag. Throwing her on his haavl, he
headed for the mining company.*

"The darztl traded her? After all the time he spent with
her, he sold her to the highest bidder?"

"You'd like my story to finish like that, wouldn't you?
It would leave you with a clear conscience. You'd no
longer ask me how I wound up here. And this ending
would reassure your beliefs in the order of things!"

"And what about you? Do you have a clear conscience?"

He remained silent.

I continued. "Because this is all about you, isn't it. This
is your story you're telling me!"

Without looking at me, he spoke, his voice barely
audible. "In Rliebkl's language, the personal pronouns
humans use have no real meaning."

I pointed an accusing finger at him. "So tell me, did
the darztl in the story have a clear conscience when he
threw his captive into the hell she had escaped from?
What a wonderful way to send her back to her own kind!
And he didn't do it out of any political conviction or
through loyalty to his own species. Not him! But just
because he was afraid to stand up, because he was
ashamed of his allegiances!"

He stood up painfully, using his atrophied arms, and
leaned against a stone. He closed his eyes and stopped
moving. Once his wounds had closed, his limbs regenerated extremely slowly, and were weaker than those I
had cut. I chased away a fleeting wisp of remorse that
was wandering about my mind and chose to ruminate
on my disgust.

§ § §

Over the following days, I had a lot of work and, apart
from feeding him and making a fire, I stayed away from
my darztl. While digging along a hill, I came across a
crevice that looked natural, but turned out to be recessed
stone doorway, its frame carved out of the mound. I was

unable to open the door, of course; it was too heavy for my frail human means, even too much for my old jeep to pull. But using a chisel and a hammer, I managed to dig out the opening enough to slip through. This cavern, no doubt like the one where I lived, had not been produced by geological movements, but by the labor of an intelligent species. Yet unlike my dwelling, which had been pillaged when the first colonists arrived on Mars II, this one had remained intact. This construction, which was certainly old enough to be considered an archeological treasure in the eyes of the darztls themselves, was possibly a temple or a castle, and contained enough ancient treasures to allow me to survive until the end of my days... or to help my kind understand the enemy's civilization.

Unable to decide whether I'd unload my archeological find in small batches that would keep suspicion somewhat at bay, sell the coordinates to our ethnologists or our military strategists, or keep the secret, I resolved to postpone the decision until I'd finished with my darztl. Still, I wanted to take a little souvenir back with me. I settled on some small plates of colored stone depicting darztls in various positions and stuffed them into my bag.

On my way out I took the time to shove a few rocks into the opening I'd made, to keep anyone from discovering my secret temple.

On my way home, I came across two patrollers. Shit! They'd seen my jeep, despite the fact that I always did everything to remain as discrete as possible. They were going to come and hassle me for the metal it contained and they might even try to steal it from me. However, the two individuals — a man and a woman — seemed too agitated to worry about my vehicle. They asked me if I'd seen anything suspicious.

"We're afraid there's a band of darztls in the area," the woman said.

"They've already killed two victims," the man said.

They told me that they'd come across some human bones at the edge of their sector, carefully cleaned by the feathered lizards, those volatile vultures that nested on the peaks of the surrounding hills.

"And what makes you think it was the work of darztls?" I enquired.

"A few miles away, we also discovered some curious symbols, pebbles arranged together, in darztl writing. So darztls have been in the area — and recently, judging by the tracks we found. We can't decipher the message they left, of course, but we photographed the site and we'll get an expert to interpret the symbols.

"And what about the bones? Do you know how long they've been there?"

"Oh, certainly for some time. Two weeks, a month perhaps... But in this godforsaken desert, you can never be sure about anything. Everything turns to dust in the blink of an eye."

"In any case, be careful if you roam around this sector," the man advised me. "What direction are you heading? Would you like us to accompany you?"

I waved vaguely in a direction other than the one I was heading in, and declined the offer politely. If they learned I was hiding the guilty party at my place, I was done for!

§ § §

"Why didn't you tell me you'd killed those men?" I exclaimed when I got home. I'd found my captive in the same position as when I'd left him, huddled against the sun-warmed stone. Occasionally, I wondered what he could possibly spend all those idle hours thinking about. I told myself that perhaps his brain, which was so different from mine, was able to totally disconnect and that he stayed there, in that position, all day, literally without thinking.

He looked at me and said nothing at first. "I'm not the one who killed them," he finally said.

"But you're aware of the story, I'm certain of that. You don't seem surprised."

"How would a human know if I'm surprised, happy or dissatisfied, simply by looking at me? You know nothing about me. You understand nothing about what I am. All you want is for me to tell my story, for me to tell you about her, for me to finally tell you where she is. After that, you'll have nothing more to do but kill me."

I pretended I didn't understand. I still needed him for something else. I held out the stone plates to him.

"Do you have any idea what these are?"

He seemed to stiffen and I concluded that he was astonished. He turned the stone rectangles over and over between his stumps. Passing his new, sensitive skin over their surface. "Where did you find these?"

"It doesn't matter. Do you know what they are?"

He shook his head, almost like a human being.

"You want to know how you can profit from the information these plates contain, don't you?"

"Not that it's any of your business. Just tell me what they are."

"When the human linguists manage to figure out the message contained on these plates," he said gently, "they'll see that the words are perfect for the illustrations."

On most of the plates, I could see some representations of darztls of all sizes in desert settings, sometimes filled with a series of mounds that looked a little like the description I'd been given of darztl homes. On some of them I saw oval shapes that looked a little like eggs, and on several animals I thought I recognized, while others were totally unknown to me.

The darztl continued, "The plates tell of an egg that fell by accident on a distant oasis. A darztl embryo emerged from it. At the beginning, he swam in the water, unaware of the world around him. Gradually, he met all kinds of aquatic animals, but he was unable to imitate any of them. And one day, he followed an animal out of the water and discovered that he could breathe. He set out to tour the world. He encountered all sorts of creatures, and briefly believed that he had found one of his own species, but he failed time and time again. Then, he came across another darztl and he understood that he had found his own kind. But his trip had not been in vain because he knew about the lives of all the other species and he never looked at them the same again."

"It's a metaphor? A religious text?"

"A religious text? No! It's a child's tale. Certain scenes are quite humorous, others are more moving. These plates are very old, and some of them are missing, but the story is recognizable. It's a story that I was told at a very young age, as soon as I left the vivarium."

That revelation struck me like a blow. My prisoner had been a child once. One must never think about one' enemies as children or nothing will ever be the same again. I leapt up.

"And what about the two murdered men? What do you know about that?"

"Well, if you want to know that, I'll have to tell you the end of my story. Are you ready to hear it now? You no longer want to settle for half-truths?"

"Perhaps I do want to hear the story."

"Are you ready to see me in a role other than that of a monster from another world, a demon that eats little children after night falls?"

"Yes, yes, the whole thing. Tell me and let's get this over with."

First, Rliebkl headed off for the mining counter, that's true, intending to trade the female for goods. He'd decided to resolve the problem by getting rid of the human for once and for all. To burst the abscess, so to speak, since he knew it would cost him dearly to leave her. Neither of them had anything to win from this contact — they could only hurt one another. Their species were too different, there were too many tragedies between them for them to ever hope to consider one another as equals.

Then he thought back on the glance she'd given him the first day and that he'd learned to decipher during the time they'd spent together. It hadn't been a look of challenge. Well at least not entirely. It had been resignation. In fact, it was a look challenging him not to resign himself, that revealed a certainty that he would resign himself to do what he had always done. And today, he had proved that look right; he was handing her over, bound hand and foot. That was the way things were.

He pulled on the halter, stopping his haavl. He was at the crossroads. In the one direction lay the mining company, where his captive would be surrounded by her own kind, all united in their slavery. In the other direction lay the desert, and on the other side of it, the human colony. His enemies, her kind. In the middle there was Rliebkl, with his stone house, his life as a tracker, his daily life where nothing would ever be the same, to which he could never return without feeling that he had lost something. So he turned towards the desert, picking up a few supplies on his way, taking into consideration the length of their trip and his traveling companion's lack of endurance.

He rode all day, stopping only when the coolness of twilight flowed over the desert. Chilled to the bone, he stopped near a rocky hill. He made a fire with hidclr — those carnivorous orchids filled with digestive gases that were everywhere in the desert and ignited very easily, burning with a beautiful, lasting flame — and arranged his belongings in as welcoming a manner as possible around their camp. Then he opened the bag that still held the human and placed her gently on the ground. He had untied the rope and she crawled out, visibly out of sorts and hunched over.

"Where are we?"

Those were her first words. Then, noting that they weren't near the mine, she gave him a smile, which faded quickly. He almost found her winsome, despite her ugliness.

"I couldn't," he simply said. "I've decided to take you to your home."

That was the first night they spent together as free beings, without any constraints. The next day, Rliebkl did not put her back in the bag, but let her ride in front of him on his haavl, advising her to hang on.

At the pace at which the animal trotted, they could have crossed the desert in a few days. However, Rliebkl opted for an erratic route to trick any possible pursuers. He doubted that the woman was valuable enough in the mine's eyes to justify capturing her again, but in these times of war, they might know enough secrets about darztl society between them to be hunted down. They rode like this for several days, talking little, but communicating the essentials as ever. The woman told him, laughing, that in the old 20th-century Westerns of her culture, he would have been a tall dark stranger and she would have been a 'white', playing the role of an Indian, and they would have wound up sleeping together in the firelight. This meant nothing to him but he smiled to himself, as he saw what a good mood she was in.

They came across the two men during the evening of the ninth day, or rather, the two men fell on them. Rliebkl had walked off for a moment, looking for water in the string of flowers that grew at the foot of the rocks, leaving the woman resting in the shade of the cliff. She found the sun harder to bear than he did and her skin, even when protected by a heavy cloth during the day, had turned bright red. It was just the opposite for him. At this latitude, large clouds sometimes gathered in the sky and he was cold, even in broad daylight, and had to stuff himself with food in order to warm up. Suddenly, as he was collecting a little water, he heard her cry out. He raced over and found a hairy man practically lying on her, as she tried to fight him off. He struck the man, who landed several yards away clutching his bloody flank. Then suddenly, Rliebkl felt a burning sensation on the back of his neck. He turned around to see a second man holding a knife covered with black blood. His blood. His vision blurred and he collapsed.

He regained consciousness, racked with a violent pain. He had been carefully trussed and thrown into some sort of trailer. He could no longer feel his tail beneath him and decided that they must have tried to drag him by the tail when he was unconscious and that, as a reflex, it had self-amputated — unless they had cut it off in an effort to avoid any unexpected whiplash from that quarter. He looked up, realizing that with the slightest movement, the chain they'd wrapped around his neck reopened the injury that the man had inflicted on his crest, causing it to bleed. The trailer was pulled by a roofless, autonomous vehicle that, although he had never seen one, Rliebkl guessed was some sort of automobile. Raising his head painfully once again, he saw the two men sitting side by side at the front of the vehicle. Suddenly, one of them turned around and saw him. "Well, well, our lizard's awake." Rliebkl didn't see the woman anywhere.

They drove that way for what seemed like hours. When the vehicle stopped, the two men climbed out. Rliebkl played dead, hoping to avoid their attention. He watched the two men walk into a sort of square shack made of stones. Then one of them came back out, headed over to the trailer and climbed into it. He kicked the darztl two or three times, forcing him to cry out in pain. "What did you do with the woman?" Rliebkl asked in a voice strained with suffering, provoking several more kicks. Finally, playing with a silver bracelet he held in his hand, the man said, "We left her behind; she's no more good to us. In fact, her testimony could be very harmful. On the other hand, you're worth a great deal. In your little lizard brain, you have absolutely no idea just how valuable you are. We're going to trade you for a real fortune." The man checked Rliebkl's bonds then, satisfied, went back into the shed.

I showed him the silver bracelet I'd been keeping in my pocket since the day I found it. "It was hers, wasn't it?"

"Where did you find it?"

"Next to you, when I brought you back here. Was it hers?"

"Yes, it was hers. She always wore it, on her left wrist. One day, she told me how she got it. It was like a trade, between blood sisters. United for life, or something like that. She was still a child. The bracelet never left her arm and soon she was no longer able to take it off."

He stared at me. "You have one like it. You look so much like her."

"You're like all the other darztls; you can't tell one human from another. We all look the same to you."

He made no comment about the involuntary irony of my words and gently continued, "Don't play that game with me. Not anymore. You're Solen's sister, aren't you? I knew it the minute I opened my eyes. But I needed to know that Solen's sister was as she had described her on our trip through the desert. She didn't speak much during those days when we both rode my haavl, but when she did, it was mostly about her sister. She told me why her sister had cut herself off from the world, disgusted with her own kind long before they had given Solen cause. She said that her sister had tried to open her eyes, to convince her not to set out on a mission as an emissary to my people. She said that her sister had called her an idealist, saying that she always had her head stuck in the clouds. Solen believed that her sister was angry with her because she went anyway and never came back. She was so happy at the thought of finally seeing her again and yet, at the same time, she was terribly afraid of being judged and found wanting."

§ § §

I headed off to the desert in the early morning, following Rliebkl's instructions. It was easy enough since I'd already been in the vicinity, including the time I had found him. I was a little groggy from lack of sleep, but I had to go to the site. All night long, he'd talked about her, telling me things he'd never had the time or the nerve to tell her. Above all, he told me the end of his tale, his terrible tale.

Rliebkl spent the night in the trailer, more dead than alive, chilled by the desert cold, suffering terribly. The men threw a woolen blanket over him but, given the lack of any source of heat, it served no purpose, barely able to help him conserve the heat stored in the wood of the trailer just a little longer. And the meager meal they'd given him kept him warm for only a brief time.

In the early hours of the morning, he was wakened by sounds of a ruckus in the shack. Using the last of his strength to lift his head, he saw one of the men rush out, hands clasped over his bloody throat, then collapse. He

*saw the other race out of the shack in turn, quickly caught
by a creature twice his size, who tore him to shreds with
razor sharp claws. Arhbkl.*

*She walked over to the trailer, carefully undid his bonds,
and helped him sit up. She took out a first-aid kit and
started cleaning his wound. Overwhelmed, Rliebkl let her
do so without asking too many questions. While bandaging
his deep gash, the female darztl explained that she'd set
out to track him down after finding that he had disappeared
with the human. It was a point of honor, she said, since
all of the trackers would be tarred by his disgrace. Moreover,
she argued, she couldn't allow him to take the human back
to her kind, not with everything the prisoner knew about
darztls, starting with the mining operations and the iron
supplies. Rliebkl felt that she basically wanted a piece of
the reward that would go hand in hand with his capture
and that of the woman, but he said nothing. Finally he
found the strength to stammer, "How did Arhbkl...?"*

*"Shh, Rliebkl must rest. He lost a great deal of blood.
I'll carry him back inside the shack and he can sleep a bit."*

"No," Rliebkl protested. "Not before I find Solen."

*"Solen? Pff... Rliebkl means the human? She's back
there."*

"I... Rliebkl wants to go there."

*Arhbkl turned an exasperated shade, but did not protest.
She disconnected the trailer from the vehicle and tied it
to her haavl. She positioned Rliebkl as well as she could
and climbed into the saddle.*

*"You'll have to hang on," she said before instructing
her mount to proceed. That's how Rliebkl retraced his steps
along a trail that became doubly painful, considering what
he found at the end.*

*Everything looked peaceful. There were no signs of the
previous day's struggle. His haavl was still there, poking its long snout between the rocks in search of tasty roots.
Nothing disturbed the tranquility of the scene, not even
Solen's body off in the distance, where she looked as if she
were sleeping, leaning against a rock.*

*Close up, however, the picture was disturbing. The
woman's body was covered with bruises. Rliebkl knew*

nothing about the refinements of the physical abuse human males could inflict on a female, and he didn't want to think about it. All he saw was her body, covered with cuts and dried blood. And he hoped, hoped with all his heart, that the mortal blow to her throat had been inflicted before the men had sliced off her thumb to remove her silver bracelet. But, looking at the blood that had flowed from the woman's hand, he had his doubts.

Since the sun had returned some of his strength, Rliebkl managed to stand up and climb down from the trailer. He fell to the ground near Solen and took her in his arms. He stayed there, rocking her, under Arhbkl's disgusted gaze. After a long time, he was vaguely aware of hearing her scratch the ground with her claws as a sign of her disgust, then climb into her saddle and ride off. Obviously, he was a complete write-off in her view.

He spent the entire day there, holding Solen's already desiccated body. When the sun set, he dug a hole in the rocky soil, using up all the strength he had stored during the day. He dug until the hole was large enough to hold his friend's body. Traditionally, darztls burned the mortal remains of their kind. But Rliebkl believed that humans preferred to bury their dead and he wanted to respect Solen's wishes.

The entire operation exhausted him. He hastily covered the body with sand and small pebbles, and marked the spot with a rock so that he could find the grave again the next day. Then he took shelter in the grotto where the flowers and animal excrement he had placed in a small heap the previous day still waited to be ignited and warm him. He soon collapsed next to the fire.

He spent the entire next day building a sort of monument to Solen's memory, painfully dragging rocks to her grave, arranging them to leave a message for posterity. By sunset, he was finished.

He spent the night there and by the next morning his mind was made up. He climbed painfully onto his haavl, which was grazing nearby, and headed off. He slept in the shack where the bodies of the two men still lay, and took advantage of the opportunity to recover Solen's bracelet. Then he headed back on his way, riding his haavl rather than taking the human vehicle, which he didn't know how to operate. However, about a half-day from his destination, the cold that crept over the desert taxed the little strength that remained in him. He slipped off his haavl. He intended to crawl toward the heat of the hill which the path wound up, but he passed out.

That's how I had discovered him, and I now recognized the spot the darztl had shown me. At the foot of a hill, he had drawn a message using rocks arranged in curious symbols, a message that could never be deciphered by the simple human passersby traveling through this desert, unless they had learned the language of the indigenous species. He had placed my sister's body under the symbol for "Solen." I dug, scraping my hands raw on the pebbles, worn by the sandy wind, and I saw her. The arid soil of the desert had preserved her body, but even if she had been completely disfigured, I would have recognized her. Her hair was sun-bleached, her body gaunt, but it was Solen, or at least it had been. Her right foot was missing, but the thumb that had been sliced off had been gently placed near the other fingers on her left hand.

I left my sister resting in her arid bed. Slowly, I returned the pebbles to their place, taking care not to disturb the rock symbols, and went home.

§ § §

Bathed in blood, Rliebkl lay in the middle of the avern. I would not have to choose between releasing him or... He had broken his chain, as I had always suspected he could. It would have been difficult for me to detect the beating of his heart beneath his scaly skin, but I knew at a glance that this time he was truly dead. His body was gray, and even stiffer than usual. The wound to his ridge had opened again and his blood had poured onto the rock in the cave.

It almost looked as if, like a cat throwing caution to the wind, he had tried to slip through the mouse hole. He had slipped his head into one of the corridors I used to get in and out of the grotto, but his body was too large, and his crest had done nothing to improve matters. Apparently, he got stuck there and, backing up in pain and misery, he had re-opened his poorly healed wound, gashing his flesh even deeper. Yet I knew that he was too intelligent to believe, for even one second, that he could slip through that opening. In his hand, he held one of the plates of the children's tale that he had described to me, the one about the little darztl who despaired when he realized that he might never find the other members of his species.

His body seemed lighter then when I had slipped him down the well in the grotto. I placed it gently on the rocky plateau that formed the roof of my dwelling, and went back down below to find twigs and fuel. I gathered materials for a few minutes, then set fire to my improvised grave. The body that had been Rliebkl caught fire easily, and I watched it transform into ash. In broad daylight like that, the smoke would be visible for miles around and I would be detected, but I didn't care about that.

I went back down to the grotto and picked up the small colored plates, as well as a few provisions, and then headed off toward the desert. I slipped into the darztl cave that stretched, untouched, below the rock hill. Once again, I looked along the walls of the room, using my pocket light. Every surface was covered with joyful images of darztls in scenes from daily life, taking part in familiar rituals so foreign to humans. I realized that I was most likely in a festival room, a place where darztls were happy, from the time when they lived alone on their planet. Solitary by nature, darztls still like to get together on occasion to recall who they are and who their kind are. That's what Rliebkl told me.

Suddenly, I thought about the darztl child my sister Solen had befriended, at a time when relations between our two species were not so tense. She saw him on the sly, in the middle of the desert. The darztls lived close by at the time; they had not as yet been forced to retreat to the south as the region cooled. I also thought about how terribly angry our parents had been when they learned who Solen had taken up with.

Suddenly I started to weep, my sobs echoing against the stone walls of the darztl cave. I wept for Rliebkl, whom I had treated so harshly, for my sister, who I had come so close to seeing again, for myself, lost and no longer able to find my way. In our culture, even less than in theirs, our little personal dramas are of no consequence, eclipsed by the Major Work of colonization, counter-colonization, and the battle against counter-colonization... I also wept for the lack of communication between species, for the pain we caused one another, for the upcoming disappearance of a civilization, for our pitiful and petty human victory. What did it matter if one member of a community disappeared if that served the greater good of the larger group? What did it matter if we lost a battle — and lives — if it meant winning the war? I wept for the century of armed battle to come, of the century it would take humans to terraform this planet, to cool its climate, to annihilate this species. I wept and my human tears served, however involuntarily, to irrigate the soil and hasten the transformation of this world.

THE DARZTL

Common name:	Darztl
Latin name:	*Chamaelo erectus*
Family:	Chameleonidae
Class:	Reptiles
Order:	Squamate
Temperature:	40°C to 55°C
Height:	Male: up to 2 m
	Female: up to 2.5 m
Weight:	100 — 150 kg
Habitat:	Mars II desert
Diet:	Omnivore (raw meat and plants)
Reproduction:	Ovoviviparus
Litters:	4 or 5
Lifespan:	In captivity: unknown
	Free: unknown

Additional information: With its large crest and sharp teeth, the darztl looks like it came straight out of the Jurassic era. Although the darztl is capable of walking on all fours, it seems to prefer standing on its rear feet. Darztl skin is covered with scales and the creature sheds its skin twice a year. As in the case of all chameleons, the darztl is capable of changing color; nevertheless, these changes are limited to the animal's wattle. Unlike certain species, the purpose of this change in color does not appear to be camouflage or the regulation of body temperature, but is instead a barometer of mood. As for the crest, which is extremely sensitive, it is most likely used as a lever for fertilization (manipulating the crest seems to stimulate the production of seminal fluid and regulates the acid level of the liquid in which the eggs are bathed). In the case of the darztl, the regenerative ability observed in other reptile species extends not only to its tail, but also all four limbs and certain internal organs. It should be noted that darztls have a complex language, consisting of a combination of deep throaty sounds and clicks.

ENEMY FIRE

To the little dragon with whom I had a special friendship,
one day, for ten minutes, in a pet shop.

And oh its so beautiful. Its like
the fourth of July. Its like a
christmas tree. Its like fireflies
on a summer night. And I wish
I could describe this to you
a little better. But I cant talk...

Laurie Anderson, *Night in Baghdad*

The sun hung deliciously over the desert. It had reached its zenith and the shadows were reduced to thin lines at the feet of rocks and the few rare bushes. Very early that morning she'd been dumped in the midst of the immense void and had been walking ever since. It had to be 50° C in the shade and yet she still felt the rays of the sun as a gentle caress on her thick skin. Her paws barely bit into the granular soil and, with her long hard tail beating time, she walked quickly south. As her body warmed, she felt a new energy flow through her. Her mobile eyes, which detected even the slightest movement around her on the desert surface, made her feel a little giddy. However, it could generally be said that she was in splendid form. It was the first day of her mission, a mission on which the fate of her kind depended to some extent, and she was prepared to literally move mountains of sand and rock!

When the molten sphere embraced the horizon, and then disappeared, she had had no time to feel any fatigue whatsoever. Her powerful legs slid through the desert at an exhilarating speed. Darkness, however, left her shivering. She hastily lit a small methane heater that she carried in her bag — and which she would have to get rid of before she met her first darztl unless she wanted to rouse suspicion — and rolled up in her reflective blanket. Then she recalled that that was exactly what she wasn't supposed to do. So she stripped down and lay on the sand to make the most of the heat stored in the soil. She spread the metallic blanket over her to let in the comforting warmth of the small radiator and lay still, waiting for her improvised shelter to heat up. She chewed on some of her rations, the most effective means she had for warming her blood. Shivering, she fell asleep, thinking that she would have to trap her first sand squirrels soon — her first osfsts — and eat them like any self-respecting darztl.

The next morning she woke, cold and weak. She had to spend several long hours lazing in the sun before setting off, bucked up, once again amazed by the astounding ability of the indigenous species on Mars II to recuperate.

Lecture by Chloé Guilimpert
Manager — Strategic Operations
Defense and Security Department
Presented to the Mars II Provisional Council
This fifth day of Sixtember, Marsian year 0040

Distinguished members of the council gathered here this morning, you know how important the decision we have to make is? Since diplomatic relations with the darztls were cut off, we've worked night and day to set up an effective yet discrete surveillance network. Of course, we couldn't, and still can't, attack them head on. Lacking sufficient energy reserves, our small group doesn't have the resources to take on an entire country, even one that is technologically backwards. No, our best weapons are patience and vigilance. Discretion as well, to avoid provoking an attack by those barbarians. The enemy's inertia to date is a factor in our favor. Let's hope that time will do the rest.

We must admit that our initiatives have only been somewhat successful to date. However, we've been working on a new strategy, one that is both innovative and ambitious, for several months now. We're convinced it's feasible. The survival of the colony depends on whether or not the board approves the final phase. Nevertheless, before getting down to the basics of our proposal, let us remind you about some of the highlights of what we've done so far.

It all started some time after the darztls cut off diplomatic relations.

We could have followed in the footsteps of the two cold wars on Earth and tried to buy off the enemy. I mean, wouldn't it have been easy enough to kidnap a darztl, and keep making him offers until we found his price, and then send him back to his own kind to spy? Well, no. No matter what we offered, we were unable to buy defection. Moreover, when we left the prisoner alone, even for just a minute, he tended to imitate his predecessors and commit hari-kari. Yet, the species seems to be almost immortal. Darztl thought patterns are completely impenetrable...

And there was no question of repeating the abduction of the Sabines! First of all, we weren't looking for any alliance with our enemy. The goal was to gain time and discover what they were up to that could upset our 100-year plan. Then, even if wartime rape had not been promoted to a crime worthy of perpetual exile quite some time ago, these extraterrestrial Sabines were far too incompatible with us.

So we decided that it would be effective to raise young darztls as humans. We didn't need their mothers for that! We would kidnap a few baby lizards or, better yet, make some of our own, using the embryos that had served, in the past, to isolate their genetic material. And that would be it! Afterwards, as long as we took charge of the baby monster as soon as it came out of the vivarium, the rest would take merely routine, patience and a lot of time. We'd entrust the wailing little creature to a normal family and let parental love do the rest, with just a little dab of external conditioning, a dozen sessions at most, nothing at all like brainwashing.

We took a chance, deciding to grow a few embryos, since kidnapping would have drawn too much attention. Let's call this little initiative Project Alpha. It resulted in beautiful, miniature darztls that screamed their little lungs out, beating the suffocating air in the nursery with their tiny tails. So as to avoid placing too many eggs in one basket, pardon the expression, we limited our initiative to a single attempt. We wanted to experiment with various forms of upbringing so as to increase our chances of success. For that, we called on our exopsychiatrist, Joëlle Lamsong.

As some of you already know, we probably took things a little fast. The experiment was a disastrous failure. You can judge for yourselves by reading Dr. Lamsong's report. Perhaps the extraterrestrials are too disgusting in the eyes of common mortals to ever be considered, even as babes, as cute little beings to be protected. In any case, the results were deplorable.

Of course, we didn't allow the families to head off into the wilderness. Without a shadow of a doubt, they would have been lynched and the young would have been seized, torn apart, and beaten to a pulp. And if the project wasn't kept secret, the results couldn't be either. No, the families were rehoused in a protected neighborhood, cleared for that purpose in the very heart of the defense department, away from indiscrete eyes. Perhaps that didn't exactly encourage totally normal behavior on the part of the family units, but it doesn't account for all the hitting, rejection, hardships the young suffered. Did the torrid climate we imposed on the families, in order to keep the young darztls healthy, contribute to the general irascibility of the small community? In any case, all of the humans involved in the experiment behaved very badly and, as a result, the experiment failed. We wanted to raise a darztl to become a real little human, to be trained by the warmth of its human hosts. But the ten baby lizards were treated like animals — no, at least certain animals are pampered by their masters, even those strange tortoises with the hairy shells that some of our kind have adopted on this planet — no, the lizards were treated like prisoners and given only the bare essentials.

And these families had been handpicked. They came from the upper echelons of our society and were aware of the stakes. Yet, on average, at least one little lizard was treated each week for a suspicious injury, malnutrition or wounds that seemed to have been self-inflicted. During the fourth year of the experiment, which should have lasted twenty, we discovered one that had been tortured to death between two buildings, the victim of abuse on the part of the children from the community — the authorities had, in fact, opted for family units that had two or more children when the experiment started. The project continued to drag on for a few months. Then, one evening, eight young darztls ambushed the community's human children. Some were seriously injured and one of them was literally eviscerated by the four-year-old lizards. That was the final blow. We ended the operation and eliminated eight young darztls. The ninth had disappeared in the meantime under suspicious circumstances. Everyone went back to life as usual and very few tears were shed for the little creatures. What did you expect? Not only do we not belong to the same species, we don't even belong to the same genus or the same order... barely to the same branch and definitely not the same world!

§ § §

She encountered her first darztl on the fourth morning, before she had time to get rid of her human artifacts. The second and third nights she spent in the desert were less trying than the first, since she had the foresight to stock up on a few rations as a preventive measure and to stop shortly before night fell to build a shelter over a burning rock which, thanks to the heater and the survival blanket, had given off a beneficial heat the entire night. That day, she set out at a lively pace, even humming an old childhood song that her new vocal faculties distorted to some extent.

Her song stopped short when she saw the stranger, obviously a male considering his size, approaching from the distance, mounted on a huge beast, probably a haavl. She'd have to switch to plan B, in which she would play an amnesia victim who had escaped from her human attackers. It was less comfortable than plan A, in which she would be discovered only after she entered darztl territory, giving her the time she needed to hide her instruments so she could pick them up again at the end of her mission. But as this was the only plan she had, she would have to make do. She took on a beaten, broken air and allowed the other to approach, without taking her eyes from him for a moment.

"Is the darztl all right?" the darztl asked as he climbed down from his mount.

"I... I'm... I don't... I don't know," she stammered. She had used the first person singular, something rare and extremely intimate for a darztl, but fortunately her translator had been programmed to automatically convert her sentences into a more impersonal form, more in keeping with the indigenous language.

The other stopped short and pulled an object from a sheath on his haavl. In case it was a long-range weapon, she stopped short as well.

"What is the female darztl doing in the middle of the desert?" the stranger insisted.

She seemed to concentrate very hard, then allowed herself to fall to the ground, faking great weakness, hoping that darztls showed their weakness in that manner. To her great relief, her action had the desired result. The darztl resheathed his weapon and rushed over to her. He knelt by her side, lifting her head with infinite gentleness. "It doesn't matter. These darztls will have all the time they need to get to know one another. The female must regain her strength."

He ran his hands over her body, looking for an injury and, as expected, he discovered fresh scars from the blows they had inflicted on her to increase her credibility. She closed her eyes, both relieved and repulsed by such intimacy.

"Everything will be fine now, the darztl will go home soon."

She felt the other pull her lips apart and pour a bitter liquid into her mouth. All disgust disappeared and she was submerged in the pleasure of lying on the burning soil under a blistering sky. She must have passed out since, when she opened her eyes, the sun was already low on the horizon.

The other was looking at her. His wattle was blue, with glints of purple. In a brief moment of distraction, or possibly because she still felt the effects of the mysterious potion, she caught herself finding the color pleasant. But the darztl opened his mouth to speak. She saw his long white teeth and his wattle wobbling about like jelly, and she once again found him repulsive.

"Does the darztl feel better?"

The stranger's wattle was once again streaked with color. She must have looked a little stunned since he commented, "This strange darztl is as myopic as she is opaque..."

She understood that he was referring to the color of her own wattle, which she still hadn't mastered like a real darztl, since she knew nothing, absolutely nothing, about this means of nonverbal communication. All the human archives said was that the wattles of the natives they had tortured turned brown when the creatures were subjected to great suffering. As for the other colors, obviously, no one knew anything....

She played the fool, "I don't understand...."

The strange darztl leapt up in a single bound. Even though she knew that she was larger as a female darztl she couldn't help but be impressed by his build and it took all she had not to get up and flee at full speed. He misunderstood the source of her distress.

"No, no. The dartzl must stay lying down. It's late. It's better to spend the night here."

Lecture by Chloé Guilimpert (continued)

We could always have repeated the experiment, changing some of the controls, but time was short. We couldn't afford the luxury of waiting another twenty local years until a new clutch reached adulthood and was ready to spy for the humans. One of our geneticists, Dieter Sych, came up with a solution that was less fastidious than the previous one. Up to that point, genetic engineering had served merely to treat hereditary diseases and modify quick-growing cultures. Yet nothing prohibited treating 'humanlife' (to use Dr. Sych's expression) as a congenital problem. Acting not on the next generation but on the current one was more problematic, but not unprecedented. Hadn't we already done as much when we had to quickly adapt the few farm animals we took out of hibernation when we arrived on Mars II? The results were not permanent (albeit not reversible) and faded to a certain extent when the medications were stopped — frequently causing the death of the subject, however — but subcutaneous implants made things much easier. Moreover, what genetic engineering couldn't hide or generate, plastic surgery could build from scratch. I'm sure you'd tell us that we should have taken our time, made sure that our project was viable, but as you know, each day counted! All we had to do was ignore certain rules of ethics.

In the case of our Project Beta, we chose ten volunteers — obviously someone in the defense department had a certain fascination with the number ten — among the victims of recent hereditary afflictions. I would like to point out that it was invariably a matter of a fresh mutation caused by the planetary environment, since, of course, most of you certainly know that no detectable congenital defect was tolerated among the passengers of the mother ship when it set out for Mars II! Thus, the volunteers were all patients who, for hierarchical reasons, could not receive short- or medium-term gene therapy. In exchange for healing them, we offered them an opportunity to sell their souls to the devil — no more, no less. Needless to say, few refused.

The experiment proceeded quickly. Soon the humans were transformed into ten authentic darztls — well, actually nine authentic darztls, since the tenth, who had a disorder affecting his internal thermostat, died a few days after the treatment, from hypothermia.

These new darztls were adults. After the genetic therapy and some plastic surgery, they went into training. Apart from their congenital defects, other selection criteria had been used, and most of them were already predisposed to take on the mission for which they had been engineered. The rest was pure routine: development of physical and psychological endurance, a quick briefing on darztl culture — the little we knew — and training on the various technological add-ons that would be hidden under their shells. Considering our initial failure, this time we made an effort to raise the hybrids in an area where they would never encounter humans. Even the training they received was handled virtually so as to prevent any frightening encounters.

Then the ranks of the new darztls were gradually decimated. First, one subject — known by the human code name Amàlia and an unpronounceable darztl name — suddenly decided to stop her therapy. But one can't stop therapy just like that, at least not without constant medical care, and Amàlia had also chosen to carve out her subcutaneous implant using a shard of glass. Her action went unnoticed for a few days, then the others found her lying skinless in her blood-soaked bed. The molting process, which is a normal part of darztl life, had not been interrupted by the reversal of the mutation, leaving her body denuded, unable to replace the layer of skin that lay abandoned about her. No transplants worked. She died a few hours later, her bodily fluids seeping out about her.

The other guinea pigs were shaken by this and had two diametrically opposed reactions. Some of them — fortunately most of them fell into this group — viewed her defection with contempt. They felt stronger and were convinced they would complete the experiment successfully. Two of the fake darztls, however, asked us to reverse the process. After prevaricating for several weeks, we agreed. About ten days later, the other subjects were gathered in a room equipped with a hologram projector. Our chief of security and defense appeared in person, announcing an embargo: any reversal of the mutation process was interrupted until further order. The process was too costly, he told them, and besides, they'd all signed contracts agreeing to stay with the experiment until the end. After that, there would always be time for reconsideration. They were kept cut off from everything and everyone, so they had no opportunity to figure out that something had gone wrong. In fact, one of the two patients had died of a particularly virulent strain of salmonella during the first two days after the gene therapy was stopped, a victim of bacteria he'd been hosting since the mutation. That's why we were hesitant to allow other subjects to return. In the case of the second individual, the reversal proceeded without any problems. Of course, that didn't prevent him from committing suicide six weeks later. Was he the victim of a sort of cyclothymia characteristic of the darztl life cycle, or had he ended his life knowing he would never be anything other than a repulsive hybrid? Either the project managers never knew or they claimed they were unable to find out.

Of the six remaining fake darztls, only four made it to the end of the experiment. One tried to escape and was torn apart by onlookers. The other died following a mysterious fever, probably caused by a metabolic conflict between the cold-blooded creature and the hot-blooded one that housed it.

At the end of a year, we finally had four beautiful, viable subjects, in the prime of their lives, ready to make the ultimate sacrifice for their race. We selected one, a woman renamed Dhrakhln (we'd once captured a darztl with that name), whose plastic surgery, hormone treatment and gene therapy had transformed her into a male darztl — in fact, in the darztl's case, males are smaller than the females, even though our hybrid would pass for a very small male darztl.

We had decided to abandon Dhrakhln in the middle of the desert, as close as possible to a native village — but not so close that they might notice us and wipe out fourteen months of work. Our valiant little agent was to cover the rest of the distance on foot, protected against the blazing heat by his new, indigenous metabolism. Once he reached darztl territory, he would recount a mind-boggling tale, telling of capture, imprisonment, cruel scientific experiments and a miraculous escape. Of course, the darztls would be suspicious, they'd interrogate him at length, examine him carefully. But we were counting on the fact that, even though the illusion only succeeded to a certain extent, local technology was not advanced enough to distinguish a real lizard from a fake one, a human female from a male reptile. As for genetics, the natives hadn't advanced beyond Mendel and had no idea what a genome is. Their investigative tools are far from advanced.

It took a month for Project Beta to fail. Dhrakhln, or rather his bloody remains, was dumped a few yards from the base camp. He was surrounded by letters traced in the sand with a pebble, like those found around darztl graves, written in the native language and that our linguists translated approximately as: "This people may not have the science of the enemy, but female darztls can detect the repulsive pheromones of a female human from miles away." So, filled with dread, we were forced to conclude that we'd have to focus on one of the enemy's other weaknesses....

As you know, that brought the experiment to an abrupt end. We wondered if we ought to eliminate the remaining subjects, but decided to help them establish a tiny colony in the middle of the desert — a colony that would not survive — since the experiment had rendered them all sterile.

§ § §

She proceeded, riding her companion's haavl, rocked by her mount's powerful legs. And yet, they were merely walking, since the darztl was forced to walk beside the powerful reptilian beast of burden, allowing her to regain her strength. They walked through the desert like that for two days, talking little, absorbing the sun's rays. In any case, what could she say, forced as she was to pretend amnesia so as to avoid making any mistake, simply hoping that darztls could actually lose their memories. He had tried to learn more about her, to find out what had happened to her, but she merely gave him a few incoherent tidbits, pretending to be in a state of shock if he probed too much.

They came across no living soul on their way, but she suspected the area was swarming with darztls. She knew that from the methane odor that floated in the air when night fell, as well as from the haavl tracks that wound through the desert. But she'd learned from her brief training that, although darztls could be gregarious and enjoy company at times, they were for the most part solitary creatures, spread over a territory that gave them sufficient living space. And yet they also had cities, which she believed served merely as transitional spaces between two moments of solitude. And now she stood at the doors to one of these cities, facing two guards who called on them to identify themselves.

Her companion walked over to the two individuals, sporting peaceful colors — at least that's how she interpreted the blue shades that flowed over his wattle. He spoke and gesticulated a little, in the purest darztl style, but managed to make them understand how he had found her and what state she was in at the time. The two guards appeared to consult, and then one of them walked over to the enclosure, handling a piece of equipment that was obviously some sort of telecommunications device, since two other disturbingly immense darztls soon approached the haavl she still sat astride. They grabbed her bag and poured the contents out on the ground, exchanging glances and... highly varied colors.

"Follow us," one of the frightening matrons said.

She must have taken too long looking stunned, without obeying, because before she had time to understand what was happening, she found her arms bound, two creatures even more immense than she was on either side of her.

"Follow us."

They took her to a sort of roughly square grotto, similar in style to most of the buildings she had noticed along her way, but much more imposing. All of the walls, with the exception of one whose lower portion was filled with large pipes, were smooth, and the very high ceiling opened directly out to the sky and the burning sun. They must have left her there for several hours since, when they came to get her, the room was plunged in darkness, although the temperature was maintained at a comfortable level by the large pipes, which were burning hot. Stumbling after her jailers, she told herself that now — more than ever — was not the time to crack.

"So, how about the prisoner telling us her little tale?" the uniformed darztl asked for the *umpteenth* time. She had been required to sit in a large room, as empty as the previous one, and a darztl as enormous as the others had come in to question her. Based on his clothing — a uniform that consisted essentially of a metal breastplate — she thought he must be a member of the police force, while she railed inside against her perspicacity, considering the cell-like room in which they had forced her to spend the afternoon. On each side of the door, two immense darztls (*The same as before?*) stood guard. In one corner of the room, a sort of clerk seemed to be carefully noting down everything that was said.

"I don't know what to tell you. I've already told you that I don't remember anything before I met..." she was surprised to note that he had not given her his name... "the one who brought me here. My mind is a complete blank."

"The darztl must know what she was doing in the desert, the bag filled with human artifacts?"

"Filled with what?" she asked sincerely, astonished and a little concerned to note that a word had escaped the attention of the translator that had been grafted into her.

"Objects that come from the enemy, strange instruments," the police officer exploded with what she took to be exasperation.

She was relieved to note that the translator had probably not been able to translate one of the words in the previous sentence since it was a neologism. But her relief was short lived. The uniformed darztl rushed at her and punched her crest with his powerful paw, causing the prisoner to cry out in pain.

"No... I... who is the enemy? I don't understand anything!" she managed to say just in time, holding her painful crest with both clawed paws.

He continued to interrogate her like this for what seemed an eternity. In the middle of his interrogation, noticing that she was prostrate, exhausted, shivering, the police officer had food brought in — disgusting raw meat that her stomach nevertheless cried out for — then renewed his questions with additional vigor. When the session had wearied him too much, he was replaced by a colleague, but the captive was given no such respite. She couldn't take it any more. If her new bodily covering had been able to weep, in the human manner, all the tears in her body would have been pouring out. She had to settle for sitting there, her soul filled with death, without knowing if her wattle betrayed anything other than pure exhaustion. She understood full well that they suspected that she was a spy for the humans and was very aware of her fate if she betrayed herself. Plan A would have been so much easier!

The midday sun pouring in through the light shaft bathed the room in a brilliant light when the first police officer, who had come back on duty a few hours earlier, interrupted the session. He struck her with his tail, throwing her to the ground, then advanced toward her, threatening. She thought he was going to hit her again, but he merely said, "Fine, the interrogation will resume later. I imagine there's no point in asking you your name again? You won't reveal it any more than you did the previous times!"

This time, it wasn't the translator that was revealing signs of weakness. The police officer had, in fact, used the second person singular, a sign of great intimacy... or great rudeness, according to the human's darztl lexicon. Looking at the clerk, he added, "In the files, we'll simply refer to her as Selmdhrakhln for the time being."

He stared at her. She held back a shiver. Dhrakhln was the name of the first spy who had been sent into enemy territory, the one who had been returned in pieces. In darztl, 'selm' meant 'two.'

Lecture by Chloé Guilimpert (continued)

That's when someone brought up an old idea we'd initially abandoned because it seemed too... esoteric: flesh-machine interface. But why not, after all? Who knew if good old cybernetic science wouldn't succeed where psychogenesis and genetics had failed? In any case, we were desperate. There had been no contact between darztls and humans for almost ten marsian years. Human kidnappings had stopped and the natives left bloody human remains on our doorsteps less and less often, but none of our people had as yet managed to successfully escape from his darztl jail to come and tell us what went on there. If they even kept hostages. For our part, the terraforming process continued, but who knew what they were working on in enemy territory to thwart our projects?

No, perhaps the solution didn't lie in transforming a darztl into a human. The two species were too different and the aversion between primates and reptiles too deeply entrenched during the brief history of this planet. Perhaps it wasn't such a good idea to make darztls out of humans either. Once again, the two species had too little in common and their knowledge of one another was partial at best. No, the true hybrid, the most viable, would be one that didn't have to renounce the one to become the other, that could continue to be the one while becoming the other. And since cerebral implants were already being used to transfer the psyche of a patient whose body was finished into a subject that was clinically dead, the technique could surely be used to transfer the mind of a human into a darztl body. And in that case, there was certainly no shortage of raw materials. After all, the research center had an impressive quantity of natives kept in a state of hibernation for our scientific experiments. All we had to do was find a sufficiently solid human volunteer who wouldn't give up along the way. However, I have to admit that the stakes weren't as high this time. The volunteer wouldn't have to give up his former life forever. During his stay in a darztl body, his physical shell would be kept alive artificially so that he could be reinstated into it without any difficulty once the experiment was over.

We had to get this up and running very quickly and our researchers worked day and night. And now, a year later, we're pleased to announce that we've reached the final phase of our project. Both our calculations and the tests we've conducted on 'guinea pigs' indicate that it is possible to implant the complete memory, the psyche of an individual, into a darztl body, without altering either the mental faculties of the donor or the physical capacities of the recipient. The darztls' primitive equipment will be able to detect both the implant and the translator that will also have to be grafted into the host, but the natives will never be able to determine the nature of these foreign bodies. They might just conclude that they're the result of recent injuries, and most likely they won't even dare extract them from our spy's brain for fear of killing one of their own kind.

However, one crucial step remains: choosing the envoy to be sent into enemy territory. For the benefit of our mission, this person must be someone who is very familiar with darztl society, even before training starts. Training will last one year and will include adapting to a new bodily envelope and a new metabolism. And it is at this point in my presentation that I arrive at the very essence of our proposal.

Distinguished council members, I come before you today to propose that I be the one to serve as the colony's secret envoy into darztl territory. I'm thoroughly familiar with the enemy, since I've been observing them for the fifteen years I've spent with the Strategic Operations division. Our staff is convinced that I will be able to fulfill my mandate and that, once the project has been completed, we'll have the information we need about the enemy's knowledge and military resources.

§ § §

Possibly because they weren't completely sure that she wasn't one of their own, they didn't really torture her. At least not physically. But they did wage war on her nerves, never once indicating that they believed, even for a fraction of a second, her tale of amnesia. She exhausted her final reserves of strength, lost all sense of time and wasn't far from doubting her own lie when they decided to resort to medical tests that could well provide scientific corroboration of her account — or discredit it once and for all. They had already given her a cursory examination, which had revealed several recent injuries and wounds, and even used a sort of ultrasound — at least that's what the machine they had placed her in looked like — that had shown a large piece of metal at the base of her skull and another smaller one, just next to it, both of which seemed to have been the source of two large scars at the base of her crest, following penetration. But this time they subjected her to a complete battery of tests that must have provided confirmation that she was, at least physically, an authentic darztl, since they quickly moved on to psychological tests.

"Selm, would you sum up everything you've told the authorities to date?"

She'd grown used to the nickname, Selm, which they used since the original was too long. Selm. She realized that it fit her like a glove as she hid herself among them. With his gentle voice and his familiar tone, the darztl shrink was once again trying to make her believe he was her friend. But beneath their endless questioning, she had to stick with the same story: she had forgotten everything, if only she remembered something she would tell them, but everything had evaporated from her traumatized brain — or at least, that's what she wanted them to believe. Except, of course, for that recent addition, which had been invented simply to pass the time, so they would have something new to chew on, perversely excited by the idea that it could put her life at risk again.

"I don't remember anything. Nothing at all. Except for a horrible, painful nightmare. I'm surrounded by monsters and they're torturing me. I want to leave, but I can't move, so I have to bear it all. And suddenly, everything is red, and everything is white, and I run out into the desert and I meet one my own kind."

They could interpret this however they wanted. In any case, they didn't seem to have given up yet on the possibility that she had actually escaped after being captured by humans whose weapons had left shrapnel in her skull.

One day, they took her into a large room, where she saw a sort of dissection table, covered with wires. They had her lie down there and connected wires from a machine to many spots on her body, concentrating on her head and torso. It had to be some kind of lie detector machine, because they assailed her with the usual questions ("Who's to say Selm isn't a spy?") intermingled with stupid questions ("What did Selm eat yesterday evening?"). Obviously, her brain waves revealed nothing. Most of her psychic activities were controlled by the implant and not the donor's brain, in which only those portions of the cerebellum and the medulla oblongata needed for motor or vital functions actually worked. If they had given her an EEG, they wouldn't have detected anything in her cerebral lobes other than the irremediably flat waves of a brain in a vegetative state.

Another time, she found herself in the middle of a debate — in which she had no say, of course — about the pros and cons of performing a vivisection on her. Some hoped it wouldn't harm her and others that it would result in a painless death. The darztls seemed to be divided into two almost equal camps with her in the middle, filled with a curious sense of the unreal. They talked about opening up her skull, seeing what her gray matter looked like and perhaps extracting the piece of metal that contained everything she was and throwing it away, and she observed them from a distance, as if floating above them on some astral trip. The hideous faces of the darztls bent over her, murmuring words she no longer understood, their wattles shimmering with colors that had never been totally familiar to her. Their silhouettes spun about her; she no longer really knew if they were above her or below her, as she lay in the middle of the room. And the movement intensified, spinning her about as if on some manic dentist's chair, until she lost all sense of direction and finally lost consciousness.

§ § §

She lay on a soft, warm surface. She jumped when she saw a monstrous face, then forced herself to regain control. Someone was observing her with what looked to be solicitude — but since when had she been able to decode darztl emotions under their thick shells? She tried to lift her head, but the darztl gently forced her to remain lying down. She closed her eyes and fell back to sleep.

She spent a few days in the cozy limbo between sleep and wakefulness. She had the impression that all of her biological functions had slowed. She allowed herself to be fed passively, like a baby, and in her confusion she thought that yes, this must be what was happening: she was being born into existence as a darztl. The days when she had clumsily had to work at moving her new body started to retreat into the distance. It had taken her an entire year to learn how to walk, make independent sounds, pick up objects, look normal — well, normal for a darztl, of course. She recalled the first time she had shed her skin, the sensation of leaving a cocoon in which she had been sealed up for a few days, and the strange sensation that followed — an immense need, an impossible desire, but for what? By looking into the matter and analyzing her reactions, she finally understood that what was happening to her was as old as the world, as all worlds that harbored life: she was in her sexually active phase, or, to put things bluntly, she was in heat and that's why she wanted to brush up against the bodies of all of the conscientious technicians around her, who would have certainly been disgusted by the idea of touching her for any purpose other than scientific ones.

Slowly, she roused from her torpor and started to grow stronger — in her mind perhaps more than in her body. She sat on her bed, or what counted for a bed, then managed to take a few steps around the room, aided by Khlearmt, her nurse — or perhaps she should refer to him as her keeper. In fact, at the beginning she had thought that she was in some sort of military clinic, but after walking to the window, and then into the garden, she discovered that she was in some kind of boarding house, in some kind of village, where the broad, low buildings reminded her of the rock hillocks that dotted the desert. There was nothing to indicate, however, that she wasn't under surveillance, even though Khlearmt, who was most solicitous, regularly railed against the treatment she had been subjected to as he spoon fed her.

"They had their reasons, of course, but really. It's true that darztls are very afraid of an enemy intrusion. But they went too far. Treating someone who needs full-time care like that. It's really too cruel. But it's over now. Khlearmt and the others will take care of Selm and she will be able to dance the brlirthl soon."

She looked at him without understanding. Her wattle must have taken on the appropriate color, since the other repeated "brlirthl," while mimicking a few steps of a comic dance. She burst out laughing — or least that's how she interpreted it, although the sound that emerged from her mouth sounded more like a moan. She remembered too late that darztls don't laugh — they turn an amused shade!

"Fine. You shouldn't tire yourself out too much. You need to sleep and get your strength back."

The interior yard at the boarding house looked more like a eastern garden than a western one, but it felt good to stretch out there in the heat. They left Selm alone more often than not, which gave her time to bone up on darztl works, bundles of thick sheets portraying scenes from this life that still seemed so foreign to her. Most often, she just looked at the images because reading gave her migraines. The translator had, in fact, been designed to decode oral language, but was of no use whatsoever for deciphering the strange signs that could not be read either horizontally or vertically, but some signs in keeping with the others on the page, in apparent anarchy. She was still too much of a novice, and had too little talent for foreign languages to do any more than browse through books intended for children. Khlearmt didn't appear alarmed by this. Blaming this disability on her selective amnesia, he often sat down next to her to read out loud. Occasionally, she even forgot that she was there as a spy and enjoyed these sessions without trying to store up as much information as possible.

She wasn't the only boarder. The other rooms were occupied by darztls all in more or less advanced stages of convalescence, some as mentally shattered as she seemed to be. The first time someone addressed her in a language other than the darztl she knew, she once again thought her translator was defective.

The immense creature, who looked slightly different than the other darztls she had seen up to then, said, "Liml, tlalm, dtlohlm," or something like that. Responding to her dumbfounded look, the other turned a shade close to lavender and continued hesitantly in a language that the translator labored to translate.

"How are you? I am Sam. From Amldl."

She didn't seem to understand, and it was the other's turn to look dumbfounded. Fortunately, Khlearmt came to the rescue.

"Sam is from the western continent. From Sliiddarztl. Selm doesn't remember her geography lessons? Well!"

The darztl's wattle turned emerald green.

For her part, she hoped that the color of her own wattle wasn't too obvious a sign of her excitement at learning something new about her hosts. For humans, all darztls looked the same. All darztls had always been treated as a group; it was assumed they had the same customs and traditions, the same language. But there were at least two separate countries? Of course the colonizers knew that there were two inhabited continents on the planet. It was just that most of the surface of the other continent was located near the equator, and it was even hotter there than here, so the humans had decided to settle here and savor the first refreshing effects of terraforming. Selm found the humans rather stupid for not realizing that two continents separated by an ocean could only house two distinct cultures!

Khlearmt was neither her nurse nor her keeper — he was essentially her escort. He was always there when she needed him; he seemed to be assigned exclusively to her and, whether this meant anything or not, he was the gentlest darztl she had ever met. But she was starting to get tired of this leisurely existence where her every need was satisfied. She was a woman — a female darztl — of action. Idleness was killing her. Plus, she wasn't there to spend her time lazing about. She had quickly realized that she wouldn't find any useful information in the books. It would take her years to decipher that strange writing and she had barely one year left, fourteen marsian months — fourteen *yanz* as they said — to learn all about darztl society. However, she would have to make her request formally. She couldn't take the chance of simply escaping. That would raise too many suspicions.

"Listen," she said to Khlearmt one evening, "I feel that my convalescence is stagnating. I feel great physically, but mentally, I'm not really improving. Only a few wisps of my past life have come back to me since I've been here, and they're just flashes that I can't weave into any coherent scenario. I have to get out of here; I have to see the country. Maybe that way, by visiting a few places, seeing some people, I'll get my memory back."

The darztl's answer was blunter than she had expected.

"Khlearmt can't answer right away. He doesn't know if the authorities will let Selm leave. They still have doubts about her and they might be afraid to let her wander about the country. Khlearmt will see what he can do."

He returned a few days later with news that made her wattle burst with color. "Khlearmt and Selm can go out. That means that Selm can start to visit the city as long as Khlearmt goes with her. Later, they will have to see if it will be possible to travel outside Sshklooreml."

"Sshklooreml." That was the name of the city where Selm was living. She had no idea what 'sshkloo' meant — maybe it was just the name of the city's founder — but she had learned that 'reml' meant land, or something like that. She was in Sshklooreml in Remldarztl, namely, the land of the darztls. It made her wonder why they'd bothered to develop translators!

§ § §

Sshklooreml was a city of gentle sandy tones, like almost everything that wove the darztls' lives. It was a lightly populated city and most of the inhabitants seemed to be just passing through. She remarked on this to Khlearmt who was no longer surprised by the candor of her questions. He even said that she helped him view his own life in a different light.

"Well, Khlearmt has no idea where Selm comes from, but here community life is not the choice for an entire lifetime. As least not for everyone. Darztls are a very anti-social species, not at all like osfts! The people like to travel back and forth between solitary life and solidarity. Indifferent to word games, the translator performed its job valiantly.

She almost added, "I understand that, you know. In the world I come from, even after abandoning the separation of the genders for hundreds of years, the human being doesn't yet seem to have completely adapted!"

But, of course, that was one of the many things Selm had to keep to herself.

In the streets — if those torturous arteries where the reptiles roamed, occasionally straddling other, even more gigantic reptiles, could be called streets — everyone greeted her host, but they all seemed to avoid meeting Selm's eyes, as if she were dangerous or, worse yet, invisible. When they entered a stall, the other darztls always addressed Khlearmt, never Selm. One day as they left an establishment, a tavern, a darztl who was apparently intoxicated — at least that's what Selm concluded — yelled something at her that she didn't understand but it seemed to make Khlearmt uncomfortable since he quickly dragged her elsewhere. Of course, everyone knew who she was. There was no television here, either 2D or 3D, but that didn't stop news from traveling.

"You have to understand them," Khlearmt reassured her after a few days. "Memory is so important. People are uncomfortable with those who have lost their memories."

"Do you think they run away from me because they're afraid I really am a spy?"

"Bah, they'll get to know you. I know for a fact you're no threat to anyone."

He stared at her, and Selm had the impression that he could read right through her with his mobile eyes. When had he started speaking to her in this familiar tone? She hadn't noticed it. But, she had not yet mastered enough of the rudiments of this language not to conclude that it was some whim on the part of her translator.

"Pardon me," he said. "Khlearmt should not be so familiar. Selm does not know him well enough."

"No, no, quite the contrary, you can be familiar with me." And the translator translated, "He can be familiar with her."

The result was totally surrealistic and Selm laughed to hide her discomfort.

"The sound you make when you laugh is strange."

That was the most difficult thing — not giving herself away. When she had had to fight against the blind authorities, all of her attention had been focused on her mission and she had been completely into playing her role, so there had been no risk that she would give away a few clues. But now that she was in a relaxing, cozy environment, now that she was being allowed to play tourist, things were much more risky. Nothing had prepared her for developing close ties with a darztl... and enjoying it of all things! She had her suspicions about Khlearmt. All of this unnatural attention. He treated her like a friend, a sister, although he could have acted like the others, mistrustful of her. Yet at the same time, he was her only contact on foreign soil.... So she had to play the game, too.

The days passed in this way, banal and uneventful. They extended the scope of their explorations farther and farther, visiting zones that were increasingly desolate, along the fringes of the city that, unlike the earthly suburbs mentioned in the books on the mother ship, harbored no industry, although military establishments stood guard in the northern sector. They had what they needed and sometimes a little more, but their lives were not filled with things as human lives were. Most of the houses she visited — three or four at most — were relatively bare. Occasionally, images were engraved in the stone walls, but no paintings hung there. The rooms were clean and comfortable, designed specifically to store and preserve the natural heat of the day but, with the exception of a few trinkets, most of the objects found there actually served some purpose. There were a lot of books, for example, and day-to-day instruments. In the city, there were a few shops selling jewelry or pieces of clothing that were more decorative than functional, but the booths were few and far between and carried little stock. The darztls were not narcissistic either. Perhaps because there was so little water on this planet, there were only few mirrors in the homes or public places. In short, day by day, she learned a multitude of picturesque details about the darztls, but nothing of any use for military purposes, and nothing that could not be found somewhere in the files they had already accumulated at the base camp. Nothing of what she was really looking for: the general status of their defense systems, their industries, the hatcheries or the place where perhaps they kept humans captive.

Gradually, she slipped in a deep depression — faked, of course. She barely ate, refused to set foot outside, slowly slid into almost total silence. Khlearmt tried to bring her out of it, proposing outings, making lengthy soliloquies — he was very chatty for a darztl. It hurt her to see him like that, with all the efforts he made. But she held firm. When he asked her what was wrong, she replied evasively or merely turned away. Then, one evening, deciding that she had kept him waiting long enough, she started to reveal herself, as if against her will, as if each word pained her.

"I'll never get my memory back, Khlearmt. I'll never know who I am."

She had used a confidential tone. The smart chip in the translator had managed to adapt over the course of her conversations and respect her use of the first person.

"Now, now. You can't let yourself get discouraged. You only started your convalescence a few short months ago. These things take time. You know, I was once like you are."

Selm's wattle must have betrayed her surprise since he hastened to add, "No, no, I didn't lose my memory. But it was the same thing. You know, I don't come from Sshklooreml, or from anywhere around here. No, I was born much farther north, in the middle of the desert. If your ears were a little better, or a little less forgetful, you would have noted my accent. I was not... well... not a good darztl. You know, life is hard in the desert. The further north you go, the colder it gets. I was raised like the others in my clutch but, I don't know, I wasn't like everyone else. I wasn't one of a kind, but let's say that we stood out from the brood by the way we always stayed in a small compact bunch. I was very attached to them, and particularly to one of them. The others made fun of us when they saw us always stuck together. The problem was that Sliermk — that was his name — hooked up with someone else after a while. The least that can be said is that Khlearmt didn't like that. One evening, when he had drunk too much, he threw himself on Sliermk. He wanted to force the other to love him."

She looked at him in surprise. Khlearmt who was so gentle, so attentive, was... Was what really? What word could she use to refer to this reality that was largely beyond her grasp? What was she to understand from his revelations? Especially if he knew that whenever he touched Selm...

"They punished me for that. I did hard labor until I was rehabilitated. At the end of my sentence, after that forced closeness, my mind was made up. I fled. I spent years on the run, wandering from one continent to the other, constantly on the move in an effort to escape from myself. Sometimes, darztls would see me in the large solar panel zone, sometimes in the stone quarries at the far east, sometimes working as a mine guard, everywhere that the bitter life gave me no time to think of anything but the present. I spent many lengthy revolutions of the planet living like that. I was trying to forget who I was. Often I succeeded, but then my past would catch up with me, someone who knew someone who had known me, and that memory reopened my painful wound, as if it had just happened. Then one day, out of some sort of morbid fascination, I returned to the place where I was born. I knew that it was in neutral territory at that time; I'd hear some vague talk without really wanting to listen, but by then I wanted to see if reality resembled the pain that my memory awoke in me. Of course, nothing was left. The places where I had grown up were smack in the middle of the buffer zone between the human and darztl territories. Those I had known, all those I had loved, and the others that I had loved less, had disappeared, chased south or carried away by the violence of the humans or... of darztls barely worse than me."

"How old are you?"

Khlearmt looked at her in surprise. Selm's translator had not translated the word "old." She recalled that darztls didn't calculate their ages as such. She started over, "Um... what brought you here?"

"Life caught up with me all of a sudden. I realized that I'd been living on the surface of my life all that time, without digging any deeper. So I came here to Sshklooreml, to recover the time I'd lost. Here I could help the lost. I think I understand them better than anyone. We do what's right without there being any obligation between us. Usually, I don't tell them where I'm from. I'm afraid that they won't understand me, that they'll judge me, that they'll... distance themselves. You see, I'm not healed yet. You're like me; you're looking for this contact. I knew that right off. There's something unhealthy in that, but it's so pleasant, isn't it?"

Selm was moved despite herself, but she was also very excited. For the first time Khlearmt had mentioned the mines, the solar panels, the stone quarries, and she juggled different ways in which she could find out more, ideally even to be taken there. The darztl was suspicious of her silence.

"I'm boring Selm with these confidences, aren't I? She has enough problems on her shoulders without having to listen to the whining complaints of a deviant darztl."

He moved as if to stand up.

She placed her hand on his shoulder, forcing him to sit down. "No, no... stay. You story was good for me. If I understand you properly, you think I can't remember anything because I have good reasons for forgetting?"

Then, holding her breath and hoping her wattle would not betray her, she added, "I would really like for you to show me those places where you roamed for all those years. I might find myself there as well...."

§ § §

Remldarztl was a rough surface pitted with rocky hills and furrowed with desiccated ravines. The people here knew nothing of motorized vehicles, only traveling through the territory on haavls. The animal, even when loaded down like a mule, pranced on quickly. During the few days she had spent with her savior at the outset, she had set her mind to learning to ride this scaly beast and now she was able to mount it almost naturally.

Khlearmt had moved heaven and earth to obtain permission to take her outside the city. First, he'd had to find someone who would take care of running the rest home. However, before wheedling the authorities into authorizing this nature stroll, he'd also had to swear that he would assume full responsibility for her and keep her under close watch at all times.

What's more, they had to register in every little town they traveled through. Obviously, no one trusted Selm. But if they had known just how right they were, they would certainly have sent her on a much longer, more permanent trip.

In this way, they crossed the desert, stopping a little before nightfall to set up their camp or staying in small, more or less deserted inns. On one barely visible road they came across other travelers, who merely waved as they rode by. Occasionally they'd encounter a group of darztls, just as reserved, perched on top of large carts carrying mysterious loads. Darztls, as Selm gradually learned, did not necessarily seek out the company of others, even though they didn't run off. Traveling on and on, she and her companion visited the places where Khlearmt had lived, and he would give her a brief account of his short stay there. When they entered a new inhabited zone, he would observe Selm's wattle, hoping to see if he could detect any sign of recognition in her. But it was all in vain, of course. She would have liked to pretend she did recognize something — it would certainly have made him very happy — but she didn't know how she would extricate herself if she took that route.

Recognize what? Invent what? Based on what? No, it was better to disappoint him than to place herself in jeopardy.

Khlearmt seemed to find his way naturally, without any need for a map. Or else he saw something in the stars unknown to Selm. In any case, however, she knew they were traveling south because the sun traveled across the sky from left to right during the day, and the farther they went, the hotter it got — even when wearing a protective suit, a human would have suffered heatstroke well before noon. But as for knowing whether they were traveling a little more to the southeast or to the southwest, she was completely in the dark. And in the middle of the desert, with no landmarks, an error of a few small degrees would condemn you to wandering for the rest of your days.

"What you see, over there, are the large solar panels. I worked there for a while, to earn some money."

In the distance, all she saw was a bright metal shine. However, as they approached, she started to make out large surfaces that looked like rounded mirrors. Darztl solar panels were not all that different from human ones. Perhaps certain good ideas were universal, Selm thought....

"And how is the energy carried to the cities?"

Khlearmt looked at her as if she had just spouted nonsense, as if she had spoken... human.

"Sometimes you say the strangest things. Come, you'll see."

At close range, the solar panel zone, as her travel companion called it, was much less desolate than it had appeared from a distance. An entire city, one of the largest she had seen in darztl territory, lay at the foot of the hill where the solar panels stood, hundreds of metal disks turned to face the burning star — Khlearmt had told her that the disks were equipped with phototropic mechanisms that always pointed them in the optimal position. On the southern slope of the hill, between the panels and the city, stood buildings that were larger than the houses she had seen so far. When they had drawn closer, she saw that the area was swarming with life — finally, here was a major concentration of darztls.

The buildings were factories. Up to this point, Selm had seen mostly artisans, manufacturing complete, unique objects and selling them in stalls out of their homes. Some items, such as books, for example, or certain tools, appeared to have been manufactured industrially, but she had never managed to discover where this was done. And for good cause. All of the plants on the planet appeared to be here! But why so far away? And why here?

"I imagine it just started like that and it became tradition. But thinking about it, why not? It gives us an opportunity to travel whenever we need to stock up. Plus, you have to consider the solar panels. At this site, the sunlight is the most consistent and the days are the longest. Look at how clear the sky is here!"

When they left the factory neighborhood — Selm would have liked to visit a few, but she didn't want to look too curious — they entered the city proper. Here, nothing was any different from what she had seen elsewhere. Barely paved, winding streets snaked among low, broad houses; buildings that were barely any larger housed the city government where they had to report; monuments carved from rock; broad, empty public squares filled with a few stone benches where ossfts jumped about, chasing sand caterpillars, which everyone here called zimmpt. There were few people in the streets, but she had to admit that it was still early and that many must be working in the factories. And, to her great relief, she observed that here she passed relatively unnoticed. No disapproving, stealthy glances like in Ssklooreml, no whispering behind her back.

"This is where I lived," Khlearmt said, stopping his haavl in front of a dwelling that looked like the others. "Well, actually, this is where I lived for a while."

The innkeeper was a small, dark, stormy-looking darztl who barely glanced at them as they registered. Then he looked up and his wattle turned bright.

"Is that... could it be... Khlearmt?" he asked.

"Yes, it's me. How are you?"

"Well... fine. Are you still wandering from one end of the country to the other?"

"Well... I've changed somewhat. I've settled down somewhere. I'll tell you all about it."

Listening to them, Selm realized that they knew one another well, and were even rather intimate. Khlearmt had told her about the technical, geographic, even philosophical aspects of his long trip, but he had never mentioned the bonds he had woven throughout the lengthy time. She'd viewed him as some sort of hermit who had kept his distance from others. But deep down it was probably something completely different. In order to flee, Khlearmt had had to lose himself in a multitude of dazzling, ephemeral relationships. Without quite knowing why, that hurt. Then she rebuked herself. No way would she be jealous of the past relationships of someone who was nothing more than her involuntary guard!

The next day, when Khlearmt knocked at her door to wake her up — the previous evening she had heard him leave his room and come back very late in the night, much more rumpled than the average darztl — she hoped he would take her to see the factories. And in fact, they headed off in that direction. But they rode past the large buildings without stopping. She followed him, a little grumpy, saying that they deserved to spend a day without riding through the desert. Yet, to her great relief, they didn't head off into the rocky expanse, but stopped at the foot of the hill, near the slope opposite the one by which they had arrived. She observed that what looked like a massive hill was really an empty shell. This side of the mountain was hollow, and seemed to open into the entrails of the planet. On the site, they found a disciplined team working busily around a series of large machines. They were connected to large pipes that rose out of the center of the planet from one side and dipped back into the rock on the other side.

"I worked here," the darztl said at the top of his lungs, over the noise of the machinery, as he handed her a suit of shimmering material. They had just walked into the belly of the mountain and Khlearmt had spent a few minutes talking with a darztl who seemed to know him.

"This is one of the three large pumping sites in the country. This is where the water you drink comes from — when you don't collect it on your own from the desert plants, of course! Normally they don't like too many visitors here, for sanitary reasons, but I have my connections, as you've seen. And I wanted to share this part of my past with you."

The corridor they walked along was narrow and filled with large, flexible hoses dripping with condensation. It sloped sharply down to the center of Mars II. They

proceeded cautiously. Selm, who had found walking
without footwear strange at the beginning of her experience as a darztl, now felt clumsy in the slippers she'd
to put on along with her suit. However, she understood
why they had to be so muffled up: it was getting colder
and colder as they descended and the heated suit barely
made up for it. But their efforts were not in vain. Soon
they reached a clearing where an unusual sight awaited
them.

There was water beneath the mountain. It cascaded
down the rocky wall, collecting in a small basin at the
bottom. It was the first time Selm had seen so much water
at one time. She had been born in the year after the
humans had settled on Mars II and knew nothing but
the colony's rations and recycled water, barely supple-
mented by the dew the colonists so laboriously collected.
Yet now, she learned that these darztls, who needed barely
any water to survive — their bodies stored most liquids,
and eliminated highly concentrated urine — had water
in abundance, while the humans, for whom water was
a necessity at all times, had to settle for an ersatz liquid
that stank of chemical purifiers. She didn't ask him how
the water was carried to the other cities; she didn't want
to confuse him as she had when she'd asked him how
electricity was transmitted from one city to another. In
any case, she now understood what was being carried
in the immense containers pulled by the giant haavls they
had met on their way.

It was a magnificent spectacle and it roused totally
human emotions in her. The desire to dive into the water,
to cleanse her body of the dust that had accumulated,
to wet her lips, to drink from this spring. But the water
had to be glacial and, despite her suit, she was already
chilled to the bone. Yet, overwhelmed by a sort of
contemplative torpor, she was unable to take her eyes
from the pure, flowing water, shining gently under the
phosphorescent lighting of the cavern. She swooned.

Khlearmt's color looked concerned. "Don't tell me
you're going to have a cold attack?"

And, thinking about it, she realized she did feel frozen. She wasn't in any real pain, just paralyzed. Khlearmt's voice, begging her to wake up and follow him, came to her from a distance. Finally, she leaned on him and stood up, less from any desire to do so than to stop the incessant murmuring chiding her.

"Come on now, grab on to me and we'll go back up."

He dragged her back to the sun.

"The water was beautiful. I can't imagine how you managed to leave here."

They were back in the daylight and she had managed to warm herself on a rock.

"It was magnificent, but as you proved yourself, one doesn't feel in his natural element there. At the end, I was tired of being cold all the time. You know, during that period of my life, I never really managed to get warm."

"Then how did you manage to work in the mines? It must be cold there too, isn't it?"

"Yes, but here, to maintain security, we have to do everything ourselves."

Selm was in the process of standing up.

"At least in the mines there are humans," her companion added.

She felt the breath go out of her. Her feet gave way beneath her and she allowed herself to fall to the ground in order to recoup her thoughts. Fortunately, Khlearmt attributed it all to hypothermia.

"Rest a little while longer. We don't have to leave right away."

§ § §

As they bounced about on their haavls after spending ten more days in Oohitlsuireml, Selm felt grumpy, sullen. Sad as well, since she now envisioned Khlearmt subduing a horde of frightened human slaves. Not wanting to rouse his suspicions, she hadn't asked him any more questions, but she didn't need him to draw a picture. The darztls had set up a work camp in the mines where they had the humans do the filthy work their own metabolism made it so hard for them to bear.

Moreover, her skin itched atrociously. She felt like rolling in the sand and scratching until she drew blood. At first, she was somewhat concerned about this new condition, but then she recalled the first time she had shed her skin. It didn't improve her mood any, but she felt reassured. Her body had knit a new envelope and would cast off the dead skin like a cumbersome sheath. Her skin was peeling off in large, dark strips that flew off in the wind.

Then, suddenly, one morning she woke up with a new sensation. The sloughing period was over. She felt supple, smooth. Her muscles rippled under her skin in perfect harmony. And when she looked at her arms, her legs, her feet, she was thrilled by the brightness of her skin. She was bedecked in new colors and shone like fire. Against all her expectations, she felt beautiful. She wondered if Khlearmt found her beautiful. She walked over to him as he continued to load his belongings on his haavl.

"I know I haven't been the ideal traveling companion these past few days."

"It's the sloughing season," he said distractedly, continuing with his business.

"I like it," she said, hugging him. "It makes me feel like I've been reborn."

She was exaggerating a little, since for all intents and purposes, this was only her third cycle.

"I think my colors are more beautiful than before, don't you?"

He finally looked at her and took two or three steps back. His wattle turned green. "Yes — my goodness! — you're all aglow."

She moved toward him, rubbing against him. "I also like the new texture of my skin."

He reached his hand out to her and she took it and placed it firmly against her belly. Without realizing what she was about to do, she jumped him. Larger and stronger than the male darztl, she pushed him back onto the ground. Stretched out against him, she rubbed against his flesh. Intellectually, she had no idea how darztls mated, but she had the impression that her body knew exactly what to do. Khlearmt's body had never appeared so desirable before. She wanted his caresses, she wanted him to penetrate her, she wanted him all for herself. She didn't notice right away that he was struggling.

"No, Selm, no!"

She stopped, surprised, and he took advantage of the opportunity to free himself. She held him, but he repeated, "No, Selm, stop. I don't want to."

With a flick of his tail, he managed to free himself and took a few steps back, obviously on guard.

"But why?" she asked, in a voice intended to sound distraught but which contained only the usual clicks. "You don't find me attractive?"

"No, it's not that," he reassured her. "I think you're one of the most... the most exciting females I've ever met. And I like you a lot."

"Then why?"

"Well... you know... Khlearmt isn't very used to having sexual relations with females."

Selm's desire evaporated as she digested this admission. What exactly did he mean by that? Was he a virgin or a homosexual? She had no idea that could apply to species other than humans. And she could hardly confess that, at least when she wasn't a reptile in heat, she didn't really like sex with males, either...

"Oh, Selm, I'm so sorry."

Realizing that any risk of excessive desire had apparently been set aside, he approached her and helped her up. But she felt that he was doing everything possible to look as gruff as possible.

"Listen, we've just about reached the city. If we gallop all day, we'll get there before nightfall. You could meet someone there, mate if you want?"

It was her turn to step back. Mate with a darztl? Any old darztl? She was too afraid. She knew nothing about darztl sexuality, she was afraid of doing it poorly, or hurting, who knew, of betraying herself at the crucial moment. Sexual relations with any darztl other Khlearmt seemed unnatural....

"No," she said. "The moment's passed. Let's get back on our way."

But she wriggled about on her saddle all day in an effort to quench her burning desire. Once again, she felt grumpy. Oh, nothing at all like she had felt when shedding her skin, it was more a sense of impatience, or impotence. Now that she was aware of them, she would not let herself be surprised by her passions, but they were just about on the threshold of the bearable. How could she, connected to this body by a tiny little implant, feel the call of the tiniest nerve endings? However, she did everything she could to delay their trip until she was certain they would not reach the city before nightfall. She was afraid of what she might do.

That evening, she lay down a ways off to avoid being overcome by a new excess of desire. She couldn't sleep. She tossed and turned, over and over. She tried to caress herself, but her enormous claws slit her skin. Suddenly, she felt something brush against her.

"Khlearmt, don't play that game."

The darztl was rubbing his paw ever so gently against her flank.

"Khlearmt!"

"You know, when I said I wasn't used to having sexual relations with female darztls, that was true. But I can't say that I don't find you desirable. I don't know what this is all about, but there's something between us, stronger than the distance that separates us."

She wondered what he was talking about, but forgot to think about it.

"I'm afraid... I'm afraid you'll find me clumsy, ridiculous." Khlearmt continued caressing her belly as he talked. "You know, in any case, it's been a very long time since I've mated with anyone."

"Bah, it's like riding a bicycle, you never forget how."

"What's a bkticlethl?"

The translator had failed to translate this. They both found her response funny, but for different reasons.

They started caressing one another, like two creatures who had found one another after a lengthy separation. Finally, she found herself on her belly and he mounted her.

She felt his penis — good grief, one of his two penises — penetrate her and, with a moan, she encouraged him to continue, wrapping her tail around him. He thrust more deeply and she moaned again, with satisfaction this time. She felt his powerful paws hold her close. Even though he was smaller than she was, he was still incredibly powerful. He bit her crest and the pleasure spread to all of her limbs. Now she knew why this part of her anatomy was so sensitive: it was also enormously erogenous. She lifted her lower body and he thrust in and out, biting her crest harder and harder and the sensation was the most delicious she had experienced in some time. For just a moment she wondered what color their wattles were. Then she felt the heat in her belly and forgot about asking questions. He immediately thrust his second penis into her; the pleasure increased and burst.

They would never mate again. The mating period was over, but Selm had no doubt that darztls were capable of sexual relations outside the reproductive periods. If she had understood correctly, and if it was true that Khlearmt had had sexual relations with individuals of his own gender, then that was a sure sign that the species was evolved enough to distinguish between reproduction and making love. In any case, what business did she have asking if they were evolved? Of course they were! Her traveling companion was much more evolved than certain humans she had encountered during the course of her life!

§ § §

By the time the mines came into sight, she had almost forgotten about the human slaves. Either that or she had voluntarily relegated that bit of information to the back of her mind. They'd been on the road for a long time. If her inner compass was right, after leaving the city with the solar panels they had headed east, toward the quarries. The quarries! Quarries for precious gems! Diamonds! Then they had set off north, traveling through numerous villages, each with its descriptive name. Drotzyreml, the land that looked like a turtle. Hidclreml, the land with the burning orchids. Sielxthblootrd, the end of the world, the city with gigantic cliffs overlooking a sea so far below it was hidden to the eye.

One day, Khlearmt stopped on a small hill formed by a pile of rocks arranged in complex figures. They had come across other elevations of a similar nature on their trip and Selm had concluded they were some sort of signs for travelers. Yet she had never dared ask. Khlearmt remained there, silent, tasting the heat of the day.

"What are you doing?" she asked.

He looked at her for a long time, as if he expected something obvious to jump out at her. Finally he said, "I'm praying."

Too astonished to ask any more questions, she remained silent and watched him. He stood there for a long time, facing a pile of rocks, then finally bent down and rearranged the rocks to his own liking. He turned to her. "You don't ever pray?"

"Well..." she said, embarrassed by her ignorance. "I don't think I remember how to pray."

"It can be learned again. Then, by doing it, maybe it will come back to you. It's a little like riding a haavl. You never forget how."

She felt her own wattle turn green, but her companion didn't see anything funny about what he had just said.

"And what god to you pray to?" she continued.

"A god? Well, it's been a long time since I've heard that word. We learned about the concept in our history classes. Don't you remember? No? Then I wonder where you got that from! No, I don't pray to a particular god. I simply pray. And I've left a sign for the individual who follows me," he added, pointing a claw toward the hill. "I used to come here for walks when I was working in the mines."

She jumped. She had forgotten the mines. The humans. The horror she might discover down there.

"So, are you taking me to the mines?" she said in a voice that was deceptively calm.

He admitted that the authorities did not have to know he was taking her there, and that he would not register their presence. It wasn't really a secret place, but they didn't want to make too much of the human presence in darztl territory. There might always be a few extremists who would want to settle accounts with the humans, regardless of their usefulness for the mining industry.

She moved forward on her haavl, next to Khlearmt, her heart pounding, eager to make one of her most important discoveries since the start of her mission, terrified at what she might find.

From a distance, she noticed nothing in particular. A few typical darztl buildings with no distinctive features apart from the fact that they were surrounded by heavy fences, despite the fact that most homes in this land were almost never locked. Several armed darztls appeared to be standing guard at the entrance to the smallest building, while several others, carrying wheelbarrows, walked to and fro between the entrance and a series of containers lined up in the yard. As they approached, she noticed that the smallest building wasn't really a building at all, but an entrance leading to a hole in the ground. It was the middle of the afternoon and activity in the mine was at its peak. Khlearmt appeared to be looking for a familiar face.

"Those who work here never stay for long; there's a high turnover rate."

Finally he seemed to recognize someone. A darztl raced over, arm raised in the sign of greeting.

After a playful exchange of spoken and body language — Selm found it easier and easier to understand the chromatic variations of the wattles — Khlearmt was given permission to spend a few days on the site. He had told the other that he was making a sort of pilgrimage — in fact, the translator had not been able to translate the exact word he had used. He was very evasive when introducing Selm, referring to her as an old friend he had come across at some point and was traveling with for a while.

The rest of the day was spent visiting the buildings outside the mine and listening to statistics about the metals extracted there. Every opportunity she got, Selm glanced at the entrance to the shaft, but saw nothing other than a few darztls pushing their wheelbarrows laden with rocks and occasionally some others, wearing silk suits, going in and out of the mine. She was bursting with impatience and yet she pretended to be extremely interested when the darztl spoke to them about the iron content of the surrounding soil. By the time they were taken to the building where they were to sleep, there had still been no mention of a visit into the mine.

Selm found it hard to fall asleep. The very thought that some of her own kind were nearby, possibly underground — did they ever let them up into the daylight? — and the prospect of not being able to act for fear of jeopardizing the entire operation filled her with rage and a sense of powerlessness. By the time morning came, she had barely closed her eyes all night and felt crumpled, her head heavy.

"Would you like to come down into the mine with me? I worked there at one point and would like to see if it's how I remember it."

She almost jumped him and... struck him, but she restrained herself.

Weighed down by the same type of suit they had worn when they went to see the spring, they descended into the mine, accompanied by an employee, who was armed.

"Are you sure you want to come?" Khlearmt asked. "Remember how the cold affected you the last time you went underground."

But she felt as ready as she ever would be to face all the cold of the world.

The first shafts they entered were deserted. But in the distance they could hear a murmur, the sound of a dozen pickaxes hitting rock. It was a real labyrinth down below and she was relieved to know that she was well guarded. Then the corridor forked and they reached the tumult. The massive silhouettes of the guards hid the rest of the scene from them. Then they took a few more steps and Selm saw her first humans in many months. Female humans above all, based on what she could make out though their genderless suits. Each and every one of them looked both infinitely sad and resigned. A few of them were very young, barely seven or eight years old, and yet each carried a pickaxe and was striking the wall with all of her frail strength. One or two toddlers, who were truly too young to work, held onto the legs of the women and one woman even had a baby lying nearby. Two guards paced back and forth behind the humans, ostensibly armed, occasionally striking a slave with the butt of their rifles, encouraging her to work harder. Selm glanced about, looking for permission and, seeing that neither Khlearmt nor the employee who accompanied them seemed to object, she bent down to one of the children. The child hid behind a woman, shrieking. She told him to be quiet as she continued her work. Selm had also stepped back, holding in her own scream. The woman had only one foot. Her other leg stopped just above the heel. Looking around, she saw that some of the other human prisoners — about twenty, counting only the adults — that she saw in the corridor were similarly maimed. Two of them, who were missing both feet, knelt on the ground to work.

Selm felt as if she were about to faint and leaned against the rocky wall. Misunderstanding, Khlearmt asked if she felt all right, if she wasn't a bit cold, if she wanted to go back to the surface. She declined his offer, of course. She couldn't leave this place so quickly, not before seeing everything, even if what she did see was as close to hell as she had ever been. They continued on their way and, at the next turn, came across the rest of the small battalion of slaves. Twenty adults again and still only two or three men. She wondered what they had done with the others. They hadn't killed all of them, however — she supposed that there were enough left to ensure a succession, for... reproduction. From the start, she had been afraid to look them in the face for fear of recognizing a familiar face — there were fewer than a thousand people in the colony so anything was possible. She walked over to one worker whose too-bulky outfit failed to hide the fact that she was almost at term and she tried to speak with her. The mine employee moved between her and the woman before she had a chance to say much, and the slave continued her work as if nothing had happened. In any case, Selm's words

would have come out in darztl and not the language she
used in her mind, and even if that had not been the case
the woman would probably have not understand any of
the words uttered by a voice box that was not human.

They left, taking a different route. Before they reached
the surface, Selm saw a door that was partially closed by
a large stone. She asked what was behind it. The guard
who accompanied them did not answer, but he cleared the
opening effortlessly. It opened into a gallery that was larger
than the others, a grotto, rather, where a series of nests had
been carved into the rock.

"This is where the humans sleep," Khlearmt explained.

And she saw that the nests were, in fact, the size of an
average human. The room smelled of human bodies, the
same odor she had noticed in the corridors they had visited,
an odor she was so unused to she found it disgusting. She
felt nauseous and suddenly vomited her entire breakfast.

The mine employee and Khlearmt helped her back up
to the surface. As soon as she was in the fresh air, she started
to run madly until she reached the tall fence.

"Wait for me," her companion called out behind her.
"Where are you going?"

Khlearmt finally caught up with her.

"I know, it's always unsettling. But we know one thing
for sure now: you've never worked here. If you had, you
would never have forgotten it."

She looked him straight in the eyes, "How could you?"

He turned a perplexed color.

She continued, "How could you have worked here, even
for a minute? Those are people who are kept prisoner here,
not haavls that can be trained or drotzs you can keep in
cages for pets! Darztls must be monsters!"

"People, eh? You mean usurpers who came here, who
invaded our planet!" Khlearmt retorted, beating the ground
with his tail in exasperation.

She didn't flinch.

He continued, "No, you know what I found the saddest the entire time I worked here? That this is the point
we've reached in our relationship with beings that we
welcomed to our world with open arms. And that we've

had to go to such lengths to entertain even the slightest hope that one day we'll be able to chase them from Sielxth. That's what I've always found atrocious."

He strode off. She remained alone with her pain, her confusion, torn between her former vision and the new one, between what she was inside and the image she projected to the world. Her pain at feeling so close to the one who should have, especially now, remained her enemy.

When she returned to their quarters, he was already packing their bags.

"I think it would be a good idea for us to return to Sshklooreml. From there, Selm can head off in whatever direction she wants. If that's what she wants."

She shrugged, remembered at the last minute that darztls never shrug, and decided she didn't care.

"If that's what you want."

She slept very badly and woke up screaming several times from nightmares. The next morning, they set out in silence and galloped all day without saying a word. Images filled her mind against her wishes, like a film playing over and over in her mind. She had not asked many questions about the daily lives of the slaves, but she could picture them without any problem. In her mind, Selm went over and over the images of humans subjected to darztls, of one-footed women forced to hammer away in the belly of the planet, to help the enemy fight their own kind. Oddly enough, she wondered if they allowed them to sing. Occasionally, however, another image took over. That of darztls massacred by humans, darztl bodies kept artificially alive until humans needed them for scientific experiments. Suddenly her own body filled her with horror, not because of its appearance or its nature but because it was the fruit of the humans' cybernetic engineering. And then the vision of all those amputated feet that she pictured stacked in the desert to dry came back to haunt her, superimposed over the real image of the mutilated remains of a darztl she had seen left behind by a bloodthirsty gang. Why did she have to come here, to the mines? Why hadn't she stopped just before? Because of her sense of duty? Her morbid fascination? Her mission, of course, her sacred mission that, right now, had caught up with her! She had to report this sinister scene of humans kept prisoner to work for the adversary. Yet she would have liked to bring back the idyllic image she had had of the darztls up to that point, the image of a peaceful, free people, both individualistic and deeply united. In that way they wouldn't have seemed so unpleasantly... human.

Once they had set up the camp, she was the first to break the silence. And, through her words, she wanted to re-establish the balance of power between herself and Khlearmt, even if he wasn't aware of it — to give him weapons to fight the enemy, weapons for which the human in her already had the equivalent.

"Images came back to me last night," she said nonchalantly.

Khlearmt looked up at her, his wattle a very pale purple.

"Because you went to the mine? You'd already been to the mines?"

"No, but I do know that I was once kept captive. At least, that's what I saw in my dreams."

He moved closer to her, looking both intrigued and pleased. He placed his paw on her arm to encourage her to continue. For once, he remained solemnly silent. She felt a little ashamed about telling a story that was totally fabricated.

"I... humans bound with me chains and caused me a great deal of pain. I was weak. I was cold. I realized that they were keeping me prisoner so that they could take me back to their kind like some sort of trophy."

She was talking about what had happened to dozens of darztls, as far as she knew, making their story her own. All darztls that had wound up in the colony's laboratories, if they weren't massacred first.

"And you escaped?"

"I don't know, I think so. Then I see myself wandering aimlessly in the desert, clutching a miserable bag containing human objects, most of which were a mystery to me."

Khlearmt thought for a moment. "Do you think the humans also keep darztls to use them against us?"

"How am I supposed to know!" she retorted hastily.

"I mean, a single human is no match for a darztl, but if there were several... Surely they've tried to find out more about us since diplomatic relations broke off; surely they tried to analyze how our bodies work, maybe they even kept a few worker darztls to work for them."

"Maybe..." she remained silent for a few minutes. "Khlearmt?"

"Yes?"

"You know, I don't feel like going back to Sshklooreml right away. Do you think you could show me where you grew up?"

"Well, there's not much to see. Everything has been destroyed. But I can take you there anyway; it will postpone our return to real life."

§ § §

It had been almost a year since Selm had left the human colony and it was time for her to return. Their travels had taken them along an elliptical route that was now bringing them close to the starting point. With each stride their haavls carried them closer to where Khlearmt had spent his childhood, bringing her closer, as well, to the place where they had met and the time when she would have to leave the darztl behind. They spent a few days in a border town, then set out for the desert, a zone that was even more desolate than what she had encountered so far in enemy territory. On their way, they rode past one or two low constructions that seemed to blend in with the landscape and, from time to time, a darztl on a haavl loaded with numerous instruments and weapons.

"Those are trackers," explained Khlearmt. "They live in the desert. They are the most solitary of solitary creatures. Their job is to patrol the edge of the territory and capture any escapees."

Selm realized that for Khlearmt 'escapees' meant humans fleeing a life in captivity. No human had ever reached the colony, a sign that the patrollers were quite efficient. But how could a crippled human outrun a healthy haavl? She shook her head to chase away a new vision of horror.

"Here it is," announced Khlearmt after a few days. She looked around, trying to find any sign of darztl occupation in the desert setting. They were standing on a vast, white-hot, irregular plateau. She shivered anyway. The wind blowing out of the north was a little too tepid for her taste. Khlearmt seemed to know where he was going. He headed straight for a small hill of the same reddish rock as the surrounding land, with a very gentle slope.

"This was the children's quarters," he said, moving a pile of rocks. He finally uncovered what turned out to be an entrance.

They walked into the enclosure, which consisted of large, semi-collapsed rooms side by side. Selm guessed they had been bedrooms. A nest carved in the rock looked like a bed, another bump could have served as a table. Of course, it was all very rudimentary, very hard, but young darztls had run about these rooms. The beds were surely soft, covered with the same spongy material she had seen in houses throughout the country. The rooms would have been decorated with handpicked artifacts. Khlearmt cleared another entrance and they found themselves in a series of larger rooms. He told Selm that this was where he had learned the basics of everything he knew.

Visiting the places where her companion had spent his childhood forced her to revise her image of him. Even though she knew that his society was based on a very different model, she had stupidly pictured him growing up as a little human being, in the midst of a nuclear family. But of course darztl life was very different. They emerged in large numbers from the bellies of their ovoviviparous mothers and were raised by the community instead of being left to the care of a single mother. In fact, when she listened to Khlearmt talk about his childhood Selm realized that 'community' was a grand word. It was more a matter of constant yet distant attention to offspring trained to be independent at an early age. That was the condition for survival in the desert.

The homes of the adults were spread over the entire plateau. Places where Selm saw only piles of rubble had once been shops, workshops, the administrative center of the small town. The site had probably been deserted when the humans and darztls had cut off all contact; perhaps they had even been attacked at that time by humans who massacred anyone who lagged behind.

They stayed there a few days, talking little, thinking a lot. It came to them like a contemplative breeze. Selm, because she knew that it would soon be time to return to her own kind and was wondering how to do so without being hampered by her companion. Khlearmt, for a reason that was known only to him, or perhaps because he guessed hers — he had always been the better of the two at decoding their wattles.

"You can't go back twice to where you spent your childhood," he said one day as they were chewing raw drotz flesh. "The first time is introspection. The second is onerous. I don't think I want to spend a long time here. I'm going to return to Sshklooreml soon. I have to get back to work."

Khlearmt's use of 'I' rather than 'we' had not slipped past Selm unnoticed. She reached for the branch he was holding out to her.

"I would like to leave here, too."

He looked up at her, "We won't be going together, will we?"

She shook her head. He seemed to understand the gesture.

"You know, I've got the power to keep you from leaving. I'm responsible for keeping watch over you. If you defect, I'm authorized to shoot you. I wouldn't be condemned for that. Or I could drag you back to Sshklooreml, bound hand and foot. And if I don't do that, my troubles will only be just starting."

"But you won't do it?"

"Khlearmt won't do it. Khlearmt won't take you back by force."

They spent a few more days there in silence. Then Selm started to prepare, imitated by a Khlearmt who was still every bit as taciturn. Once again, it was Khlearmt who broke the silence.

"This is too stupid. Now it's as if I have dozens of things to tell you, dozens of things I want to learn from you. But I don't know where to begin. And at the same time, I don't want to tell you too much. And there are things I don't want to know about you."

"You realize that we probably won't see each other again."

"Yet you know where to find me. I'm a creature of habit. I get attached to people and places."

"Me too, Khlearmt. And that's my entire problem."

"But you can't come back. I have matters to settle as well."

Selm had finished saddling her haavl. This time she wouldn't travel the entire way between the darztls' land and the meeting point on foot.

"I know that a normal darztl doesn't do such things, Khlearmt, at least not when he doesn't intend to mate. But can I hug you?"

Finally, they separated and Selm mounted her haavl. She waved at her companion and set off without a word. After riding several hundred meters, she turned back. Khlearmt was standing where she had left him. She waved once more and headed northeast without once turning back.

She was afraid she wouldn't find the meeting point. Originally, she was supposed to hide her human objects there so that she could pick them up on her way back, but she had encountered her first darztl earlier than planned and had had to switch to the alternative plan. Fortunately for Selm, another, more romantic alternate plan that required her to end her life before revealing her secrets to the enemy had not been needed. Lacking her tools, all she could do was head in the direction of the colony, hoping that once she arrived in the vicinity, she wouldn't miss it by a few kilometers and wander aimlessly north of the oasis. Fortunately, her stay in the desert with an experienced darztl had taught her how to survive in this austere land. She knew which scraggly plants were edible, which provided water, which flowers produced a lasting flame.

She didn't have to test her newfound knowledge for long, though. Humans ambushed her one afternoon. A band of barbaric humans swooped down on her with a barely controlled rage, killing her haavl with precise high-caliber fire. She fell on her back under the animal and they took advantage of the opportunity to pounce on her. In any case, there were too many of them. Panicked, she tried to hit them with her tail — a single blow of a darztl's powerful tail could do quite a bit of damage — but she was out of practice and merely whipped the air. She injured a few with a swipe of her long claws but, in the end, they captured her and bound her, tail and all, laughing wickedly and butting her with their guns. She tried to protest, to beg, to explain what she was, deactivating her translator so that they would understand, but her pronunciation was marred by her darztl tongue and they laughed harder, mocking what they took for clumsy begging. Then they dragged her on the ground behind their truck, shrieking like madmen. When she came to a stop on the sand and pebbles, her body broken and scraped, weakened and at their mercy, they stuck a large hook in her crest, causing her to cry out in pain, then hoisted her into the truck where they fastened the chain that was attached to the hook. That evening, they started by setting up camp, then they threw her on the icy ground under the truck.

"It's not what you think," she tried to say again. "I'm not really a darztl." But she was so weak that her words came out like an inaudible grinding.

They threw a handful of cooked food at her that, since her hands were tied, she ate off the ground, not so much because she felt hungry but rather because she knew she had to eat. They ate and drank their fill, burping and making crude jokes. They spent the night there, outdoors, taking turns guarding her and, on several occasions, torturing her. Finally, numb from the cold, she no longer felt anything.

She welcomed the first rays of the sun gratefully and felt her body return to life, although this revived the pain as well. Everything was quiet around her, with the exception of the snoring of the men, even the one who was supposed to be guarding her. When her torturers started to move about and wake, she pretended to be asleep, to make them believe she was weaker than she was. They seemed to have forgotten her presence, but her relief was short-lived. By way of greeting, one of the men kicked her forcefully, causing her to double over with pain.

He bent down to her, saying "Looking at you, you'd never know that you're worth one month of paid vacation for each of us!"

As the men lingered at the camp, smoking, bickering, she stayed rolled up in a ball, her belly torn by an atrocious pain. Suddenly, she felt something hot flow between her legs. She stood up with an effort and noticed five sticky spheres on the sand.

"Hey come and see this. We've caught a female. She's just laid five eggs for us!"

The others ran over and looked at the small white rosary that lay in the dust with expressions of morbid fascination. The spell was broken by the man who had made the discovery.

"We don't want any more of these now do we?" he said as he crushed the frail spheres under his heel.

Once again, they forced Selm into the truck. During the night, her flesh had started to close around the hook, but the movement reopened the wound. The pain was horrific.

Plea by Chloe Guilimpert
In her own defense
Mars II Martial Court
January 22, Marsian year 0043

I feel that it would be judicious for me to tell you the end of my story, my version of the story. A story that, no matter what I said before, started in a way that was not glorious at all, ranging from failure to partial success, most often stagnating. When I look at the report I wrote shortly after I volunteered, I feel as if I'm reading words written by someone else. A stranger who speaks of *us* and declines all responsibility. A stranger who never takes a stand when her own kind commit atrocities. Someone I no longer am, fortunately.

It's too bad, since I was acting with complete impunity at the time. You know, I've held the fate of dozens of innocents in my hands and no one ever asked me to account for my actions. Whereas now...

You know the facts; you've read all the official reports; you know all the details of what happened, before my departure, during my mission, after my return. But do you have the slightest idea of what could have been going on inside me during all that time? Do you even want to know?

When I was crossing back through the desert, bringing an entire year of my existence to an end, I was extremely excited. Within a few days, I would see my own kind, I would leave this foreign envelope behind and become as I had been before. It's ironic, isn't it, that I could only return to the land of my birth thanks to the powerful legs that carried me through the desert, the body that was designed to withstand the heat of this world, the knowledge I had acquired from the darztls.

Then I ran into the mercenaries. As they abused me, I told myself it was fair. I had taken advantage of the benefits of this body, now I had to pay for usurping it. At the very least, it was not my own body they were torturing, it was a borrowed envelope, it was not really me they disgraced, not me they spat on, but just the life form I was pretending to be. I didn't even hate them when they ignored my pleas, refused to listen to my revelations, since my own human words sounded so poorly pronounced to my foreign ears that I wondered if these humans could even understand what I was saying. Moreover, I thought I deserved to suffer, retrospectively, prospectively. I even thought that I was lucky to get out of the situation alive, unlike several darztls that arrived here dead rather than just seriously injured.

When I finally found myself in the presence of someone from the Defense and Security Department who knew who I was, I was suddenly very eager to return to my original body, so I could finally break the spell. Technically, the

transfer was easy. The darztl body was reconnected to the
artificial life support system, while I was torn out of it,
transferred into my former envelope and resuscitated. But
psychologically it was an entirely different matter. Have
you ever sky-dived? Of course, you have. That's part of
basic training. So you've already experienced that sensation
of heaviness, of inertia, as you touch the ground and you're
filled with an undeniable certainty: you are not a bird. Well,
that's exactly how I felt when I returned to my human body.
I knew that I belonged to that body and that it belonged
to me, but I recalled being a bird and I dreamed of the day
when I could fly again.

No one around me noticed the change; no one noticed
that I had become someone else. And I have to admit that
my training made me very good at dissimulating. If I could
spend an entire year deceiving the darztls, a species that
is completely foreign to me, imagine just how good an
actress I was when it came to humans! As a good, impassive
soldier, I continued my mission, I wrote my report, and
I betrayed those who had welcomed me among them for
more than a year, and particularly Khlearmt, my beloved
Khlearmt. But if you only knew how heavy I felt, beaten
by the heat and the weight of what I had experienced. I
understood what the little darztls raised as human beings,
what the hybrids I had helped to create, must have felt.
Neither flesh nor fish, I balanced between two species
without being able to turn to one or the other.

This was a time of joy for the Defense Department. In
a single year, I had collected enough information to ensure
a peaceful existence for us on this planet. You knew the
extent to which the darztls have been affected by the recent
climate changes; you had been informed about the existence
of water in darztl territory; of the magnificent mines that
could be a source of virtually inexhaustible energy for us;
about the human slaves they had captured to work in their
place. I also told you just how civilized they were, how
cultured, how they stood together yet remained fiercely
independent. All in all, they were hardly any crueler with
their enemies than we had been with ours. But you didn't

want to hear a thing about the good side. All you wanted was for me to tell you about the atrocities, the massacres, the threats, the monstrosities. And yet, almost every evening, in secret, I would go into the room where my darztl body was kept artificially alive and was healing. I found it beautiful, a hundred times more attractive than my pale human body that was made for a cooler world.

I didn't want to return to that darztl body. No, it didn't belong to me and I no longer belonged to it, particularly since I had betrayed those with similar bodies. I didn't want to return to that body, yet, at the same time, it felt as if I had never left it, that it stuck to my skin. When I went to visit it at night, I pictured crossing through the desert, sunbaths, physical exploits that are impossible for humans. If the chief had not come up with the absurd idea of destroying my darztl body, I would no doubt have continued to drag my uprooted carcass from one camp to the other, finally sinking in a permanent yet innocuous depression.

During my trial, the experts spoke about the Stockholm syndrome, where the victim identifies with the attacker. But Stockholm is twenty-five light-years away! Plus, I sincerely believe that we have to set aside our outdated methods of analysis. Clichés won't help us settle on this planet for good. We have to prove that we are open. That is what I am asking the court today.

I knew that the chief was considering having me assassinated. He told me up front, as if it were a formality. I tried to protest, to present my objections in an official tone, and I managed to hinder things. If you examine my files, you'll see that I'm excellent at everything that concerns administrative paperwork. However, since I came back, I've been a little more disorganized, undisciplined. I've had more trouble dealing with the jargon used by my superiors. And then one evening, as I usually did, I slipped into the room where the darztl envelope lay and I heard the chief of the Defense and Security Department discuss its *termination*, as if he had just finalized some files that had been dragging on for far too long, and I realized just how imminent the danger was. It was as if they had the poor taste to plan my own execution without thinking about inviting me. And at the same time, it was me they were going to execute, in my own absence. I mean, how interested would you be in having your heart cut out, your liver plucked out, having any healthy organ essential for your survival torn out? Well, it was as if they were slowly planning an excision like that without my knowledge. Why? To symbolically bring the experiment to an end? A little like humans' once-celebrated circumcision? Imagine that! I saw us like the members of some barbaric tribe dancing around their enemy's remains.

Events occurred as you've been told throughout this trial. That night, I was fully aware that my hours were numbered and I went into the senior offices at Defense and Security. It was him or me. So I killed my boss — in cold blood, or almost. And I felt like I was saving my life. In fact, things didn't go down that peacefully. We talked. He made a decision. There was a quarrel, resistance, a struggle. But by the time the guards ran in, I believe he was already dead. I didn't resist arrest. I let them cuff me quietly, peacefully, finally, as if I were mad. All I knew was that I had prevented an atrocious crime. I had the bitter feeling that I had saved my skin. It was my life, Your Honor, that I had been protecting that day, and that's why I decided to plead self defense.

I have no illusions, however. You may reject the charges of first-degree murder and accuse me simply of manslaughter, or you may find that there were extenuating circumstances. But you will adamantly not accept a plea of self defense. And yet I would have defended my life as strongly if someone had attacked my poorly adapted human envelope!

But, you will not agree that I killed to save my skin, and you will undoubtedly inflict the sentence usually administered in such cases. For this, our ancestors had a sentence they called the death sentence, but we're more open. Eternity in prison for someone convicted of murder; exile in case of involuntary manslaughter. Personally, I would have opted for the opposite, but then I'm not a legislator. No matter, whatever happens, I do have a favor to ask of the court, my last favor before I retire from your view and put an end to this lengthy argument. If you have to banish me, can it be in my darztl body? My lawyer has managed to obtain an injunction, so no one has touched that body yet. I know I'm asking the court for a lot. I mean, this is the first time since the colony was founded that a murder has been committed, so there is no precedent. However, I'm fully cognizant of the fact that, out in the desert, I could still be of use to my kind, learn more about the climate and survival on this planet. Destroy my human body if that's what you deem appropriate, but leave me my other identity. That, at last, will not condemn me to the death that will be mine if I am chased out with only a protective suit to cover my milky white human body. And it will prevent you from having the impression — at least unofficially — of reinstating the death penalty that was abolished three hundred years ago. Since I no longer belong to the human group, and since I will not be able to rally the enemy — obviously the darztls will tear me to shreds as soon as they see me — I will join the small colony of hybrids that was established in the midst of the dunes and, if they decide to accept their former torturer, I will spend the rest of my days there in peace. Those living on the fringe should be able to get along....

§ § §

Off in the distance, she saw the rock hovels. The dwellings were less discrete than the darztl buildings. Two silhouettes were busy working around the house. As she approached, she saw a child playing in the sand. A real darztl child, about ten years old, ran off, shrieking as soon as he saw her. Perhaps the child had come from Remldarztl and been found wandering in the desert, but Selm had another idea as to his identity: one of the Project Alpha young, of course, that had been kept aside at the end of the experiment. That would explain why his body had never been found, and suggested that one of the guinea pigs had, perhaps, been loved. The child stopped near the two silhouettes, claw pointed in her direction. Everyone went into the stone dwelling, then not two but four individuals came back out, each of them armed with a rifle. She raised her arms and walked on, slowly.

She stopped a few dozen yards from the rifles.

"I come from the base camp," she said, hoping to clear up her identity. She made an effort to pronounce each syllable carefully, to make sure they understood.

"What's that mean to us?" asked one of the creatures with pronunciation that was far too clear for the darztl she claimed to be.

"I have my sentencing document with me. Mine. I'm coming to live with you. I'll hold the paper out for you. Better yet, I'll roll it up into a ball and toss it over to you."

One of the hybrids picked up the ball of paper and read what was written on it. The four of them remained standing there for a minute, then the one who had read the court order shrugged. He turned and went back into the shack, imitated by the others. But the door to the dwelling remained open. It was a start.

TERRAFORMING 101

1. Definition

Terraforming a planet means transforming an inhospitable planet into a livable and habitable world, with a breathable atmosphere and a bearable temperature. Everything else depends on the actual conditions found on a given planet.

2. Economics of terraforming

One of the first elements of the project to be considered is feasibility. Does the planet satisfy the conditions for terraforming. So as soon as we started discussing terraforming, Mars, the planet next to Earth, was considered one of the easiest planets to be terraformed. In fact, the average temperature on Mars was -60°C on the surface and its atmosphere was 0.7% of earthly density. If we had wanted to terraform Mars, all we had to do was multiply its atmospheric pressure by 200 (considering its lower gravity) and increase its temperature to an average of 0°C. Mars II would be even easier to change. In fact, its atmosphere and gravity are similar to those of Earth, whereas the average temperature is 50°C. Terraforming will, as a result, be minimal. Some people have even said that it would be superfluous and stress the indigenous species unduly. However, by decreasing the average temperature by only 20°C, it is estimated that the climate would be modified to such an extent that conditions on the surface of the planet would be similar to those in the tropical and subtropical regions on Earth, making it much easier to colonize the planet.

3. Water

One of the factors important when it comes to terraforming a planet is the presence of water. For example, major sources of water were discovered frozen beneath the surface on Mars. And on Mars II, there are water sources under the surface, in liquid form this time. By modifying the ecosystem, we could free up a portion of these reserves and, as a result, irrigate the desert zone, which covers 90% of the emerged land on the planet.

4. Metals

The presence of the minerals needed to maintain life is to be considered. Thus, Mars had vast reserves of the necessary metals and other important elements. The same applies to Mars II, which has significant deposits of iron.

5. Ethics of terraforming

Of course, the very notion raises one fundamental question: why should we and, above all, are we entitled to terraform a planet? Opinions differ. We will deal with this issue in our section, "Ethics of Terraforming."

The Worst
of Both Worlds

To all the little turtles
I called "Turtle,"
who lived out the last
of their days
in the sewers.

Jet stream cuts the desert sky.
This is a land could eat a man alive.
Say you'd leave it all behind.
REM, *"Low Desert"*

The darztls could have eliminated me at birth, but fate intervened. Two days after giving birth to me, my mother died and I was taken in by none other than the mine boss. Once he saw me, he watched me with a mitigated tenderness, both touched by the tiny, wailing creature before him and disgusted by my humanness. Realizing that I was hungry — after all, no one had thought to feed me for two days — he ordered the humans to provide a nurse for me. She would be exempted from working in the mine every time she came to breastfeed me. But my new master never left me alone with her since she tended to take revenge on me for the deprivations of her own life. The rest of the time he took care of me, clothing me, rocking me, playing with me as if I were a small osft, leaving me only to make his inspection of the mine. Apparently the others made fun of him behind his back, but he didn't care.

At the age of one, I was weaned. And it was a long time before I came near a real human after that. From then on, Sshlurltr — that was my master's name — took care of all my needs on his own. He fed me — making an effort to prepare meals that were digestible for a human baby, yet he was not always successful, occasionally triggering alarming reactions. And he educated me in a just, gentle manner. He never beat me or locked me up unless I deserved it. He watched over me and, above all, made sure I had no contact with my own kind whose bad manners — or so he said — might contaminate me.

He had named me Skllptiastlt, which means 'saved from the mines,' but for the sake of convenience he called me simply Skllpt. It is a female name and, in fact, Sshlurltr believed I was female. The sexual organs of the masters are not visible, hidden inside the bodies of individuals of both genders. So whenever they had to separate human males from human females, they stuck to the obvious. Anything with a penis was labeled male. Generally, this system worked. Except, of course, in the case of someone whose mother had decided to amputate him at birth, for example.... Until I rejoined the human group, I'd always believed I was a girl. Not that it played much of a role in the development of my identity. The real difference was the one I experienced with the masters who, apart from the fact that they stood upright, had little in common with me.

Yet I loved Sshlurlt no less as a father — if that word had any actual meaning for me. In my eyes, he was the handsomest, the largest and the strongest, and I feared — with good cause — that I would never manage to look like him. For his part, he behaved like a father — even if that word had a different meaning for his species — making sure that he transmitted his culture, his values, his knowledge to me. He did not treat me like a human.

I didn't go out very often during the day, because of the liirzt — the sun. My master only allowed me outside for brief periods of time or else either at night or at dawn and dusk, when the sun's rays were more tolerable. The darztls allowed me to come and go as I pleased within the enclosure, which was surrounded by a tall fence topped with barbed wire. I could go everywhere except near the shaft and I knew my own kind only from a distance, when I saw them taking their weekly walk in the fresh air under the moonlight.

But that doesn't mean I felt like a darztl! The masters were too numerous to make me feel that I was one of theirs. Whenever Sshlurltr turned his back to me, some of his subordinates would make the most of the opportunity to hurt me or torment me. One day, Sshlurltr had to send a foreman back down into the mine for dragging me out into an empty field. Once there, the foreman had asked the others to hold me still. I'd been forced to witness the punishment they were inflicting on a human they had just captured, a few days after escaping. I can still see the blade, that shone for a second or two in the sun, before striking the woman's one good foot, cleanly slicing it off. I can still hear her cries of pain when, following the amputation, her wound was cauterized with coals. That's when my master arrived, tore me away from the guard who held me back by force a few yards from the scene and carried me off. Later, after he had told me that some darztls are naturally cruel and that they are the ones who complain the most, he asked me to decide how my tormenter should be punished before being sent away. Obviously, I chose his foot. I never found out if the punishment was applied but, in any case, it wasn't fair. The darztl may have cried out like the woman did, when he was held down, then at the sight of the blade falling, but I knew that the limbs of the masters, unlike those of their slaves, could grow back.

I found myself a little hiding place. The master would have thought it was a little too close to the mine, so I kept it secret and went there when he allowed me outside to play. It was a sort of ditch dug from the main shaft and closed with a rusted metal fence at ground level, condemned and hidden by large stones. It was probably one of the former cells where they used to keep the humans, before they had decided it would be more convenient to have them sleep directly in the mine. I discovered it by chance when playing in the area. One of my toys had rolled away and fallen into the ditch. By moving a few rocks, I managed to open the door in the fence. My little top had fallen to the bottom, like a rock. The next day, I returned with a rope. From that time on, I went back whenever I got a chance. I'd take toys there, shiny rocks gathered in the mine enclosure, dried food. I hid there, taking great care to make sure no one found my hidey-hole, making an opening that was barely large enough to let me through. I went there to dream, inventing stories, a world.

Occasionally my master took me into the children's area. These children, the offspring of the masters who worked in the mine and occasionally left them behind, were raised apart, outside the enclosure but not far from it. The master said it would do me good to see darztls of my own age. I didn't dare contradict him, but I viewed each of these outings with terror. As soon as the master left and the supervisors turned their backs, the young darztls would either go back to their own games and totally ignore me or they'd torment me. Timidly, I mentioned this to my master but, although he never denied that things were difficult for me, he told me to be patient, that the young darztls needed time to get used to me. So I allowed my-self to be abused like the straw dolls the darztl children usually played with, quickly setting these dolls aside as soon as I was brought to them. A living doll was ever so much more fun! The children, who usually played on their own or in small groups, would suddenly gather around the new attraction. Of course, there were some that didn't take part in the massacre game and who, as soon as my tormenters left me alone in a corner, would take the op-portunity to be nice to me, to watch over me, both curi-ous and well-meaning. Unfortunately, the group of young darztls had two leaders, a male and a female, larger and stronger than the others, who were like night and day. Their favorite game was "masters and the slave." Taken straight from the daily lives of their elders. I don't know where the young masters got their information, since darztl children were not allowed to get close to the mine, but they knew completely how it operated, as I discovered all too well.

They gave me all kinds of tasks to perform, and when I didn't work as fast as they wanted, they would hit me with the harder toys or lock me in a stifling closet. Of course, when my master came by to pick me up, he would notice the bruises and cuts, but while bandaging my wounds he blamed it on the frailty of my human body. When I tried to tell him about what was going on, he merely promised to tell the young ones to play more gently with me, to let them know I was not as resilient as they were. The others, once they had been dutifully admonished, of course tormented me even more the next time.

One day, the female leader proposed a game. "It would be interesting to determine what effect the liirzt has on its skin, wouldn't it?"

Some of the others opposed this, saying that I might get really hurt, but the majority won. They dragged me outside, formed a circle around me, tore off my protective suit and, after overcoming their surprise at my physique, they left me exposed to the burning rays. When I attempted to escape through a breach in the compact hedge of children around me, I was invariably pushed back into the middle of the circle. Finally, exhausted, my head buzzing, my body on fire, I lay face down on the dusty soil. After I had stopped moving, one child touched me with his foot to see if I would react, but I fell back, inert. Some of the young darztls became frightened and cried out. One of them went to find a guard. Someone finally came. When my master returned, I was only half conscious and talking incoherently. They gave him my slack, burning body. He took me back to the house and lay me down in the relative cool of my room. I shivered with fever and my skin was on fire. Not knowing whether he should heat me or cool me, Sshlurtlr simply stayed there, watching over me, occasionally dribbling some cactus juice between my lips. When I regained consciousness after three days of delirium, he continued to take care of me, giving me liquids to drink, feeding me, changing the sap-soaked bandages he placed on my blister-covered body. One day he told me that the young darztls had been punished in keeping with their action, but I never returned there to reap the fruit of that tardy discipline.

Yet you should not think that my childhood was a
perpetual hell. I'd even say that, until I met Inès, that was
the happiest time of my life. Master Sshlurltr was highly
educated. He would have me sit at his feet while he pas-
sionately told me his darztl's history. He taught me to read
at an early age, astonished by my intellectual abilities. He
also taught me mathematics and natural science. This is
how I learned that the history of the darztls dated back
to the dawn of time, when the surface of the planet had
dried, leaving only the hardiest species — mostly reptiles,
along with a few small mammals and crawling insects, and
plants that could survive in a semi-arid climate. There were
fish, as well, in the oceans that surrounded the two continents. Darztls, however, had very poor sea legs and trade
between the two species was kept to a minimum. The continents had been occupied since before the darztls had
crawled out of the oceans, which accounts for the morpho-
logical differences between the inhabitants of the planet's
two countries. My master also spoke to me about recent
history, and above all, the arrival of my kind, "those sand
troglodytes who came to usurp a land that was not even
made for them." He spoke to me of human duplicity and
the bloody confrontations that took place when the darztls
finally saw through my peers' tricks and schemes. I almost
hated myself for what I was and understood why the
darztls treated us as they did.

Some evenings, other darztls would come to visit my
master. A few were horrified to find themselves in the same
house as a human. On those occasions, I would be locked
up in my room earlier than usual and told to stay quiet
so they would forget about me. But several of my master's
friends liked me well enough. When they came, I was
permitted to stay up later. I think they found me amusing. They would ask me to recite my latest lessons and their
wattles would turn turquoise streaked with green. My
master also instructed me to show them how well I did
at the standard tests given to darztl children of my own
age. I took pride in what I knew and I enjoyed pleasing
the master. Then I would be told to let the big darztls talk.
I would roll up in a ball at my master's feet and allow

myself to be lulled by the clicking of their conversations. They would have to wake me to send me off to bed.

Occasionally, Sshlurltr would turn thoughtful in the middle of a lesson. He would look at me for a long time and then tell me that it would take more people like me to build any real peace between his people and my own. On my own, all I could do was convince them to go back to where they came from. When he said this, my master would turn a very sad hue. I would kiss his feet, promising to change my kind. Then he would stare at me and announce that class was over for that day. He would stand up painfully and go off to fulfill his duties as the master of the masters of the human slaves.

I knew that Sshlurltr was in more and more pain. His wattle turned darker day by day. Sometimes I'd watch as he moved about with great difficulty, grabbing onto a wall to keep his balance. He had less and less appetite, saying that food did him more harm than good. One morning — it must have been about twelve revolutions after my birth — he did not get up at all. I know that because each morning he came to open the door to my room, which he always locked the night before. That day, I was a prisoner in my room for several hours, powerless, crying out for help, but knowing full well that the thick stone walls muffled my voice. Finally I heard a noise, footsteps, then voices. But no one came to tell me what was going on. An hour or more must have passed before anyone thought to come and release me. I was taken to my master, who lay in a carriage that was prepared for travel. He beckoned me to come closer.

"Skllpt," he said, "I'm very ill. You may not realize this, but I'm very old. They're taking me away for treatment. I'll get better soon and I'll come back to watch over you and complete your education. Meanwhile, be a good little darztl. No one will hurt you if you're a good little darztl."

My throat tight, unable to reply, I watched the carriage as it moved off, pulled by two large haavls.

The entire time my master was ill, they kept me locked in my room. I believe that the others weren't quite sure what to do with me. I was Sshlurltr's creation and I'd never really had any close contact with the other adults. So they continued to feed me, without paying much more attention to me. All day long, I was locked inside my four walls, reading books I had already read, thinking about my state, and weeping, as well, since there seemed to be no end to my imprisonment.

One day a female darztl, wrapped in a shimmering suit, came and told me to follow her. I asked her where we were going, but she didn't answer. When I noticed that we were heading to the mines, I protested, saying that my master didn't want me to go there. The female darztl simply said, "Your master is dead." I protested, I struggled, but the darztl was powerful and I was no match for her. She had me climb down the ladder that led to the middle of the planet. It was cold below and I shivered. She told me to take off my suit, which I'd put on clean that morning, and held out another one to me, all stained and tattered. The suits my master had given me had always been altered to fit me. This one had already belonged to a young master who had probably abandoned it since it didn't protect him from the cold or fit him anymore. The arms and legs were too long, the body too short and the sleeve for the tail had been cut off and sewn shut hastily.

The darztl pushed me ahead of her into a labyrinth corridor. In the distance, I heard the sound of metal striking rock and shouts. We entered a hallway filled with activity. There I saw humans spread out through two galleries. Some were standing, while others sat on the ground. They were all using some kind of metal instrument to hit the walls. Some turned to look at me, visibly surprised. The four masters watching the humans also turned a surprised shade. The female darztl who brought me into the mine told the other masters that the new boss would be arriving the next day and that, when she had learned of my presence, she had asked them to remove me from her future quarters and clean everything carefully.

While the darztls were talking, the work slowed. When they noticed this, the masters shouted at the humans to pick up their pace. The first darztl placed a tool in my hands and indicated that I was to do as the others did. I started

to strike the rocky wall. Small pebbles came loose, but that
must not have been enough because one master told me
to work harder. All day long, stunned, trying to look for
a way out of this situation, I struck the wall with the energy
of despair. All too soon, blisters formed on my hands, then
burst, leaving my flesh exposed. But as soon as I tried to
slow my pace, a master would order me to get back to work.
No one hit me, however. At first, I thought it was because
I was being conscientious, but later I learned that the
masters who had known me up above were giving me
preferential treatment.

The pace at which we were forced to work quickly
exhausted me. My suit was soaked with sweat despite the
coolness in the mine. I felt dizzy, starving. They had forgotten to give me my ration that morning. However, I didn't
dare ask for anything to eat, thinking that they would feed
us eventually. Little by little, I digested the news they threw
my way: Sshlurltr was dead and I would never see him
again. So who was going to take care of me? But I had no
time to wallow in despair — I had to break the rock. The
only time we stopped hammering away at the wall of the
underground gallery was when we loaded our harvest into
a wheelbarrow that human workers pushed up and down
the corridor behind us.

Finally, at the end of a long day, the masters ordered
us to put our pickaxes down. They had us line up in rows,
cutting off even the slightest murmur. We walked back
along the corridor that led to the shaft. Some hobbled along,
hampered by their mutilated legs. The few humans who
were missing both legs had to lean on others for help. I
was happy at the thought of finally going back out into
the fresh air. But we didn't go back up. A master shoved
aside a large rock that blocked the entrance to a corridor,
opening up a big square cave, where the only source of
light was a few weak candles the humans lit. One by one,
counting us, the masters had us enter the nauseating room,
ordering us to remove our suits and shoes. I tried to protest
but the master told me to shut up and do as the others did.
So I undressed in the chilly mine. As the glacial under-

ground air wafted over my sweat-covered body, I shivered. I stepped nervously into the humans' room. Once everyone had been packed in, the masters pushed the rock back in place, locking us up for the night.

Slowly conversation started up and some children cried or shouted, a deafening murmur of which I understood nothing. The humans looked at me curiously, but no one spoke to me. I glanced about the room. I was the only one, standing there in the middle of the room, who did not know where to go. They had automatically gathered around two large containers from which they drew a sort of stew and a ration of water. Still shivering, I got in line with the others and picked up a brownish, bitter-tasting paste that I gulped down. The room was not terribly warm, in both senses of the word, but the food warmed me up somewhat. Then I stayed there, feeling like an intruder. Each of the other humans seemed to have their own place; several huddled together to keep warm, while others stretched out on what looked like beds, hollowed out of the rocky wall, and still others gathered in small groups, excitedly discussing something while pointing in my direction. A young human male walked over to me and addressed me. I had no idea what he was saying, but the other humans laughed. An older woman said something in an authoritative tone and the laughter stopped. A female, barely older than I was, walked over and said something, but I didn't understand her, either. Seeing that I didn't understand, she pushed me away from the candlelight, towards a wall. Showing me a bed, she indicated that I was to lie down there. Groping around in the dark, I climbed into that strange bed. Lying on the stone, chilled to the bone, I wondered why the masters were so cruel as to remove our suits and then abandon us to the underground chill, then guessed that it was to leave us naked, exposed to the rays of the sun, if we were crazy enough to think of escaping. The female handed me a rag barely large enough to cover half my body, rolled into a ball and lay down next to me. I snuggled against the stranger's body and this warmed me somewhat. The sounds gradually died out. Darkness swept over the cave as the candles burned down. The room was soon completely black, with the exception of a pale shaft of light from a tiny hole in the ceiling that provided air. My arms and legs chilled, trying hard not to cry, I allowed myself to fall asleep.

The next morning we ate the same mush, cold this time, then the entrance to the cave opened. After we were given our clothing, we were herded back into the corridor where we had worked the day before. And the cycle started again.

I was as miserable as the rocks I broke. I felt like I was the victim of some injustice, that I had been handed a sentence I didn't deserve. Master Sshlurtlr had always told me that the humans who worked in the mines were paying for the frightful crime they had committed. But I had done nothing wrong, and here I was, imprisoned underground in atrocious conditions. And all these people around me, what could they have possibly done to deserve such a fate? And what about the children — no more than five or six years old — what had the children who were forced to work done that was so wrong?

That second day, I summoned up all my strength and tried to explain my situation to a master, to make him see the terrible error that had been committed. Because of the protective suit he wore I could not see the color of his wattle, but I could have bet that it had taken on a well-meaning hue as the master patiently listened to my demands.

"Poor Skllpt. The grand master has been replaced by someone who... well... who has different views. But you have to work. The other darztls can't do anything for the human. If Skllpt works hard, she won't have any problems."

"Does that mean she will be able to go outside?"

The darztl didn't answer and, looking away, indicated that I was to get back to work.

Another evening passed, the same as the previous one, and another morning. The third day passed uneventfully, every bit as dreary and exhausting as the two before it. I worked as hard as I could to keep in the masters' good graces. But that evening, when I wanted to get my portion of the food, the female who served the stew shook her head at me, pushed my bowl away and served the human behind me. I held my bowl out to her again, but the female spit into it and threw it to the ground. Everyone turned to look at us. Another female, this one with fine features, stood between us and talked with the serving female. The other shrugged. The fine-featured female took her own bowl, from which she had just been eating, and had it filled. Then she gave it to me and indicated that I should move away. The young female who had given me a place in her nook pulled on my arm and dragged me into a corner with her. I ate in silence, unable to understand what was being said around me, then went to bed, exhausted and desolate.

The hardest part, I believe, was being among the slaves while feeling closer to the overseers. Some of the masters looked unhappy; others seemed pleased with my treatment. I could hear them talking about me as I worked.

"As far as this darztl is concerned, Boss Roemlskt is wrong," a darztl I had met at the master's house said on my third day in the mine. "This little human has been raised in a civilized manner. It's cruel to make her come back here. It's like abandoning a pet drotz in the desert."

"Humans have no place among darztls," objected another master.

"But she was raised with darztls! She can't go back to this life after spending her entire childhood with the boss," said the first darztl.

"This darztl has always found such a relationship unnatural," declared the other master. "It's a good thing the mine is no longer under the sway of a boss who was too fond of little human females."

"This darztl will do what the new mine boss wants," declared a third. "She's threatened to fire anyone who doesn't agree with her. So if darztls don't agree, they can leave."

"What's the human doing there, listening to darztls instead of working?" shouted another darztl walking into the corridor." Get back to work," he roared, slapping me on the shoulder, the first time I had been struck since they had brought me down into the mine. The others glared at him balefully, and encouraged me with a glace to get back to work. My shoulder in pain, I went back to digging.

Another two days passed, then it was time for our weekly day off. One evening, rather than taking us to our hole in the wall, the darztls had us climb us the rope ladder that led outside. Everyone had to go up — even the children, who were helped by the adults; even babies, carried in rags tied to their mothers' backs; even the footless, who climbed up on their stumps. We were told to take off our suits and I did as the others were doing, rubbing their suits with sand to clean them. Then we were told to take a sand bath, which I found somewhat comforting. Our chores done, the darztls picked up the clean suits and, even though we were under constant supervision, we had some free time. It was the first time in five days I'd been outside, the first time I'd found myself naked outside. The air was warm, the sky magnificent. The immense moon bathed the mine yard in a bluish light. As alone as ever among the humans, I still managed to feel more confident. Happier days lay ahead of me, days when I'd be allowed to return to my past life. Then I got in line with the others for the routine examination and my nightmare took a different turn.

The night sky provided more light than the few meager candles that lit our den at night. The darztls inspected us in silence, looking for poorly healed wounds and infections that could degenerate into serious illnesses. One woman carried a baby. They took the infant from her, to examine it as well, then returned it. I had already been inspected by other darztls under the magnifying glass in the children's area where, even though they didn't abuse me, they still treated me like some kind of strange beast. But I felt uncomfortable, as if I were no longer a person, but an object they were inspecting to see if it still served some use.

A female darztl I didn't know appeared. Based on her badge, which was encrusted with precious stones, I realized that she was someone important and guessed she had to be the new boss. She examined us again, one by one. Imposing, she was almost twice as big again as the largest of the human adults. When she got to me, she stopped. The master following her told her who I was. She looked me up and down. "So this is my predecessor's little pet!"

I took advantage of the opportunity to make my appeal "It's all a mistake," I said, throwing caution to the wind. "Skllpt does not belong in the mines. The boss master kept her..."

She lashed out with the full force of her tail, throwing me to the ground, knocking the wind out of me. I hadn't even seen it coming.

"Roemlsk does not believe she addressed you, human female. She has learned bad habits," she added, addressing the other masters. "This will have to be corrected."

Standing up painfully, I persisted, "Skllpt can be of great use if the boss master keeps her at her side."

Then she lost her patience for good. Her wattle black, she rushed at me and pulled me out of the line. Throwing me at another master as if I were a sack of potatoes, she said, her voice dripping with scorn, "Make sure she loses the taste for begging favors. Make sure she loses any desire to massacre our beautiful language as well."

As my own kind watched in silence, two masters held me still in front of the wall of the stone shelter that protected the mine shaft. I knew one of them fairly well, having met him at my master's home.

"Skllpt must be brave. It will all be over soon," he whispered in my ear.

Their grip relaxed a little and I managed to turn around. Out of the corner of my eye I saw a third darztl taking off his chain belt. The other darztl looked as if he was about to hold him back, but then did nothing. I tried to defend myself, but the two masters were too strong. They tightened their grip. The chain struck me once, then a second time, then a third and then... With each blow the metal dug deeper into my skin. I glanced at the masters, who held me firmly, beseeching them, but they looked elsewhere. The pain of the blows was hard to bear, but it became even worse when the beating stopped and the darztls let me fall into the dust. My entire body was ablaze and I felt each blow again with each heartbeat. And the shame of the beating mingled with my lack of understanding. This was the first time I had even been punished without cause. And I didn't know which I preferred: being beaten by an unknown torturer or by masters for whom I felt affection.

Yet I had to stand up. I was the last to climb back down into the mine. The master I knew well gently helped me to stand up, while avoiding my eyes, then helped me step down onto the ladder. As I stumbled into the common room, all eyes turned to me. Several seem to glance at me with compassion, although I could have sworn that others seemed to mock me. I headed straight to my stone nook, not stopping for my share of the mush. I climbed into my bed painfully and stretched out on my belly, both because my back pained me so and because I didn't want the others to hear me cry. My sleeping companion came over to me with a bowl. She said something, but the only word I understood was "eat." I turned my face toward the rocky wall. She caressed my hair, murmuring comforting words. During the night, I rolled over in my bed without thinking and cried out in pain. She was still there, awake. She lifted my head and gave me a little water to drink.

The next day I was given no time off work, despite my condition. I dragged myself painfully through the corridors of the mine, my pickaxe seeming heavier than ever. The masters did, however, allow me to work shirtless so that the rough fabric of my suit would not rub against the wounds the chain had left on my back. From that time on, whenever we went up top for our weekly outing or during surprise inspections in the mine — whenever the boss was around — I would tremble with fright. She stopped by me frequently, looking me up and down, visibly pleased with the fear she read in my body. There always seemed to be good reason for punishing me. All too soon, my body was covered with scars. I was the only one she vented her spleen on. As far as people could remember — or so the slaves said — a boss master had never imposed such a cruel regime in the mine. But I think she took particular pleasure in knowing that I was at her mercy, as if I posed some sort of threat to her, as if I wasn't just a captive teenager.

My days were frightful, caught between masters who were less and less familiar to me, new faces replacing old ones, and humans who looked like they would never consider me one of theirs. No one spoke to me, with the exception of my sleeping companion, and most of the time I didn't understand what she was saying. At least at the beginning. I found human pronunciation hard to learn. I'd never managed to articulate darztl words as well as I should have, but I was used to the clicking and the slurring characteristic of their language. Human sounds were both more complex and more difficult to discern in the midst of all those vowels. Yet I learned quickly. And although I was unable to sustain a fluid conversation, I soon acquired a basic vocabulary, which meant I could both understand what they were saying to me and make myself understood.

Anaelle — that was her name — was the only one to treat me well. Thanks to her, my nights were less glacial and my days less unbearable. There were not enough beds for all of the humans so the youngest, as well as some of the adults, slept in twos or threes in the narrow nooks. Anaelle, however, was the only one who wanted me.

"People here find you strange," she told me one day.

Since it was obvious that I didn't understand she placed ten black pebbles, all the same, on the floor in our cave. Then Anaelle selected a red one, which appeared out of nowhere, and placed it in the middle of the other pebbles. Repeating the word 'strange,' she pointed at the red pebble, then at me. I understood what 'strange' meant. It was like Reimstl, the little lost darztl in the children's tale, who was a stranger among all of the species until he found the one he belonged to. Then, as she repeated the word 'strange' yet again, she pointed to my crotch.

I didn't understand what was strange about me. I'd always been told I was a female. My master had believed that as well and had given me a female name. Lacking any point of reference, I couldn't contradict him. Moreover, when I looked at the other females around me, their genitals looked like mine. The few males in the group had an extension that bobbed about between their legs as they walked. The females simply had a triangle of flesh between their thighs. The adults had more hair than I did, but apart from that I didn't see any difference. Finally, in an effort to make herself understood, Anaelle took some sand and shaped a long hill surrounded by two small, round mountains. I realized that she had made male genitals. Then she hit the ground at the base of the two small mountains and swept the sand away. She pointed to the space she had cleared, then touched my crotch with a finger, as if to indicate that something had also been swept from me. I shrugged and went to bed, still confused.

Anaelle lay down facing me. The lights gradually dimmed. She gave off a strong, pungent scent of sweat, mingled with dust, which had initially disturbed me with its strangeness — before going down into the mines, I'd never breathed in the human scent from close by — but I had learned to like it. That evening, her scent was particularly heady and I pressed more closely to her, placing my nose against her throat to breathe it in more deeply. She placed her mouth against mine and I tasted the freshness of her lips. Then her tongue slipped into my mouth with a delicious contact. She took my hand and drew it between her legs, where it was hot and moist. She guided my fingers to her genitals and pushed my index finger into flesh that was soft and slightly damp, then deeper into a cavity in the middle. I pulled my hand back, frightened. I patted the space between my legs and found nothing but relatively smooth flesh with a little hole in it, from which my urine flowed and which grew larger towards my rear, to form the cavity between my legs. That was not like what lay between Anaelle's legs! I *was* strange! She took my hand again, but I didn't want to feel just how different I was so I pushed her away a little more roughly than I meant to. I wanted to be close to her and yet, at the same time, contact with her burned. She turned away without a word, leaving me to reflect on my new identity.

One day, when I reached a point where I understood their language sufficiently, she introduced me to Dahain, the matriarch, an ageless woman with long gray bushy hair, the woman who had defended me at the beginning and had allowed me to eat out of her bowl. Anaelle and I had never spoken again about the night when she had allowed me to explore her body and I'd almost managed to forget the event. The following nights, as soon as she tried to caress me, I disengaged myself, gently but firmly. But deep in my being, I knew that something was wrong with me. That explained the looks the other humans gave me, the muffled laughter of the youngest behind my back, the sad looks some of the adults gave me. The feeling that I was different followed me everywhere. The matriarch had me sit down next to her and started to speak, slowly, so I would understand.

"I knew your mother well," she started. "Lorna was an exceptional woman who provided numerous services for the colony. A very beautiful woman and an accomplished politician, like few others. From mother to daughter, the women in her family were diplomats and, back on Earth, several of your ancestors had settled numerous conflicts that had appeared insoluble. Your mother's mother was responsible for interpersonal relations on the mother ship. One of the wave of births that followed our settlement on Mars II, Lorna naturally followed in the footsteps of her genitor."

I managed to decode most of the words, but I didn't understand much of what she was telling me.

"Koloni"? "Politician"? "Muthership"? These concepts meant nothing to me. Only later would the pieces of the puzzle slip into place for me. Unaware of my confusion, Dahian continued, "Naturally, in time she joined the team of emissaries sent to the indigenous population and she stayed there until the end, even as relations became increasingly tense between the two camps. Obviously, when things turned bitter and communications were cut off once and for all, she was at the forefront. Caught, as I was as well, in the wrong place at the wrong time, she was in the first contingent of prisoners sent to work in the mine. When she was brought here, in the first days after contact between humans and darztls broke off, she was a proud individual; she made her views known, even to the masters. But she had to repent of her ways on numerous occasions, since certain masters did not like to be dictated to by an impertinent slave. Twice she tried to escape, and twice she was brought back. The second time, when the darztls, those filthy pigs..." She spit on the ground. I had no need to ask her want a 'filthypig' was.

"... when the darztls amputated her second foot, the wound became infected and we almost lost her. But she finally recovered and was once again the Lorna we knew. She was still a beautiful woman, you know, despite the hollows carved in her face by working in the mine."

She looked at me for a moment, thoughtful. She stroked my cheek, in a very gentle gesture.

"You have her eyes. And you also look a little like your father."

I was dumbfounded. I had a father as well? A minute earlier, I had had no family. And now they were telling me about my roots. Of course I knew that you needed a father and a mother to make a child. I didn't know quite just how it was done among humans, but I had learned how darztls reproduced and I figured that it had to be similar for us: a male deposited a fertile liquid in the part of the female's body that sheltered the eggs. That encouraged the eggs to grow and finally, after a few moons, little babies, almost fully formed, emerged, immediately piercing through their soft envelope.

"You knew my father too? Where is he? Where is my mother?"

"Unfortunately, boy, they're both dead. Your father died first, then your mother. But, you know, they loved one another a great deal, despite the multiple partners the masters made us take to ensure the survival of the herd, when they found we weren't reproducing quickly enough."

She had pronounced the word 'herd' in a strange way, biting into the consonants, yet at the same time sounding distracted, as if talking about someone else.

"I think the fatal blow to your mother was losing the three earlier babies. And when I say lost, I don't mean stillborn or dead from natural causes. No, they were all taken away a few days after she delivered, during the weekly inspection, because the masters felt our group had enough males. The third time, she had picked up a stone and threw herself on a darztl, hoping to strike him. They could have killed her for that, but she was spared. All the same, it cost her a week in solitary, a week in a corner of the mine where it's so dark you can't see your hand in front of your face."

Judging by her tone, I realized that she had certainly suffered a similar punishment.

She continued, dreamily, "It's strange all the same. We keep on making babies... babies who are conceived and born in captivity, who will never know what it's like to be free. We should stop welcoming the slaves of our masters into our bodies. And yet, life is stronger. We make love to prove, no doubt, that we're still alive. And we get attached to our babies even though we know they can be taken from us at any time. Finally... when your mother came out of the hole, she came back to us thinner, but prepared to get back to normal life — life as it's imposed on us here, I mean. Your father was also shaken by the events, but he remained devoted to your mother. A fourth pregnancy in four Marsian years was the final straw. Lorna, who had always done her best, who had always worked herself ragged so as not to give the master any more reason to take their vengeance on a human, seemed to have given up. And the repeated blows they gave her could not encourage her to work harder. Most of the masters left her alone — they were always kinder toward pregnant women — but one female darztl in particular took advantage of the opportunity to be even more violent. You know her well, that female darztl, you've already tasted her medicine since she's come back to the mine, assuming even greater responsibilities. Roemlskt knows who you are. It's no surprise she concentrates on you."

The matriarch stopped speaking, giving me a chance to digest this news. Roemlskt had been a master at the mines during my parents' time. This gave me some insight into her cruelty towards me, and yet I didn't understand a thing.

"Roemlskt is one of those darztls who detests humans just as we humans detest vermin. She knows that her people need us to operate the mines, but she doesn't think we should get off so lightly. One day when your mother, pregnant with you, was throwing up her breakfast in a corner, Roemlskt struck her in the stomach with the barrel of her rifle. Your mother fell to the ground. Your father — who was usually so cautious, who frequently moderated Lorna's desire for vengeance — saw red. He rushed over to Roemlskt and raised his pickaxe against her. He struck her in the shoulder, causing black blood to flow. The female darztl also saw red. She grabbed him with her powerful paws, planting her claws firmly in his back, and threw him against the stone wall. Your father never got back up. She had broken his neck. The boss at that time — the one you called your master — asked Roemlskt to leave the mine. But he couldn't change the course of events. Your father was dead and your mother prostrate, losing blood, unable to get up and go back to work. Your birth didn't improve matters. When the midwife took you out and showed you to your mother, she saw nothing but your tiny penis mocking her. Lorna held you to her breast, weeping, and never stopped sobbing, in despair as much as rage. You both cried your lungs out. It was painful to see and hear. During the day, we had to stifle your shrieks under a pile of rags, for fear that they would bring the master's wrath on us, since they had little appreciation for such troubles. But at night, we could hear your mother raging against her curse, her ability to bear only boys."

I didn't want to understand. "But why is it so bad to give birth to boys?"

"Look around you," the matriarch said, staring at me. "Tell me how many men you see."

I turned around. The room was plunged in shadow, lit only by a single, wavering candle, but I knew the members of the little group by heart. I'd say there were about eight men. About fifteen males in all, counting the young ones. On the other hand, there were a lot more women, almost thirty adult females and as many young girls.

"You haven't wondered about this lack of balance? You've never thought about it? The darztls don't want too many males, I think, because the first ones captured were much less docile, much more aggressive than the females.

They only keep a few alive to ensure that our species continues and to ensure new workers for the mines. Your mother knew there was a very good chance that you would be taken away once the masters examined you. She mulled over her decision for two days before taking action. That evening, when everyone had gathered here for the night, your mother suddenly fell silent. Forty surprised faces turned towards her, as she held you in her arms. Before everyone, she lifted your frail, naked body, as if you were a sacrifice to some bloodthirsty god. Before anyone could stop her, she took your tiny little penis into her mouth and closed her eyes. A tear rolled down her check. Then with a precise, deliberate move, she clenched her teeth, taking away your masculinity from you for all time. Then she spit that little piece of flesh out and held you to her."

My stomach hurt and I suddenly felt a hot liquid flow between my legs. I had urinated! Suddenly, I no longer wanted to hear this story. I wanted to leave, but the heavy bolder at the entrance to the cavern would keep me from going too far. In any case, I was paralyzed, unable to move or speak. The matriarch, pitiless, continued her tale in a monotone voice, looking straight ahead.

"In the cave, filled as it was with your strident shrieks, everyone was dumbfounded. Then the others tore you from her arms, and she didn't resist. They quickly wrapped you in rags that were all too soon drenched in blood. Your mother no longer moved, no longer sobbed. She sat there, quietly, a smile on her lips, as if she were the first to understand a good joke and was waiting for the others to react. She no longer wept, but she no longer spoke either. She no longer seemed to hear the others, as they begged her to explain. Two days later, during the weekly starlit outing, your mother followed the others out, limping on her two stumps. Like the others, she rubbed her clothes with sand to clean them. Like the others, she sat out under the starlit sky. When it came time to go back down below, she ran ahead of the others, racing to the shaft, running as fast as her mutilated legs would let her, stumbling, grabbing onto the others for support. Before the masters had time to see what she planned and stop her, she dragged herself to the mine shaft and pitched forward. We all rushed after her, but the masters pushed us back, striking us frantically and furiously in an effort to keep us from looking as they brought her body back up. Nevertheless, we could clearly see the puddle of blood that lay at the bottom of the pit when they finally made us climb back down into the mine and shut us in for the night."

"But how did I survive?"

"Well, against all expectations, you did. Just like that! Under the filthy compresses, the hemorrhage stopped and, needless to say, the antibodies you had as a newborn prevented you from succumbing to a bacterial infection. You didn't die, yet your destiny was radically changed. In fact, one of the masters — and not just any master but the mine boss — had witnessed the entire scene. He inquired into the accident and because there was some good in him, despite the fact that he was a master, he inquired about you. Two days after your mother died, masters came to get you and took you to him. After that, we only saw you from a distance, growing up with our enemies."

"But are you certain that, if my mother hadn't... bitten off my penis, the masters would have killed me?"

"That, poor child, we will never know."

I didn't say another word. I walked away, followed by Anaelle, who had been there for the entire conversation, listening to a story she already knew, that everyone but me had already known for a long time. Everyone knew that I was abnormal, that I had been mutilated by my mother who, while wanting to save me, had handicapped me for life. No need to paint me a picture. I was old enough. I knew why I heard all that rustling, those moist noises during the night, I'd seen the men and the young boys caressing their penises in the shadows, even Anaelle had seemed to find it enjoyable to allow me to explore her moist flesh. But when I placed my hand between my legs, all I touched was skin, neutral and somewhat sensitive, that would always bear the scars of my mother's teeth.

And yet I felt desire. The act of the woman who had given me life had not taken everything from me. At night, touching Anaelle's skin roused all my adolescent senses.

Anaelle had beautiful large breasts that bounced grace-
fully as she walked, that grew round when she lay down.
The penises of the few male adolescents in our group grew
as they moved into adolescence. Yet in my case, my breasts
would stay those of a child, my penis did not exist, and
I was flat everywhere. Sexless. Anaelle was beautiful. I
loved her scent, her skin so soft in the places that were as
yet untouched by the masters' sticks. I wanted to caress
her, embrace her, penetrate her, let her into me. But my
desire stopped short, hampered by the lack of means to
assuage it. Instead, I felt like hitting her over and over
again, to hurt her, since I could not pleasure her.

Instead, I plunged into a stubborn silence. She asked
me what was wrong, but I replied evasively — when I replied at all. I think she guessed what I was feeling, but she
didn't have the words she needed to talk to me about it.
The distance between us grew, my silence pushing her
away. One evening, she didn't slip into our nest. In each
of the nightly noises, I heard her coupling. The next
morning, I examined each of the males who was old
enough to be her lover. From that time on, she was away
frequently. Some time later, I saw that her belly had grown.
She wasn't even an adult yet and carrying her first slave.

We had come around to the time of year when my master
had died, the previous revolution. I knew it because it was
the season when the desert was filled with the scent of
hidclrs, those lovely large, purple, carnivorous flowers.
During our weekly outings, their perfume plunged me into
my memories and, at the same time, filled me with despair.
One evening, seeing that my thoughts were tearing me
apart again, Anaelle came over to me and sat down, her
belly heavy. We hadn't had any real conversation for a long
time.

"What are you thinking about?" she asked, in an ordinary manner. Since I didn't reply, she continued, "It's been
a year, fourteen earth months according to the elders'
calendar, that you've been with us, sharing our daily lives.
But you never talk about your past life."

This pulled me from my silence. "My past life? My past
life? You want to talk about the life in which I was treated

like a darztl and not an animal, when I considered myself a normal individual, when I could still dream of tomorrow? There is no life here, just one long day that keeps playing over and over, to infinity. One day and each of its variations. In one of those variations I get beaten, and in another I escape. It's completely arbitrary. In one of the variations, a woman weeps because she's had a stillborn baby and in another a woman weeps because she has just given birth to a daughter who will become a slave. Depending on the variation, sometimes the masters are cruel and sometimes permissive, but I'm still at their mercy."

I looked up at her. "In one of the variations," I said, my voice quavering, "my best friend talks to me and comforts me, whereas in another, she finds something better to do and allows herself to be impregnated by someone with all the right parts."

She took me in her arms. "Oh, Skllpt!" she exclaimed. "You've got everything all mixed up. It's your head that's missing pieces. You didn't grow up among us. You still don't know what it means to get used to this kind of life. There's something stronger than the feeling of captivity, and that's the survival instinct. Besides, I find it much more agreeable to choose my own lovers than to be locked up for an entire week with the most repulsive male and forced to mate with him. I want to live, despite the masters that bury us alive. I take my pleasure where I find it. You should forget your past life and try to make an existence among us."

"Maybe. But some of the members in the group will never accept me as one of yours. You're not the same. You accepted me the very first day. But some of the others..."

I fell silent and thought about all of those legs that suddenly stretched out in front of me, tripping me, setting off muffled laughter and, occasionally, the ire of the masters as they told me to look where I was going. Several times, when no one was looking, some of the adolescents had forced their hands between my legs and pulled back, feigning extreme disgust. And all too often, when I walked over to a group, even after all the time I had spent in the mines, I would hear someone whisper: "Shh! The masters' little pet is coming!" How many times would I have to be beaten for them to consider me a full-fledged human? How much would I have to suffer? Things had been going well since I'd been accepted by Dahian, but I would always be an outsider.

"It's as if people hate me for my past life," I concluded. "As if I had chosen to be raised among the darztls, and all the magnificent things that happened to me." I stressed the word 'magnificent.'

"You don't have a monopoly on misery, you know. Before I was five years old, my mother had time to escape, get caught by the human hunters and have a foot savagely cut off. The only memory I have of my mother is of a mutilated woman who never took care of me."

I was dumbfounded. I'd never asked Anaelle about her past, figuring that it blended in with the gray routine of the mine.

"You never spoke of your mother," I said gently.

"I never told you about my mother because there's nothing to tell. Solen left me behind and escaped a second time. We never saw her again. No one ever said a word, but everyone believes she didn't make it back to the colony. She surely died in the desert. Her bones, picked clean by vultures, are turning into dust."

"Don't talk like that, Anaelle! Why do you hurt yourself like that?"

"I have some news for you, Skllpt. This misery... this is life. Skllpt, people hate you because you stay on the surface of their world, as if you were just visiting here. You have to accept the idea that you're here to stay, buddy."

She stood up painfully and walked off. I did the same, since it was time for roll call.

Just visiting! So I was just traveling through! I had to escape to get back to my real life. This conversation sowed the seeds of a plan in me, a plan to get out of this situation, to get out of it alive. I had to escape. I was completely certain of that, as if it were my destiny. I had a head start over the other humans. I was familiar with darztl society and I knew the site. I would succeed where the others had failed.

My plan developed very quickly. I didn't mention it to anyone, out of fear of being denounced. When our masters weren't paying attention, I would slip into one of the heavy wheelbarrows that the strongest humans carried to the shaft, attached to large hooks and then hoisted up. There, the darztls would collect the load and stow the wheelbarrow on a large conveyer belt, that would take it to a container, where it would be dumped. No one would notice that the wheelbarrow carried something other than rock and, wounded by the rock that would be unloaded on top of me, I would wind up in the container. Of course, I knew that someone must have tried this already. The tricky part of the plan would come when the masters counted us before locking us up for the night. It was only when someone missed roll call that they hooked the haavls up to the containers and hauled them out of the mine enclosure to be searched. However, I had something new to add to the plan. I'd sneak out of the bin before nightfall. The sun would burn me to a crisp, of course, so I'd have to be quick about it. Instead of heading over to the wire mesh fence, which would be closed in any case, or staying in the container and waiting for someone to find me, I'd head to my childhood hiding place, that narrow stone cave. No one had ever found me there before. Maybe no one would find me there now. No one would think of looking for me inside the mine enclosure. I'd stay in my den for a few days, nibbling on the dried fruit I'd left there over a year ago. At the outset, I'd hear the hubbub in the enclosure and I'd curl up in a ball, expecting detection at any moment. But as the hours passed, my confidence would grow. And a few days later, once everyone thought I was long gone, I would slip into another bin and wait to be turned free.

I was really excited. For the first time in over a year, I enjoyed something. This plan became the very core of my life, it was a new, imaginary den where I hid and, all too soon, I thought of nothing else. In my mind's eye, I left the mine over and over again, looking for the right time, and then I'd be free. I added details, I embellished the story, I distilled the risky elements. At one point, a darztl would be on the edge of searching the bin; another time, someone would walk past the cell where I hid, looking for an opening in the wire mesh fence; and yet another time, someone would denounce me, having uncovered my plan as I talked in my sleep. In the best scenarios, I was strong and brave and overpowered the immense darztls who pursued me. In every case, however, I succeeded. From that time on, they would use up the last of my energy on the mine walls, beat me until I screamed in pain, but nothing affected me. I would be free soon, I told myself, so I could put up with one more inconvenience.

"Skllpt, what's wrong?" Anaelle frequently asked me. "You were always taciturn, but at least, before, you answered me!"

I was more alone than ever, but I cultivated that solitude, enjoying the impression that I had knowledge known only to me.

In fact, I spent far too long finessing that plan before putting it into effect. A few weeks later, Huhoy, a young man in the group, caught me by surprise and escaped in a wheelbarrow. Too bad for him since the rest of his plan was weaker than mine and the masters caught him as he tried to get out of a container, his body covered with bruises. Usually, the punishment for escaping was a foot. But considering his age and the fact that he was too stupid to even get past the fenced enclosure, the masters were merciful. They assembled us all and a master had him lie on the ground, then clasp his ankles and raise his legs. The boss master, who was always up for this type of operation, administered the punishment herself. She beat the soles of his feet until his skin broke, until the muscle and bone below was visible. The punishment lasted an eternity, or at least it seemed like that to me, an eternity during which the masters forced us to watch and listen as Huhoy screamed in pain, striking us if we turned our eyes away or covered our ears. That male never walked normally again, even though his skin healed. And it was more than enough to discourage anyone from trying something similar. Enough to prevent a young boy from putting any other plan into action. Enough to definitely wipe away all my own plans for escape.

I'd had enough of that kind of violence, of all that blood. The boss master was completely crazy. She'd kill us all if no one stopped her. And her underlings were barely any better, blindly following her orders. All of the good darztls had left, disgusted. Roemlskt only kept masters of her own ilk, who would never stand up to her. Why would living beings impose this kind of life on other living beings? My master had been wrong when he said that the humans in the mines had committed crimes in keeping with their punishment. No one could deserve such a fate, such degradation. The worst part was not being imprisoned, but the power games that came with imprisonment. Captivity weighed heavily on me, but largely because of the powerlessness it filled me with. And things were no better with my own kind. I was as fed up with belonging to the human group as I was with not being a darztl. Had that only been a figment of my master's imagination? Anaelle was right. I glided over this existence without plunging into it. I was with them for the time being while waiting, unconsciously, to return to my past life.

My friend was just about at term. She walked heavily and found it hard to perform adequately. Most of the masters seemed to understand this and left her more or less alone. Others, however, took advantage of her condition, and were even crueler than usual. I thought back about what my master had told me about people: that their cruelty hurt them more than it hurt the others, and I thought, once again, that my master had been wrong. It was much easier to beat someone than to be beaten. One day, Anaelle leaned against a wall, doubled over with a cramp. One of the masters walked over to her and told her to get back to work. Since she failed to obey quickly enough, he hit her on the shoulder. She stood up in pain and misery, but all too soon, she had another cramp, one that left her kneeling on the ground, trying to catch her breath. The master kicked her and hit her again, either not understanding or failing to see what state she was in. I stepped between Anaelle and the darztl.

"Stop," I said in his language. "The darztl can see that the human is unable to work."

I had been very polite. The darztl shoved me aside with a smack of his tail and went back to hitting my friend. I threw myself at him, pushing him back with the handle of my pickaxe, knowing full well that he was stronger. At least, I thought, he'll spend his fury on me and might even forget about hitting Anaelle. And, in fact, the master did turn his anger on me. He sent me spinning with a powerful blow of his paw — backwards, fortunately. Otherwise, considering the force he had used, he would have injured me mortally. I tried to stand up, but he hit me again, and sent me flying against a pile of rock. He forced me to stand up, then struck me again, pushing me to the ground. I was afraid. He seemed to want to kill me. I started to run down the underground corridor, but he caught up with me in a few leaps. He grabbed me by my long hair and dragged me down the corridor. I screamed and fought with all my might, but he was more powerful. He dragged me to a rocky cavity, tore my suit off and threw me in. Before I had time to stand up, he blocked the opening with a heavy rock. I stayed there in the dark, in that tiny hole, too low for me to stand up, too narrow for me to lie down. My mouth tasted of blood, but in my heart I felt that I had done what I had to do.

The masters left me there for a long time, almost six days, or so they told me. They gave me nothing but water, handed to me in a gourd slipped through a crack. Once, they gave me the flesh of a cactus. I chewed it slowly, to get as much as possible out of it. The ground was hard. The walls were rough. I had nothing with which to cover myself, to protect my skin from the rock. It was cold, the hole was damp, my joints hurt and I was chilled to the bone. My prison became viler and viler as the days passed. And yet, at the same time, I was almost comfortable. In the dark, everyone looked the same.

A master came to get me the evening of the weekly outing. Covered with shit and piss, I was so weak and so hunched over that the darztl had to help me climb the ladder to the surface. He was so gentle that I almost felt I could love him. On outing evenings, the masters let us eat outside. Feeling a little dizzy from lack of food and the clean air I was breathing in, I stumbled over to the stew pot and threw myself on the food that a woman poured into my bowl. Then I rolled in the sand to clean off the filth that covered me. Then, and only then, did I look around, searching for Anaelle. She was sitting in the middle of a group, breastfeeding a tiny baby. I walked over to her timidly.

"Skllpt! Come over here! I hope you're well. We were all so worried about you."

The others nodded.

"You know, that was very kind of you, to do that for me. While the darztl that had been beating me took care of you, nicer darztls allowed me to rest. The baby was born a few hours later."

She held out the little thing she carried in her arms to me. A bald, red baby with a tiny penis. Alarmed, I looked at Anaelle.

"They don't know about it yet," she said, faking disinterest, in answer to my unspoken question.

"The masters haven't conducted the inspection yet."

I looked at her. I wanted to ask her how she could live with the uncertainty, with the possibility that the infant, whom even I loved already, would be torn away from her. But words were useless.

Time for roll call came and we stood in rows. The boss master didn't always take part in the inspection with the others, but this was one of the evenings when she decided to come out. I glanced furtively over at Anaelle, standing a little farther along in the row, pale and trembling. The masters progressed slowly, occasionally asking a human to step forward, feeling his muscles, inspecting ears and teeth, more to humiliate us than out of any real need. When the boss master got to Anaelle, she stopped and tore the baby from her arms. Holding him by the feet, as if he were some sort of vile object, she walked over to the master in charge of our files. He consulted his log and checked a box. Taking her time, without allowing us to see which direction she would take with the baby, she returned to Anaelle and gave the baby back, almost as if she regretted it, as if giving up a valuable object, then wiped her paw ostentatiously in the sand and returned to her inspection.

§ § §

Life went on in relative tranquility, punctuated by the quick blows of our pickaxes on the rock, alternating with the heavy sound of clubs striking our bodies, and the slower rhythm of our weekly outings. I'd managed to make a living space for myself, tuning out under the rain of blows, pretending to find satisfaction in fleeting moments of pleasure, taking one day at a time. The others gradually seemed to grow used to my presence. Perhaps they thought that I had made up for lost time with my time in isolation and they could show me a little consideration. But I was different, handicapped both physically and emotionally, the improbable combination of being half-human and half-male. One day — it must have been almost two years since I'd been slaving in the mine — a rumor ran through the humans: the boss master was about to be replaced and perhaps the new darztl would be as considerate as Master Sshlurltr has been. During the next weekly outing, in fact, we saw a new master approach for the inspection. He walked up and down between the rows, looking at us with what I took for benevolence, distant of course, with the look of a parent faced with young who are a little rowdy, but he had nothing of his predecessor's evil. Nevertheless, when he reached me, I panicked. He looked me up and down. One of his subordinates whispered something in his ear. He nodded.

"So this is she. Skllpt," he said, addressing me in his language. I jumped. Even the Dartzls who were the kindest to me had never treated me with such deference. And it had been a long time since anyone had taken me for a female. And in the most ridiculously normal tone of voice, considering the circumstances, he added, "Skllpt will have to drop by soon to see the boss. Khlearmt has things to discuss with her."

I almost replied sarcastically, saying that I would see if I could get free, but I bit back my words, deciding it would be better to be cautious and see what tricks the masters had up their sleeves.

"What did he say to you?" Anaelle asked me once we were shut up for the night. I shrugged, pretending disinterest.

"I don't know. I didn't understand. You know I don't speak the masters' language much any more."

The very next morning, as I was getting ready to swing my pickaxe against the rock for the first time, a master came looking for me.

"The boss is waiting," was all he said. The others watched me leave as if I was about to have a foot cut off.

When I stepped out of the mine, the sun — the liirzt — struck me like a whip and the heat squeezed the air from me. I realized that I hadn't been outside during the daytime in two revolutions. Even with my eyes closed, I was blinded by the light and had to cover my eyes with my hands. The darztl immediately handed me a blanket to protect me from the rays that were so dangerous for me. I baked underneath it, but at least my skin wasn't burning. I allowed myself to be guided, not knowing where I was headed.

When we arrived at the boss master's quarters, my eyes had become somewhat used to the light. It had been such a long time since I'd left the rooms of my childhood that they'd changed somewhat in my memories. I didn't remember the rooms being so bright or the rock walls so smooth. The boss was waiting for me there, stretched out in a chair carved from a hollowed out cactus. Calm and serene, if I was right about the color of his wattle. He pointed at a stool, smaller than the furniture darztls usually used and, as a result, suitable for me.

"Skllpt can sit. Khlearmt must talk with her."

His wattle turned purple, with lighter streaks. I thought that he would say something, but he remained silent for a while, obviously looking for the right words.

Finally he said, "The darztls did not treat Skllpt well."

He stopped talking again and then leapt up.

"Skllpt's master had big plans for her. Unfortunately he died too soon. And, well... Roemlskt did not understand those projects. She did not understand them at all. Or else she understood them too well and did everything she could to compromise them. But that's already history. She's gone now. And Khlearmt is in charge. He can correct the errors of the past, repair what has been broken."

I said nothing, by now too used to remaining silent in the presence of a master. Occasionally, when we looked as thick as boards, the masters would lose interest in us and stop hitting us.

He continued, "Khlearmt has projects too. Skllpt will not stay underground for long. She will come back here to live."

I jumped, despite my resolution to hide any emotion. But I triumphed inside. Although the boss was treating me with a deference darztls granted only their own, he was still treating me like an inferior, making all the decisions for me.

As if he could read my thoughts, he added, "If Skllpt agrees, of course. Meanwhile, would Skllpt like a drink of agthrlt?"

Agthrlt is brewed from a blend of dried herbs. I'd always found the taste unpleasant, but it had been so long since I'd had a hot drink, and this concoction was so closely associated with my past life, that I agreed. Tears in my eyes, both as a result of the bitterness of the brew and because memories crowded into my mind, I drank my tea in silence.

The boss was delicate. He didn't ask me to move in with him right away. He told me that he'd give me time to think about his offer and had me taken back to the mine. The next few days I lived in a dream world, working on automatic pilot, getting up and going to bed like a mechanical doll. The others looked at me, curious. They would have liked me to tell them about the sophisticated punishment the new boss had administered to me, but I couldn't open myself up to them and tell them just how refined that punishment was.

I was torn in two. On the one hand, there was life in the mines, suffering, punishment. There was less and less of that, however. Already we were feeling the effects of the new administration. The masters were less violent; they weren't encouraged to beat us for no good reason. Yet it was a life that went nowhere, the truncated destiny of an animal that lives one day at a time and depends on its master for everything. On the other hand, there was existence with the darztls. It was a gentler fate, of course. The boss didn't seem to be lying. He had actually promised that I could go back to my past life. Yet, was that life any freer? Would I be trading the life of a beast of burden for the destiny reserved for a favorite pet, exchanging one form of captivity for another? I wasn't a darztl and there would always be someone around to remind me of that. But I had to admit that the idea of returning to the life that my master had promised me — a life that had been torn away by his death — was appealing. I'd spent the last twenty-seven months underground, yet I had spent most of my young existence on the surface of this planet, and I found the first phase more successful than the second. In the meantime, leaving the mines and returning to the surface of Sielxth, would mean abandoning everything I'd found below. I hadn't found much to enjoy in the mine, but there was Anaelle, the few others who had been kind to me, the entire group of humans who were my own species. No one underground would ever forgive me for returning to my former world. My bonds with them were too fragile. Yet how many of them wouldn't trade their current situation for a gilded darztl prison?

The boss gave me several days, then he had me called, just as the masters were locking us up. I'd already entered the common room, but a darztl told me to come with him. Khlearmt was waiting for me at the top of the shaft. He handed me a clean suit.

"This darztl knows that humans prefer to be dressed rather than go naked, so he brought this."

I slipped the clothes on, but remained barefoot on the warm sand. We walked around the mine yard, the darztl taking small steps, me taking large strides to keep up with him. I waited for him to say something. He remained silent.

Before speaking, I still had no idea what my answer would be. My idea took shape as I linked the sentences together and, by the end, I knew that my decision was made.

"Skllpt was born almost fourteen revolutions ago. The mine workers did the calculations and told me that this is about sixteen human years. This means nothing to Skllpt, whose references are essentially darztl ones, but it seems to mean that she... that she is almost an adult. Yet between the time when she allowed herself to be educated by her attentive master and the period she spent in the mine, this adult period seems to have bypassed her for good. Skllpt seems destined to remain a child forever, to be guided as a child, both cosseted with love and corrected for some obscure mistake, but always immature, unable to make her own decisions, buffeted about at the will of the masters."

I stopped and looked up at him. "And at the same time, she already feels old, she has seen too many things for her fourteen revolutions or her sixteen years, whatever, tragedies that are too painful for a single lifetime, horrors that have been written on her body, in her head, a series of atrocities, one of which alone would be enough to scar an existence."

"And what answer is Khlearmt expected to hear?" the boss asked, gently.

I continued, without really answering him, "Skllpt does not know what her life would have been like if she had had a normal life. On this world, she was not even destined to survive, so..."

I stopped, but the boss did not seem to understand what I wanted to say.

"Yet," I continued, "she knows that destiny has little to do with the long present of the human slaves. She has met people who are born, will grow up and die, probably earlier than they should, in the mine. If Skllpt knew that, by staying below she could save a single human, she would choose to die there. Unfortunately, even though most of the humans will hate her for the rest of her days if she chooses another life — they already hate her for coming from somewhere else, speaking with a different accent, having a different past — that will change absolutely nothing in their lives."

I stopped, out of breath. It had been a long while since I had spoken so long and the need to refer to myself in the feminine was exhausting.

"Does Skllpt want to ask something before answering?" the boss asked me.

I looked at him, astonished. I didn't think I was in a position to negotiate. But my answer was on the tip of my tongue.

"Yes, if the master will allow me. Two things. First, not to be so hard on those in the mine. Deep down, Skllpt would prefer for there to be no mine at all, but she is realistic. Second, for Khlearmt to make sure that, even after he leaves, even if he is replaced by a bloodthirsty boss, that Skllpt will never be sent underground again. It's not the abuse she fears, as much as having to face her own kind again."

Khlearmt's wattle turned a bluish hue. "Skllpt can move into her new quarters immediately."

Stupidly, I expected to return to my childhood room in the boss's home. But I was grown now. We walked past it without stopping and went to a little house just a few steps away. The master opened the door and gestured for me to go in. There was only one room in the shack, but it was clean and decently furnished. In one corner, there was a table with two chairs, built for my size. In the other, a bed, a real bed. On the back wall, a radiator that sent a comforting heat into the room. And above all, running the length of one wall, was a bookshelf, filled to overflowing. I wanted to hide my excitement, but I couldn't contain myself.

"Skllpt and the darztl will have all the time they want to speak tomorrow and the following days. For now, it would be good to sleep. Khlearmt is tired."

He saluted me and left, closing the door gently behind him, leaving me in the middle of the first house I had been inside in two years. I didn't hear the door lock behind me.

I waited a few minutes, to give the master time to walk off, then I went to the door and pushed. It opened without any difficulty. For the first time in my life — whether it had been to protect me from the others or to protect the others from me — I was not locked up. I was about to go to sleep in a room where I could open the door at any time. If I wanted to. I closed the door and lay down.

I was so very excited I thought I'd never manage to fall asleep. Randomly, I chose a few books that I had read before and lay down, fully clothed, leaving the light on. I leafed though page after page, unable to concentrate. Then I fell asleep, my nose in a book.

In the days that followed, the boss allowed me to get used to my new life. He told me that I was free to come and go inside the enclosure. I walked about as twilight approached, of course, and I avoided the side where the mine was located, even though I knew that, apart from the weekly outing, there would be no risk of meeting humans.

One morning, the boss handed me an object. It looked like a darztl book, but opened from right to left, rather then top to bottom. And the minute I opened the object, I knew it was no darztl artifact. The symbols were too different, arranged in compact rows like slaves during roll call.

"Skllpt can press here," the boss said, pointing a claw toward the screen. "It seems to function only when touched by a warm-blooded creature."

I pressed on the symbol he indicated and a word emerged from the book. "I." I jumped. I pressed the other signs and a sentence formed. "'I can't play with you,' said the fox. 'I'm not tame.'"

I glanced inquisitively at Khlearmt who seemed to understand.

"The darztls finally realized that it is a human book. When someone presses on the words, the book pronounces the sentence. It's very ingenious. Darztls tried to dismantle several of them, but it's not possible to figure out exactly how they work. All that we know is that if certain parts are removed the image disappears, and that if certain other parts are removed the sound is deactivated. And the object seems to be powered by tiny solar batteries, somewhat like those in the suits the darztls wear in the mine, since it stops working when kept in the dark too long."

And, as if it had waited for that specific moment for permission, the human book turned off.

"There are several books like this one in the mine warehouse," he continued. "There are plates that can be slipped into them, to change the story. The books have been there for several revolutions and no one remembered they were there. If Skllpt wants, she can play with these objects as long as she wants."

"But where does it come from?"

His tone sounded regretful when he replied, as if he had anticipated this question and knew that he would have to answer it sooner or later.

"The humans we captured had these books with them."

The darztl raids, of course. The other humans had mentioned them to me. The oldest had been sent willingly into darztl territory and it was only after they had arrived that they were captured. My master had told me the same story, although the humans and darztls didn't play the same roles in the two versions. He had also spoken to me about the humans they had gone to trap where they lived, but that had all remained a little vague.

"At the beginning, when the darztls understood that the humans intended to remain on Sielxth, they thought they could frighten the humans by capturing their emissaries. In this way, the humans would learn how powerful the people on this planet were, they would see what darztls are capable of. Then they would demand their own back and they would return to where they came from. But the humans never demanded what the darztls had kept. So, Khlearmt's people decided to go a step further. Some humans had settled in the desert, between the oasis and the darztl territory. On several occasions groups of darztls attacked them, killing several and kidnapping the rest. But the humans never asked to have them returned, either. It's almost as if they meant nothing to them. So the project was abandoned. The darztls had enough humans, enough workers for the mine. Certain darztl ethnologists viewed the humans like osfts, allowing their kind to be cooked on a spit while going about their daily activities."

Reality struck me like a whip. Humans had been working in the mine for almost twenty revolutions. First there had been those of my mother's time, who had been enslaved following a burst of darztl anger, followed by those who were caught in the raids. And now, the second generation had reached maturity and was producing a new generation of little slaves. Fewer and fewer of the humans in the mines had any knowledge of a free human society. Apart from myself, who came from up top, a growing number of the humans seemed to be accepting this life. Several spoke a sort of pidgin, a mixture of human grammar and poorly mastered darztl vocabulary. And not once in all that time had the humans from the colony appeared, even though the mine slaves secretly hoped they would. Was it possible that my kind could be so insensitive to the fate of their own? Yet the people in the mine seemed to be attached to their kind. Was it possible that the work in the mine had... civilized them? Or that the humans didn't have the resources they needed? That was the most plausible explanation, as I told Khlearmt.

"Perhaps. But Khlearmt doubts it. Does Skllpt want to follow him to the warehouse? Khlearmt will show her the books, along with something else that is very interesting."

I pulled on my suit and followed him. He led me to a little stone shack with no opening other than a heavily locked door. He played with a series of keys and opened the door. The small, dusty shed was filled with human artifacts piled every which way on stone shelves. In the midst of other mysterious objects there were dozens of human books, more than enough to keep me occupied for some time. I hoped that all the books were accompanied by a little voice that would help me understand the stories and gradually learn to read human writing. When I opened them, most of the books remained lifeless. But Khlearmt placed one in the sun for a moment and it sprang to life. I was incredibly excited.

"Skllpt can take as many books as she likes. And when she has finished with them, she can read more."

"But Khlearmt said that there was something else of interest to show the human," I said timidly.

"Skllpt pays close attention. That's good," the darztl said joyfully, plucking an object off a shelf.

It was a small, ordinary cube, equipped with a few buttons. Khlearmt played with some of the buttons and an image literally leapt from the cube. I stepped back, alarmed. Two tiny humans were running about in front of me, one seeming to chase the other, in a dark setting filled with right angles. However, when I timidly reached out to catch one of the humans, my hand passed through the image. I pulled it back, frightened. Khlearmt's wattle turned various shades of green. Obviously, he found my reaction amusing.

"It's always strange the first time. But it's better to look at this indoors. In full liirzt, the image is not as good."

Once I got back home, I asked Khlearmt to leave me alone. It was a lot of information to digest in a single day and I needed to go over it. He appeared to understand what I was experiencing and told me he would be back the next day. I was upset. I had known nothing about these artifacts until that day. I wondered why my master had never spoken to me about them, but I decided that he must have thought I was too young and had been waiting for the right time. After all, he'd prevented me from associating with my own kind from very early on, so he must have thought that human knowledge would corrupt me if he let me have access to it too early. Without knowing why, I still felt that he had intended to show me all these things one day. He'd spoken to me too often of the great mission that lay ahead of me to have intended to keep me from ever knowing where I came from.

I was eager to read through the books, but the cube was too appealing. I pressed a few buttons and an image appeared again. It was true that the quality was better inside than in full daylight, but the shapes shifted somewhat as soon as I passed my hand through them. It wasn't the same image as the first time, however. Now I saw two men sitting on strange pieces of furniture — boards with four legs — talking. By playing with the buttons, I managed to hear what they were saying. I didn't understand everything, since their language was a little different than the one I spoke, but I could clearly see that the two men were angry. Then a woman entered the room and the conversation stopped. She sat down next to one of the men and caressed him as if she wanted to make love with him. The other man left, saying that they would see one another again, or something like that. I pressed a few buttons and the image changed. This time, the man — one of the two I had seen earlier — stood with his back to a wall. Standing in front of him, another man was threatening him which what looked like a darztl gun. Suddenly, I saw a silhouette take shape behind the armed man. A bright light burst from the silhouette. The armed man shone for a moment and then disappeared. When the silhouette stepped out of the shadow, I saw that it was the woman. She ran to the man, who gripped the wall, and embraced him. I pressed another button. The scene played again, but in reverse. The man reappeared, then shone, then the ray of light withdrew from him. I pressed yet another button and the scene played again, as it had the first time.

I put the cube down. The images continued to flow, but I no longer paid any attention. I was disturbed. I didn't know how this fabulous object worked, but I figured that the humans must have been able to capture reality and put it in a box so they could play it over and over. The oldest of the humans in the mine spoke of our superior technology, but they had never mentioned an object such as this one. Or I had never understood. In any case, they had never spoken of the humans' formidable destructive weapons, weapons that could make someone disappear in a few seconds. How could a people with such extraordinary means not have found a way to free its own people who had been suffering in the mine for over twenty human years? It was not a matter of fear or a lack of means. What was the reason?

I pressed a few buttons on the cube and managed to turn it off. I turned back to the human books, which were more familiar to me. I had placed a book in the sun, hoping it would absorb enough energy. Khlearmt had shown me how to change the plate and bring up another book. The one I opened was very different from the first. The symbols were larger and placed next to images. When I pressed on one or the other, the voice that spoke was that of a child. I understood that the book was used to teach children to read, a little like the simplified books given to darztl children. It was perfect for me, since I was looking at human writing for the first time. Even if the oldest humans in the mine had known how to read in the past, they had certainly not seen any books since being locked up. And, obviously, they had not had either the time or the energy to teach the younger ones how to write. Patiently, I set about studying the book and gradually discovered how certain words were written, certain words I was already familiar with, of course: father, child, house, hand, foot.... I didn't understand all of the vocabulary, and certain concepts were completely foreign to me. What was a car, a dog, a computer? But I learned quickly.

Khlearmt allowed me to learn as much as I wanted, keeping an eye on my progress from a distance, coming to see me in the morning, asking me if I needed more plates, and inviting me on long walks during the evening so I could tell him what I had learned. Those plates contained everything: school texts, works of fiction, and even technical manuals, although I really didn't understand those. He looked pleased to see me dive into the knowledge of my own kind, as if the darztls had not cut the slaves off from all human knowledge.

As I concentrated on my learning, months passed, months that brought me closer to the culture of my kind while distancing me from the humans in the mine. Occasionally, during the evenings, when Khlearmt had to take charge of the weekly inspection, I would set my books aside and discretely leave my house. Hidden behind a building in the distance, I would watch the humans climb out of the mine shaft one by one, walking slowly, some of them limping painfully, and go about their cleaning activities. Anaelle was among them, holding her baby to her breast. Then apparently quiet, but keeping a watchful eye out for the slightest movement on the part of the masters who supervised them, they lay down on the sand to rest for a while. Then I heard a darztl shout something and the humans got back up. Naked in the night, they stretched out in a close, shivering line. Never again had I witnessed punishments like those imposed by the previous boss, but the human slaves were still in thrall to the darztl masters they feared. I went home, closed my door and dove back into the imaginary world of human books to keep myself from thinking about those who were going back down below.

Large areas of the human world remained a mystery to me. Several of their short stories, probably intended for young children, resembled darztl tales. These were moral tales in which the children successfully completed major trials in order to find happiness. Along the way, they would run into both evil creatures and people who came to their aid. All of these encounters were intended to teach the reader a lesson. For example, the first story that came into my hands was about a little boy a man met in the desert — I was happy to come across that word since I knew what a desert was at least. Among other things, I learned that you can't love people despite themselves and that dangerous beasts cannot overcome their nature. In that story, I understood that a 'snake' was a sort of hesstdl, like the ones I occasionally saw in the mine yard. The stories for adults were harder to understand. All they talked about was murders, chases, violence and betrayal, as if my kind, even when they were free, took pleasure in locking themselves up in mines they had dug in their imaginations! The books also told of confrontations among groups of humans, called 'wars' in their language, which left dozens of humans dead and prisoners, human prisoners who were beaten by other humans. In all of their stories, the humans seemed to strive to make life hard.

Perhaps freedom left my kind too idle and they needed to tell atrocious stories for entertainment....

And then there were scenes in which humans loved one another. I found one in a three-dimensional book — I had finally realized that the animated images that came out of the cube were not actually reality, but invented stories where the three-dimensional image replaced the universe we see in our mind's eye when we read. But some of the books were more explicit. I read them with a morbid fascination, caught up in a desire to pitch the storybook away, but riveted to a world that would forever be beyond my reach. Already, I felt ill whenever a book talked about love. Love of any kind — between a mother and her son, between friends, between lovers — was a mystery to me. I had adored my first master, but with a naïve love, the love of a child who idolizes an adult. And then, in the mine, there had been no time for love. I believed that I felt affection for Anaelle, that I was attached to some of the humans... but love? Did Anaelle love the men she sought out at night, while refusing to speak to them during the day? My mother and father, according to Dahian, had loved one another. And then I was born after my father died and my mother had mutilated me.... Out of love? No, something definitely eluded me.

And as for understanding sexual relations... Some of the books described mating abundantly. Not only in biology texts, but also in tales the humans called 'novels.' I recognized some of the gestures I had seen in the common room in the mine, and others I had guessed from the moist noises heard in the dark. There were stories about men and women, two men, two women, several individuals, but I didn't see myself in any other them. And what was strange about the books was the connection with nudity. The simple act of undressing seemed to excite the humans in these tales beyond belief. After spending two revolutions in the mine, undressing evoked the cold of stone against my body and the need to snuggle with a warm-blooded creature, as well as the master's blows after they removed our suits....

Once the initial exultation was over, these books plunged me into despair. I slowed my reading, unable to concentrate, and then, as the weeks and months passed, I completely stopped reading the books the boss brought me. I merely stayed in my bed, eyes wide open, seeing nothing, welcoming sleep with gratitude. When Khlearmt came by to see me, I'd tell him that I was tired, that I had worked too hard. Occasionally, I'd agree to go for a short walk with him and then I'd try to hide my discouragement, forcing myself to appear animated when talking about my discoveries, but increasingly I had nothing to stay, no readings to summarize.

"What's wrong?" the boss asked me one evening, as we strolled about the mine yard.

I jumped. I hadn't thought I was so transparent. I shrugged.

"Khlearmt can see full well that the human is not as enthusiastic as at the beginning. Is all this reading tiring her? Does she want something?"

Yes, but I was unable to tell him what was missing. He would not have understood. And it could have been dangerous for me. I hesitated to tell the boss that he was keeping a male in the house next to his own.... So I sidestepped that issue, but when I did speak it came out like a liberating admission. I told him, a darztl, about all the thoughts that ran through my mind when I dove into the culture of my kind, through books, about everything I found strange in their free world, in their non-darztl world.

"I don't understand my kind... excuse me, Skllpt should not be so familiar with the head boss."

His wattle turned a pacifying color.

"We're friends, Skllpt. We can ignore formalities."

Khlearmt stopped and looked at me. "Skllpt, tell me, would you be happy if you could see how your kind live? I mean, not in books, but in real life?"

"Well... I don't know." I replied, surprised by his question. "It all depends on the kind of book I find myself in," I added laughing.

"Skllpt, I'm not joking. If I told you that I had the means to send you to the human colony, would you want to go?"

When I realized he was serious, I stopped laughing and stared at him. What was he thinking? And why was he asking me for permission? Since I'd been born, no one had ever asked me for permission for anything at all. Or perhaps, just once. And that was when I was allowed to choose whether to live on the surface or not. But it had been a dishonest bargain and a lose-lose situation.

"I don't understand," I said. "You want to send me back to the free humans? Why?" Definitely not to make me happy, I thought.

"Come," he said, "I'm going to show you something at my place."

Once we were inside his home, he had me sit down and brought out a bundle of papers. He produced a diagram with various curves.

"What you're looking at Skllpt, is a graph of the temperatures on Sielxth during the course of recent revolutions. Each dot represents the temperature at a specific time in a revolution and the curve lines are made by connecting the dots. The white line you see indicates the date on which the humans arrived. What do you notice?"

The curve wavered slightly up to the white line and then for a little while after that. Then, increasingly winding, it started to drop slightly. The highest temperature recorded that year was two degrees lower than the highest temperature recorded during the year when contact between humans and darztls had been broken off.

"I admit I didn't notice that the weather was cooling," I said as a joke.

"It's not funny, Skllpt. Our planet is not as hot as it was. And several darztls think the humans are behind it."

I burst into laughter. "Khlearmt, your hatred for humans has blinded you. I know my kind have a great deal of knowledge. They can travel through the heavens and the cosmos, they can explore matter in depth, they can make sophisticated calculations using machines that defy the imagination, but to go from there to changing the climate of an entire planet..."

Khlearmt showed me other graphs taken, or so he said, in the inhabited desert between the darztl territory and the zone where the humans had settled. This time, the curve dropped more abruptly and the temperature difference was four degrees.

"Of course, we were not able to measure the temperature farther north because the humans prevent us from approaching. But we think that the temperature difference would be even more noticeable. Already, in our country, the drop in the temperature is noticeable. The need for energy is greater and homes have to be heated more at night. Darztls are getting sick more frequently and, if I showed you the mortality graph, you'd see that it follows the thermal graph. In short, our world is cooling and we're dying from it."

Recalling how this conservation had started, I asked, "And how would my going to live with my own kind heat the planet back up?"

"Strangely enough, you can help us by cooling the atmosphere between our two peoples! Skllpt, we know that the humans are very powerful, and more technologically advanced than we are. They came to our planet, yet we are unable to go to theirs. However, certain darztls say that the humans no longer have a planet of their own. That they destroyed it and wander aimlessly through space, settling on one planet for a while and then leaving after depleting its resources."

"What do you think?"

"I don't know. It could be so, but I don't believe that. I don't think they're any more monstrous than they think we are! However, I do believe our meteorologists when they tell us our planet is changing. But I don't promote the extreme means others are proposing. Skllpt, if the most belligerent of those among us win, all the humans on this planet will be exterminated or, at the very least, their culture will be annihilated and they will be our slaves for all time."

I jumped. I realized that I was used to the current balance and that I thought it would always be maintained. The darztls had never attacked the humans head on because they knew that they would suffer heavy losses in any such confrontation. Yet if they felt threatened enough and took on the colony, the humans, despite their technology, would never hold their own against a nation of angry darztls.

Suddenly, I understood why the humans had never come back to look for their captives. They knew all about it and simply wanted to gain time while waiting until they had radically transformed this planet. Khlearmt was right. The humans had the ability to do that. Nevertheless, I still didn't understand what role I was to play in the entire situation.

"I belong to the camp that believes we must give the humans one last chance. But we have no means for communicating with them. None of the emissaries we've sent them has ever returned. I must admit that we didn't treat the emissaries they sent us any too kindly.... In short, we need an ambassador."

He looked me straight in the eye. "And I want that person to be you."

Our conversation ended there that evening. The head boss, skillful as ever, told me to think it over. I went to bed with a new destiny ahead of me — a destiny I could refuse, but at what price!

I went back to my books and tore through them with a new idea in mind: understanding what I would be getting myself into if I accepted. There were few books about the colony, as if most of the human books had been imported from their original planet. But there were a few plates, somewhat larger than those used for books, that could be slipped into the cubes to change the three-dimensional images there. Some of these plates contained additional works of fiction, but others seemed less well developed, left to chance, homemade. Their images looked like daily scenes caught live, and several seemed to have been captured here on Sielxth. One of the plates contained images of a few adults and several children. The children ran about chasing bouncing spheres and the adults seemed to find them very entertaining. The image shook as if the observer had been moving. Other 3D scenes had been filmed in a metal house where all the rooms were connected by dark, narrow corridors. Someone had immortalized the image of two lovers kissing while other humans applauded.

After allowing me to consult the books and other animations for some time, Khlearmt brought me additional plates for the cube one day. Rather than leaving me alone, as he usually did, he stayed with me as I watched them. The image projected by the very first plate was horrific. Darztls mounted on large haavls approached a square house. Humans poured outside and started to run. The darztls chased them down, firing their weapons at some of them, crushing others under the powerful paws of their mounts. The observer had to be moving quickly since the image jumped constantly. Darztls, humans — adults and children — ran in all directions. The din was deafening. One darztl threw a net over a small female and threw her into a bag tied to his haavl. Then a warrior grew larger and larger in the observer's eye, his enormous paw finally covering the entire field of view. The image wavered, then disappeared.

Without realizing it I had stood up from my chair, and had watched the entire scene tense, rigid.

"But darztls are barbarians!"

"I thought you knew that already. But wait until you see the rest. It's very interesting."

He handed me another plate. I took it, my hand shaking, and slipped it into the cube. Another scene took shape in the middle of the desert. This time, there was only one darztl. He was tied behind a large animal, where several humans rode. He struggled in vain. Suddenly the animal started walking, with a powerful grumble, and the darztl was carried along with it. The observer was on the animal, facing the darztl, as he was dragged over the pebbles and the sand. The darztl cried out in pain, but when the observer turned to the other humans, I could see they were laughing. The animal stopped and the men got down. That was when I noticed that it was no animal but a vehicle that could move forward on its own, without having to be pulled by haavl. The darztl lay behind the vehicle, flayed, begging the humans to kill him. But one human walked over to him with a large knife and, rather than cutting off his head, cut off one of his back feet, then the other. The darztl screamed with each slash. Then the human hacked his crest and the darztl stopped shouting, either dead or unconscious. One of the men went over to the darztl and removed that rope that bound his upper limbs and took a comical position next to him, as if the man had just discovered something wonderful. Each of the humans imitated him. The darztl wasn't dead after all, moaning weakly at the end.

All of the plates the boss brought me that morning were filled with similar images. Sometimes groups of humans were being attacked by furious darztls, sometimes darztls were victimized by humans. On one of the plates, a darztl lay tied to a bed. An entire web of wires were tied to his body and connected to a machine at the foot of the bed. He was being asked to admit something or reveal something. I didn't understand which. Each time he refused to reply or gave an unsatisfactory answer, a human in a white smock would press on a little button he held in his hand and the darztl would writhe in pain. I turned off the cube, disgusted.

"Why did you show me all that? Do you think I didn't see enough horrors when I was in the mine?"

"I want you to understand that our two species are destined to kill one another. We're too different and we come from worlds that are too dissimilar. And too much blood has flowed between us. Go, Skllpt, go see your kind. And convince them to leave. Otherwise, they will live to regret it. This no idle threat. This is your people's last chance. You know, there are fewer and fewer darztls who, like me, are willing to give humans a little more time. Go. I'm counting on you. And I'll stand up for you with the other darztls. I know you and I know that you're good. If Master Sshlurltr kept you near him it was because he had good reasons for doing so and he trusted you. And I trust Master Sshlurltr."

"Will you free the slaves? How will you mine the metal then?"

"I swear that we will not keep a single human on this planet. Before you arrived, we didn't need as much metal. It's being used to make weapons to fight you, you know."

"But how do you know that I won't bring an army of humans back to the mine to free the slaves you're keeping?"

"Yes, you could do that. But if your kind manage to make it this far, they will all be eliminated. Or they will join the slaves in the mine. The pacifists, including myself, will not be able to prevent that."

"But my people are powerful. They can attack your cities, your children...."

Once again, I saw the image of a small darztl in a cage, carried throughout the colony while onlookers threw rocks at him.

"Even if they're ten times stronger, we're a thousand times more numerous."

§ § §

I left without saying good-bye to anyone. There was no one I could say good-bye to, not even Anaelle, who would not have understood. There was no one I wanted to see, afraid to see anyone. Khlearmt insisted on taking me into the middle of the desert himself. He couldn't just let me go. The human hunters would have caught me within a few days. No human had ever evaded them. And not only would they take me back to where I came from, they'd have their way with me first. I allowed myself to be shut up in bag, hauled up on a haavl like a piece of merchandise and jostled about through the desert. This means of transportation, as uncomfortable as it was humiliating, was necessary according to Khlearmt. This was how escaped slaves were returned. If we came across a hunter, my presence would be relatively easy to explain, although Khlearmt would have to justify his presence in another darztl's territory. The bag, moreover, would protect me from the sun. The boss had me dress in a slave suit that would not filter out enough of the sun's rays.

I found it stifling in the rough bag and lost all sense of direction. Slaves who were tied up in bags would have no way of guessing where the hunters were taking them. It would also prevent me from making my way back to the mine. I knew we were heading north, of course. That was where the human colony was, but the bouncing of the bag on the haavl made me feel as if we were traveling in circles. At least this would be the last time I would allow myself to be handled like an object. Soon, I thought, I would be free among my own people.

It was with a great sense of relief that I finally felt the haavl come to a stop. Khlearmt unhooked the bag and placed me gently on the sand, then opened the bag and let me out. I was covered with sweat after my day in the bag and shivered in the coolness of twilight. Fortunately the boss had lit a fire that provided comforting heat. He cooked a small animal for me. The meat was bland and tough, but I devoured it hungrily while my traveling companion gnawed on raw flesh.

"Why are you so committed to saving the humans?" I asked him as we settled down for the night. "Why don't you allow your kind to eliminate every last one of us?"

"I am one of those darztls who believe that every civilization should be preserved, even if we find it barbaric."

The next day, I crawled unwillingly back into the bag and the day started as the previous one had. However, after a few hours, Khlearmt's haavl stopped. I didn't know quite what time it was, but I felt that it was too early for us to call it a day. I heard another haavl trot up and stop as well. An unknown voice greeted the boss and they exchanged a few pleasantries.

"What is the darztl carrying in this bag?"

Something struck the bag, hitting me in the ribs, forcing a moan from my lips.

"Well, well, well, a human. Does the darztl know he is in another's territory? This darztl should be the one carrying the human back to the mine."

"Oh, no. There must be some mistake. Khlearmt is no hunter of humans! He works in the mine. He's simply giving the human a little lesson."

I was hit again, not as roughly this time, a blow administered by the boss to demonstrate his good will. Finally, the other darztl accepted his explanation and rode off.

"That was close," Khlearmt whispered as we set out once again.

That evening, when I crawled out into the fresh air, I noticed a large bruise on my flank. The boss looked at me with what appeared to be solicitude and went to pick a tiny plant that grew between two rocks. He broke off a leaf and rubbed the sap over my injury. I immediately felt cool.

"I've never met a free human close up, not really. But I met someone once who made me think about humans. The authorities believed she was a human disguised as a darztl. Can you believe that! But they were never able to prove anything and she was given to me. We spent a certain amount of time together and, during that time, I discovered that we could feel farther from our own kind than from a stranger. Or closer to a stranger than... You know, Skllpt, I haven't always been at peace with my own kind and I've often felt like a stranger within my own community. On the other hand, I find that we understand one another, you and I, despite everything that might separate us."

Never had a darztl, not even my first master, spoken to me like that. Not too many humans had either, for that matter. They had all been too busy working in the mine — and some of them had been too interested in humiliating me — to develop any kind of bond at all. I felt a little tug at my heart thinking about Anaelle, whom I had left behind. At that time of day, she would have been pulling the last few rocks from the mine wall before undressing and being locked up for the night with the others.

"I know what my people are doing is not right," Khlearmt continued. "Oh, I'm no better than the others. I worked underground at one point and I've beaten more than one human who didn't work hard enough. Since I've been the mine boss, I've tried to improve the slaves' living conditions, but they're still slaves. I know that. We're not all as perverse as some of the guards I've known, but...

There's a sort of carryover effect and we find ourselves working as masters, beating other living beings, without truly realizing what we're doing. It all becomes abstract, automatic. And those who can't get used to this kind of work leave, without changing the system at all."

Without thinking, I ran my hand along his crest. It was the first time I had touched a darztl other than my first master. He pulled back, as if my touch had been icy.

"Don't do that, Skllpt. It's not decent. And I'm already on edge."

The other days passed like the first one. In the morning, after a small breakfast, I crawled into the bag and bounced about on the haavl all day long. In the evening I would crawl out, crouched over, and then we would chat by the firelight until we fell asleep. The fifth evening, however, Khlearmt told me that we would go our separate ways the next day.

"We're already too close to human territory. I'm afraid for my own safety."

I knew what he meant. I'd seen the images on the cube.

"So this is it? Tomorrow, we'll part and never see one another again? And if everything goes as planned, my people will head off into space, leaving this planet for good?"

Khlearmt's wattle turned brown, then streaked with green.

"That would be best for all," he said.

The next morning, the boss left me supplies and the bag. Along our way, he had taught me to recognize both the edible plants and the carnivorous flowers, their bellies filled with methane that I could use to start fires. I could not take any tool or weapon since the humans that would pick me up had to believe I had escaped. I hoped the humans would, in fact, find me before I lost my way since, despite everything, I wouldn't last long in the desert.

Our farewells were brief. During the evenings we had spent chatting, we'd had time to say everything we had to say. Yet it was only when I saw the master's haavl ride off that I realized just how alone I was.

I walked for a few more days, heading straight north. Compared to the time I traveled by haavl, I advanced at the pace of a drotz. The hills I saw in the distance seemed to get no closer. My feet were soon torn to shreds and I had to wrap them strips of the bag around them, which I had torn with my teeth. Despite my suit and the bag I used as a screen, the sun scorched my skin and I was soon on fire.

One afternoon I noticed a cloud of dust in the distance. It came closer and I saw that it was one of those horseless carriages I'd seen in the 3D images. I approached the humans, my heart light, as quickly as my painful feet allowed. Suddenly I felt a burning sensation on my arm. I looked down and saw an arrow stuck there. I tried to pull it out, but my arm was too weak. My body, too, and my legs collapsed under me. I fainted.

I heard a voice. "Come see this, guys!"

A human male came into my field of vision, followed by two other males and a female. I wanted to say something, but my muscles wouldn't obey me. I lay there on the ground, unable to speak or move.

"Well, I can't believe my eyes! We've caught ourselves a human!"

I saw one of the males nudge me with his foot, but I felt nothing.

"Completely paralyzed. Help me carry him into the jeep while we wait for him to thaw out."

The men lifted me up and carried me to the carriage.

"Close his eyes, or they'll dry out."

Everything went dark. I heard the machine start moving.

After what seemed like an eternity, feeling came back to me. But that was even more excruciating than being paralyzed. It was as if thousands of needles had been stuck in me. And it was even worse when I moved. Finally, the unpleasant sensation dissipated a little and I could move again. I opened my eyes and saw that the humans had thrown a blanket over me to protect me from the burning sun. As I shifted, I also noticed that my feet had been bandaged and they now hurt less. I pushed the blanket off and lifted my head. I was at the back of the carriage, which was racing through the desert.

We stopped at nightfall. The humans helped me climb down from the carriage, which they called a jeep. I sat with them by the fire and they gave me something to eat, a sort of white meat that was fairly tender, and other pale objects I didn't recognize. They also drank a spicy liquid. After tasting it, I asked if I could have some water. Laughing, they handed me a bottle.

They chatted and laughed while eating, without taking too much interest in me. I didn't understand everything they said, or every reference they made. It was the first time in my life I had been with so many males and I found it strange. I stayed in my own little corner, silent, trying to go unnoticed. However, at the end of the meal, one of the men came over to me.

"You're not very talkative!" he exclaimed. I shook my head. "How about telling us your name?" he continued.

"Skllpt."

"Skllpt? That's not a name!" one of the males burst out. "Is Skllpt a boy's name or a girl's name?"

The others laughed, but I didn't understand what they found so funny.

"Skllpt is the name the masters at the mine gave me," I replied.

"The masters? You mean the darztls? You've escaped from the darztls? Hey, did you hear that? Our find will bring us a bundle!"

"I want you to take me to the colony government," I said in a voice that was less assured than I had intended.

"To the government? Don't worry, we'll take you there! They'll pay us a small fortune for you!"

While the others celebrated their good fortune, one of the males came over to me. He reeked of the spicy liquid they had tried to make me drink earlier. He sat down next to me, too close.

"Thing's couldn't have been easy for you," he said. "It must be terrible to be kept prisoner by the darztls."

He rubbed his hand through my hair.

"I bet you could use a little comfort."

The female in the group intervened.

"Leave him alone, Lalonde. You can see the little guy is all confused. He needs to rest."

I slept in a bag similar to the one Khlearmt had left me, but it was warmer and a lot more comfortable. Early the next morning, we ate and then set out on our way. But this time, the humans had me sit with them in the jeep, on the seat behind the driver, between two males. The one called Lalonde sat to my left. He spent the entire day caressing my thigh, making jokes he seemed to consider amusing but that I didn't understand. Occasionally, he would take my hand in his and place it along the inside of his thigh, laughing. The others told him to stop, but allowed him to harass me anyway. I was very uncomfortable and would have liked to hide in the back of the jeep.

That evening, I was awakened by a hand covering my mouth. I felt a sharp object against my neck.

"If you move, if you make a sound, I'll slit your throat."

Around me, I heard the three others snoring. Threatening me with his knife, the man forced me to climb out of my bag and dragged me over to the jeep. He pushed me inside and forced me to lie down on the bench behind the driver's seat.

"It must be a long time since you've enjoyed human warmth," he said, unbuttoning my suit, his knife still pointed at me.

He rubbed a large, moist hand along my face, saying how soft my skin was. He placed his large, wet mouth on my lips. The male was barely any taller or stockier than I was, so I should have been able to resist, but I was used to submitting to the individual who seemed to have power over me. I was terrified that he would stab me or, worse yet, discover my infirmity. However, he turned me on my belly, pulling the clothes from my back. He rubbed his hand along my spine and uttered a muffled exclamation, "Good grief, your back is covered with scars! My poor little one, I will make you forget all that."

He pulled my suit down to my buttocks and pressed against me. I felt his skin against mine. I bit my arm, holding back my cries of disgust.

"Don't be afraid. I won't hurt you," he said as he started to do just that.

Once he had finished, he abandoned me there, half naked on the seat of the jeep. I waited awhile, then went back to my bag to lie down. I didn't sleep all night. The next day I refused to touch my breakfast, too disgusted at the thought of having to sit next to my nocturnal attacker, too frightened to denounce him. Yet, to my immense relief, he seemed to have no more interest in me. Without looking at me or making any comments similar to those he had made the day before, he sat up front with the female, leaving me stuck between two less threatening males.

We reached the base camp later that day. The colony was surrounded by a tall wall, supervised by heavily armed guards. They asked us to identify ourselves. The driver of the jeep got out to speak with one of the guards. The man uttered an exclamation and poked his head in through the window. They negotiated some more and then motioned for us to advance. Our jeep drove on, escorted by two other vehicles, identified with the word "Police."

Everything I saw was new to me. First there were the cubic houses, made of metal and strewn haphazardly along winding roads. And the humans, large numbers of them, all different shades, walking free. Some houses were open to the streets, offering passersby strange, appealing merchandise. Children ran among the adults and the stalls, seemingly happy. There were also large green plants, taller and larger than any I had seen in my life.

Our little procession stopped in front of a strange, immense building that stretched out to infinity with its angular, tortured shapes. We were instructed to climb out of the jeep and enter the building through a large sliding door. The four males were stopped at a counter, but I was told to continue walking. None of the men said good-bye to me. I was guided through a maze of corridors, then pushed into a room. There, I was instructed to sit at a table and wait. I didn't know how long they left me waiting there, but I was starting to get cold. It was very cool in the humans' building, almost as cold as in the mines where at least, when I didn't warm myself through working, I could cuddle with Anaelle.

Finally a woman came in and sat down in front of me, placing a pad of white paper on the table.

"Are you the government?" I asked. "I have to see someone from the government."

"The men who brought you here stated that you claim to have escaped from darztl territory," she intoned, as if she had heard nothing I said. "We'd like you to explain this to us. Start with your name."

I looked at her without understanding.

She stated, "Tell me your name. What you're called."

I replied.

She looked surprised. "Sklip? That's not a human name."

"Skllpt. That's the name the darztls gave me. It's the only name I have. Are you going to let me speak with someone from the government?"

"Fine, we'll make do with that. So I'll write down: Sklip. Gender?"

Once again, I revealed my lack of understanding.

"Male or female?" she specified.

"Well... male."

"Age?"

"You want to know how many revolutions I've been alive? Sixteen."

This time, she was the one who didn't understand.

"In human time, that's about eighteen and a half," I added. "Listen, I have to speak with those in charge of the colony.

"Place of birth?"

Once again, I was confused.

Interpreting my reaction, she sighed and said, "Where were you born?"

I didn't have any clear response to give her. All I knew was that I had been born in the mine. But I had no idea where the mine was located.

She delved into the matter. She seemed determined to learn everything about me and completely ignored my request. She wanted me to sum up my sixteen revolutions in a flash. I decided that if I told her everything she wanted to know, she would do as I asked. I started telling her about my birth, voluntarily omitting the episode when my mother castrated me. Also, as Khlearmt and I had agreed, I didn't tell her that I had been raised by a boss darztl for twelve revolutions. I had barely started my tale when the door burst open. A female human, dressed in white, raced in, breathless.

"I came as soon as I could," she said. "Why is this individual here and not in a hospital? Before you question him, there's his health to consider."

She turned to me. "Sir, I'm Dr. Smythe. I'll take you with me."

Once again, she turned to the woman who appeared to be a member of the police. "As soon as I've examined him, you can have all the time you want to ask your questions."

Two people in white suits came in, pushing a bed on wheels. They had me lie down on it, bundled me up and set off. We went into a tiny room. The doors slid shut and I felt as if we were falling. But the room didn't move and the doors soon opened again. We were in a large, well-lit hallway and the two individuals in white pushed the bed on wheels to another room. Lifting my head, I saw a sign on the door that read, "No entry." The white suits went back out.

I was not left alone for long this time. The female in white came in, surrounded by two men I hadn't seen before. All three put some white fabric over their mouths and slipped their hands into supple envelopes, which were white, as well. They started to examine me, asking me to open my mouth, looking in my ears, just as the masters had done during the weekly inspections. Then the two males started to take my suit off me and I was filled with fear. Their reaction was immediate. Once of the males stifled an exclamation.

"Look at this," he said to the other man and the women, who both looked amazed.

They abandoned my other orifices and bent over my mutilated genitals, poking at this, touching that, asking me if it hurt. But the scar was sixteen revolutions old and the only pain was in my mind and my heart. I felt more naked than ever as they examined me.

"What happened to you? Who did this to you?" the female asked me gently as she helped me up.

But my throat was too tight and I couldn't answer. I simply shook my head.

"It's not a problem," she said. "We'll have all the time we need to talk about it. Now, I think a shower would do you a world of good."

I didn't understand what she meant by that. She spoke to me slowly, as if addressing a simpleton.

"A shower. To wash in. With water."

Washing I understood, but with water?

She addressed the two men, "Give him a bath, it will be easier. And then put him in a room."

The two men gave me a white piece of clothing that did up in the back and took me into a completely white room with a slippery floor. They had me undress again and left me standing in the middle of the room while they filled an immense container with water. A woman came in, covering her mouth with her hand when she saw my naked body. However, she recovered her composure and, as if she had seen nothing strange, she pushed me over to the water-filled container and told me to get into it. I hesitated. She wanted me to step completely into the water? To put my body in that? She took me by the arm and encouraged me to do just that. I stepped into the water, terrified, but too stunned to protest. It was very cold in the room and the water was hot. I found the contrast very strange, but it was not as unpleasant as I would have thought. The woman had me sit down in the water. As I grasped the edges of the container, she rubbed my body with a cloth and a scented cream. She also wet my hair and rubbed it. When I stepped out of the water, I saw that it had turned brown and that the bottom of the tub was covered with sand. The woman wrapped me with a piece of fabric and patted me. Following this, she had me sit down and untangled my hair with a long comb. I'd seen combs in the mine before. One woman kept one hidden in her nest, but this one had all of its teeth. She cut the clumps of hair she couldn't untangle. Then she had me put on some clothes that came in two parts, one for the top and the other for the bottom. She gave me something for my feet, but they were still too swollen, so she let me go barefoot.

The two men in white escorted me to a room, which was white, just like everything else. They had me lie down on a surface that looked like a bed. One of them took a tube from his clothing and pressed it against my arm. I felt a little pinch. Then they left, after pressing a button that plunged the room into darkness. I waited a few minutes. Then, feeling my way around, my legs quaking, I walked over to the door and tried to open it. Either they had locked it or I didn't understand how it worked. But I didn't work at it for long. I was very sleepy. I allowed myself to slide down the wall and I fell asleep there, on the chilly floor.

Early the next morning, a small female came into my room, carrying a tray of what looked like food. During the night, someone had come in while I was sleeping on the floor and helped me back to the soft bed.

"Good morning Sklip," the blonde female said in a cheerful voice as she placed the food in front of me. "My name is Inès. I'll be taking care of you."

Then she fed me. I was capable of eating on my own, of course, but I didn't stop her, too intimidated to react.

She was cute. She reminded me a little of Anaelle. She didn't look anything like her — she was much smaller and much rounder — but she was every bit as vivacious.

"Apparently, you've come from darztl territory?" she asked, without any preamble. "Your life must have been hard."

She took a piece of cloth and wiped the corner of my mouth. The food she fed me tasted strange. The food in my plate varied from dark yellow to pale beige, and it was all relatively soft and easy to chew. After a few mouthfuls, I got used to the taste.

"They'll treat you well here. They want to give you a series of tests, but you shouldn't be afraid. You're a big boy."

She pushed the tray back and helped me stand up. I towered head and shoulders above her.

In fact, they subjected me to a battery of tests for several days. Mostly physical tests, but a few psychological tests as well, and certain examinations involving machines I didn't understand. They took my blood with long needles, they tested my urine after asking me to pee in small vials, and they inserted probes into my body to take internal samples. I imagine they wanted to determine the scope of the damage caused by my extended contact with the darztls. I complied without protesting, hoping that, once they had finished exploring me, they would finally allow me to talk to someone rather than insisting on an interrogation. At the end of each day I returned to my room, exhausted.

Inès was a great comfort to me. When I talked with her, I felt that I was something more than an interesting case for the doctors. Inès told me she was a nurse. That meant she was paid to take care of me, but she was so graceful about it that I soon felt as if I were being treated like a friend. She rubbed my feet with a special cream that helped them heal faster. Soon I was able to accompany her on brief outings, during the morning or evening, in a room they called the "physiotherapy room" and in another, larger hall, called the "common room." These rooms were always deserted when we went there and we never met anyone along our way, as if the hospital had either been evacuated or they took special precautions to keep me away from curious eyes. Two giants dressed in white accompanied us for every outing. I asked why we never went outside and Inès said that it was because I wasn't ready yet.

Only after performing numerous examinations did they finally take me outside the hospital. Inès helped with my preparations, then smiled at me in encouragement. I wasn't taken outside, but rather into a cubicle I now recognized as an elevator, and I went down to the basement. We

walked along a maze of corridors. I didn't enjoy this time
below the surface of the planet — it reminded me too much
of the mine. Finally, we went back up, into a wing that was
more colorful than the one reserved for the hospital and
similar to the first area where I had been taken when I
initially arrived. Suddenly, seeing all the people around
me, with their dark suits, staring at me inquisitively, I felt
ridiculous in my white clothing. I was taken into a room
where two men and three women were already seated.
There was an empty chair in front of then and I understood
I was to sit there. As I approached it, I noticed that my
physician, Dr. Smythe, was already positioned in a corner of the room.

"Mr. well... Sklip," said one of the females. My name
is Waltrid Meyer. These are my colleagues: Dams, Dubois,
Ndiaye and Carrols. We're here to listen to you."

"Is this the government of the colony?" I asked. "I have
to speak with one of the leaders."

"We are the colony council," the woman said. "I hope
you understand the scope of the privilege you have been
granted. But I have to admit that your situation is somewhat... unique. Since diplomatic relations were cut off with
the enemy, you are the first human who has managed to
escape. We have questions to ask you about your detention
in darztl territory. And about your escape as well, of
course."

She slumped back in her chair and started with a direct question. Obviously, she was in charge of the interrogation.

"We noted several scars on your body. Did the darztls
cause them?"

I thought I would be done in a few hours, but the interrogation lasted several days. Days during which I had
to recount everything in the smallest details, then repeat
it all over again, so they could see, I imagine, if the second version corroborated the first. Then several times again
to verify all the details. From time to time one of the council
members would ask Smythe questions so she could confirm
what I told them.

Each of their questions brought back a dark period in my short life, moments I would have preferred to bury deep in my memory for all time. During the examinations they had subjected me to, the humans had also taken photos, which the council members now handed from one to another, exclaiming darkly. The first day, as if the photos were not enough, the council also asked to see my back so, as they said, they could have a clearer idea of the cruelty of my treatment. Hardening themselves, they then asked if they could see my entire body.

"Mr. Sklip, we know that this is all very painful for you, but we would like to see your other... um... injuries. We need to be able to put all of the pieces of this horrible puzzle into place. We would like you to take off your clothing so that the council can observe the extent of the ravages... your captivity by the enemy has caused your body. It should not take very long. You don't have to do this, of course, but it would help us prepare our file. Doctor, could you please explain exactly what we're seeing?"

However, after spending most of the day in silence, Dr. Smythe came to my aid in a most unexpected manner. She stood by my side and helped me put my white shirt on.

"No," she said. "I won't help you peeping toms. You don't think this patient has undergone enough tests? You have the photos there and the young man and I will answer your questions. That should be enough for you."

For half a day, the council studied the photos of my body like a map. Dr. Smythe pointed out the scars and explained how they had been inflicted. They simply asked me to confirm what she said and, throat tight, I merely nodded. Obviously, what fascinated them the most was my emasculation. They looked at the photos from all angles and studied me as if they were trying to see right through my clothes. During the examinations, I'd been asked on several occasions how it had happened, but out of a sense of modesty, I'd simply said that it had happened when I was very young and I didn't remember. They asked me if it was the work of the darztls, but I neither confirmed nor contradicted that hypothesis.

"Mr. Sklip," said the council member introduced to me as Dubois. "You've already told the doctor and the psychologist that you don't recall the circumstances of this... regrettable amputation. Of course, as you said, you were very young. Yet when you grew older, you must have asked people questions, you must have wondered, you must have asked the people around you why you weren't like the other little boys. What did people tell you?"

"I've already told you that. They said I'd had an accident. I've described our miserable existence in the mines in detail. Accidents are common. I imagined that a stone fell on me or something like that."

"Yes, but why didn't they tell you exactly what happened?"

"Maybe they did tell me and it was too much for me to bear and I forgot it." I had kept my eyes down the whole time my body was served up on a platter for the council. Now I looked up. "Tell me, why are you talking to me as if I were the guilty one? I certainly didn't do this to myself!" I burst out. Then I fell silent, my throat tight, just like every time I lost my temper. I now felt like bursting into tears. The council members looked at me in surprise. This was the first time I'd ever shown anything other than servile docility.

The woman called Nadiaye got up, walked around the table and over to me. She placed her hand gently on my shoulder. I stiffened.

"Please excuse my colleague's clumsiness," she said. "No one is accusing you of anything. We're simply trying to understand what happened to you, in order to get a better idea of the enemy."

"What good will that do you? Having a better understanding of what those you abandoned there suffer each and every day? Those you never went back for even though they've been hoping for exactly that for twenty revolutions? You want to expand your theoretical knowledge while they suffer the effects of darztl medicine every day?"

"Mr. Sklip, we're political strategists! We need to know everything there is to know!"

"Well since you insist, I'll contribute to your education,"
I said as I started to undress. Dr. Smythe moved as if to
prevent me from doing that, but she stopped, powerless,
as I finished undressing.

"I'll tell you the story of a woman who had been crouching in the mine for four Marsian years, weakened by a
series of pregnancies and abuse, abandoned by those who
had sent her to the front. In her culture, every birth was
a happy event. But down there, underground, it was a completely different matter. When women had the misfortune
to give birth to a male child, they were plunged into total despair. Most of the time, the male baby would be torn
from their arms and they'd never see him again. When this
woman gave birth to her fourth male in as many revolutions, she broke. She told herself that the darztls would
never take this one from her. She played a trick on them.
She transformed that little boy into a little girl. But afterwards she was no longer able to live in a world where a
female has to eat her young to protect them. So she killed
herself."

I stared at them, defiant. They all looked at me, eyes
filled with concern, carefully avoiding any glance at my
crotch. The two men in particular smiled with what looked
like a grimace of pain.

"Do you want more details?" I asked, weeping with
rage. "Do you want me to tell you how my mother managed it, how she took my little baby penis between her
teeth? Do you want me to tell you about the little piece of
flesh that cooled on the stone? Do you want me to tell you
about the blood that flowed on my mother and onto the
floor in the cavern, about how I screamed my lungs out?
Or maybe I haven't given you enough details about the
punishments they inflicted on us. I've got a whole bunch
stored up. All you have to do is ask."

Now that I'd started, there was no way I could stop the
flood. Dr. Smythe tried to take my arm gently, but I shoved
her aside. She went to the door and two people in white
came in. She indicated that they should to help me dress
and accompany me. I allowed myself to be escorted out.

My faithful Inès waited for me back in my room. It was only as I took my clothes off that I noticed my pants were wet. I had pissed myself as I recounted my mutilation and I had pulled my pajama bottoms back up my wet body. I smelled. I was dirty. I was mortified. But Inès behaved perfectly. She cleaned me, murmuring comforting words. She gave me a clean pair of pajamas and helped me slip between the cool sheets. Abandoning any free will, I allowed myself to be cosseted like a small child.

"Inès," I said, "sometimes I wish I hadn't left the mine."

She looked at me, visibly surprised.

"The rules in the mine are so simple. You work, you eat, you sleep. If you work less, they beat you, so you eat less, you sleep less, because you hurt all over. But everything is so simple! You don't have any decisions to make. You don't have to disclose anything. You stand before everyone completely naked. And you know all the rules in advance. Whereas here..."

I fell silent. Inès looked me, encouraging me to continue.

"Whereas here?"

"Whereas here, I don't understand anything. I don't know why the council keeps asking me all these questions instead of settling for what they can see with the naked eye. What do they think? That I'm a darztl disguised as a human who has come to blow up the colony?"

Inès nodded her head. She gave me two little pills, which I swallowed, taking refuge in a dreamless sleep.

The rest was never as bad as that first day, but it still left me exhausted. Every evening, I would go back to my room, my head buzzing, and I'd curl up in my bed after picking at my dinner. The following days, however, they made a point of asking less personal questions. I still found answering every bit as difficult, but it was less painful for me to speak about the operations at the mine, how frequently we were punished, the work they required us to do. They also wanted to know how I had escaped, of course, and I told them the tale of my imaginary escape. They seemed to believe it. In any case, it was the story of many slaves who had tried to escape, except theirs invariably ended with capture or a horrible death in the desert.

In the midst of all these questions, I tried not to lose sight of my mission: to convince the humans of the danger that threatened them, to persuade them to leave the planet. As I was crossing the desert, I had told myself I had an easy task. I would make them understand the peril that faced them, they would believe me and that would be that. But then I felt like I was speaking to a wall and that the council only heard what it wanted to hear.

Yet they must have been listening to me a little, because on the fourth day, after the council had exhausted all the other questions, one of the women, the one called Adams, asked me, "Now, if you could tell us why you keep saying that the humans have to leave this planet?"

I jumped. I had expected anything but that question.

"Because it's the truth," I finally stammered.

"And why are you so certain of that? Did one of those you call the *masters* confide in you, a slave, when you suddenly found yourself in his good graces?" Meyer asked me, chuckling wickedly.

"No, I didn't need any confidences. All the darztls in the mine talk like that."

"And you speak their language?"

"A bit. You have to, to be able to understand their orders."

"And they talked politics in your presence? Even when they knew you might overhear them?"

"Do you refrain from talking in front a piece of furniture because you don't want it to understand you?"

I saw that I had made my point. The members of the council looked a little embarrassed.

Meyer continued, "And, if I understand you properly, if the humans do not abandon the colony, the darztls will attack us?"

I nodded.

She continued, "But if the humans decide to leave, what will happen to the humans in the mine?"

"I've heard that they will release them."

"What guarantee do we have of that?"

"None. But even if they don't release the humans, that won't change a thing. Up to now, it's not as if the colony has shown much concern for the freedom of the prisoners...."

The council member named Dubois leapt up. "I don't know about you, but I can't swallow this story! The darztls apparently discuss politics in front of the humans and, just at the right moment, a little eunuch manages to escape as if by magic? No, this story doesn't hold water. I'm not saying that this boy is lying, but I can't rule out the possibility that he's been manipulated, that some mysterious agent helped him escape."

"I agree with Loic," said the man called Carrols, a council member who had remained relatively silent throughout the interrogation. "But I'd go even further. How do we know this boy isn't working with the lizards?"

"Come on, Louis!" Meyer said. "You've seen his mutilations. Don't be obscene!"

"There seems to be some grain of truth in this story," Carrols said. "But the boy may have been forced to act in this manner to redeem some fault. Or he may have been brainwashed."

"In any case, it goes against everything we know about the natives. Our studies have shown that these creatures do not know war. They have no weapons, no military strategists. I can hardly see how they would attack us!"

"You're right. The darztls are simply trying to intimidate us. And this boy is their creature."

And they continued on like that as if I weren't there, as if talking about someone else. As if they hadn't already discussed this matter in my absence and hadn't already made up their minds.

"Does this mean you won't leave?" I finally dared ask.

"Dear Mr. Sklip," Meyer replied, "That's up to the council to decide. But whether you were sent here by the darztls or came here in good faith, we'll simply tell you one thing: the council doesn't usually give in to outside pressure and particularly not pressure exercised by the enemy. You know, we have means to find out if you're telling the truth. However, we won't use them since you're a victim of the situation."

She stared at me and the others followed suit. Five pairs of eyes stared at me as she added, "Plus, how do you want us to leave this planet? We're tied to it now, for better or for worse. There are now five times more of us than the mother ship can carry."

§ § §

As the sun set in the sky, the colony came back to life. I got into the habit of strolling about the alleys in the market, not to buy anything, but to make up for lost time and plunge into the culture of my kind, scraps of which could be found strewn on the counters. Occasionally Inès accompanied me, but I preferred to take part in this activity alone so I could study the odd assortment of artifacts to my fill: jewelry in all shapes and textures, trinkets and mismatched plates. Strange foods. There were also a great many plates of various sizes, like those used in books or cubes. But there were also devices you could walk straight into, at least in your imagination, to experience a borrowed life for a few minutes or hours. One day, Inès showed me how to connect to one of them and for an hour I walked on Earth, the humans' home planet, wearing clothes that clanked, responsible for meting out justice. She also told me there were plates people could use to make love by proxy, but that they were hard to find. I kept an eye out for them, both impatient and fearful.

I had moved in with Inès when they discharged me from the hospital. For a few days before, she had taken me on walks throughout the small town and then brought me back to my room. Then, suddenly, I was released and found myself in the street, forced to make my own way. So she took me home. Otherwise, I would have been reduced to begging — or worse. Now that it had extracted everything it wanted, the council was no longer interested in me. I think that if I had told them I could read darztl they would have given me a job with the government, but I was too afraid they would hold that skill against me and ask me where I had acquired such knowledge. So I had to live from hand to mouth. Everyone knew that I was in the community and some people might have been prepared to hire me for rather questionable tasks, but I settled for accepting small manual labor contracts here and there.

I had given up on the idea of convincing the council how serious the threat was and decided to work on a smaller scale. I tried to convince the people around me about the danger they faced. As soon as I had enough money to buy paper, I printed warnings and distributed them at the market. I held information sessions that attracted only a handful of people, always the same ones, all more or less cut off from reality.

Everyone thought I had some kind of inner light. Everyone whispered behind Inès's back, I think, finding her decisions to share her life with me more than a little perverted. Yet our relationship was purely platonic. Inès had her own love life and I continued my asexual one.

"You know, your condition could be changed. There are operations." But after checking, the operation alone, not to mention the convalescence, would take Inès' entire salary. I took that news with a certain amount of relief and Inès said she was pleased with my choice. I had been formed around this body; it was part of my identity. It was proof that people can get used to anything.

I had become accustomed to my condition just as the humans had become accustomed to life on a hostile planet. My predictions fell on deaf ears. There was a human expression I liked a lot: "to preach to the deaf." That applied to my situation. Everyone preferred to believe the leaders of the colony, who denied any danger, rather than listen to me, who had returned from the front. Life in the desert slowed everything. Both the humans and the darztls had allowed the situation to drag on too long. It was too late. Deep down, I knew the humans would never leave Mars II. The mother ship, of course, could not leave without abandoning a large part of the colony, a colony that would be even more vulnerable when deprived of the stores on board the ship, including the hospital and the government quarters. Not to mention the mechanisms used for terraforming.

Moreover, not only did the humans not have the means to leave, they no longer had any will to do so. Those who spoke of Mars II/Sielxth as their homeland were four times as numerous as those who had arrived here on the mother ship. Most humans had no desire whatsoever to leave. The humans were trapped on a planet they wanted to occupy. Inès, for one, had never seen Earth, being born thirty revolutions after the humans set foot on Mars II. Neither had her parents, who came from the artificial uteruses the humans had started up as soon as they had arrived on the planet to accelerate demographic growth. Sielxth was her world. Inès knew no other. She waxed poetic about the sand storms, the arid land, the burning sun.

"You know, Sklip," she often said to me, "I can't imagine living anywhere else."

I understood her and, at the same time, I don't know if she could imagine what her life would be like if the darztls attacked us and did not kill her.

I missed the desert — the real one — far from the air conditioned buildings, the homes where people swept the sand out on a regular basis. I missed the sand baths, the desolate landscapes. I grew accustomed to living freely with the humans and nothing in the world could have convinced me to return to my former life, and yet I occasionally found the temperate zone cold. Khlearmt had been right. The humans were changing the planet's climate. They didn't bother to hide that fact; it came up in every conversation concerning the weather.

"It's hot today isn't it?"

"Yes, it is. I'll be glad when we control the climate of this planet."

Occasionally, I would go traveling in the desert with Inès. These expeditions were expensive, since we had to rent a vehicle, and we could not afford to go every week.

Yet we would go as often as we could. We would leave near the end of the day and stop late at night. We would camp in the desert, next to our little dune buggy, under the milky light of the Marsian moon.

It was in the desert that Inès and I became lovers one night. It happened just like that, without warning. Otherwise I would have stopped it, terrified. We had never really discussed the issue. Inès maintained a respectful silence and I never brought it up either. Yet, that evening, Inès broke our unspoken agreement. I have to admit, we had been drinking a bit — a warm beer that had bounced around our vehicle all afternoon and sprayed in all directions when we opened it. We lay down, each in our own sleeping bag next to a fire of sand orchids. I had shown Inès how to use them. Wrapped up like a sausage in her sleeping bag, she had wriggled over to me and placed her head on my belly.

"Sklip," she said, "can I ask you something indiscrete?"

She looked up just long enough to see me nod, then placed her head back on my belly.

"I'm warning you, it's delicate. Only answer if you want to."

I felt myself stiffen, guessing where she was heading.

"What's it like being like you? I mean, what do you feel inside? Do you have desires, I mean sexual desires, or is that all foreign to you? Oh! I shouldn't have asked you that," she said as she lifted herself up. "It's none of my business."

I took her head and placed it gently back on my abdomen. I remained silent for a moment, looking for the right words.

"No," I finally said, "it's all right. I'll try to answer you."

I was glad that she was in that position. She would only see my face from below and would be unable to read my expression.

"I don't know what it's like to be normal."

When she protested, I added, "Or, if you prefer, to be whole and not mutilated. It's the same thing. I don't know what it's like to not have genitals, because I don't know what it's like to have them. Yet everything around me shows me what it must be like. At night, when I was in the mine, I would hear the other humans caressing one another in the dark. Sometimes I would cover my ears, sometimes I would be straining for the slightest sound. No one ever came to join me in my nest, not even Anaelle — I've told you about Anaelle — since everyone took it for granted that if I had no genitals I could not be a sexual person. And I believed that myself. Sometimes, I would try to caress myself and the sensation that provoked would be imperfect, incomplete, frustrating, leaving me filled with the desire to tear off the few strips of sensitive flesh that remained."

The words died in my throat.

Inès stretched out the length of my body, until her face was in front of mine.

"Your skin is so soft," she said, rubbing her cheek against mine.

I cleared my throat and continued. I told her everything. I told her about my slightest frustrations, all of my disappointed hopes. I told her about my one and only contact with the brutal sex forced on me by one of the mercenaries who had found me. Finally I noticed, without having realized it, that I had started to weep.

"But the memory of that man penetrating me by force is not the worst image I recall. No, the worst image is one I can only imagine: the image of my mother, who saved my life by mutilating me forever. Oh no!"

I climbed hastily out of my drenched sleeping bag.

I sat down, naked and shivering, to allow my soiled body to dry in the desert night. I don't know what made me shiver more: the cold of the night or this conversation, that forced me to remember everything.

I sighed, "Every time I think about my... my mutilation, I urinate. As if this spillage could take the place of the blood that flowed, or something like that."

"Sklip, don't stay there!"

"But I'm disgusting!"

"Come here."

She opened her sleeping bag and I slipped in beside her. She took me in her arms.

"I'm sorry, Sklip. I should never have made you talk about all that."

"No, Inès. I have to talk about... about all that. I never say a word about it because it hurts too much but if it hurts so much it's that..."

I burst into sobs.

I wept for a long time. Inès simply stayed there, next to me. Wiping my tears with her hand. Then she sponged my tears away with a kiss and finally embraced me, gradually intensifying her hold on me. I allowed her to do that, without protesting, without resisting. She held me for a long time, then she slid her mouth down to my chest. She took one of my nipples between her lips, then between her teeth, while her other hand caressed the other. A strange sensation spread through my abdomen, like an intense hunger. She continued to nibble at my nipples as her hand caressed my belly, then my pubis. I felt uncomfortable for a moment at the idea of her touching my mutilated genitals, but her hand was so gentle it swept away all my apprehensions. She didn't spend much time on my scar and positioned her hand between my thighs, gently running her fingernails over them. Shivers ran through my body. Finally, she pushed her hand deep between my legs, right up to my buttocks. She inserted a finger in my anus, pushing in and out. I felt a heat rush through my belly and I cried out.

We continued our little trips into the desert and she gradually taught me how to caress her. I felt like an adolescent discovering his sexuality. I was insatiable. I wanted to try everything. And Inès went along willingly. We loved one another and, for the first time in my life, I believe I was happy.

The darztls could have killed both of us when they attacked the human colony, but that wasn't what happened. We were in the desert the morning darztls swarmed over the base camp. We had just spent the night under the stars and were preparing to return. In the distance, we saw a cloud of sand approaching. I'd been with the humans for four revolutions and had almost managed to forget the threat. I had completely stopped trying to convince my kind that they had to leave Sielxth and I had almost convinced myself that the darztls would leave us alone. But I immediately knew what was happening and, after hiding our dune buggy behind a large rock, I dragged Inès behind a hill from which I hoped we could watch without being seen.

The darztl army was several thousand strong. From the top of our hill, looking through our binoculars, it looked like a cloud of vermin with shining abdomens — they must have been wearing armor. The insects raced toward the colony, as if it were a heap of food. Four small cruisers emerged from the entrails of the mother ship and shot on the darztls. We saw the sand explode and the debris the lasers left behind. Using the binoculars, I saw insects lying immobile in the dust. But the body of the army continued to advance, all too soon nibbling away at the settlement. Soon there were no longer any darztls left in the desert to shoot. They had all rushed into the colony, striking, killing, capturing — although from our position we could only guess this. Suddenly, the mother ship started to vibrate. Even from our distance, we could feel its powerful motors. Then the immense ship lifted off the ground, drawing the sand up in whirlpools. Those in the ship could have shot, but they would have had to shoot at least as many humans as darztls, so they did nothing. The ship hung in the sky for a second. Then it rose up and moved off, leaving four-fifths of the colonists in the darztls' claws. The four smaller vessels didn't fly for long. As a result of the lack of water and the shortage of metals, hydrogen supplies were minimal and could not be stored for long. All of the remaining fuel had been reserved for the mother ship. One of the vehicles crashed to the ground with a deafening roar. Two more small shuttles landed and groups of darztls raced at them, tearing them into shreds. One of the cruisers disappeared over the horizon. We never knew if it crashed or managed to take refuge somewhere.

Inès and I witnessed the entire scene, powerless, pet-rified. My friend looked terrified; she shook in fright next to me. But she would have been even more frightened if she knew, as I did, what would happen if the darztls ever managed to find us. Our safest refuge was that hill, where we stayed hidden, close enough to witness the horror of the spectacle, but far enough away that no one could see us. Above all, we were not exposed to the desert.

The natives remained in the colony all day, fighting humans and capturing, or so we concluded, the last resist-ers. Familiar as I was with darztl metabolism, I knew that it would not be in their interests to let things drag on, and they would want to finish up while it was still light and hot — although the temperature was noticeably cooler at this latitude. When twilight fell, they still hadn't left the base camp. Inès and I spent the night entwined in each other's arms, shivering despite the heat of our two bodies, together in the sleeping bag. We ate the food that remained from the night before, surprised that we had not felt hungry all day.

The first morning dawned over the conquered colony. We hadn't shut our eyes once all night, jumping at the slightest sounds, fearing that a darztl was coming to capture us. When we looked through the binoculars, everything looked calm. Suddenly, Inès passed the binoculars to me.

"Look!"

The darztl army was slowly leaving the settlement, like a cloud of insects returning to their nest. But they were not alone. They escorted smaller, weaker insects — humans. The exodus lasted a long time. The caravan did not progress quickly, hampered by the slowness of the humans who walked beside the conquerors' haavls. I wondered why the darztls had decided to take prisoners, then answered my own question: they needed slaves. The darztls had become accustomed to the idleness that this servile labor pool allowed, which was definitely more intelligent than a herd of beasts of burden. Individuals like Khlearmt had lost.

At the end of the day, once the dust had settled back in the desert, we returned to what had been the base camp, approaching cautiously, fearing the enemy might have left guards behind to capture the last living humans. But everything was calm. The darztls had destroyed everything, but they had not pillaged anything, obviously not knowing what to do with human artifacts. They had left bodies behind, hundreds of mutilated bodies. Some of the humans had been killed by the exhaust fumes of the mother ship, but most had fallen before the fury of the darztls who, for their part, seemed to have left few bodies behind in the battle.

We picked up some food and essential articles, siphoned some methane out of the abandoned vehicles, promising that we would come back to get everything we needed once we had found somewhere to settle. It wouldn't be in the colony in any case. It had been transformed into a cemetery. Then we set off into the desert, more terrifyingly free than ever before.

THE HUMAN CODE

[EXTRACTS]

Article 28

These darztls declare that the slaves cannot have anything that does not belong to their master, and all that comes to them by industry or liberality of other persons or otherwise in any manner whatsoever is acquired is the full property to their master, without the humans' children, their father or mother, their parents or others being able to lay claim to anything whatsoever by inheritance, provision of a will between living people or because of death. We declare such provisions null and void along with all promises or obligations that would be made, as being made by creatures unable to dispose of property and contract on their own.

Article 33

The human who has struck his master in the face or has drawn blood, or has similarly struck the wife of his master, his mistress or their children, shall be punished by death.

Article 44

These darztls declare humans to be charges, and as such enter into community property. They are not to be mortgaged, and shall be shared equally between the co-inheritors without benefit to the wife or one particular inheritor, nor subject to the right of primogeniture, the usual customs duties, rights of option or territorial charges, and they shall not be affected by the details of decrees in case of disposal by death or bequeathing.

ROCK AND FURY

To the large yellow snake
I wrapped around my neck like a necklace
and who, I hope, is enjoying himself in Florida.

I dream of rain
I dream of gardens in the desert sand
I wake in vain
I dream of love as time runs through my hand
Sting, *"Desert Rise"*

From where he was posted, Kthloold could observe the entire scene. The rocky landscape that stretched to eternity. The gutted stone mountain. The tiny silhouettes of the humans as they gnawed away at the rocky eminence. The slightly more imposing silhouettes of the darztls who urged them on with their whips. He lowered his head and caught his breath.

Mounted on his haavl, he had followed them there patiently, making sure no one saw him. First he saw Rhtiralmt, dirty and haggard, climb into the cart, looking around him for help that would not come. The darztl had continued to follow the vehicle and he saw other slaves shoved, thrown in and covered with an insulating sheet. He saw the guards chain them up, not caring whether the rings were too tight. He saw them strike the humans, forcing them all to jam into the wheeled box. Then the crew set off, waiting for the next shipment. The vehicle disappeared behind the hill which, as Kthloold knew, sheltered the rock quarry where the rebellious humans were taken,

for forced labor harder than anything they had been required to do up to that point in their lives. The darztl left
his haavl a little ways off and walked the rest of the way.
From a distance he saw the vehicle, stopped at that point.
Humans were climbing out of it, chained together. The
masters forced them to lie down, one after another, on a
large rock. There they stripped the clothes from their lower
backs and branded their flesh indelibly with the sign of
the work camp. Even from where he stood, Kthloold could
smell the odor of grilled flesh that arose when the hot iron
came into contact with the slaves' skin. Then, since night
was falling, the masters set them immediately to work.

As silently as he could, Kthloold moved even closer to
the scene, taking care not to set any stones rolling as he
walked. And he crouched down yet again. It may have been
night, but the moon was full and he could make out the
bodies clearly now, focused entirely on striking — humans
on rock; darztls on humans. He thought he could see
Rhtiralmt among them, but from that distance, he couldn't
be certain.

As soon as he saw that the human, Rhtiralmt, was going
to be condemned, Kthloold had made his decision. He
would follow the human to the work camp and take him
away. He'd heard about the atrocious site where the undisciplined humans were sent to work and, often, to die.
He'd been given explanations about the implacable logic
of this system under which a human that had bitten will
bite again. A slave who strikes a master is no good as a
slave.

Even at night, there were many darztls there. Not as
many as the humans of course, but still enough to make
one wonder why they didn't do the work themselves. The
masters were so large and strong compared to their slaves
that they could easily have brought down the mountain
on their own in much less time. Since they could work
during the day, they wouldn't have had to stand about
shivering in their heated suits, beating the slaves regularly
to keep their joints from going stiff and to stay awake. But
of course, that wasn't the point. The principle was to impose

meaningless work on the humans, work that was too much for them, and to criticize them for not doing it well.

Kthloold shivered in his heated suit. He opened one of his bags of travel rations, hoping to generate a little heat. He might have been in the south, but that didn't make the nights any less cold.

§ § §

For five days now, he'd been camping out on top of the hill. The darztls never patrolled the perimeter because they had nothing to fear. The slaves were chained so closely together, they were so intimately riveted to the mountain, that they barely had the space they needed to take a swing and hit the rock. They were there, in a rock desert, abandoned by all save their new masters, who never forgot to beat them regularly.

Kthloold hardened himself and moved closer. He had spotted Rhtiralmt. He was with the others, in the lower group. Obviously, it was a group of new arrivals — they stood straighter and there seemed to be fewer scars on their backs. He watched as Rhtiralmt struck the rock in time with the others, his sweat glistening in the moonlight, despite the cool night air. Since it was nighttime, the darztls didn't have to make them wear suits. They forced the slaves to work shirtless. Kthloold figured it made it all the easier to beat them.

Suddenly, there was a disturbance near Rhtiralmt. A darztl struck a slave, who fell. The master continued to beat the slave, but she didn't get up. Straining at his chains, what Rhtiralmt did next was crazy. He raised his pickaxe to the master and moved as if to strike him. Kthloold tensed. *No, Rhtiralmt, don't do that!* A slave who has struck, will strike again. But another darztl nearby grabbed the pickaxe, pushing Rhtiralmt roughly aside. He unchained the slave and dragged him by the feet over the rock.

It was a well-oiled routine. Another master waited for him in the middle of the quarry. There was a ring in the rock and what looked to be blood around it. First the darztl tied Rhtiralmt's hands firmly, with a leather thong. Then he tied him to the chain. Rhtiralmt was on all fours in a stone basin, hands motionless on the ground. The master stepped back to admire his handiwork. Kthloold watched, powerless.

A master threw a rock and missed his mark. His colleagues seemed to find this very amusing. Behind them, the other masters forgot to whip the slaves, and leisurely turned about to watch the scene play out. A darztl threw another rock, hitting the captive on the back. He stifled a cry. One by one, the masters tried their luck. They didn't all hit the slave, but those who did injured him cruelly. The rocks in the quarry were sharp and they didn't just strike flesh, they occasionally dug into it as well. The human shielded himself as best he could, but his hands were bound. All he could do was turn away from the stones, but the darztls circled their prey too soon, the slave's body was red and blood flowed down his face.

Over and over again, Kthloold had to stop himself from intervening. Over and over again, Kthloold grabbed onto the rock, telling himself to stay down. Racing towards the darztls, protecting Rhtiramlt's body with his own, would do no good. He would be caught, compromising any chance he had of freeing the slave.

But dawn was coming and the game had to come to an end. The masters had to take the slaves inside to spare them. That way, Kthloold thought, they could play with them even longer. The darztls released the chains that bound the humans to the mountain, but they left them tied to one another. Slowly, punishing any outburst with blows, they forced the slaves down into Sielxth's belly. Once all of the slaves had gone in, two darztls pushed a large rock in front of the hole, imprisoning them there for the entire day.

They had forgotten Rhtiralmt. He was still prostrate in the middle of the quarry, his body broken and bloody, held still by his bonds. Oh no — they remembered him. Finally a master walked over to him and nudged the slave with his foot. He moaned. The darztl's watttle took on a satisfied color and he walked off.

Kthloold shook. The sun was rising. The slave was still riveted to the ground, powerless. No one came to free him. Didn't the masters know that his skin was sensitive, that exposing him to Sielxth's sun would cause cruel injuries, that leaving him outside too long would kill him? He thought, of course, they knew that. It was part of the game. It was the game of the last chance and the slave had lost. A slave who strikes a master is a dead slave, sooner or later. *Why didn't you wait, Rhtiralmt? Kthloold could have saved you. I would have saved you and you wouldn't have had to go through all this.*

§ § §

The daytime star reached its peak and then started to set. No one had come to release the male broiling in the dust. From time to time, a master strutted past him, making sure that he was still breathing. Someone even threw some water on him, precious water so very rare in this corner of Remldarztl. But it was worth it. Rhtiralmt started, then appeared to come back to life. The master seemed satisfied. The torture would last longer.

Everything was calm then. The slaves were in no position to intervene before nightfall and the masters were taking a sunbath. Night work is exhausting for darztls and they need to recharge their batteries during the daytime. Kthloold, too, was exhausted by the five nights he spent watching. But this was no time to give up.

Now, no one was interested in the human, as he roasted in the middle of the yard. No one was guarding him, either. The male looked too weak and he was chained too firmly. No one knew that he, Kthloold, was waiting, crouching on top of the hill. The darztl knew that if anyone ever saw him help Rhtiralmt escape, that would be his last chance for rescuing the slave. Yet if he did nothing, the male could die. He could choose to creep out his hiding place slowly, moving from rock to rock down to the middle of the quarry. But once he reached Rhtiralmt he would be exposed. On the other hand, if he rushed over to the human and unchained him as if he were in some position of authority, the others might think he was acting legitimately. He decided to take the gamble and, walking with a step that was intended to look assured, he strutted over to where the slave was tied. No one stopped him.

Rhtiralmt looked lost and didn't react immediately. His skin was red, both from the beating he had received and from the intense rays of the sun. His blood had congealed, but some of his wounds had not closed properly and he was bleeding in several places. His wounds would have to be tended to, but not right then. There was no time for delay.

Finally Rhtiralmt recognized him. "Kthloold! What are you doing here? Kthloold, I've done something stupid."

"Shhh! Don't tire yourself. We'll have time to talk about it. First, Rhtiralmt, you have to be brave a little longer. If I'm going to get you out of here, I'll have to hurt you some."

He cut the bonds that tied the slave to the ring set in the rock. Forcing himself to look as brutal as possible, while trying to limit the damage, he grabbed the male by the leather thong that bound his wrists and dragged him off, walking briskly. Rhtiralmt moaned when his sunburned body grated against the sharp stones of the quarry.

Once he was certain that no one could see them, he cut the leather thong binding the slave's hands, but Rhtiralmt remained still, wrists welded together as if still bound. As gently as possible, Kthloold took the male in his arms and placed him on his massive shoulders. Rhtiralmt had never been very heavily built, but it seemed to the darztl that he was even lighter than usual. He continued to race off.

The haavl waited for him a short distance away. There was no reason to delay, but the human could not be exposed to the sun a minute longer. Kthloold had brought a spare suit with him, which he slipped onto the slave's body, taking special care not to reopen his wounds. Despite all this, the man moaned. The darztl placed the human on the saddle and threw a blanket over him. Then he climbed up on the haavl behind him. He urged his mount to gallop off, even though he knew that each jolt caused the human new suffering.

§ § §

They stopped at nightfall. No one had intercepted them. Kthloold had led his haavl on an erratic route, hoping to lose any possible pursuers. The masters expected to track slaves, who were in poor condition, on foot, and they would be astounded to learn of a darztl accomplice.

Kthloold was starting to feel a little cold, but he was afraid they would be seen if he lit a fire. So he pulled on his heated suit, hoping that the battery would last long enough to let him spend a sixth night in relative comfort. Besides, he had other worries. The human, whom he placed on a blanket after lifting him down from the haavl, was in a bad way. His teeth were chattering. Every inch of his body appeared to be causing him pain. Yet he hadn't lost consciousness.

"Kthloold, you know deep down I was hoping you would come and rescue me. Yet at the same time, I didn't believe you would."

The human's clothing was stuck to his wounds. Kthloold lifted the fabric gently and spread ointment on his wounds. It was an all-purpose ointment darztls used on all humans, without really questioning its actual virtues. Then he gave the human a little agthrlt, which he carried in a gourd. The tea had cooled, but its calming properties should still be effective.

Dozing fitfully, chilled to the bone, Kthloold spent the night next to the human, wondering which way they would head the next morning.

§ § §

Knowing full well that he might come across humans, Kthloold decided to head north. Only there could the man hope to find safety. If the darztl authorities ever laid hands on him, he would certainly face death, an atrocious death like the one Kthloold rescued him from, but lengthier because they wouldn't have the clemency to weaken him first.

Kthloold, a darztl, risked punishment for himself, of course, but his imprisonment or community work was nothing like what darztls did to humans. In the north, of course, he could well lose his own skin. But he owed Rhtiralmt.

The man lying across the haavl was in bad shape. His injuries, which were not deep, were slowly healing. But his exposure to the sun had weakened him and given him some sort of 'fever' — Kthloold was forced to use the human word covering all slave problems of this nature because there was no darztl equivalent. Rhtiralmt seemed barely aware of what was going on around him.

Even if it was risky, since they could have been detected by both humans and darztls, they traveled by day. Kthloold had never been very good at astronomy, and he left without thinking to bring tracking instruments, so he needed the sun. In any case, he was so exhausted that he needed the nights to recuperate. He couldn't afford to crack and abandon the human.

§ § §

By the time they encountered another darztl, they'd been riding randomly for five days, and probably two or three days since they had left the inhabited zone of Remldarztl. Considering the other darztl's frightening appearance and his equipment, Kthloold immediately concluded he was a slave hunter. Moreover, there was a canvas bag, jiggling feebly, tied to his haavl's saddle. Most likely it contained an escaped slave being brought back for sale.

Kthloold made as if to continue on his way, but the other darztl motioned for him to stop.

"Hello, stranger," he said. Then, pointing at the human lying in front of Kthloold, he added, "What does the stranger have there? Is that a human?"

Kthloold felt stupid. He should have prepared an answer for this type of event. He should have said that he was out riding with his slave, or something like that. In broad daylight, in the middle of the desert, something about killing him... As punishment, of course. It was not without precedent. He remained silent.

The other persisted. "Yet the stranger is not a hunter. That's obvious. In any case, no one but this darztl is allowed to hunt in this territory."

The darztl swept his hand across the broad desert as if the world belonged to him.

"Nnnn... no," Kthloold finally stammered. "This darztl is not a hunter, but a walker. On his way, he found this slave and he thought it would be a good idea to take him back to his masters."

The other darztl's wattle turned a lighter shade. "Ah, well. Well, then, the stranger will not object to transferring his prey to this darztl!"

He nudged his haavl closer to Kthloold's and made as if to grab Rhtiralmt. Kthloold thought quickly.

"Night will fall soon," he managed to say. "Would the stranger like to share a meager meal with this darztl?"

In fact, the sun had several degrees to travel before reaching the horizon, but Kthloold was trying to buy time. Fortunately, the other seemed delighted by this offer.

"Why not? This darztl has been riding since dawn and deserves a little rest. Especially since the hunting has been good this time out."

He slapped the bag, which certainly contained another slave, while staring at Kthloold's passenger.

Kthloold dismounted and helped the human down.

"This darztl thinks the stranger is very cautious," the hunter mocked.

"The human is injured. Kthloold found him in the middle of the desert. He's surely been exposed to the liirzt for a long time. His skin is burnt to a crisp."

"These humans merely get what they deserve when they escape!" the other darztl said, scraping the ground with his feet. "If this work didn't pay so well, Ltamlt would be prepared to let them all turn to dust in the desert."

Thinking about the long night ahead of them, Kthloold started to set up camp, imitated by the other.

They'd been chewing their meal for a few minutes when Kthloold noticed that the large bag was still tied to the hunter's haavl.

"Doesn't Ltamlt want to take the bag down from his haavl?" he asked.

"Of course, Ltamlt is stupid. The bag should not be left on the haavl. That poor beast needs to rest."

He walked over to the haavl and removed the bag, whispering words of comfort in the beast's ear. Then he tossed the bag off a way. Up to that point, Kthloold had wondered if there were something other than an escaped slave in the bag, but he heard a cry of pain as the bag hit the ground.

Suddenly, Kthloold lost his appetite.

"But isn't Ltamlt going to feed the human?" he insisted. He had already given Rhtiralmt something to eat before setting down to supper, which earned him a critical glance from his guest.

"Yes, yes. It wouldn't be good for it to die before we get to our destination, now would it? Once Ltamlt has finished, he'll give it some scraps."

A few minutes later, the hunter got up and headed over to the fire. He speared his scraps with a knife, then placed it over the coals. Once the food had been cooked somewhat, he went over to the bag, which he opened a little and tied around the human's neck, allowing only the head to emerge. The slave shook his sweat-drenched hair. Then the darztl threw the food down, forcing the human to eat off the ground. The human glared at the darztl, but gobbled up the food, obviously famished.

Disgusted, Kthloold turned away.

§ § §

The other darztl slept, but Kthloold watched. Once he felt that his companion was sleeping deeply, he stood up slowly. Rhtiralmt was sleeping nearby. He told Rhtiralmt not to make a sound, but he didn't know if the human heard him. He picked up his belongings as quietly as possible and loaded them onto his haavl. Then he helped the human up onto the animal. He was just settling himself on the beast when he heard a noise behind him. Ltamlt was pointing a weapon at him.

"Ltamlt knew it. You're trying to steal his prize."

"This darztl isn't trying to do anything. This is his human. He's entitled to leave with..."

"Your human. Ltamlt will put it in a bag like the other and do what he will with it. As for you, you're going to get down from that haavl slowly, without making any sudden movements, and sit down on the sand."

The darztl motioned Kthloold off with his gun.

Without thinking, moving past the mouth of the gun, Kthloold jumped on the other darztl, trying to disarm him. A shot was fired, but was lost in the desert. The two darztls fought for a moment, slashing each other cruelly with their claws. But Ltamlt was either stronger or more used to combat. With a sudden slash of his tail, he stood up, astride Kthloold, claws digging into his skin, powerful paws pushing against his chest. Kthloold fought well, but the hunter had the upper hand. Crushing Kthloold's throat, Ltamlt brayed in triumph, "Filthy thief! Ltamlt will truss you up and bring you back with him, dragging you behind his haavl. The authorities take slave thieves seriously. You'll be sent away for two or three years."

Suddenly, the darztl turned a surprised shade and wriggled about as if trying to dislodge an insect. When Ltamlt looked around to see what was happening behind him, Kthloold noticed a knife — his knife — planted in the hunter's crest. Carried by the weight of the individual who thrust it, the blade had traveled a certain distance before coming to a stop. Rhtiralmt collapsed at the darztl's feet, out of breath, haggard, feverish. He was covered with blood. The darztl lay very heavily on Kthloold, then collapsed to the side, gasping.

Kthloold took a certain amount of time to react, then frantically freed himself. First he headed over to Ltamlt, who was seriously injured, but still breathing. When Kthloold pulled the knife out, he moaned deeply. Without wasting a second, Kthloold looked around, searching for a rope or chain of some kind. There were chains hanging from Ltamlt's haavl, but the rings were too small for a darztl. Finally, he took the ropes from one of the hunter's bags to tie the darztl's limbs and tail as securely as possible. Then he bent down over Rhtiralmt, who seemed to have exhausted all his strength for the evening.

"He was going to kill you. He was going to send me back there," the human said, teeth chattering.

Kthloold helped him roll up in a blanket. Then he re-kindled the fire and sat down to think.

He was in the middle of the desert with a human who was ill and a darztl who was injured by an escaped slave. He was a party to the escape and he had helped the escapee put the hunter out of commission. They were in the middle of nowhere, with nowhere to go. If they were to go back to Remldarztl, they would be caught. Rhtiralmt would be executed and Kthloold would be exiled for some time. If they were to go too far north, they would encounter some horde of humans. If, by chance, they welcomed the human with open arms, they might well not do the same for his former master. If they were to stay where they are, they would be caught in the crossfire between humans and darztls. And if they were to let Ltamlt go, if they released him and waited for his injuries to heal, he would go after them for the ransom.

That was when he realized that two eyes had been following him the entire time, two eyes in the middle of a dark face peeking out of a bag. The hunter had not seen fit to settle his slave down for the night and had left him on the ground, in the bag, close to where Ltamlt had fed him. Kthloold walked over to the bag and opened it. As a safety precaution, the man was stripped and chained. The darztl took the human out of the bag and searched through Ltamlt's belongings for a key. He finally found it in the slave hunter's belt. Releasing the slave from his chains, Kthloold noticed fresh wounds on the male, either the result of his flight or possibly inflicted by Ltamlt. He also noticed that the slave had only one foot — or almost. One leg ended at the heel. Was that punishment inflicted the first time he tried to escape, or meted out as a preventive measure? Kthloold decided there would always be time to ask questions later. He gave the escapee a blanket. Humans didn't like to go naked.

Once free, the human wrapped the blanket around his body and took a few steps back, gauging his reaction. Kthloold remained where he was, not wanting to frighten him. But the other didn't really seem to be afraid. He stared at Kthloold without saying a word.

"Your slave is ill," he finally said in laborious darztl. "I don't know how he managed to find the strength to jump down from the haavl and stab the slave hunter."

Kthloold didn't balk at the familiar tone the slave used to address him. Slaves were taught to speak like that, as if they could never become adults.

"He's not my slave," he replied. "He was before. But not now."

Kthloold looked at Rhtiralmt, who had fainted. He got up and walked over to him. He ran his hand through the human's sweat-soaked hair. The male was burning up, far too hot for a human. His lips were cracked. His skin was dry. The darztl picked up his gourd and poured a little water into his mouth. The other swallowed mechanically.

"He'll have to be protected for several days."

Kthloold jumped. The other human had walked over. He touched Rhtiralmt's forehead. "His fever is very high."

"And do you know how to treat a human's fever?" Kthloold inquired, filled with hope.

"Without medication, I don't know.... But one thing is sure, his fever has to drop, and to make sure that happens he has to be placed somewhere cool."

He started to remove the blanket covering Rhtiralmt.

"What are you doing? You're going to kill him!"

"Just the opposite."

The human undressed the patient and, after digging a sort of bed in the sand, placed him in it, far from the fire. Rhtiralmt was wracked with shivers.

"Give me your gourd," the human said in an authoritative voice.

Kthloold was too dumbfounded to protest, so he obeyed. The man wet a corner of the blanket and moistened Rhtiralmt's skin.

In a quaking voice, the male said, "I've never been so cold."

But when Kthloold touched him, he found him abnormally hot.

Along with the human, Kthloold watched over Rhtiralmt the entire night. In the wee hours of the morning, the fever had dropped a little and the male was no longer shivering. The human hunter, on the other hand, was starting to wriggle about. Fortunately, he was tied securely.

Yet that didn't prevent him from uttering threats.

"Sub-darztl!" he spat out. "Animal! Human lover! Stay with your own kind! I bet you don't hate it when your little slave..."

Kthloold gagged the hunter. The darztl could then only communicate through his wattle, which was black with anger.

The time had come to set out, but Kthloold didn't know which way to go. He was burdened with two humans — one of whom was ill — and a trussed up slave hunter. On the one hand, if he abandoned the other darztl, injured, in the middle of the desert, bound and without a mount, he might be condemning him to death. Kthloold concluded that the lives of the two slaves were worth that of a hunter and decided to leave him there.

"Do you know how to ride a haavl?" he asked the human.

"What do you think?" he exclaimed.

Humans, Kthloold had discovered, liked to answer one question with another.

"Well, you're going to have to show me that humans can learn quickly!" retorted Kthloold. "We can't gallop with three on my haavl. Unless I put you back in the bag."

That argument worked. They broke camp and installed Rhtiralmt on one of the haavls, for better or for worse. Following this, Kthloold dug through his bag, looking for some clothing to give the other male, then helped him mount the large animal. The haavl stoically put up with it as the human made several attempts. Finally the male managed to sit astride of the enormous beast, looking tiny on his perch. He stayed there, tense, barely able to hide his fear. Then Kthloold walked over to Ltamlt.

"You've got to leave him there to die," murmured the human, who had tasted the hunter's medicine.

In fact, Kthloold knew that if he didn't free the darztl, he would certainly die there in the desert. So, he finally decided to loosen Ltamlt's bonds, hoping that they would already be long gone when he managed to free himself. The former prisoner glared at him, but said nothing more. The two humans and the darztl rode off on their two haavls, Kthloold guiding the human's mount by its halter.

§ § §

They galloped across the desert the entire day, heading straight north. They spoke little. The human held on to the haavl so tightly his knuckles were white. From time to time, however, he asked Kthloold how Rhtiralmt was doing. In the middle of the day, as they traveled in silence, the human asked Kthloold where he intended to go.

"I don't know," replied the darztl. "And what about you, where did you plan to go when you escaped?"

"I don't know. I just escaped. The slaves talk about a place, in the middle of the desert, where free humans live. I imagine it's some sort of pipe dream I'm following..."

"I've heard about a place where humans and darztls live together. I don't know if that place exists, but I'd like to believe it."

"We may be headed for the same place..."

When they finally dismounted from their haavls to set up camp for the night, the patient's fever had climbed and he was muttering incoherently. Kthloold tried to make him comfortable, not knowing if he should cover him up or expose him to the cool air. He sat down near the patient and placed the human's head on his thigh. He caressed his hair, speaking to him gently in darztl. Rhtiralmt opened his eyes a bit, but did not appear to see the darztl.

"You care for him a great deal."

Kthloold jumped.

The other human spoke again, "You love him a lot. Your wattle is chestnut brown. This is the first time I've seen a master weep over a sick slave."

"Not many of us would. My people have gone mad."
He looked at Rhtiralmt, whose face was flushed with
fever. "Yes, I'm very attached to him. I imagine you could
say I love him a great deal."

"Did you help him escape?"

Kthloold nodded his head slowly, knowing that this
was how humans indicated agreement.

"Seriously, where are you taking him?"

Kthloold shook his head.

"I haven't the slightest idea. My only goal is to put
as much distance as I can between us and Remldarztl.
Then we'll see."

Suddenly, as if they were in the most ordinary situation in the world, the human stood up and declared,
"Kthloold, my name is Nayel. The one who said he was
my master gave me another name, but that doesn't
count."

"And what about you, Nayel, I imagine you're fleeing
from something as well?"

"Yes, from the one who said he was my master. I no
longer have a master. And I'll never have another one
again."

Kthloold stood up painfully. The last night spent
watching over his patient, combined with his worry, had
exhausted him. He dug through his bags, looking for
something for their evening meal. There wasn't much
left. He had already exhausted a large portion of his provisions, but there were three to feed now. And he was
never much of a hunter. He thought about the food he
left in the bag near the other darztl and his stomach
rumbled. But Kthloold was no murderer. If he had left
Ltamlt without resources, he would have condemned him
to a slow death. Particularly since he'd taken his gun.

The two ate the travel rations in silence. Earlier, they
soaked a few crumbs in cactus juice for Rhtiralmt. The
fire cast a comforting heat and yet Kthloold felt icy. He
was afraid. Not afraid for himself, but afraid that he had
made the wrong decision. Then he pictured the darztls
who took pleasure in throwing rocks at the hobbled slave,

who laughed as they walked past him under the broiling rays of the sun, and he decided that death awaited Rhtiralmt there, as well.

He saw Rhtiralmt again, as a child, running freely about the yard. His little community had never been hard on slaves, adopting them like little pets rather than killing them with work. Of course, the darztls did make them do some work, but life was hard for everyone and each individual had to contribute. Their houses, constantly eroded by the sandy wind, had to be re-built. There was water to gather. And for the largest and the most skillful, there was game to hunt. There was also a small herd to take care off, but it wasn't enough to feed everyone.

Kthloold and Rhtiralmt were both boisterous by nature. And whenever they got into trouble, the darztl was punished as well, since the elders said he was responsible for his human's actions. They settled for tying up the slave in a corner of the barn until his master finished his chores and could take care of him again. Of course, only Kthloold received an education, but he in turn taught the human everything he learned. One day, the adults caught him teaching Rhtiralmt to read and write. He was given the most formidable punishment of his life: a week in seclusion. They never caught him at it again: he and the human found better hiding places after that.

The years passed and the community slowly dispersed. Several went to join other groups. Some went off to spend a few years living in solitude. His kind were like that — never too close, yet never too far from their own. Kthloold went off to live on his own. On his own with Rhtiralmt, whom he had come to consider a friend.

"You look exhausted."

Kthloold left his thoughts behind and looked at the human.

"You're tired," said the other. "You should rest."

Kthloold looked down at Rhtiralmt.

"I'll take care of him," said Nayel. "Sleep a little. You need it more than I do."

The darztl agreed. He had no energy left. He went to lie down next to the fire.

§ § §

Kthloold sat up. Day had already come. He had slept straight through, without dreaming. He looked around. Nayel had disappeared. One of the haavls was gone, too. Rhtiralmt was still lying in the same place, but someone had built a shelter with a blanket to protect him from the sun.

Kthloold leaped up, to see how the human was doing. His skin was cooler, as it always was in the morning. It was in the evening that the fever rose, making him delirious. For now, he was sleeping deeply.

He picked up their belongings. Nayel had not taken any food with him. He was crazy! But if the human preferred to ride off on his own, that was his business. Kthloold had no rights over him. Still, he felt more alone than ever. He had gotten used to relying on what the human knew about caring for Rhtiralmt. Of course, given
· the lack of resources, the real scope of his knowledge was limited, but the care the human had given his patient did bring down the fever a little.

Kthloold was preparing to lift Rhtiralmt up and place him on his mount when he heard a haavl galloping. Ever on the alert, he picked up the rifle he had stolen from the slave hunter. But a familiar silhouette was perched on the haavl that emerged from the dust. Nayel was back, feverish with excitement.

"I went exploring. That hill you see over there... well we can reach it in an hour. I checked. There's a place where we can take shelter. The cavern isn't very deep, it's just an indent really, but it's cooler there. And there's water."

"But we can't stop in the middle of the desert!"

"But we don't even know where we're going! Plus you can't just keep on carting your patient around on your haavl. He needs to stay in one place for a while if he's to heal. Your friend will be comfortable in the grotto I've found. He'll be less exposed to the sun."

Kthloold couldn't find any arguments to oppose this implacable logic. Obviously, the constant traveling wasn't good for Rhtiralmt. They had been on the run for six days by then and, rather than improving, his condition had worsened.

"I'll follow you," he conceded.

§ § §

The cavity was neither spacious nor luxurious, but the human was right, it was cooler. Kthloold, helped by Nayel, had stretched the human out, after first making him a bed of sand and foam. Rhtiralmt hadn't really regained consciousness, but he did smile. Then he slept, moaning quietly.

Kthloold sat down on a sun-warmed stone. The heat was good for his reptilian body, but deep down, he was still cold.

"It's all my fault," he said.

Nayel, sitting in the shade of a rock, two feet from the grotto where Rhtiralmt was sleeping, asked, "What's all your fault?"

Kthloold started. Listlessly, he swept his arm about the desert surrounding them.

"All this. The fact that we're here. The fact that we were forced to flee. Everything."

His wattle betrayed his defeat.

"But you helped him escape!"

"Only because I condemned him first!"

Kthloold stretched out on the rock, perfectly immobile, body melding into the mineral surface. He didn't want to answer the human's questions. He didn't want to think about all that. Nayel remained silent for a long time, appearing to mediate on what the darztl had just disclosed. Finally, he gently asked, "What do you mean, darztl?"

Kthloold rose out of his torpor again, grumpy, sad. "Just what I said. I don't want to talk about it."

Silence stretched out between them again. Heavy. Torrid. The only sound was the whistling of the wind between the rocks, the click of grains of sand hitting rocks. And, from time to time, Rhtiralmt's moans. Strangely, Kthloold was disappointed. He would have liked the other to insist. He needed to talk about it all, even if only to feel as if Rhtiralmt was there beside him, healthy, rather than lying in the shadow, weak and feverish. Finally, he broke the silence.

"It's not right to raise slaves as if they were free. It's dangerous for them."

"You raised your friend as a free human?"

"Yes. Well, when we were still in my community, I can't say that he was truly an equal. But let's say that he was one of us. Inferior, an eternal child let's say, but one of ours. We never hit our slaves where I grew up. And, because we treated them well, they were faithful to us."

"Like a haavl you feed and care for..."

Kthloold looked at him, his wattle sad. "Yes. Something like that. But when I was a child I didn't understand all that. I thought it was normal to sleep in a house while the slaves slept in the barn. I thought it was normal for my toys to be taken away while Rhtiralmt would be locked up for two days for the same offense. I was used to eating, then taking my leftovers to the human who played with me. And he found nothing odd about it, either."

"How old are you, darztl? It's impossible to tell with your kind."

"I realize that humans are fascinated with knowing how long it's been since their birth. That's of no consequence to us. I was born shortly after the war between my kind and the humans. I imagine that was about twenty revolutions ago."

"You're young. You haven't seen everything. You haven't been out and about much, because if you had traveled about your beautiful land a little you'd have seen much more flagrant injustices."

"I know. I spent a day in a camp. You know, darztl children are sent out to spend time in various parts of the country to learn different ways of becoming adults. I was an adolescent. The adults didn't want the young to take their human friends with them. I found out why. In that camp, I saw humans beaten, locked up, starving.... It disgusted me. How could my kind do that to other living beings?"

The human sighed. "Ever since the darztls captured me, I've been asking myself the same question. I've met slaves who've lived in captivity for three generations and still ask that question. When their masters give them time for that, of course," he added, his voice hard as he stroked his mutilated leg.

Their conversation ended there. They had to ensure their survival. They had water there, although it would have to be boiled for the humans to drink it without risk. But their supplies were running out and they didn't know how long they would have to stay here. Perhaps the rest of their lives... Kthloold had a gun then, and they'd seen small animals running about. He always tried hunting but the prey would run off, untouched, seeming to mock him. In any case, if they had to rely on his skills, they would be fasting for quite some time. Nayel offered to hunt. He said that it had been a long time since he had held a gun, twenty-one revolutions to be precise, ever since the darztls had captured him, but he had been a good hunter back then. When he was young, his mother often took him into the desert at twilight to catch a little game for the evening meal. Of course, he didn't know how to use darztl weapons and this gun was very heavy for him, but he wanted to try. Kthloold hesitated. Never before had a darztl given a human a gun. But Rhtiralmt needed food. Kthloold did, too, if he was to keep up his strength and watch over the human. So he decided to give the weapon to the former slave, hoping he would not regret it. When the sun set, he congratulated himself. Nayel, who left as the sun was already low in the sky, returned, limping along, carrying two osfts. During his absence, Kthloold picked up materials to make a fire and, his heart light, sat down to eat and pass the night.

He gave his patient something to eat. His fever seemed to be less intense than previous nights, but he was still half conscious. Yet he accepted the food they give him.

They had been lying down for a while when Nayel's voice rang out through the night, "You know, one of the first services you could do for your human is to stop feeling guilty for the acts he commits."

§   §   §

Days passed with no surprise. Rhtiralmt's condition was not improving, although it did not look like he was getting worse. Kthloold spent many hours with him, moistening his skin as Nayel had recommended. However, his friend was still delirious. Occasionally, the darztl felt as if his friend was regaining consciousness, but his words were incoherent when he woke.

Then one morning, just after dawn, Rhtiralmt woke. He sat up in his bed and asked, "Where am I?"

Kthloold presumed that the human was still delirious, but his friend looked at him and seemed to recognize him for the first time in ten days.

The darztl leaped over to him. Nayel, who had wakened as well, got up and touched Rhtiramlt's forehead. He declared the fever over. The patient was surprised to see this male near him and asked who he was.

"Another human your master has rescued," Nayel said simply, getting up to prepare the morning meal.

That day Rhtiralmt really seemed better. He managed to swallow a few mouthfuls of osft and some water. He was still weak, but his sleep was peaceful then. When Kthloold examined him, he noticed that all of his wounds were healing. Quickly, he chased the image of a mocking darztl aiming a large rock at the human from his mind. The human's skin was also healing, where the sun had burned it.

"Rhtiralmt," he said, caressing the human's sticky hair, "I never thought we'd wind up like this. I never should have taught you everything I did. Not in this world..."

"Don't blame yourself. If you only knew how good it made me feel when I hit that darztl! Ever since I saw him beating the human who worked for him, I swore that one day he would hit him once too often!"

"But if you had killed him, I could not have saved you. They would have executed you on the spot."

"They did almost execute me. But you saved me. Thank you. And thank you for making it possible."

The male fell asleep, a smile on his lips. Kthloold decided that if his human friend got better, hope was still possible.

But later that day, Nayel returned from his hunting out of breath, sweat beading his dark skin.

"A darztl," he said as soon as he came within talking range. "I saw a darztl on the other side of the hill. He looked like he was searching for something. He looked like a hunter!"

Kthloold felt the blood suddenly drain from his body. Several times, since he left, he had felt like standing still and allowing the desert sand to cover him. Yet knowing Rhtiralmt was free and helping him build a life far from the darztls helped him go on. For all they had gone through, he couldn't let the slave fall into the clutches of a human hunter. He regained his composure with difficulty.

"Do you think he saw you?"

"No, I don't think so. I was in the hills and hid as soon as I saw him. And my haavl was farther off. But that doesn't mean we're safe here. It means they're coming. We have to kill him!"

Nayel clasped the gun he always carried.

"If he comes here, I'll kill him."

Kthloold tried to sound soothing. "Come on, Nayel, he won't necessarily find us. Give him time to ride off and we'll be as discrete as possible."

But Nayel looked fiercer than the darztl had ever seen him look before.

"I'll give him time all right, but if he approaches, I'll kill him."

Kthloold stepped forward to take the weapon, but the human stepped back.

"And if you stop me from killing him, watch your step. I'm not going back there. They'll skin me alive if they capture me, darztl. They'll beat me to a pulp and then they'll cut off my one good foot! Think about it! They'll take your human and finish what they started. And you, you may want to play at being a pacifist, but there's nothing you can do to stop them."

"Listen, Nayel, I understand, but..."

"Oh! You understand, do you? I'd like to know how. If I cut one of your feet off, it will grow back, and if I cut it off a second time, it will grow back again. So don't tell me you understand. If they catch you, you'll be given a reprimand and released. No, you can't understand me! And your little pet slave can't understand me, either! A slave who only speaks the masters' language. A slave whose sole heroic act was to strike a big bad darztl one day and then immediately ran off to hide behind his masters' skirts!"

Realizing what he had said, Nayel stopped, petrified. He turned to Rhtiralmt, whose eyes were wide, and mumbled his apologies. Then he sat on a rock and hung his head. But he didn't give up his weapon.

That night, Nayel refused to release his weapon. He slept with it cradled in his arms, like a lover.

§   §   §

The next morning, Kthloold's mind was made up. They would go out to meet the darztl as soon as they saw him roaming about the vicinity. He would speak with the darztl, feeling out the individual, and convince the stranger that he was a darztl just like any other who had decided to lead a solitary existence in the desert. He explained his plan to the two humans. Rhtiralmt had improved since the previous night and could sit up, leaning against a rock. He declared it a good idea and said that, in any case, they couldn't allow a darztl to walk into their lair. Nayel agreed grudgingly, but insisted on keeping the human hunter's weapon. Kthloold understood his fear and, at the same time, knew that the human was right. Kthloold would never really understand. He didn't know what it was like to be a slave and live in a world that did not belong to him.... He imagined how he would react if someone took Rhtiralmt back and placed him in chains again. He knew he would do everything in his power to prevent that. However, he would also do everything he could not to become a murderer.

A day passed. Rhtiralmt was getting better and better and, one evening, leaning against the darztl, he took a few steps outside their grotto. However, when he took Rhtiralmt's clothes off to clean him with sand, Kthloold noticed just how much weight he had lost. He helped him, fearing that his friend was so frail he would break in two.

"Do you think we'll end up spending our entire lives here?" the human asked before falling asleep.

"I don't know whether to hope for that, or fear it."

The human indicated that he shared Kthloold's sentiments and closed his eyes.

Another day passed. Then as night fell, Nayel who had made it a habit to patrol from dawn to dusk, raced back, saying he believed he had seen a darztl in the distance, possibly the same one he had seen earlier, to the south, riding a haavl. He was heading straight for them. Kthloold shivered. He could not believe things were happening so quickly.

"Stay here and let me handle it," he ordered.

"I'm not your slave, darztl," said Nayel. "I'll do as I please." Then, softening his stance, he added, "Go and do what you have to do."

Kthloold saddled one of the haavls, hastily loaded his bags on it and galloped off to prevent the other darztl from approaching their hill.

As he approached, he noticed that the stranger was a female. And that, beyond any doubt, she was a slave hunter. She had all the right equipment. Above all, there was a canvas bag tied to her mount — full. The darztl shivered at this sight and asked himself how he was planning to get out of this situation, how he would ever get out of this mess. As he reached the female darztl, she was preparing to get down from her mount. She was certainly setting up camp for the night.

"Good evening, stranger! It's a little late for a stroll!"

"This darztl was on the point of stopping. Can he join the stranger?" Kthloold said, counting on darztl hospitality — which was matched only by their need for solitude.

As expected, the other replied, "Of course, as long as the stranger doesn't mind sharing this darztl's modest meal."

However, before preparing their food, the female darztl unhooked the bag tied to her saddle. Gently, she placed her load on the sand and opened the bag. A female human crawled out, wearing a chain on one foot, distrustful. There was a wound on the female's flank, hidden by a bloody bandage. The female darztl dug through her gear and pulled out a first-aid kit. Then she walked over to the slave, approaching her slowly, so as not to frighten her. She removed the bandage and Kthloold noticed that the wound was a serious one. With tender, almost gentle gestures, the female darztl cleaned the wound and applied a new bandage. The human allowed her to do so, grimacing.

Only after she had completed this task did the human hunter set up camp, aided by Kthloold, who hoped the other would not notice that he didn't have anything of much use in his bags. First, the female darztl heated a little food, which she offered to the human. Then the two travelers sat down and started to eat their meal in silence.

"The female stranger prefers the gentle approach," Kthloold said.

"What does the male stranger mean?" the other darztl replied, on the defensive, her wattle reddish.

Feeling that he had used a bad approach, Kthloold made another attempt, less abrupt this time, "This darztl means that the stranger is not any rougher than necessary with the human. He appreciates being with someone who does not use gratuitous violence with the slaves."

"This darztl does not believe that it is necessary to brutalize the humans."

"And yet, the stranger is a slave hunter..."

The female darztl remained silent, looking for something to say. "Mirnlt has chosen a trade, but that does not mean she shares the philosophy," she finally replied enigmatically.

Silence floated between them. Kthloold looked at the human. She was lying on the sand, taking shelter in the bag that the slave hunter had left her. She was staring, apparently thinking about nothing. But Kthloold had the impression that she had not missed a word of their conversation.

"This darztl had a slave, which he treated well. But the slave was sentenced for hitting another darztl. Kthloold found this very difficult. The law is harsh."

"Remldarztl is very hard on slaves," the stranger said.

The conversation ended there. They set up their beds for the night and went to sleep, without Kthloold knowing what kind of hunter he was dealing with.

§ § §

Rustling. Metallic sounds. The galloping of a haavl. Kthloold opened his eyes. It was morning. He looked around. He was alone. He stood up. He saw a haavl riding off, mounted by a female darztl. Heading north. Heading straight to the grotto where Rhtiralmt and Nayel were hiding!

He leaped onto his haavl, abandoning everything, telling himself he would have time to come back for his belongings. What counted just then was catching up with the darztl named Mirnlt who was heading straight for... straight for what? For the gun Nayel had trained on her.

Kthloold was a good rider, but the stranger's haavl was faster. He couldn't catch up. He saw her riding closer and closer to the hill, and he shivered. What welcome awaited them there?

When he finally reached the edge of the grotto, the female darztl was motionless, a gun pointed at her. Obviously, it was Nayel who was holding the gun, red and furious.

"Get down from your haavl, darztl, and don't make a move. Fine. Now, untie the bag holding the human you so savagely hunted down. That's it. Untie the rope and let the human out. Now, put your filthy paws up."

The female human retreated on all fours, hampered by the chain around her foot. Kthloold got down from his haavl gently, so as not to upset the human.

"Nayel, I don't think..."

"Shut up, Kthloold!"

"But Nayel..."

"I told you to shut up. Let me handle this. This darztl will not take from me the freedom I fought so hard for. That won't happen!"

He walked over to the slave hunter, who made no move to resist. She had her hands raised and was looking around her, frightened, obviously looking for a means of escape.

"The human must allow me to explain," she said in human language. "It's not..."

"You shut up, too. Do you allow the humans to explain before you throw them in bags and take them to their torturers?"

When he reached her, Nayel lowered his weapon and, in cold blood, shot her point blank in the arm. The female darztl fell to her knees, pressing one paw against her injured limb. Kthloold jumped. Nayel pointed his gun at him.

"Get back!" he barked. "I won't think twice about shooting you, too!"

Then he pointed his gun at the darztl and shot her in the leg. She collapsed with a cry. Once again Kthloold moved to step forward.

"I told you not to get involved with this, darztl. It's none of your business. This is between the hunter and me."

Combining action and words, using his mutilated foot, he pressed on the wound he had inflicted on the darztl with his weapon. The hunter shrieked in pain.

"Stop, Nayel, you have no right—"

"I have no right? What rights do you, you darztls have? Yet, darztls give themselves all the rights. And you, you're no better. You may be kind to your human, but that doesn't stop you from treating him like a lap dog."

He fired a third shot, into the darztl's tail this time. She cried out again. The sand around her was spotted with blood. As if he found all the blood exciting, Nayel plucked up his courage and struck the darztl in the face and she rolled over, conscious but dazed.

"Nayel, stop."

Kthloold threw himself between the female darztl and the human, who backed up, gun aimed.

"Get back," he said. "I don't want to kill you. I know that I owe my freedom to you, but I will not allow you to get in my way. This darztl is a human hunter and she doesn't deserve your pity. In any case, for your kind, this type of injury is nothing more than a superficial scratch. Isn't that so? You do worse to us and in a much more final way!"

"Nayel, there's no need for us to be murderers. And you can't blame one individual for the group they belong to. There's been enough killing between humans and darztls. We're not going to get into that game..."

"So you shouldn't have started it. You shouldn't have killed my family, you shouldn't have taken away my freedom, or locked me up in your factories and mines, or mutilated me, or beaten me every day until my back lost all sense of feeling."

He stepped forward, up to Kthloold, his gun pointed.

"Get out of my way, Kthloold, or I'll shoot you too."

Suddenly a gun shot rang out. Kthloold closed his eyes, certain that he must have been hit, waiting for the pain to surge through him. But he felt nothing. He opened his eyes. Nayel had crumpled to the ground at his feet, his weapon smoking. The female human was crouched down a little way off, motionless. The female darztl, eyes wide, stared dumbfounded at the scene. Behind them stood Rhtiralmt, a large rock in his hand, motionless, overwhelmed. Finally, he managed to stammer, "Did I... did I kill... him?"

Looking down, Kthloold saw that Nayel's hair was drenched in blood. He bent down and noticed that, fortunately, the human was still breathing. Looking both relieved and defeated, Rhtiralmt collapsed, his head in his hands.

"The masters are right, Kthloold. A slave who has struck once will strike again."

§ § §

From where Kthloold was positioned he could see everything. The rocky landscape that stretches on for eternity. The hollow rock mountain where the village stood. The tiny silhouettes of humans and darztls busy rebuilding a life. In the midst of them, even though he could not see him, was Rhtiralmt, for whom freedom would bring no danger here. It was morning. The shadows cast by the houses slowly pulled back. He stayed up there on his perch, fascinated by the peaceful scene, the scene that proved not everything on Siexlth was rotten, the scene he could spend his entire life watching. Then he slowly climbed down.

The night before, they had reached the village after allowing the female darztl to recuperate for two days. She had had the time to tell them, that a few days away by haavl, where she lived, humans and darztls lived together without killing one another.

"However, Mirnlt cannot tell you where this place is. If the human and the darztl want to go there, they must agree to be blindfolded. As for him..."

She pointed at Nayel, who they had tied up in the rocky cavity after wrapping his head with a clean cloth.

"As for him, the village will have to discuss his status."

As she slept and recovered from her injuries, Kthloold and Rhtiralmt discussed the opportunity of following her and decided the risk was well worth it. They could not spend their lives alone in the desert, and the female darztl didn't look like she was a hunter like the others. Moreover, they questioned the female human she had captured and, although she seemed very overwhelmed by what was going on around her, she shook her head when they asked her if the hunter had brutalized her. Perhaps Mirnlt was telling the truth.

"And even if the society she's offering us is not the idyllic world she's described to us," argued Rhtiralmt, "it can't be any worse than life on the run in this never-ending sand...."

"I'm ready to try my luck, too."

The darztl and the human jumped. It was the other human who had spoken, for the first time since Nayel had released her from the bag.

When they set out, since she was still very weak, Mirnlt asked Kthloold and Rhtiralmt to put a bag over Nayel's head and make sure his wrists were firmly bound. He glared at them, furious, but said nothing. In fact, he hadn't really said anything for two days, merely grunting when they asked him how he felt or offered him food. The female human allowed herself to be blindfolded as well. Mirnlt said there was no point in putting her back into a slave bag.

"In any case, if Mirnlt and the others come across a darztl, this crew will look decidedly strange!"

Rhtiralmt and Kthloold then lifted each of the two humans onto a haavl. The male human climbed up behind the female and Kthloold behind Nayel. The female darztl handed them blindfolds that they voluntarily tied up. Then the strange little group set off.

They trotted like this for three days, slowed by the fact that the female darztl had to guide their mounts. They stopped when the sun set, and started again at dawn. They only took off their blindfolds when night fell, putting them on again in the morning. Mounted on his haavl like this, not knowing where he was headed, Kthloold felt slightly dizzy and he suddenly understood how the slaves must feel, jostled about on the flank of a haavl all day long. On the evening of the third day, he started hearing more noise around them and their darztl guide said they could take their blindfolds off for the last time.

They found themselves in the middle of a small group of humans and darztls. Everyone was looking at them, eyes filled with curiosity, but no animosity. Nayel still had a bag over his head, but the blindfold had been removed from the female human and she looked around, confused. They climbed down from the haavl. Someone took charge of Mirnlt, who had not recovered fully from her injuries, and a female human told Kthloold, Rhtiralmt and their female human to follow her. Nayel tried to get free when two darztls grabbed him, but he could not keep them from carrying him off.

§ § §

Kthloold walked down the hill, thinking about the day ahead of him and the days to come. Humans and darztls lived there in relative peace, Mirnlt told him, without any form of pre-established hierarchy or power roles determined by membership in one of the two species. Rhtiralmt and he would do well here. No one would ever criticize them again for their unlikely friendship.

Before returning to the room that the people here assigned him, Kthloold went to visit Nayel. On his way, he saluted the darztl sitting near the door. In the cell, which looked more like a guarded room, the human was already up. He was sitting very straight in a foam chair, his head immaculately wrapped with a bandage. He didn't move when the darztl entered. Impassive, moving only his eyes, he watched as Kthloold walked over to him and sat on the bed. He continued to stare, without saying a word. The silence stretched out between them.

Finally Nayel closed his eyes and murmured, "I wouldn't have killed you. Not you."

Kthloold figured that's why the ball whistled past his ear so close when Rhtiralmt struck Nayel.

"They asked me if I want to stay here, and they told me they had to discuss it as well," the human continued. "But I don't want to stay here. I could never live with all these darztls around me, pretending to be my equals."

"You don't want to give them the chance to show you it's possible?"

"No. Maybe twenty years ago I would have, but not now."

"Things seem different here."

"As long as there are darztls things will always be the same."

"But Nayel, if you don't stay here, where will you go?"

"Into the desert. I'll find groups of free humans."

"And what if you run into a slave hunter?"

"I'll die fighting him. You know, I resisted for a long time before the other hunter managed to catch me. It's not true that humans are completely powerless against darztls."

"Especially if they have weapons."

Nayel finally opened his eyes and stared into Kthloold's. But he didn't say another word. A few minutes later, the darztl stood up and left.

§ § §

The haavl trotted peacefully through the desert, visibly pleased to be back in its own element. The sun was already low in the east, stretching their shadows out ahead of them. In the sandy silence of the desert, the only sound to be heard was the wind in the rocky dunes and the scratching of the animal's claws in the dust.

A few hours earlier, Kthloold had left behind a village darztl who had taken them out to the middle of the desert. They spent the last two days winding their way through the desert, heading west on a relatively erratic trajectory. Kthloold understood that this was one way of misdirecting any potential pursuers and completely disorienting the human they carried. However, for a few hours now, he had been alone with Nayel. The region was too dangerous and both individuals had been lost in their own thoughts.

Kthloold insisted on bringing the male back himself. Rhtiralmt was hesitant to let him go. He spoke of accompanying him, but Kthloold made him understand that the human was in even greater danger than the darztl was. However, no matter how reassuring Kthloold was, he knew that the expedition was not without risk for him. If a band of humans came across them unexpectedly it might well be the end of him. Yet even though the darztl understood why the village decided to let the human go, he could not agree to abandon him to his unhappy fate. Nayel might not be forced to live among darztls, but he did not deserve to die or to be put back in chains.

The darztl stopped his haavl and climbed down from his mount. He untied the bag that was hooked to the saddle. He opened it and let Nayel out. He untied his hands. He hesitated about untying his feet since he knew just how dangerous Nayel could be to him, but he resolved to do it, telling himself that if he wanted to help the human become free, he could not start by leaving him hobbled.

Everything else — making fire, setting up camp, preparing the meal — was just routine, a routine established after wandering for several days in the desert. Kthloold heated the human rations he was given when he left the village and offered a plate to Nayel, who grabbed it and started to eat in silence.

The evening before, the male did not say a single word from the time Kthloold took him out of the bag until he fell asleep. He didn't utter a word the next morning, either, as they set out. He didn't say a word when, two days earlier, Kthloold informed him that the village had decided to delegate someone to escort him into the desert and that he, Kthloold, had volunteered. That evening, however, Nayel was the one to break the silence.

"So you decided to do the dirty work yourself?"

"If by 'dirty work' you mean taking you to a band of free humans, yes, I decided to do it myself."

"You're not taking me back to the darztls?"

"Nayel!"

Kthloold put his food down and stood up suddenly. He strode away from the human and the warmth of the fire in an effort to cool his temper. This male was not reasonable. After all these days traveling together in the desert, Nayel still didn't trust him. The darztl shivered. The desert night was icy at this northern latitude. He headed back to the fire.

"I'm curious about something, Nayel," he said. "What was driving you, all that time we were in the desert, the three of us — well, the two of us since Rhtiralmt was unconscious much of the time? Were you looking for a good time to shoot me in the back or was I right to think you actually trusted me?"

This time it was Nayel's turn to stand up. He walked toward the fire and made as if to stoke it, then nervously arranged his blankets on the sand. Finally, he remained standing, shifting from one foot to the other.

"I'm sorry, I've been unjust," said the human. "It's the disappointment that is making me talk. I know that the village could not allow me to stay after what I did to that female darztl and..."

"Nayel, the village didn't throw you out because of what you did. They *let* you go because that's what you wanted. No one is forced to stay there against their will. That's against the community's principles. Of course, they also decided that if they kept you there by force, other unfortunate, possibly with more tragic consequences, could occur...."

His words hung in the air. Neither Kthloold nor Nayel said another word that evening. When they went to bed, they simply wished each other a good night.

The next afternoon, they found human tracks. In a small plain between two hills, humans had stopped in the past. They saw the remains of the fires they had made, and the small stone walls, now half covered with sand, that they had erected to protect themselves from the sun and the desert winds. Kthloold even found a human doll, almost completely buried. Nayel got down from his haavl and absentmindedly picked the doll up.

"I told you that I was born free, but I never told you how I lost my freedom," he started, twisting the doll. "I was born free and grew up in the colony, and then my life was interrupted when your people attacked mine. I was eighteen Marsian years old at the time. I'm thirty-nine now, which means that I've spent more years in captivity than free...."

Without releasing the doll, Nayel sat in the shade of a small wall, legs bent, elbows resting on his knees, hands clasped around the toy. Kthloold climbed down from his haavl and sent it off to graze with the other. He walked over to the human, not daring to speak, waiting for Nayel to talk about himself.

"That morning, when the darztl army entered the base camp," the human continued, "I was busy with my usual chores. I was a maintenance worker at the pumping station. Basically, that involved watching over the machines to make sure there was no sand build-up that would shut them down. So I was inside the building, not far from the mother ship, when I heard the sounds of fighting. I raced outside. People were running every which way. No one could see the darztls yet, but everyone

was screaming that they were coming. I didn't know where
to go. You know, we humans have plenty of war stories
in which courageous men and women fight to the death
against the enemy. Everyone in the colony had been given
military training. Yet most of the civilians were unarmed
and mostly what I saw was people racing for a place to
hide. Me too — all I wanted to do was hide somewhere
far away when I saw the first darztl, then a second, then
an entire battalion, all of them immense, mounted on haavls
twice as tall as I was. I felt like this doll here standing next
to a giant like me. I ran this way and that between the
enormous mounts, as human bodies piled up in the streets,
expecting to be struck dead at any moment. But I noticed
that the darztls were killing as few as possible, throwing
some kind of net over the others, immobilizing them in
just a few seconds. Suddenly I heard a roar. When I felt
the ground vibrate, I realized what was happening. The
mother ship was taking off, abandoning the colony. And
in fact, just a few seconds later, I felt an intense heat. I lay
face down on the ground, expecting to be burned to a crisp
by the exhaust. But I was already a few yards from the craft
and I was untouched. On the other hand, that made me
an easier prey and I found myself trapped in a net. That's
when my life as a slave started."

Kthloold looked around. He found it hard to imagine
a human village, but he could picture places swarming with
humans. He imagined the terror that would be sowed by
a darztl army attacking a camp — or flowing over the
village, killing or capturing humans and darztls indiscrimi-
nately. Nayel continued his tale. He said that he tried to
get free of the net, but the links were woven too skillfully.
The more he moved, the tighter the net closed around him.
He called out to others for help, but they already had their
arms full — they were busy trying to save themselves,
fighting an unfair battle against an enemy that was too
large, too numerous. The fighting slowed. The humans fell
one by one, dead or captured. At the end, a heavy silence
fell over the colony. All that could be heard was the scratching of haavls' claws and the clicking of darztl conversations. A few human wails as well, followed by a final cry

when a darztl finished off some injured human. Finally the darztls assembled the survivors in what had once been the marketplace, but was now completely ravaged.

"As for me, a darztl dragged me behind his mount," Nayel said. "Those who weren't in nets were brutally beaten by darztls mounted on haavls. Laboring to speak our language, a darztl told us that the humans had lost the battle and we were now their prisoners. We were going to be forced to work for the darztls in order to compensate for all of the harm our kind had caused on this planet."

"Did some of the humans try to resist?" Kthloold asked.

"Yes, briefly. Some people stepped forward to object that this was against all the conventions of war. Some darztls rounded up the protestors from the group of humans and had five or six of them lie down in the sand. Then, their large swords raised, an equal number of darztls walked over to the humans and, as we watched in terror, they brought their weapons down on the rebels' bodies, slicing them in two and, if I may say so, cutting off any protest. I was at the front. I saw it all. I don't know if you've ever seen a human body cut in two, but let me tell you it's not a pleasant sight.... All of those fluids and substances that spilled out and flowed over to our small, terror-stricken group..."

Nayel shook his head, trying to chase away that horrific image. He continued to speak in a monotone, as if trying to remain detached from his own story. After that first show of force, he explained, the darztls could have done almost anything they wanted with the humans. One by one they took them out of the group, freeing them from their nets if necessary, and placed chains on their wrists and ankles. Once everyone had been hobbled, they chained them to one another, and that's how the humans spent the night, one on top of another, chained too closely together to lie down anywhere but on top of their neighbor, too chilled to refuse that contact. The next morning the darztls had lined them up and told them to get walking. This was how their painful trek across the desert started. Not everyone survived. Several fell — some succumbing to the heat and the cold, others to the darztls' blows.

"And when you got to the end, that's when the forced labor started?"

"Not right away. First they parked us in a type of camp that looked like a zoo, since we were organized in small groups in cages that were too low and too small. The cages were sheltered from the sun and we were locked up there, naked and dirty, and forced to eat off the ground. They humiliated us day after day, treating us like animals. I think they wanted to start by breaking us so we would be more docile. Perhaps they were also waiting until they decided how they would use us. You don't become a society of slaves overnight...."

The darztls were particularly ferocious with respect to the males, according to Nayel. He'd seen masters take men from their cages and execute them just like that, for no good reason, just to reduce the ranks of males. Slowly, either one by one or in small groups, the humans were separated from one another and taken far away. Nayel found his mother and one of his brothers in the group of captives, along with several other acquaintances. But he was locked up with humans with whom he was less familiar, and was taken off by himself to start his new life as a slave.

"And what happened to your family?" Kthloold asked.

"I heard some rumors," replied Nayel, shrugging. "If I can trust what I heard, my mother didn't survive long. And as for my brother, the last I heard he was working in a sort of factory. I hope he was luckier than I was, although I doubt that, as a male, he managed to keep both feet."

Nayel sat down cross-legged, the doll between his legs, holding his mutilated foot with both hands. As if each word pained him, he described the icy hell where he spent his first few years of captivity, a new project apparently designed just for the humans, for the new, fresh slaves. There were about twenty slaves in all, males and females, who were forced to wade in an underground river, looking for gold. The water was cold and they had to wade in it up to their thighs, then explore the bottom, holding on to one another so they wouldn't fall in. But the river bed was smooth and, hampered by their chains, the humans often slipped on the smooth round stones.

"We were always wet," Nayel said, wrapping his arms around his body. "We were always freezing, and the masters' whips striking our backs were all the more painful. Our rations depended on what we dredged up during the day, so I often went to bed with an empty stomach. At night we slept in the mountain, chained to one another, guarded by darztls who were grumpy from lack of sleep."

"You spent twenty revolutions there?"

"No. The darztls had us mine the river for about five local years. But our efforts didn't produce much during the last two years. When I finally left the mountain I felt washed out, bleached by all those years bathing in water, without ever once seeing the sun. I was lucky to get out of there alive because several died of cold and hunger. I traded one underground prison for another, since I was sent to work in a mine. I spent the next fifteen years hammering away at a rock wall, looking for precious iron. That's where they cut off my foot."

Nayel stopped, white as a sheet, and as he continued to hold the end of his footless leg, he rocked back and forth. He grimaced, as if reliving the moment when they cut off his foot in his mind's eye.

"You escaped from the mine?" Kthloold asked, to draw him out of his atrocious memories.

Nayel nodded. He took advantage of an outing up top and the inexperience of the darztl who was responsible for counting the humans for the night. He made mistakes frequently, mixing up human faces, so the male took advantage of a new error on his part and hid in an unused shaft.

Of course, a few days earlier, they'd caught an escaped slave.

"I'll spare you the details of the treatment reserved for escapees," Nayel warned Kthloold. "But let's just say that the sight of their bodies hung out to dry, exposed to the masters' blows, usually serves to discourage others. The darztls weren't expecting any further escapes for some time.

But I didn't allow myself to be discouraged and I escaped after a few days."

Nayel fell silent and closed his eyes, his mind certainly filled with new visions of horror. Kthloold told himself that was what it must be, visions of the horrors his people inflicted on the humans day after day. He could not have tolerated living anywhere near all that. He regretted having decided to escape with Rhtiralmt rather than fighting the system head on. On occasion, he had talked with other darztls who opposed the stance Remldarztl had taken with respect to slavery and so he knew he was not alone, even if only a few dared oppose the system or defy the establishment openly.

"And you swore you would never trust a darztl?" Kthloold asked, to bring their conversation to an end. "Even a darztl who says he is your friend?"

"I swore that I would never trust an intelligent race that is capable of enslaving another intelligent race without any sense of remorse."

"And wasn't that what the humans were trying to do?"

"Yes, but they're my own kind."

"Yet you seemed to trust me for a time."

"You're not the same. I knew that you would never willingly hurt me. I saw you weep for your ill friend. You wanted to save him too much."

"You don't want to give those in the village another chance?"

"I know that I could never trust anyone. I know that I'm someone the darztls can never trust. I'm not even sure I can vouch for myself. I can say it to you now — I took too much pleasure in hurting that female darztl."

§ § §

"Kthloold, there are humans over there," Nayel said as he held out the binoculars to the darztl.

They had taken refuge in the hill to the south-east of the plain where they found the former human camp. They both presumed that humans traveled through there regularly. For the past twenty days, they had been hiding behind the rocks, hoping they guessed right. Their patience was now being rewarded.

"It looks like there are a lot of them, Nayel. Perhaps you should set out to meet them."

"And what will you do? I suggest you get away from here as quickly as possible. I know what my kind can do to a darztl. When I was young, I saw one massacred by a crowd."

Nayel hastily packed up his belongings. He didn't have a lot to carry — a few supplies at most. He could not afford to arouse the suspicions of the band of humans. They had to believe that he got here on his own. Kthloold tried to make him promise not to talk about the village, but the human simply said that he would try to remain discrete. In any case, the darztl thought, he would never be able to find the village on his own.

Even though he ran the risk of being discovered by the approaching humans, Kthloold remained hidden in the hill, curious to see how things would turn out for Nayel. He watched as Nayel walked slowly ahead, a small, anonymous figurine in a setting that was larger than life. He knew that the others had seen him when one of the vehicles carrying humans — he had already heard about those carts driven by internal engines — moved to the head of the caravan and reached Nayel before everyone else. The humans surrounded the former slave. Everyone was waving their arms about. Nayel indicated the desert around him, without specifically pointing in the darztl's direction. Slowly, the rest of the group arrived. Kthloold watched them for a moment as they started to set up camp, Nayel standing in the middle of them, either free or else a captive of his own kind.

Kthloold was relieved, knowing that Nayel was with his own kind and that, for the time being, Nayel would not betray him. Kthloold would not have to rush off to escape a human horde agitated by Nayel. He would not have risked his life to save the human. With a little luck, the human would convince the others that not all darztls are rotten. His heart relatively light, Kthloold told himself that he could now head off in the direction of the small community where darztls and humans lived in peace. A place where Rhtiralmt and he might have a chance to find what they had always been looking for, a place where they could live as a free darztl and a free human. A village where no one was kept by force. A peaceful oasis in a troubled world. An island of sand and rock in the middle of a sea of sand and rock.

HER RIGHT ARM

Her right arm was growing back well. Every day as the liirzt rose, when she still felt all alone in the camp, she measured its progress. Her arm had already lost some of the sensitive color of new buds and the tissue was almost completely functional. She worked the muscles, measured the elasticity of the tendons. She observed the skin in the early dawn. Obviously, it was still just a ridiculously tiny arm, like a child's, but it would not take more than a dozen days before she would have a beautifully formed darztl arm again. A beautiful arm to lose to her torturers for fodder.

§ § §

When they caught her, she had all her equipment with her: detention bag, tranquilizers and enough weapons and munitions to overcome a small band of poorly equipped humans. She was on patrol, looking for a human, a female, as is often the case, a particularly cunning type that could not be recaptured easily. An animal at large in the desert, no matter how tiny it may be, is still awaiting its sentence, as darztls on both continents liked to say. It was true that, in the immense wilderness of stone and sand, it was hard to avoid capture once you had been spotted. While thinking about her prey, she repeated this implacable law of her world over and over. She had forgotten that it could also apply to her....

§ § §

She heard the little human approaching. She had no idea if he could decode the colors of her wattle, but it was possible that he noticed just how much pleasure she invariably took in his arrival. Joy was a rare commodity under the circumstances.

Every morning she wondered if he would come. But it was an idle question she asked to keep her mind occupied. He always came to see her. Not a single day had passed without him coming to take care of her basic needs, her hygiene. He was the only one who didn't appear to be either frightened or disgusted by the sight of her. He stayed with her as she gobbled up her meal — a nourishing broth that tasted disgusting. She recalled that the first few days she had refused to eat it. But they force fed her and she could do nothing about it because the humans had pulled all her teeth out. After her meal, the little human cleaned her body, rubbing it with handfuls of sand.

§ § §

Occasionally, as was the case of all new limbs, her arm itched. It was as if an entire colony of strulzs — those small burrowing insects that lived in the stems of the succulent plants in the desert — were building a nest there. She would have loved to scratch, gnaw it until she tore the flesh off, but that was impossible of course. For that, she would have needed another arm, a real darztl paw. For the time being, all she had was an embryonic left arm and feeble sprouts of legs emerging timidly from her body. Her bud of an arm had not attained the size of a fully formed arm, and even if it did, it would be too weak to ease her torment. So she rubbed on the ground. But her jailers were not stupid. They kept her in an enclosure with smooth walls where there was no risk of damaging the merchandise. She had to settle for meditating to set aside the discomfort.

She had mediated a great deal in recent moons, since she had experienced a great deal of discomfort.

§ § §

Any normally grown darztl could overcome a single human, even a group of humans, with no great difficulty. A few blows with her tail, a few well-placed strikes with her claws and any humans still alive would run off like frightened osfts. But the group that had swarmed over her had been too strong, an entire horde, and the humans were armed. Plus, she'd been overconfident, softened by years of uneventful patrols. She hadn't taken the elementary precautions that would have allowed her to detect the presence of a group of humans, to spot them before they spotted her and blend into the landscape before they saw her. In short, she'd been caught like some rookie and, by the time she saw them, they had already encircled her. A hook in her crest stopped her in her tracks. She collapsed in the sand and when she regained consciousness they were discussing her fate.

§ § §

The little human was sitting near her, watching her.

When he came to see her and the others were not paying too much attention to him, he spent some time in her enclosure, studying her as if hypnotized. She knew that she didn't look like much with her butchered body, but the fascinated gaze of the young human gave her a certain sense of magnificence. He was not afraid to sit near her; he knew she wouldn't hurt him. She, too, examined him sidewise, despite her disgust. If she could, she would take him in her arms. She would sing songs to him in a language he didn't understand. But neither of her arms was long enough and the songs of her people would make him too sad. Furthermore, her songs would not calm the human child; they'd be merely noise to him, just as the human language hurt her ears.

§ § §

The rest of the time she sat motionless in her enclosure, watching her limbs grow for no good reason, or in any case, not for her. They must have cut off her legs and each arm two or three times, but she got tired of the morbid

count. An animal waiting for slaughter didn't count either
the days that go by or the slashes of the knife — it
allowed itself to be fattened, then eaten. Soon, if she
didn't keep watch, her human jailers would have transformed her into a brutalized beast that allowed itself to
be eaten alive at regular intervals. From time to time, she
looked at this recent arm that would soon mature and
she decided this was her last chance, that it was all that
still connected her to a civilized species. When they cut
off this limb, the process would be complete. She would
be converted into a piece of cattle for once and for all.
That was why she must act right then.

§ § §

After capturing her and seriously wounding her, they
had dragged her mercilessly to their camp and, since that
time, they had been carrying her with them as they
migrated. They kept her near their quarters. She owed
her survival, this state of partial survival, to the fact that
one of the group's males — not the leader, but someone
important — was on hand when they dragged her in and
had a good idea. The others were already discussing how
they would cut her up and distribute the pieces. But he
found a way to make the pleasure last. She didn't understand much of their language, of course, but she
harvested the fruit of his cruel inspiration. She finally
realized that, instead of slicing her up once and for all,
they would sample her in small portions, and her arms,
her legs and her tail would be transformed into choice
dishes within the clan, meals served to the elite. Like an
exotic plant that was allowed to grow so that its tender
shoots could be served as a delicacy.

And of course, this solution would the best way to
keep her from escaping....

That day the little human had a new injury, a bruise
so large his right eye was essentially closed.

The child was abused. His living conditions were possibly even more atrocious than those most darztls imposed on humankind. They treated him almost as badly

as they treated her, a stranger. Except they didn't slice him up for dinner, of course. In addition to taking care of her needs, he was responsible for all kinds of filthy tasks that were visibly too arduous for his body, which was still not fully grown and already deformed by the work they made him do. Obviously, he was beaten when he made a mistake or wasn't up to his task — which happened frequently, considering the scope of the work and the masters' lack of sensitivity. Not that they needed a reason to beat him. Apparently the slightest pretext was enough. His little back was covered with scars and his left arm, which must have been broken when he was even younger, had never set properly and was more twisted than the other. That touched her all the more since his little deformed arm reminded her of her own buds, in miniature.

The little human had never tasted her darztl flesh.

§   §   §

The first time they cut off all her limbs she fainted. Just because darztl limbs grew back didn't mean that amputating them was not terribly painful. Without a doubt, it must have hurt as much as when her own kind chopped off an escapee's foot.... But in her case, it wasn't just a foot they cut off, but arms and legs and tail.

Later, they learned to be more frugal, not to use up all their pleasure at a single time, to make the food last. But that first time, they seemed to take great pleasure in cutting her into little pieces and watching her suffer since, each time she lost consciousness, they waited for her to come to before cutting off the next piece. She suffered throughout an entire afternoon and thought she would go mad from the pain. But when evening came, she was still alive. Weakened, prostrate, powerless, lying on a piece of canvas, she couldn't even raise her head to see what the humans were doing. She smelled the odor of grilled flesh, her own flesh, and the outbursts of human voices indicating that the entire little community — or at least those who were fortunate enough to take part in the feast — dug into this macabre banquet with relish.

§ § §

For months they held her captive, imprisoned inside four solid fenced walls, a chain around her neck. Not that she could go very far in her condition, but she viewed this as part of the humiliation they wanted to impose on her, and on all her kind through her. Perhaps, as well, by treating her like an animal, the humans managed to convince themselves that she could neither think nor suffer. Or maybe they were fully aware of the barbaric, yet refined, torture they were subjecting her to and derived pleasure from it. She didn't know. What she did know was that when the human, and it was always the same one, came to amputate one of her limbs, his eyes shone as he sliced through her flesh with the ax while the others watched, impassive. The group reacted afterwards, when the leg or arm was detached and they held a piece of meat in their hands. Then they all looked triumphant, while she felt defeated.

§ § §

The little human looked at her so gently, so sadly. It was hard to believe that one day he would turn hard, that he would join the ranks of her torturers.

Except when they had no choice, the other humans kept their distance, even when shouting at her or mocking her. She preferred that, in fact. They were so repulsive, with their smooth, pale skin, their fragile constitution, their limbs that didn't regenerate when cut. The little one's body was also that of a white larva and she had no idea why he found grace in her eyes. Maybe because he fed her. Obviously, because he shared in her misfortune. His life was barely any better than that of the prisoner for whom he was responsible, and they could not even use the excuse that he was a monster. They were the monsters.

That provided food for thought about how people treat their own, namely how the monsters treated their humans, and about the harsh measures they imposed. This was a savage species, raised in violence, naturally inclined to be brutal. During her time with the humans, she'd seen horrors such as she had never seen anywhere on her planet — despite the fact that she had traveled the two continents extensively. She'd seen humans respond with an eye for an eye, or turn violent without even the slightest provocation. She'd seen the strong take advantage of the weak. She'd seen one human take another by force, using that human sexually, and she'd seen a group of males do as much with a lone female. More than once. In front of her eyes, they had fought and torn one another apart like animals. She had even witnessed a murder one day. How could she trust a species whose members killed one another in cold blood?

§ § §

From the very first day she had constantly tried to find the means to end the atrocious cycle. She didn't want to spend the rest of her life being cut up and served as fodder for the humans. Her body's ability to regenerate was a curse for her. Who knew how many more times her limbs could grow back before her body gave out? She didn't want to live long enough to find out. Of course, she had nothing on hand to end her torture, to cut it short. Her torturers would never let her treat their food that way! However, a few yanz ago — here she had heard them called moons — she came up with a plan and since that time she had been trying to put it into action. It was a cruel solution, a project in tune with the world around her. A project that would alienate the only being with whom she had bonded since the early days of her captivity, but a plan that, if it worked, would free her once and for all.

§ § §

She had played the scene over and over in her mind, in secret, repeating by night the words she heard during the day. In the beginning to test the sounds in her throat, then gradually, understanding the words she was saying.

Then one morning, as the child brought her pittance, she broke her silence of the past months and addressed him for the first time in that unpleasant language. He started, dropping her meal at his feet and ran off. When the masters discovered that some of the food had been wasted in the sand, they made him pay dearly. But after that, he never again ran off. She didn't think he had any fear of reprisals. He simply seemed curious. At least that's what she understood from his expressionless, colorless face. Gradually she started talking to him, more and more frequently, for longer and longer, more and more intimately. Simple greetings at the start, to which he merely nodded. Once he was used to hearing her talk, she talked to him about anything, about her life in captivity, her people's culture, the quiet days she spent with her people, about the time when she wasn't an animal in a cage. Obviously, it wasn't all smooth going and, on several occasions, when what she said sounded stupid or made no sense, she saw the child's face light up. Under other conditions, she thought, they could have got along together. He had never spoken in return, never responded, but from time to time he nodded — the human way of indicating agreement. Or simply, that they were listening.

§ § §

The little human was still near her. He was waiting for a signal from her. Soon she would have to take action; otherwise the opportunity would be missed for all time.

"Do you have the knife?" she asked him in his language.

Without saying a word, he showed her the shiny metal. She knew that her wattle must have turned emerald.

§ § §

One day, carefully choosing her words from among the few rare synonyms she knew, she started her work. The little one was attached to her; she was almost certain of it by that point. He was spending more and more time near her enclosure. At least, just little enough, just infrequently enough not to attract the others' suspicions. Despite his young age, the child must have learned to keep a secret a long time ago. First, it seemed strange to her that she was the one to be giving him such attention. Partly because she had a plan in mind, of course, but also because she was developing a strange affection for the miniature human who, nevertheless, stood for all that was disgusting to her. Then she made him her confidant, her accomplice, knowing full well the danger she placed them both in, but aware that the child was her last hope of escape.

§ § §

She had to take action. Already, the camp was stirring. She looked at the child. His face, burned by the liirzt, looked pale nonetheless, almost as pale as the white suit he wore during the day, to protect him from the deadly rays — deadly for them, of course. She nodded at him. Suddenly, she could no longer speak the humans' language; she could no longer speak any language.

For several yanz, she had prepared for this moment. She had patiently trained the child. Gently, she told him what she expected from him, she made him realize that this was the best solution. If he were to get rid of her, he'd make both of them happier. He'd be better off because the other humans wouldn't hate him so much for being the one who had to take care of the darztl. She'd be happy because... well... she wouldn't be unhappy any longer. She didn't know if he understood the first reason, the selfish reason. He'd always looked bleak (humans' eyes leaked when they were sad) when she told him how happy he would be without her. On the other hand, he nodded his head when she told him that she couldn't go on like that, imprisoned by the humans, a living larder for the enemy.

§ § §

She motioned for the little one to approach. He was nearby, the knife blade gleaming in the light. He had to do what he had practiced dozens of times, his small hands clasping the knife, his small body arching to pierce the darztl's thick skin. Except that this time they were using a real knife. But she was confident. The child had seen enough humans kill one another that he knew what to do.

Patiently, she told him where to hit, where he could pierce through the artery that would spill out her life. And how, just before she died, he had to help her turn over and plant the blade of the knife in the sand to make them believe she had acted alone. She was not quite sure they would swallow that, but all she wanted was for the child to be left in peace. That was why she had told him, over and over again, that he had to be strong and play out the scene. He had to run and shout, to warn the others. He couldn't say too much and he couldn't say it too clearly. She was counting on the fact that he was too insignificant in their eyes to be considered a viable suspect.

That was the best she could hope for. If everything went as planned, she wouldn't be there to reap the fruit of this ultimate outburst of her captive will. The act of an insect killed with its own stinger.

§ § §

The child lay next to her. They hadn't even bothered to pick him up. Weeks of work undone by this butchery that, for once, didn't solely target her.

She was prostrate, weak. She was bathing in a puddle of blood. Both darztl and human blood. The child had managed to make her blood flow, but he had not had time to strike the source of her life, her artery. The other humans had surprised him before he could and spilled the child's blood. To teach him once and for all not to play with the food, they killed him, just like that, with a well-placed blow when simply backhanding him aside would have been enough. When she felt him fall on her, she understood that the little one would never get back up, that he would never feel blows or hear her rough darztl voice again. She should have realized it. Meat was too precious a commodity for the nomadic humans. By making the little one an accomplice to her escape, she had condemned him. Even if he had managed to cast aside all suspicion, they might have killed him anyway, since they had to take their vengeance on someone. When she realized he was dead, she heard herself cry out, "No!" Not in her own language.

She hadn't been spared either. For once, they didn't have the patience to wait until her arm reached maturity. But she was already weak. She barely felt the long knife, the same one that had just killed the child, slice through her flesh, amputating her arm just below the shoulder.

§ § §

She didn't know how much time had passed. The sun was high in the sky. Its rays warmed her, preventing her from dying. She stayed there, still, immobilized, miserable, wondering what would become of her. Life, no doubt, would continue. This state of survival would persist. Forever, or until her regenerated body gave out. Or until she found a better solution. Nothing, apparently, had changed. The child was a negligible quantity, a grain of sand in the desert. Nothing had changed except that... except that they had learned she could speak their language. At least they had to have some rather strong suspicions. All it would take was for one human, a little more aware than the others, to decide to test her resistance and she would crack. Of course she would. She was drained, both physically and emotionally. They would make her talk. And once they had confirmed that she could speak their language, they would decide that that gave her an edge, an advantage over them. But the days when humans tortured darztls to draw out State secrets were long gone. These days were much simpler. There was no doubt about it. One of them would be creative enough, after first learning how to prepare her arms, her legs, her tail, to go on from there and, prepare them a little delicacy, after tearing out her tongue.

Desert Soul

To all those who dream,
who believe in utopia,
to all the optimists and
naïve people of this world.

Oh, give me that night divine.
And let my arms in yours entwine.
The desert song, calling.
It's voice enthralling.
Will make you mine.
Sigmund Romberg / Otto Harbach / Oscar Hammerstein II
From the operetta "The Desert Song" (1925)

The little human female tore off like a frightened animal when she saw me. She ran as fast as her puny legs could carry her. I walked toward her slowly and caught her quickly. From my seat on top of my haavl, she looked tiny. I dismounted. She ran a little farther off. I took a few steps toward her. She bent down and picked up some rocks that she threw at me in a futile effort to defend herself. She was red with fever and terror. In an effort not to hurt her with my large paws, I threw a net over her and gradually pulled it tight. She wriggled weakly, caught in the solid mesh, looking at me, eyes filled with fear as she tried to appear defiant. When I started to slip her into the bag, she swore at me, using all of the swear words she knew in human language, along with a few more in darztl. I closed the bag, stifling her cries. As gently as I could, I slung the bag across my shoulders and tied it to my haavl. Then I got back on my way.

The early afternoon sun tickled my skin deliciously. My job was a filthy one, but there were certain compensations: living a free life in the immense desert, the ability to choose when and where I worked, the solitude of being on my own. The haavl's gallop rocked me gently, putting me into a trance. The beast and I cut through the burning desert air at breakneck speed. Suddenly the animal's stride became rougher and the bag holding the human bounced brutally on its flanks. I heard a cry of pain and slowed my mount.

I stopped at dusk to make the most of the last rays of daylight to set up camp. I picked the hidclrs that would keep my fire burning all night and spread a tarp over the sand. Then I took the bag containing the human from my haavl and placed it carefully on the ground. I untied the ropes and took the female, who was still tangled in the net, out of it. She seemed even more pathetic than when I had found her, but when she saw me approach to free her, she tried to back away, visibly frightened. I picked up a chain and turned back to her. I untied the bottom of the net. She kicked her foot about in all directions, but I caught it easily and locked the chain to the manacle already around her ankle. I also took the opportunity to remove a cactus needle that had dug into the sole of her foot. She started to pull on her chain madly, arching as if to break it or topple me backwards. Finally, she tripped over the chain and collapsed.

"Be careful," I said. "You'll hurt yourself for no good reason."

She looked at me, surprised to hear me speak the slaves' language, then went back to struggling. I put the other end of the chain under a large rock she would never be able to move. Then I took a few steps back. As it grazed, my haavl approached the human, calming her. Obviously, she was even more frightened of the large beast than of me, and didn't dare make a move for fear of upsetting it or getting stepped on. It rummaged through the sand looking for forgotten roots. I led it a short distance away.

Carrying a jar of ointment, I once again walked over to the human, who stepped back as far as the chain would let her. I placed my foot over the metal links to hold her still, and told her to undress. Through the holes in her shredded suit, I could see that her skin was red. But the human merely glanced at me in terror. I mimed taking off her clothes. The young girl didn't trust me and probably thought I would beat her. She slipped her coveralls down.

Even though I was used to such sights, I was surprised by how thin she was. Her ribs showed through skin and her breasts barely peaked out of her chest. Either the master she had fled from did not feed her enough or she had been wandering in the desert for days. As I lifted her damp, tangled hair off her reddened back, I noticed tracks on her skin. No more numerous than what I had seen on backs of other humans I had intercepted, but nevertheless recent. This young girl's life was certainly similar to that of hundreds of darztl slaves. At the lower end of her back was a scar, a brand, like those found on more and more humans, indicating who she belonged to. She couldn't have been more than thirteen or fourteen marsian years old, and yet the marks on her stomach indicated that she had already been a mother. I applied some of my ointment to her back, hoping that the cooling effect would calm the fire on her skin, and told her to get dressed. Then I broke the lock of the rings she wore on her wrists and ankles, leaving only the one tied to the chain.

I dug through my bags and took out food for a meal. I had some hiistml meat, which had been seasoned and dried, and heated it over the fire. As the food warmed, I nibbled on raw meat and some vegetables. Then, realizing that the human must be parched, I gave her some water. She grabbed the gourd, looking at it suspiciously, then swallowed it so greedily I had to tear the container out of her hands to keep her from making herself sick. Once the meat was heated through, I gave her some. She took it with the same air of distrust and dug into it. I wondered how long it had been since she'd had anything to eat or drink.

"What's your name?" I asked her.

The human looked at me, but said nothing.

"My name is Miekl. Don't be afraid, I won't hurt you."

The human remained silent, fiddling with a lock of hair as she stared at me. Suddenly, she cast a frightened glance behind me. As I turned around, I saw a darztl approaching, riding a haavl. I had been paying too much attention to the human and had not heard him coming.

"Good evening," he said. "And good hunting."

I nodded politely.

He continued, "Can this darztl spend the evening with the stranger? The desert air is cold."

The color of my wattle showed that he was welcome. He sat down and I offered him something to eat.

At the end of the meal, he stood up and walked over to the human, who had remained motionless the entire time, glancing at us in fear.

"Not bad," he said. "She'll be worth a fortune on the market. Unless her previous owners want her back."

"Is this darztl's guest a human hunter?" I asked, in an effort to find out what I was dealing with.

"By times, yes. But it's unpleasant work so he takes time out between hunts. This evening, he's just out for some fresh air."

That meant that if I was in his territory he wasn't worried about it for the time being.

He nudged the human with his foot.

"Fortunately, humans aren't very clever, which makes hunting easy."

I nodded. He moved his face closer to the human, who retreated to the end of her chain. The darztl's wattle turned a cheerful green.

"And they're so easy to frighten."

He poked at her with the pick he had used for dinner. The young girl tried unsuccessfully to get away.

"They can even be entertaining! As for the rest..."

He whipped the human with his tail, throwing her into the sand, where she moaned in pain.

"... as for the rest, they just need a little discipline."

I leaped up.

"The darztl shouldn't hurt the human for no good reason. It's cruel."

He glanced at me, startled, then back at the human. "Of course not. They're used to it," he said, as he kicked her. "That's the only way darztls can make these stupid animals understand. And they're not like darztls — they don't feel pain as deeply."

I stepped between them. "This darztl said no. The human should not be hurt."

His wattle turned a dumbfounded shade. "This human hunter can't have been plying his trade for long. Otherwise he would be more used to it."

Then his color turned an amused, perplexed shade. "Ah, this darztl understands...."

He returned to his place and started to pick up his belongings. I looked at him, astonished. He placed his belongings on his haavl.

"Well, well. The host will excuse this darztl, but he feels it would be more judicious to be back on his way. He will leave the stranger alone with the little slave."

He rode off, leaving me dumbfounded.

"Thank you," the human said weakly.

She had spoken in darztl. *Tzliendty* was always the first word taught to humans. But that was the only word I managed to worm out of her that evening. The next day, not far from the camp I'd just left, I noticed the remnants of a recent camp. The darztl I had met the previous evening must have decided it would be better to spend the night away from the company of the pervert he thought I was.

The next evening, the human looked less frightened when I took her out of her bag. That uncomfortable means of transportation was necessary if I wanted to go unnoticed. This way, if I came across any other hunters, I could account for the human's presence and my behavior would raise fewer suspicions. The young girl shook herself and stretched, then allowed me to apply the ointment to her sunburn. Then she docilely sat down in the sand and waited for me to decide her fate.

She was pitiful. I almost felt like taking her in my arms and rocking her. I could read so much fear in her nervous body, so much unexpressed disgust. I would have liked to tell her not to be afraid of me, to explain to her that I was not taking her back to the masters, but I had to remain quiet her protection. And for my own as well. Now if we ran into a group of darztls that might claim her or, worse yet, a bunch of humans who would take her from me, she wouldn't know anything compromising. I'd already lost one slave to a band of humans and, as I had galloped off on my haavl, I had taken great joy in my discretion.

"Marie," the human said.

I jumped and turned to look at her. She had just finished devouring her rations for the evening.

"My master called me Armiiltd, but my real name is Marie. The master can choose whatever name he pleases."

I smiled, but she didn't seem able to decode my expression. I didn't reply right away, fearing that I might alarm her again.

"You're nicer than the others," she finally said.

"The others weren't gentle with you?" I asked stupidly, knowing full well what her answer would be. The human shrugged.

"Not any less so than with the others."

She sat in silence and I didn't dare ask her any more ridiculous questions.

The night before, she had stayed in her corner, shivering, her only protection against the desert dew was the blanket I had given her. This second evening, she slowly moved closer to the fire, dragging her chain behind her. I watched her from the corner of my eye.

She spoke very quickly, as if afraid I would interrupt. "If you don't want them to hurt me, don't take me back to where I come from. They'll beat me for sure, probably hard enough to kill me." She lowered her head as if ashamed.

I finally broke my silence. "Listen, Marie, I can't tell you where I'm taking you, but I can assure you that no one there will hurt you. If everything goes as I hope, no one will ever hurt you again."

She seemed to think about what I had just said and concluded it was good news, since she dropped her guard another degree. I said nothing more. When I looked back at her again, she was asleep, apparently trusting me. She

made me think of a little pet I was training. I did everything possible to chase that impression away, but it was
the only analogy that came to mind when I saw her curled
up in a ball next to the fire, reassured by the simple idea
that, for that evening at least, she would not be beaten.

And that was heartbreaking.

The next morning, she slipped into the bag on her own
and patiently waited for me to close it. I would have liked
to allow her to breathe a little, but I couldn't allow her to
see where we were headed.

The third day passed and I met no living being. And
saw no haavl tracks or tire tracks to indicate that someone had been that way recently. I trotted gently on my
mount, not too quickly so as to spare the human. It was
a beautiful day, the sky turquoise, a burning wind whipping my face. I felt good.

That evening, when I took the human out of the bag,
she indicated that I was to sit down. As I lounged in the
last rays of light, she arranged everything, as if she had
always been doing that. She lit a fire, prepared our meals,
spread tarps on the ground and told me to sit down. I let
her be, torn between pleasure at seeing her so enthusiastic
and guilt at knowing that she was serving me. But when
she sat down behind me to massage my crest, I grabbed
her wrists.

"No, don't do that."

She stepped back as if I had frightened her or as if... I
had insulted her.

"Master Miekl doesn't like what I'm doing?" she asked.

I was uncomfortable. I didn't how to answer her without
hurting her feelings.

"I don't like you to do that. You are not to do that."

"Master Hisstdl liked it."

"That was your master?"

"Before. But not at the end. He's not the one I escaped
from."

She closed in on herself as if afraid that she had revealed
too much by telling me that she had escaped. As if I would
have believed for a single moment that she had just been
strolling about the desert when I found her!

Finally she added, "Master Hisstdl left without taking me. He was replaced by new masters and I escaped."

"The new masters were the ones who beat you?" I took a chance on asking.

"Yes. Master Hisstdl corrected me sometimes, as well, when I did something stupid." She looked up at me and said, "I often do stupid things, you know, Master. But the new masters beat me for nothing at all. So I ran away."

Now that the word had been uttered she seemed to enjoy telling the world out loud that she had escaped.

"But you're nice to me, so I won't leave."

Her last words appeared to frighten her and she added, "Oh, that doesn't mean I'll leave if you aren't nice. You're entitled to be nice or not and decide what is nice or isn't. I'll be a good girl and do everything you want!"

She knelt down before me and took on an innocent air, but the speed with which the ideas seemed to take shape in her mind indicated that she wasn't as stupid as she was trying to look. Looking stupid meant a long life for a slave, from what I understood. Those who played dumb were always beaten less than those who looked intelligent.

We sat down to supper. Marie moved as if to serve me, but I indicated that I was all right and she could eat while I did.

"That mark on your back," I asked her while I chewed a piece of raw meat, "did your last masters put that there?"

"Yes. Everyone had one. As soon as we arrived there, they branded us. You know, it doesn't hurt at all."

Of course not, I thought. They press a piece of white hot iron against your skin and it doesn't hurt at all. Then they do it again to perfect the design, and you don't feel a thing. Not you.

"What did you do in the house of these new masters?" I asked, simply to keep the conversation going.

"It wasn't a house. It was a large building where we made things for darztls. Mostly clothing, but also other objects from fabric. It was detailed work. I had never done anything like that for my old master, so they beat me at the beginning. Then I got better at it. But then the masters would beat me again because they said that wanted me to continue being good. That's why I didn't like being there as much as I did with my old master. Especially after the baby."

She stopped then and went to check the fire. When she came back toward me, she didn't start talking again. Seeing that she was making a great effort to look very tired, I asked her if she wanted to go to sleep.

The next evening, I stopped earlier than the previous ones. It was our last evening on our own. The next day we would reach the village, and then there would be no more time for confidences.

I indicated that Marie should remain sitting while I set up camp. She looked upset, but obeyed without a word. As I worked, she started the conversation as abruptly as she had the other evenings, as if continuing a discussion interrupted the night before.

"They took him away from me," she said.

I immediately knew who she meant by 'him'. I turned toward her, but she looked away.

"It's not that I want to criticize or anything, but you masters are very odd. You tell us to be good humans and make lots of babies, but when they come you don't want them. Yet I accepted the male the new masters gave me. I let him have his way without saying a word. The male wasn't so bad. He smelled a little because he didn't work in the factory like I did, but I let him make me a baby. And it was a healthy baby. And then the masters saw that it was a boy and they took him away. I don't know if they killed him or just took him to some special place for boys, but I never saw him again. So I didn't want to stay with those masters. I don't think Master Hisstdl would ever have done anything like that."

I sat down near her, unable to eat after listening to a story like that. Marie stared off into the distance.

She continued, her tone almost bland, "Do you know what the worst punishment I ever received was? A master tied my wrists and ankles together and then placed my arms under my knees. Like this."

She showed me what she meant.

"And then the master placed a stick there, in the space between the fold in my arms and legs."

She held that pose, like a good little girl sitting down, legs closed, holding her elbows. A slave immobilized in the position of the good little girl.

And she continued, in the same bland tone, "If you try, you'll see that it will keep me perfectly still. Except for my head, of course. In that position darztls can beat a human and she can't defend herself or ward off the blows. The slave is totally at the master's mercy. He can lift her up, like a parcel, if he finds places on her body that haven't been beaten enough. Or he can keep on hitting in the same spot over and over, without any fear that she will move. He can drop her roughly to the ground, as well, or drag her along it. Or he can leave her there a long time and she won't be able to get away. And he can come back and hit her whenever he wants to. Or tell her that it will be over soon and then start beating her again. If she cries or begs too much, he can put a rag in her mouth, or he can take pleasure in making her cry out even louder, varying the intensity of his blows. That can go on for several days. He can use a stick, a whip, a chain or any other available object. Several of them can beat her, taking turns. Soon enough, they don't even have to beat her at all. They can just revive the pain of her existing injuries. If it's cold in the cave where they keep her, she'll feel even colder than usual because she can't move. The master can give her a little water, to make sure she doesn't die, and he can give her a little food, but he has to feed her himself because she can't lift food to her mouth. Maybe she refuses to eat because it hurts too much and then he forces her to swallow the broth. And when he finally unties her, he can continue to beat her and she won't stir, because her arms and legs have gone numb. He can also—"

"Stop!" I shouted, putting down my untouched plate.

"He can also call her lazy, once she's there, untied, at his feet, and beat her to make her—"

"Shut up!" I shouted, louder than I had planned, whipping the ground with my tail. She looked frightened and fell silent for a moment, to my utter relief since I couldn't bear another second of her tale.

When she started to talk again, her voice sounded completely dead, "Well, when the masters took my baby away, it was 100 times worse than the punishment they gave me after I struck the master who had taken him."

§ § §

Marie was born when the colony was still a colony. She lived in the protected human enclave, in the oasis their machinery worked to expand day after day. At the time of her birth, people were less afraid of the darztls. They had stopped raiding the fringes of the base camp and the terraforming process continued as planned. The children were all taught this in history and science at the school.

She was a little girl even though, during the time of the colony, that didn't make much difference. In fact, in the base camp there was no real social difference between the genders. Everyone was taught skills in keeping with their talents, and not because they belonged to one gender or another. As for reproduction, it could happen naturally, of course, but often gestation continued in vitro, making each birth something that belonged to neither men nor women. That is how the biology textbooks she used at school discussed the process.

At that time, all humans still remembered Earth. Most spoke about it nostalgically, although they had never really seen it close up. A large majority of the colonists had been born on Mars II. And yet not a day went by without you hearing someone complain about the sun, the sand, the heat, the dreary life in the colony. She and the other children learned to convert Mars years into Earth years. They were taught the names of important people back on Earth. They were never taught to speak the language of the natives, the barbarians who would one day be civilized.

She lived like that for twelve years, in a sort of bubble in the middle of a planet where her kind had imposed their will. About fifty local years earlier, humans from Earth had made an emergency landing on this world and they wound up staying. Never, however, did they ever speak about an aborted mission, a ruined landing, an alternative solution. Those in her community learned to view themselves as pioneers who had fulfilled the glorious mission they had taken on when they left Earth (when her parents' parents took off) and spent each day fighting to tame a hostile planet. Never were they described as usurpers who would lead the indigenous species on the planet to a slow death.

§ § §

By the time the master let her out of the bag, she had already been aware of a general hubbub for a few minutes, like that in a darztl community or slave quarters. When she finally emerged, she found herself in a large village swarming with people. It looked like the village near the factory where she had worked. She had walked through that town briefly on the day she had been sold, and she'd been able to see all the activity through the wire mesh. Master Hisstdl had never taken her into the city. He didn't let her out much either, so everything she saw was new to her. But this village was very different from the town she had seen before. Here humans strolled about, completely free, nodding and waving at the darztls they encountered.

They were at the entrance of the small town. The new master turned his haavl over to another darztl and he grabbed the halter as if that task was not reserved solely for human stable hands. Then Master Miekl motioned for Marie to follow him. Trotting in his wake, she saw that all eyes turned toward them as they moved past. Master Miekl waved cheerfully at darztls and humans alike. This was truly a strange place.

He took her to a building that was larger than the others. Marie hoped that it wouldn't be another factory. But when they entered it, she noticed that it was too clean to be a factory, much cleaner even than Master Hisstdl's house. The new master took her into a well-lit room and instructed her to sit down. He said that he would be back soon, but her old master had said that he would come back to the factory to get her and never did. She was filled with anguish, but tried to hide it. She sat down and waited, forcing all thoughts from her mind. Often, when you think of nothing, the masters believe you really are thinking about nothing.

A human in white overalls approached. Marie was disappointed. She would have felt more important if a darztl had come to collect her, even if it was only to take her to work. The human, who said her name was Lukden, looked nice anyway. She told Marie that she was going to examine her to make sure everything was all right. Then she inspected Marie's ears, the inside of her mouth, the whites of her eyes. Marie allowed her to continue despite being upset by having to obey a human. In the factory, the human guards were always the worst. They saw everything and betrayed your deepest secrets to the masters. So Marie did everything the female human told her to. Even when that meant climbing in a strange tub of water that the white-clothed female told her was for washing.

The human, Lukden, then allowed her to choose clothing from a variety of items. Some came in parts; some had legs. Marie chose coveralls that were most similar to what she was used to and pulled on an outfit that was more beautiful than anything she had ever worn before. Wearing her new clothes, Marie felt good. The human suggested that she cut Marie's hair. Marie agreed. That would remind her of the time when she lived with Master Hisstdl. He always kept her hair very short, telling her that this made her less ugly and look almost as clean as a little darztl. Yet the entire time she had spent in the plant, no one had ever worried about her hair and now it was just a mass of tangles and knots, like the skeins of thread she had to collect and untangle each evening after working in the plant.

Finally, Master Miekl came back. He told Marie that he would show her where she was to live, but that he would first show her his house in case she needed him. His house was good and she felt comfortable there. The late afternoon sun entered through the skylight, painting the entire room with pink light. She wanted to spend the rest of her life there. But they left it immediately and walked through the village. For the first time Marie noticed that the town was surrounded by a long wall that rose high into the sky, as if it were in a tub. There was no roof, but the village was literally encircled by a rocky wall. That must be for keeping the humans in.

They walked over to a house that was larger than the others. Miekl knocked at the door. A female darztl answered. She was gigantic. Marie hunkered down in an effort to become invisible. But the darztl was not angry. Marie could tell by the color of her wattle. Miekl said that she was a friend of his and that Marie should not be afraid. She motioned them in and told Marie, using human language, that her name was Mirntl. She told Marie that she would show the girl to her room. They walked into a corridor, and through half-open doors Marie saw rooms that looked like the masters' bedrooms. The female darztl opened one of the doors and told Marie that it was her room. Inside, there was something that looked like a master's bed, along with other furniture. She wondered how many would have to sleep there, or if a master would sleep on the bed. But she was too afraid to ask.

Miekl finally took his leave and the female darztl asked Marie if she was hungry. She took her to a room with an enormous table. Humans and masters were already sitting there, much too Marie's surprise. Where she came from humans were never allowed to sit at a table, particularly if darztls were already seated there. She had always been fed on the ground, after the master had completed his meal. The female darztl took her over to a sort of chair and told her to sit down. She went along with that, fully expecting to be kicked out of the seat at any moment. But the entire meal was completed and no one bothered her. The food was good and she made the most of her time by eating as much as she could. Some people asked her questions, but seeing that she was too overwhelmed to answer, they let her be.

After the meal, everyone else got up, but Marie stayed there, not knowing where to go. No one told her what she was supposed to do then. A female human came over to her and tapped her on the shoulder. She told her that after the meal there was a recess — Marie didn't really understand what the word meant — and that she was free to come and go as she wanted in the house and meet the other residents. Never before had Marie had access to so much space at a single time. Master Hisstdl's house had only one large room, and just a small corner of it was accessible to Marie, except when she did her chores. During the daytime, she had never crossed the border that marked off the space allotted to her or she was shut up until the master trusted her again. At night, she had slept in an alcove behind a wire enclosure. It was true that the factory had been large, but her chains had restricted her movements. And at night the workers had been locked in the cellar.

She strolled about the house a bit. The others had gathered in a common room or in their bedrooms, humans and darztls mingling. When she walked past them, several of them smiled at her. But she merely lowered her head and rushed off in the opposite direction. She decided to hide in the room where they told her she would sleep. There was no one else there. She didn't know if she was to sleep in the bed with other humans or if she would have to sleep in a corner and leave the bed for a master. Finally she lay down on a small rug on the floor. She felt as if she would never manage to fall asleep, and yet sleep took her quickly.

In the middle of the night, she woke up, startled. She looked around and noticed that she was alone. She felt ill at ease, uncomfortable. But she recalled that she was not in the factory basement. Here, the floor was warm. She didn't have to snuggle up to other humans to get warm enough to fall asleep.

§ § §

She was twelve years old when the darztls decided to terminate the humans' project. Her people had been living on Mars II for over fifty years and had almost managed to forget the danger. In the anthropology courses at school they taught the children that the natives were a solitary, apathetic species, unfamiliar with the art of war, and not highly developed, either. Well, their surprise attack on the colony demonstrated that they could learn quickly when they needed to.

The morning they struck, she was at school with the other children. A rumor raced around the school, then the teacher received an emergency call. When they heard shouting, the children knew something was wrong. The teacher hung up, then told them, his voice bleak, that the darztls were on the verge of attacking. The humans would make quick work of them but, in the meantime, the children should go home and take shelter. All of the children at school — about two hundred in all — went outside in a relatively orderly manner, under the watchful eyes of the teachers who tried to look calm. But, once they were outside, they realized that it was total chaos in the colony.

There was nowhere to hide. The teachers had sent the children home because they didn't know where else to tell them to go. The school was a large, flat box with no basement. All the camp barracks were bolted to one another to make small dwelling units, and installed directly on the ground, thrown together hastily with materials from the mother ship. They were temporary shelters, intended to be replaced by dwellings built with local materials. But there were so few resources in the desert of Mars II that they had transformed them into permanent constructions — at least until their terraforming of the planet was completed.

She ran home, but found no one there. Her parents worked in the mother ship, in the administrative quarters. Since they weren't high ranking, they couldn't live there and had to make do with a stifling little shack in the middle of the colony. They were certainly on board at the time of the attack and she thought they must be sick with worry about her. Yet she was too afraid to go into the streets to join them.

§ § §

When I wasn't hunting humans, I was, like everyone else, assigned to various chores in the village. My specialization was biological research, but that didn't exempt me from the more menial chores. One of the greatest challenges faced by our community was keeping the new arrivals busy without neglecting the rest of the group. The most serious challenge, of course, was protecting the village. The darztls, for obvious reasons, were assigned to this duty on a priority basis. That week, however, I asked if I could take care of the new arrival. There was something about her... I didn't quite know what... that was quite touching. I wanted to keep an eye on her progress. And I had already established a contact with her, which was something no one else had managed to do, even after a few days.

I have to admit that, the second night, when I woke up, I found her sleeping at the foot of my bed. She had come into my home without making a sound — which wasn't all that difficult since no one ever locked their doors in the village — and slipped into my room. My dwelling wasn't very large and I had no room for a guest. I think she would have willingly agreed to spend all of her nights on the floor, but I couldn't agree to that, of course. And letting her spend her nights in my bed was even less acceptable. I had no intention of mixing things up. I shook her gently and she looked at me, still half asleep.

"I'll take you back to the rooming house," I told her.

"No, Master," she replied. "Let me stay here. Rhtizliendt!" *Rhtizliendt* means *please* — the second most important word in a slave's vocabulary.

I protested. "But I have no room for you!"

"I can sleep anywhere, anywhere at all. I'm used to making myself small. Rhtizliendt, Master."

She knelt at my feet, head bowed.

"Marie, I'm not your master. You don't have a master here," I said as I helped her up. "Listen," I said, hoping to reassure her, " I'm going to take you back to your room, but we can spend some time together tomorrow. They told me you didn't leave the boarding house today. So tomorrow, if you want, I'll take you on a tour of the village. Now, come with me."

I stood up. I realized full well that she would have preferred to stay, but was afraid of making an issue out of it. She allowed me to accompany her back without a word. I told her that I'd stay with her until she fell asleep. She wanted to lie down on the floor, but I encouraged her to use the bed, telling her that it belonged to her. Docilely, she did as I wished.

"The master must think I'm stupid," she finally said, her voice slowed by sleep. "But I'm not used to sleeping alone in a place that's so beautiful and warm." Her words faded into a sleepy murmur. I stayed there, watching her as she slept, then went home.

Over the next few days, I toured our village with her. Even though our community was growing at the speed of light, it still wouldn't have taken us long to complete our rounds, so I showed her everything in great detail. The municipal building where our elected officials met, the solar panels we had built to replace the methane generators, the library with the meager collection we had managed to salvage from the ruined colony, the spring under the mountain that provided us with water that was drinkable despite its unpleasant taste. I showed her everything except, of course, our laboratory. I decided to keep that for later when I was certain we could trust her. I also introduced her to as many people as possible to help her fit into our community as quickly as possible, but she continued to cling to me, replying only in monosyllables.

After five days, I had to get back to work. The village could not allow any member in full possession of his faculties to wallow in idleness. I had to return to the laboratory and do my community work, before setting out into the desert on another tour. That was my life.

Since I thought it might be good for Marie to have some responsibilities, I asked her what she wanted to do.

"Anything you want, Master."

Ignoring the title she stubbornly insisted on using, I told her that in our community people chose their own occupations, and that they could change jobs whenever they wanted to. She said nothing. I asked her what she knew how to do.

"Everything, Master, I can do everything."

I asked her if she wanted to handle maintenance, and she said she did. I asked her if she wanted work that required attention to detail, and she agreed. I asked her if she wanted to work in the kitchens, and she agreed yet again. Although she didn't know how to read, I believe that if I had asked her if she wanted to work in the archives she would have gone along with it. So I took her to our school, gave her a brush and a bucket and asked her if she wanted to clean the classroom. She seemed surprised about having to clean with water, but she set to work without complaining. When I left, she was smiling as she washed the floor.

Later that day, during a break, I returned to see how she was getting along. I had to order her to stop or she probably would have washed the entire village before nightfall.

"Am I cleaning the way the Master wants me to? Master Hisstdl liked everything in his house to be very clean."

"You were your master's only slave, weren't you?"

"Yes, so I had to work very hard to make sure everything was perfect."

"Well, here several people do the work and you have to leave some for the others," I said, laughing.

Marie started to laugh as well. "Not you, Master. You don't wash floors."

I sighed. I wondered how long it would take to deprogram her. She was silent then, in the abrupt way that was characteristic of her, before she suddenly said in a dreamy voice, "I cleaned everywhere and then I wasn't allowed to go anywhere because the master said I'd get it dirty."

Then her mood brightened as quickly as it had turned dark. "Do you want me to clean your house, Master? Then I could clean you, too."

I shook my head.

This human was a mystery to me. Of course I'd seen former slaves before who had been completely obsessed by their former status, incapable of interpreting the world other than through the framework that had been imposed on them from birth. Most of the humans I'd rescued from the desert had been in bad shape, torn between their impression that there had to be something more than a life spent in servitude and the image of themselves that had been forged by the lash. Several had been beaten, locked up, abused beyond all belief. Others had psychological damage that was just as severe. And yet those who managed to escape were among the strongest, those whom the darztls had not beaten to death or mutilated beyond repair. As a general rule, we asked them no direct questions and waited for them to tell us their tales. We encouraged them to confide in our psychologist, but they were never forced. Some were very vocal and disclosed everything on the first day. Others remained closed for a long time, and some never revealed their pasts. Those who had agreed to speak told us that the most difficult part of a slave's life was totally abandoning their free will to another, although this made life easier. They no longer asked questions, they obeyed, and were grateful to get through a day without a beating. Curiously, the humans who had always worked in teams of slaves in one darztl factory or another were better off, psychologically speaking. They were abused more frequently, but they retained a sense of belonging to their own species. It was the others, those like Marie, who had lived alone a long time, isolated in the darztl world, who were more difficult to reach.

Marie spoke to no one but me. She replied to the other darztls, of course; she would have been too frightened of incurring their wrath otherwise. Yet I was the centre of the world for her. That made me uncomfortable and I could no longer think straight about it.

"You know, Master, if I do something you don't like, you can correct me. That will help me learn and it won't really hurt me."

I took her back to the boarding house after making her promise she wouldn't clean anything else that day.

In the days that followed, I continued to provide support for Marie. She seemed to accept instructions only from me

and she obeyed everything I asked. I would give her a
schedule for the day and come back in the afternoon to
make sure she wasn't killing herself at work.

§   §   §

*She hid in the house. In the distance, she heard a deaf-
ening din, the sound of thousands of haavls running on
the desert sand, thousands of sets of armor clanking. She
heard explosions, as well, but the noise of the war was
moving closer to the center of the colony. She risked a glance
outside and saw people running for their lives. She'd
already seen darztls, beaten or in no condition to hurt
anyone, dragged through the city under the curious eyes
of passersby. But now she felt as if she were truly seeing
darztls for the first time in her life, sitting enormous on
their monstrous mounts, lashing out every which way.
The humans fought as well as they could but, since no one
in the colony was equipped for anything more than hunting, they didn't cause too much damage to the enemy. The
security team, which was better armed, was not up to the
task. The natives were too numerous. All too soon, darztls
swarmed over the base camp.*

*She heard a rumble. The ground shook, the air turned
even hotter than usual. Then, hugging a wall near a window, she saw the mother ship rise into the sky, abandoning
them, her parents on board the mother ship, leaving her
behind. At that point, she felt truly overwhelmed. She was
twelve years old and all alone on a hostile planet. She
realized that she would have to take care of herself from
then on.*

*She knew that if she stayed in the house the darztls
would find her soon enough. Making the most of the dis-
array caused by the ship taking off, she went out the back
door of her home. Behind the group of dwellings where
her family lived, there was a dip in the ground of rock and
sand. Pilings held the house in place but, along with some
of her friends, she had discovered that by digging a little
they could slip under the houses. When the adults had
discovered their makeshift cave, they had been angry, saying*

that the children would suffocate if the soft ground shifted. They had closed up the opening and forbidden them to play there, but she knew she only had to remove a few rocks and she could hide there. Hoping that no one would see her, and working as quickly and discretely as possible, she made an entrance under the house. She wriggled into it and pulled a rock behind her to hide the opening.

§ § §

Yet again, the master showed Marie the village today. People here lived closer to one another than the darztls she knew. What was strange as well was that certain humans lived alone in their houses, with no masters to watch over them, and that certain darztls had no slaves to serve them. At the boarding house, she was still waiting for the darztls living in the rooms near hers to give her orders, but they paid no attention to her other than to greet her as they passed.

She was not used to sleeping alone in that room. At the beginning she had tried leaving the door open, imagining that a master was nearby, supervising her, but a human guard had come to tell her that she could have a little more privacy here. And she closed the door. Marie was afraid to disobey and stayed alone within the four walls, in a room that was not too cold, on a bed that was not too hard.

Whenever they had taken her to the factory it was evening, so they didn't put her to work right away. She had been sent down into a cave with the others. That was the first time since the master had bought her — so long ago — that she could recall being surrounded by so many humans. But the hard ground was familiar and they had to cling together for a little warmth.

She had never been so confused as she was in the village. Master Hisstdl and the other masters were harsh, but their orders were clear. She had always known what she had to do. And when she didn't have any more work, it was time to sleep. Not for long. Never for long enough, since she had to start all over again the next morning.

Here, everything was different. There wasn't enough work to do, and too much time for thinking. She couldn't spend the entire time sleeping! Master Miekl had told her that they would start teaching her to read soon and that reading was a very interesting way to pass the time.

She understood what he meant. Master Hisstdl had often sat down in the sun to read, telling her to work hard while he was out. During the evening, he also sat next to the fire, reading, while she finished her chores. One day, the master went out without saying anything. He failed to secure the fence to the alcove where he always kept her locked up. She had never dared touch a book when her master was there, but strangely enough, instead of trying to escape that time, the first thing she did when she realized she was free to come and go in the house was to open one of the large volumes that filled the bookshelves. She didn't understand anything that was written, of course, but there were images. She turned the pages, fascinated by everything she discovered. There were portraits of darztls involved in all kinds of activities. Some images were stylized versions of reality but others were surprisingly real, as if the book had managed to capture everything the eye saw. One of the images showed an immense darztl on a desert backdrop, looking proud, armed to the teeth and mounted on a monstrous haavl, surrounded by bones. That picture could tell all kinds of stories. She decided that it had to be one of those mythic slave hunters who people said ate their captures raw.

As she looked through the book, she lost all track of time and Master Hisstdl surprised her in that position. He was terribly angry when he came in and this was one of the times he beat her especially fiercely. He grabbed both her arms in his powerful arms and shook her every which way, asking her what had come over her. Then he threw her in a corner of the room and moved toward her, gigantic and frightening, telling her that he would make her understand she must never touch books. She cried, she wept, saying that she would never do it again, but that did not calm the master's anger. He took a strip of leather and whipped her until she fainted. When she woke in her alcove, her entire body hurt. The master brought her a little water and some food and applied an ointment to her wounds. He bent down near her and spoke to her gently. He explained that he had beaten her for her own good. Humans should not touch books. They didn't understand books and books were bad for them. He made her swear that she would never touch his books again. She promised, in a weak, frightened voice. When the master finally let her out of her alcove, she noticed that all of the books had been placed out of her reach, on the highest shelves.

A few days ago, Master Miekl had taken her to visit a house filled with books and told her they contained valuable knowledge. She wondered if everyone in the village, darztls and humans alike, hadn't gone a little crazy from reading all the books.... Then she decided that she must be crazy to judge a master's behavior so.

There were so many protocols she didn't understand here. Like the right to speak. At Master Hisstdl's house, the rules were clear. She never spoke unless ordered to do so, and she had to be brief when replying in darztl. When she had a specific request to make, she always had to expect that the master would refuse to listen to her, would not respond or, most often, would tell her to shut up and get back to work. In the village, on the other hand, she was expected to talk a lot, often, and about everything.

Yesterday, Master Miekl had taken her to see a human she had never encountered in the village. Master Miekl had left, but this time she was almost certain he would come back for her. The human had her sit down and asked her if there was anything special she wanted to say. She asked him what he wanted to know.

"I don't know," he replied. "That depends on what you want to tell me. I know that you've had a difficult life. Maybe you've never had an opportunity to speak openly with anyone. So we're going to see one another several times to give you a chance to decide if you have anything you want to tell me. If you decide you don't, we'll leave it there. So maybe you could tell me a little about yourself?"

Marie was uncomfortable about having to speak to a human. Not that she would have been any more at ease speaking to a darztl. Often they asked you to speak and then what you said angered them and they told you to shut up. But she had never spoken much with humans. Of course, during the first few weeks she had spent in the factory, she had had to relearn how to speak human on a daily basis. With Master Hisstdl, she hadn't had much opportunity to meet other humans, except when she had come into contact with other slaves or when her master's friends had come visiting with their humans. Yet there was always so much work to do that there wasn't much time for talking, especially since the master didn't like human babbling.

The human insisted on asking her questions for a certain time, questions to which Marie gave the briefest of answers, which the other constantly used to start up again. Finally, he told her that the session was over and invited her to come back.

One day, Marie had nothing more to do. Master Miekl took her to a large kitchen where another master set her to work peeling vegetables, but she worked too fast. When he saw that she was finished, the darztl told her she could leave. She wanted to keep working, but the other would have none of it and gently dismissed her. And then she found herself wandering aimlessly around the village. She could have gone back to the boarding house as she did other days, but Mirntl, who seemed to run the establishment, had told her to stop doing that, to take more time and explore her new adoptive home. So Marie was afraid to return to her room.

She walked around the village, passing behind the house, getting as close as she could to the rocky wall, to avoid as many people as possible. Her wandering finally took her to where the haavls were kept. Through an opening, she noticed that, like in the masters' houses, the huge beasts were kept in large enclosures, in a vast stone building where the roof was left open at all times so the animals could make the most of the sun's heat. The immense her-

bivores were rooting through the sand, placidly searching for the food hidden there just for them.

Marie had always been fascinated by the haavls. The
day when Master Miekl had caught her, she had pretended
to be frightened by the immense animal, since it was always a good idea to look frightened when a master was
around. Besides, since the masters weren't too fond of the
idea that slaves could escape, they loved to see humans
who were frightened of haavls — except for those who took
care of the livestock, of course, but they were kept under
close watch. But in actual fact, she had already been close
to these beasts, and noted that, contrary to what people
said, they weren't any more dangerous for humans than
for a darztl. That was the time that Master Hisstld had gone
on a long trip to a sort of farm in the middle of the desert.
Since the trip was to take a lengthy amount of time, he had
taken her with him, carrying her in a bag on his haavl as
he did whenever he took long trips with her. At the farm,
she had joined the team of slaves and, instead of sleeping in her master's room, she had spent the nights with
the others, in a small shack adjoining the stable. On the
farm, they didn't worry too much about locking up the
slaves because they were too isolated, too deep in darztl
territory for any human to be able to escape the masters'
attention. One morning, when everyone was still sleeping, she had managed to slip into the immense building
and watch the large reptiles. They had looked harmless
enough and she had slowly walked over to one of them.
He'd moved over to sniff at the air near her hand, then went
back to grazing as if nothing had happened. Every morning
after that she went to see the enormous beasts, even getting
her nerve up to touch them. One day, a master got up earlier
than usual and gave her a few excellent reasons not to try
that again.

"You like haavls?" said a voice behind here, shaking
her from her memory.

Marie leaped about and saw a large darztl. She started
to back up, uncertain of what lay in store for her.

"Don't be afraid. I'm not angry."

Marie was on the verge of running off but the darztl
said, "Wait!" and Marie froze, used to obeying orders.

"Would you like to see them up close?" the master asked.

Marie nodded, both because she didn't want to anger
the master and because she really did want to get close to
the animals.

"Come."

Marie docilely followed the master.

§ § §

*Trembling, she waited there a long time, a very long
time, knowing nothing about what was going on in the
colony, but too frightened to leave her hiding place to find
out. At one point, she heard an enormous hubbub overhead
and decided that the darztls were exploring the living
quarters. She heard less and less noise, but that didn't mean
there were no darztls lurking about. Judging from the bluish
light that filtered through the cracks between the rocks,
she knew that night was approaching. She was thirsty,
she was hungry, but she decided it would be better to stay
hidden for the night.*

*The next morning, there was still a ruckus outside and
she resolved to stay hidden for a while longer. Then suddenly, a deadly silence invaded the human camp. When
she finally dared to go out, everything was deserted. Hiding
behind the demolished barracks, she toured the colony.
When she reached the entrance to the town, she saw a cloud
of dust off in the distance. The enemy was riding off. She
threw herself down on the ground, afraid that she would
be seen.*

*She returned to what was left of her home. Obviously,
the darztls had made a serious attack on the human buildings, reducing everything that had fallen underfoot to a
shambles. All that remained was a pile of scrap metal. All
that could be seen where the mother ship had stood was
a black circle that faded at the edges. Some of the buildings that had been located too close to the mother ship had
melted from the blast. Carbonized bodies lay in the ashes.
The entire colony smelled of dust and smoke. She walked*

on, taking care not to cut herself on the shattered metal. There wasn't a single living being; she felt entirely alone in the world. She was the only living being there anyway, since bodies littered the base camp.

She wandered aimlessly through the colony for several days. The darztls had destroyed everything and seemed to have carried off the survivors with them. Yet they had left some usable goods behind. In the ruins, she found food as well as clothing that was intact, for the most part, and replaced her sole outfit. Over time, she noticed that she was not alone. Gradually, other people who had managed to hide in time, as she had, without being detected, emerged from the ruins of the colony. There weren't many of them, but they soon developed a sort of solidarity. There was enough merchandise left behind for them to survive several weeks, and not one of them believed that they would have to wait any longer than that before the mother ship came back for them.

§ § §

When I learned that my protégé had finally found an occupation she enjoyed, I felt relieved. Not because I disliked watching over her, but because I was pleased to see her gradually settling in. I was surprised to see her choose the haavls, but I decided that they must appear easier to understand than humans and darztls living hand in hand in the village. The large reptile's thick shell probably ensured a certain stability, providing reassurance for someone who had been thrown into an unknown world and had to rebuild all her benchmarks. When I went to see Marie at the stable, it always pleased me to see her throwing herself wholeheartedly into her new passion. Yet as soon as she saw me, her face would light up. She would come over to me and wait for me to give her permission — or to order her back to work.

However, a few weeks later, Mirntl, my dear Mirntl, the female responsible for the boarding house where Marie lived, came knocking at my door one afternoon. She brought bad news.

"Your protégé is a little thief!" she announced.

Noticing my disbelief, she invited me to go back with her to the boarding house. She took me to Marie's room, since Marie was busy with the haavls at the time.

"Look under her bed," she said.

I lifted the mattress that lay on the stone block and saw an entire array of objects hidden there.

"As you can see, she has a particular fondness for sharp objects."

Under the matters, along with a few books and trinkets, I found a long-distance walkie-talkie, (one of the few rare ones we had recovered from the defunct colony), a pocket computer (which was just as exceptional), a watch and a compass.

"But what is she planning to do with all this?"

"That's what I intend to ask her when she comes back!"

"Listen Mirntl, if you don't have any objections, I'd like to speak with her myself."

"As you like. In fact, I'd prefer that. I'm quite angry and my tongue might run away from me. She's still so frightened of darztls that I wouldn't want to give her new cause for fear."

I didn't go to the stable to speak with her. Night was falling, so I sat down in her room and waited for her to come back. When she came in and saw me, she smiled broadly and took a few steps toward me. Then when she noticed all the stolen objects I had placed on the table, her face crumpled. She stopped short and stood in front of me, trembling. I tried to speak to her as gently as I could.

"We found this in your room, Marie."

"Oh, I'm so sorry, Master. I should never have... I didn't mean to... I didn't know..."

"If you didn't know, as you say, why do you look so guilty?"

"Because you seem angry, Master. But I promise I won't do it again."

"What I'd like to know is why you took all of these objects."

She stood up and slipped her suit down to her waist. Then she placed her upper body down on the stone table, arms raised, leaving her back exposed.

"Beat me, Master. I know I deserve it."

And she stayed there, motionless, waiting to be punished.

I didn't know what to say. I felt powerless. How could I teach her the rules of our world without whipping or beating her? She knew no other form of explanation. I stood up and walked over to her. I ran my hand through her short hair. She shivered, as if expecting me to tear off her head or something.

"Listen, Marie, I simply want to understand, to understand you. Here everyone has everything they need, including the objects you took without even using them."

She turned to look at me.

"Does that mean you're not going to punish me?"

"That means I'm not going to punish you, that no one will punish you."

"But I'll forget! I'll start over again!"

"Here, Marie, in the village, we're convinced that hitting someone doesn't make them understand any better. Of course, it might prevent her from committing the same stupidities, but not because she understands the reasons for her punishment, only because she's afraid of being beaten again."

"Master Hisstdl called that learning. He said it was the only way to make us humans learn anything at all. After beating me, he always explained that he had done it for my own good. You don't want to correct me for my own good?"

"Marie!"

I made her stand up and pull her overalls up. Then I drew her to me. She stiffened, surprised, but as used as she was to doing what was expected of her, she gave in. Rather than beating her, I repeated my explanations from before, as I continued to rub her back. Over and over again, I told her that she was not in the darztl world, that here we respected each individual, that she was the same as everyone in the village and that we held all these things to be the truth. From time to time, I asked her if she understood and she agreed, in a tiny voice. However, I had the impression that she was forcing herself to take me at face value.

I spoke to her for a very long time. Then I asked her if she was tired and she nodded. I helped her get into bed and left the boarding house where everyone else was already asleep. I hadn't noticed how late it was and the night cold rushed over me. I walked home quickly and took refuge there, exhausted.

In the days that followed, Marie and I didn't mention the thefts again. Her landlady, however, who continued to inspect her room every day, never found anything under her mattress again.

One afternoon, my protégé brought the subject up without any preamble.

"My mother stole things too."

It was the first time she had mentioned her mother. Oddly enough, I had always pictured her as an orphan, taken by a master at an early age. But in fact, she informed me that she had stayed with her mother a fairly long time, at least long enough to remember her. From what she said, I understood that she had stayed with her mother until she was four or five years old.

"We lived in a large house with several darztls. We didn't sleep in a cave, but in a shack that was adjacent to the building. My mother worked very hard because they didn't have many slaves to keep house. I imagine that my father was one of the males who worked there too, but my mother never told me who he was. Maybe she didn't know...."

Marie fell silent.

"But, Master, maybe you don't want to hear all this."

Since her silence grew longer still, I reassured her. Yes, she could tell me her story. I even wanted to hear it. I suggested that she sit on a bench near me where we would be more comfortable. She allowed me to get comfortable then sat at my feet, her head on my knees. She continued where she had left off.

"The master forced her to have me, but he didn't give her enough food for two. At night, he gave her the same ration as before I was born, so things were very difficult for her. She breast fed me even when I was old enough to be weaned. As far back as I recall, my mother was always very thin. Her bones stuck out through her skin. Anyhow, things went fairly well until I was forced to work as well. But little humans have to be put to work young so they can be taught good habits.

"What did they make you do at that age?"

"All kinds of things. Wash the floors. Polish metal objects. Carry things. The masters weren't too harsh with me when I was little. And the more I grew and the stronger I became, the more food I needed and the more my mother had to give up for me. So she got into the habit of stealing food from the kitchen when the master had her work there. She would slip it into a rag she kept tied at the waist, under her clothes. It was darztl food, of course, vegetables and raw meat, but it helped us survive. One day, a master wanted to correct her because she had broken something. He told her to remove the top of her suit, because that makes it easier to whip people. That's when he saw her little bag and notified the grand master of the house. He tied my mother up and punished her in front of all the others. Then, saying that he had more than enough mouths to feed, he took me away. The last picture I have of my mother is of a distraught woman, bleeding, begging the master to let me stay with her."

Marie's head was still on my thigh. I bent down to look at her. She wasn't weeping. She had told me one of the saddest stories I had ever heard in my life, and her eyes were dry. She had related it all in a monotone, in a voice without tremors, as if talking about some else's life. Powerless, I caressed her thick hair.

§ § §

Then the mercenaries came into the colony. She'd seen these groups of human rebels, who spent most of their lives in the desert and only came to the colony to drink cactus alcohol and wreak havoc. Once, when she was very young, she'd seen them come to the base camp dragging an injured darztl behind them, exhibiting it like some trophy before turning it over to the authorities. When she replayed the scene in her mind, she could still hear the cries — the mercenaries, of course, but most of all the darztl's — as if it had happened the day before. This time the mercenaries were looking for new recruits, and she found them as frightening as the darztls who had decimated the settlement.

She managed to escape their clutches for several days, hiding where she had hidden during the darztl attack. They may have been armed to the teeth, but there was just a handful of them and they couldn't watch everything. She reassured herself, saying that they wouldn't stay for long and would hear the call of the desert wind again. But she needed to eat and had to venture out into the settlement from time to time to renew her supplies. It was on one of her forays that a mercenary caught her.

"Look what I found," he said to the others as he dragged her back by the hair. "Fresh meat!"

The other humans in the camp laughed in a way that boded no good.

The mercenaries didn't keep slaves in the same sense as the darztls. However, their band was based on a hierarchical system that meant the most recent arrivals and the youngest had to serve the senior ones. Plus, since the mercenaries didn't consider the settlers they had captured — as if they had won the war and the survivors were their trophies — as their own kind, she knew just where she fit into the hierarchy. And they brooked no complaints. In the beginning, the mercenaries had no qualms about killing the few adults who opposed their authority.

§ § §

The haavl masters were very kind and Marie liked working in the stable. Kthloold, the darztl who worked there, had a rough exterior but was a good master. He gave her clear explanations about what to do, and never hit or scolded her. In fact, Marie would even sleep in the stable if Mistress Mirntl wasn't so insistent that she come back to the boarding house every night. She felt closer to the haavls than to anyone in the village. Except for the master, of course, but that wasn't the same. Despite their monstrous appearance, the beasts were very gentle. And they were all that remained of her former life, a life she had fled without regret, but which never seemed to leave her.

Yet life in the village wasn't as difficult for her as it used to be. She began to understand certain rules, to have a clearer idea of what they expected of her. And when she didn't understand, she tried to do as everyone else did. Master Miekl seemed so determined — and he was so nice to her — that she did everything she could to satisfy him.

Every afternoon, the master visited her in the stable. At the beginning, he took her to see the human he called a psychologist on a regular basis. Marie didn't like those meetings and fortunately, after a while, the master stopped taking her there. Now he merely strolled about with her and had her talk about her former life. He never forced her to say anything, and she often surprised herself by confiding in him about things she thought she had long forgotten. For some time now, these walks ended at the library. The master, in fact, had decided to teach her how to read, as if he didn't realize she was too stupid for that. So she set herself down to her task with pleasure and learned to read short texts almost correctly.

Then suddenly, one evening the master told Marie that she would not see him for a few days. He had to make a trip into the desert, but would be back soon. Marie didn't know if she was entitled to ask him questions. But she did know that he wouldn't appreciate it if she threw herself at his feet and begged him to stay. He never beat her for that — he never beat her for anything — but she knew that such behavior displeased him. The next morning he came to the stable to say goodbye to Marie. He mounted a haavl and rode off. She watched him leave without a word.

But she was troubled the rest of the day. The haavls managed to take her away from her thoughts a little, but the master's absence weighed heavily on her, particularly at the time when he usually came to pick her up for their daily walk. She did her work very poorly, and yet the master didn't get angry. Instead, Kthloold suggested to Marie that she leave earlier than usual and Marie, afraid to protest, found herself in the middle of the village with free time she had no idea how to use. She went to the library and forced herself to read a book written for children about a little human whose parents abandoned him along with his brothers, and who found themselves in a giant's house. The letters danced before her eyes and she couldn't finish reading the tale. But her little trip to the library did use up some time and she could go back to her boarding house without upsetting Master Mirntl.

She didn't eat that evening and went straight to her room. There she undressed and lay down, not on the bed that they insisted on, but on the floor where she always felt more comfortable. And she tried to empty her mind, like she used to do before, when she had been beaten and wanted to forget everything. When you've been corrected, you have to forget it quickly, otherwise you're punished a second time, in your mind. But they had put too many things in her head lately, and she couldn't keep her thoughts from spinning.

The boarding house had long since fallen silent and she was still awake. She spent all night like that, eyes wide open in the dark, thinking thoughts she could no longer escape.

Over the days that followed, she continued to go about her tasks, but was less and less able to complete them. She made mistakes, she forgot everything, she no longer had her mind on what she was doing. And the more obtuse she became, the nicer everyone treated her and the more she missed Master Miekl. And as time passed, she became convinced that he had abandoned her to the village. If Master Hisstdl could do it, why wouldn't Master Miekl be capable of it as well? He may have treated her nicely, but he was still a darztl and in real life darztls had always imposed their wills on humans. That was the way of things.

After a week, she knew it for a fact. Master Miekl was gone for good.

§ § §

While the former inhabitants of the colony had all lost at least a few members of their families and close friends, the mercenaries had lost their main source of income: the revenue and privileges they received every time they brought in a darztl, particularly if they brought in a live one. Knowing that hard times were coming, they scoured the colony looking for the smallest bit of recyclable metal, the smallest bite of food. Or rather, it was the young and the prisoners like her who were drafted to do the work, while the band leaders shouted orders at them, hitting and threatening to cut off their supplies if they didn't work hard enough. At night, they controlled the distribution of the supplies and, from the time of her capture, she went to bed with an empty belly more often than not. She didn't understand why they kept them if they cared so little for them. Later she came to realize that for those people, it was one way of feeling alive.

One of the mercenaries, however, didn't treat her as badly as the others. When no one was looking, he would often give her sweets or some tidbit he had recovered from the ruins. Yet when he came to see her, he made her uncomfortable. He stood too close, he caressed her too often, he was too interested in her. One evening, he asked her if she wanted to eat with him. She didn't really want to, because she didn't feel comfortable with him, but no one in the small group of outcasts ever had enough to eat. From the leaders' quarters they could always smell the odor of grilled meat, so the offer was tempting.

She entered his shelter, and she ate as she hadn't in weeks. But in the end, she had to pay. They were sitting on a blanket that had been spread on the ground as they finished their meal. Mr. Williams — that was his name — started to caress her, saying that she was a pretty little girl and he would take care of her. She remained silent, although she stiffened a little. Then he moved even closer and tried to kiss her. She moved away and told him to stop that. He spoke to her gently, telling her over and over how

*pretty she was. Then he pushed her back onto the ground
and slipped his hand between her legs. She fought back.
At the beginning, Mr. Williams seemed to find it all entertaining, but then he got angry. He started to hit her
and tore her clothes, telling her that she was ungrateful.
He held her down and raped a twelve-year-old girl. Mr.
Williams never again treated her so nicely, but he did
force her to stay with him. By day she obeyed everyone's
orders, but at night she was all his. She ate as much as
she wanted.*

§ § §

After ten exhausting days in the desert, I came back
from my tour. Empty-handed this time. In fact, more often
than not, like the other trackers, I found no humans and
returned to the village alone. After all, the mesh of the
nets cast by the darztls was tight, and few humans
managed to escape. Others were recaptured all too
quickly and steps were taken to make sure they were in
no condition to escape again. Several didn't survive their
escape, finding death along with freedom. I sometimes
found human remains in the desert. And the desert was
also inhabited by other marauders, human ones, who
greedily sought to capture former slaves who were easy
to order about — another form of servitude.

From a distance, the village looked as it always did:
one hill like any other, although it was the tallest in the
area. It was only once you were inside that you noticed
that the hill was not only hollow but also cut off. After
walking through a cave, you found yourself in an enclosure that was protected by the walls of the hill and
swarming with life. That afternoon, everyone was agitated. Limpa, one of the human stable boys, came running
over to me as I was about to climb down from my haavl
to find out what all the hubbub was about.

"Miekl, you're too late. The human girl, you know,
little Marie, the one you take care of? Well, she ran away
this morning!"

"What?" I shouted.

"Yes! When we were opening the fence, she raced off on a haavl. I didn't even know she knew how to ride."

"Did they find her?"

"I don't know. A team set out after her. But she got a good head start before they got organized."

I stayed on my mount and headed back into the desert as quickly as my haavl could go. What had gotten into her? Why had she run away? And just when I thought she was starting to settle in!

I had been galloping in the desert for about an hour when I came across a group from our village. All three were riding haavls and they brought a fourth with them. Riderless.

The only human in the group said it was Marie's haavl.

"But where is she?" I shouted.

"She stayed behind."

"You left her there? You didn't bring her back?"

"She didn't want to come back."

"But you should have convinced her."

"We tried. And failed."

"Then you should have brought her back by force. You know as well as I do that abandoning a human in the desert means condemning her to certain death!"

The one who had been speaking from the start shrugged.

"And you, Miekl, you know as well as I do that we've never kept anyone against their will."

He handed me a bag.

"Particularly not someone who has tried to escape with things that belong to the community."

I looked in the bag. It contained a sampling of items similar to those we had discovered under Marie's bed that day. I didn't know what to think. I had nothing else to say. I bid them farewell and headed on my way, following the tracks the group had left in the sand.

I galloped for a while, then saw a tiny silhouette in the distance. It was Marie. She had collapsed in the sand. I don't know if she heard me ride up, but she didn't move. I climbed down from my haavl and walked over to her. I touched her shoulder. She jumped and moved away, half dragging herself, half crawling across the sand. I moved closer again and knelt next to her. When she tried to escape, I held her gently. She turned as if wanting to strike me, to fight, and that's when she saw who I was. A light flashed in her eyes, but it was short-lived. She curled up into a ball in the sand, hands covering her face. I lay down next to her, wrapping my body around hers, both to protect her from the rays of the sun and to get closer to her. Without looking up, she said, her voice heavy, "I thought you had gone for good."

"But I told you I'd come back, Marie."

"Yeah, that's what you all say."

Finally she looked at me and asked, as if anxious to hear my response, "Did you come to beat me?"

She curled up in fetal position on the sand once more, but this time facing me.

"No, I know that you haven't come to beat me," she responded on her own.

She placed her head on my chest and when I felt her shaking in my arms, I realized that she was weeping, more silently than I had ever heard anyone weep before. The saddest sound I had ever heard. The first tears I had seen her shed. I held her close and let her weep until her tears ran dry.

"Master," she finally said, between sobs, "Master, I can't do it. I can't get used to this life. It's too different from my life before. I believe you when you say that no one wants to hurt me, and yet, every time I do something stupid and every time I hear someone walk up behind me, I expect to be hit. I'm even more stupid than you think, you know — I can't even believe that I'm free. I escaped because I didn't want to be hit anymore, because I didn't want to be afraid anymore, and yet I'm still just as terrified, everywhere, all the time. The nicer people treat me, the more I think I'll have to pay for it."

She was weeping and talking at the same time and stopped, caught in a fit of coughing. I said nothing and waited for her to continue.

I didn't dare say a word, afraid that she would stop talking. She had never confided in anyone before. I realized that everything she had told me up to then had only been superficial — about what had happened to her, but not what she felt.

Finally, she started to speak, "You don't know what real fear is. No one in the village does, except for those who come from where I come from. When I escaped I was very frightened, but I was even more frightened of staying. I was afraid of dying. I was afraid of not dying quickly enough. I would never have fled from my other master, but in the factory things were different. Master Hisstdl hit me too, but I believed him when he said it was for my own good. In the factory they beat me simply because... because I was there..."

She stopped, overwhelmed by sobbing. Finally she continued. As she spoke, her weeping calmed.

"After my baby was born, after they punished me for protesting when they took him away, one of the factory masters said they were going to transfer me again. At the factory, they wouldn't tolerate a human that hit its masters, so they were going to send me somewhere where they'd take away any desire I had to rebel. The darztl who told me all this was so excited, his wattle was streaked with colors. I decided that if there was somewhere worse than the factory, death would be waiting for me there. And when it came down to dying of thirst in the desert or being beaten to death, I chose freedom. The entire time I was in the factory, I had hoped that Master Hisstdl would come back for me, but time passed and I had lost hope. I decided to take the first chance I got to escape."

Marie's tears had completely stopped by this point. She stood up and I followed suit, as I continued to screen her from the afternoon sun.

I risked a question, "And how did you manage to do it?"

"I used another's escape! When I had recovered a bit from the correction they had administered to me, new masters came looking for me. They dragged me outside roughly, despite my begging. They had me climb into a cart covered with a tarpaulin. There were other slaves there, and from their terrified expressions I knew they shared my feelings. I was afraid, Master, you can't imagine how afraid I was. They chained me to the others and our trip began. It was stifling under the tarp and the masters refused to give us enough water. They lashed out at us through the tarp, not caring where their blows landed. I believe that all those in the cart had, like me, committed a serious offense in the eyes of the darztls. So, our punishment began. The next human the masters stowed in the car was a male. Suddenly, as a master was about to bind him to the others, he struck back, hitting randomly, frantically. Confusion reigned for a moment and the man ran off. That's when I noticed that the chain that bound us to one another and to the vehicle was not connected properly. I looked as if I were bound to the others, but I was in fact free — with the exception of the manacles around my wrists and ankles. Gently, terrified that they would notice me at any moment, I slipped out of the cart. Instead of running off right away, I slipped between the wheels, hanging on to the metal structure, hooking the irons that impeded my movements onto to it the best I could. A loud death cry rang out and I almost let go. I decided that they must have caught the fugitive and were punishing him, or most likely, killing him. Quaking, I tightened my hold on the frame of the cart. In the hubbub, the masters forgot to make sure all the slaves were present and accounted for. And no one denounced me to earn favors. Either that, or no one had seen me escape. Or else, none of the slaves had any illusions about their fate. We started off again.

"When did you manage to really escape?"

"During the night. You know, Master, when the cart stopped at twilight, I was exhausted. I was afraid I would lose my grip at any moment and, at the same time, with the masters guarding the cart, I couldn't flee right away. So I waited some more. They had the slaves climb down from the cart and chained them even closer together for the night. And that's when the masters finally decided to do a head count and realized I was missing. At that moment, I was paralyzed with fear. I expected them to find me at any second and I hardly dared think about the fate that lay in store for me if they did. But the masters thought I was already far away. Two of them set out to patrol the vicinity. At least that's what I guessed when I heard two haavls gallop off. During that time, the other masters unleashed their anger on the remaining slaves. I know that because I heard the blows and the shrieks. I was more terrified than ever, but I held firm. Finally, I heard the two haavls return. The masters came back empty-handed, of course. I heard them joking, saying that, in any case, I wouldn't get far and would soon be dragged back to them in a net. And that then they would settle their account with me.

I held her closer. Poor little human... I would have liked to remove all these memories from her head and replace them with more peaceful images.

"I can imagine how terrified you were."

"No, Master, you can't imagine that," she said gently. "These things are beyond imagination. I myself wonder how I managed to hold on, to stay under that wagon until everyone went to sleep. When I finally dared to leave my hiding place, everything was quiet. The darztls were snuggled into their heated coveralls, and the humans, who had been stripped naked for the night, huddled, shivering, in a tightly chained little group. Two of the masters were standing guard, but they weren't looking in my direction. In any case, they weren't expecting me to run out in front of them. I looked around me. A short distance off, the haavls were grazing, but if I rode off on one of the beasts, I would attract the masters' attention. My only option was to flee on foot, even if that meant there was little chance I would escape alive. I crawled off as quickly as I could, taking care to keep the manacles on my wrists and feet from clanking. It took an eternity. I expected to feel a rifle barrel against my back at any time, to hear a master ordering me to stop, to feel a club dig into my flesh. But I managed to put enough distance between myself and the group until they could no longer hear me. Then I stood up and walked on, taking small steps, hampered by my irons. When I decided that I had gone far enough, I huddled down behind a rock to catch my breath. At one point, I hammered rocks against my chains to break them. It took a long time. I don't know how I managed to make my way out of the inhabited territory without being seem. I knew that I had to head north. People said that free humans could be found there. But there were human hunters, as well. I expected to be caught at any moment. And that's exactly what happened. But it was you, Master, who caught me. And you didn't take me back."

She fell silent, obviously exhausted, and leaned against me. I felt her frail body relax suddenly. Her body was hot against me and I suddenly realized that I was chilled to the bone. I looked around and saw that night was falling over the desert. I was cold. I had to find shelter as quickly as possible. Yet one matter remained to be settled.

"Yet you decided to go back."

She looked up at me, astonished.

"Who told you that I had decided to go back?" she asked.

"All these objects you're carrying. You decided to give them to the masters?"

"You have to understand. It was like a... a guarantee for me."

"In case a hunter caught you?"

"When a hunter caught me."

"But why did you leave? You knew what would happen!"

"That's it, Master, that's it..."

"Do you realize you've placed our community in danger? The darztls would have only been too pleased to have proof that the village exists. Why do you think we take such pains not to let the humans see where we're going?"

"I would have never told them where you are."

"And you think your former masters don't have the means to make humans talk? After everything you've told me?"

"I wouldn't have told them!"

Suddenly, her face crumpled. She was once again the fragile little girl I was used to seeing, a little girl who had, perhaps, been able to soften darztl hearts occasionally.

She looked down. "You think I'm stupid, don't you?"

"Not at all, Marie. You're very skilled at surviving at any cost. I think that, in order to have survived all that you have, you must be more intelligent than most beings I know, myself included!"

I shivered despite myself. It was starting to be far too cold for me in the desert. There was good reason that darztl territory ended farther south. I did have heated coveralls in the bag on my haavl, but, knowing that I was going home that day, I hadn't recharged the battery. Marie understood that the situation was becoming critical for me.

"Do you want me to make a fire?" she asked.

I nodded. She raced over to my mount, which had spent the entire time snuffling through the sand, foraging for food.

She pulled a blanket from my bag. It would, at least, protect me from the icy dew that was falling on the desert with the night. She also gave me rations to eat. Then she set out to find fuel for a fire. I stayed behind, shivering. Even the heat from the fire was unable to warm me. That's when inspiration struck her.

"Pull on your coveralls, Master!" she said.

"But Marie, you know the battery is dead! The coveralls are made from an insulated fabric, so I can retain my body temperature, but they certainly won't warm me!"

"Put on your overalls, Master!"

I was too numb to protest any further and, above all, too astonished by her bossy tone. I pulled on the clothing that was as icy as the night desert. As I did that, she took her clothes off. Then, facing me, she slipped into my over-alls, sliding her arms and legs along mine. My reptilian body and her slim one barely fit into the overalls. I closed the zipper as well as I could. The insulated clothing pro-tected us from the coolness of the ground. Her body tem-perature was at the lower limit of my comfort zone, but the contact was beneficial. Soon I stopped shivering. We spent the night entwined, Marie's tiny human body heating my larger darztl one.

§ § §

Once the colony had been stripped of its resources, the mercenaries set off. They didn't like to stay in the same place for too long and they traveled from oasis to oasis, hunting the small desert animals they found on their way. Life was even harder during these migrations. The band leaders traveled in large, stinking trucks that ran on methane, but there was never enough space for everyone or for all their equipment. So along with several others, she was forced to travel on foot, carrying a heavy load, weighed down even further by her tattered coveralls.

Essentially, they lived by hunting. They lived off tiny osfts, fighting over the rare meat. But there were also large hiistmls that provided more food. Care had to be taken when hunting and preparing the animals since, once the shell was broken, it released a substance that poisoned the meat. And there were darztls, too. Now that they had no value for barter, the mercenaries said people might as well eat them. A single darztl could feed the group for several days. But she had never been able to swallow a single mouthful.

For five marsian years, she remained with the mercenaries, aging twice that amount over that time. She was unable to develop any relationships with anyone. No one did. Life was too hard, too unnatural, too basic. All relationships were based on power, force, coercion. She felt alone, isolated, abandoned. All day long she had to work, fight for survival, fight for food. And the night brought other concerns.

It was hard for the boys but, for the most part, the mercenaries left them alone at night. The girls were the prey of choice. Mr. Williams kept her for himself most of the time, but he was occasionally generous. On festive evenings, she wouldn't sleep all night. And the women who had made their way into the elite of the band let their males be, without interfering, completely ignoring the girls' distress. The only help they ever gave her was to help rid her of a baby a mercenary had made with her, on two separate occasions. The second time she lost so much blood they thought she would die.

§ § §

They headed out on haavl after a short night. They left early, hoping to arrive at the village before the noon-day sun hit the desert. Despite everything, the heat was already stifling and Marie was glad of the small shadow the master's body cast over her. This time, she was not traveling in a bag, but on the haavl, seated in front of Master Miekl. She hadn't seen the village when she set out on her desperate race, but he trusted her for the trip back. For the first time in a very long time, for the first time in her entire life, her heart felt almost light. The master brought her back to the village, brought her back to the house. She wasn't sure that she understood all the rules yet, but she was starting to realize that they would give her all the time she needed to get used to her new life and that, above all, she would not be punished if she didn't learn quickly enough.

She had done the stupidest thing in her entire life and she realized that. For less than that in darztl territory, they would have slaughtered her like an animal. Here, even though she had placed the entire community in danger, acting like a stupid slave... like someone terrified... like a female saving her skin... Miekl said that he understood. This morning, he had assured her that the others would not chase her away. No real damage had been done, and she probably wouldn't even be given chores to make amends.

When they rode into the village, the welcome was almost cordial, considering the circumstances. Limpa, the human stable hand to whom Marie had practically never said a word, came over and told them both that he was glad she was back. Kthloold, the darztl responsible for the haavls, was less welcoming, but he greeted her anyway. At the boarding house, Mistress Mirntl seemed sincerely happy to see her, as if Marie had been gone for several months and not just a day. She placed a bowl of soup on the table, which the human devoured, ashamed to discover that not only had she not eaten much the previous day, but it had been two weeks since she had had much of an appetite.

She suddenly felt very tired and asked if she could go to her room. Mistress Mirntl said that she was free to do as she pleased, of course. But before that, Marie took a shower, a long shower. The water smelled bad, but it made her feel good. Bathing in water was more beneficial than bathing in sand. In the case of humans, it cooled their fevers, washed away a great many pains. That might be the problem. Masters and slaves were not made from the same element: water for humans, sand for darztls.

She chose coveralls that fit. Here, there was wide range and people could get clean coveralls every day. Miekl had shown her where to clean them. That was one of the chores people could choose to do. It was very different from the darztl world, where she was only given new clothes when the old ones fell to pieces. Unless it was essential for your work, no one let you wash very often either, not with sand or with water. Darztls preferred to blame humans for their unpleasant odor.

Before dressing, she looked at herself in the mirror. Darztls didn't have many mirrors and they were reserved exclusively for the masters. Since she had come to the village she had never looked at herself naked, as if she expected to hear some master making fun of her behind her back. In the mirror, her body looked like a book in which all the shames, the fears of her life, were written. At the base of her back, an indelible mark proclaimed that she had belonged to someone. She was thin, too, thinner than most of the females in the village. In fact, her body was almost that of a boy. Yet, on her belly, lighter streaks revealed that a child had grown there for nine months. Her breasts, as well, were once swollen, painful... useless.

The male they had forced on her told her she was beautiful. Their intimacy lasted three days, after which time she found herself pregnant. Three days of grace during which the masters had left them alone. As for the male, Marie had found him ugly and stupid, but he had been relatively kind to her the entire time they had spent together. They both knew what they had to do and they had made the best of it.

Marie sighed and slipped on her overalls. Her experience had been atrocious and yet there had been a few rare moments of relative gentleness to which she clung as if they were gold. She decided that's why most of the slaves kept on living, rather than killing themselves. And then, one day, the masters would exceed the limits and find themselves with a slave who was either dead or escaped.

She went to her room and lay down, fully clothed. On her bed. It was in the middle of the day, but it was neither too bright nor too hot in the room that, in order to be kept cool, had only one tiny window that was usually covered with a piece of cloth. Outside she heard the murmur of the village, an entire free world where humans and darztls lived in peace.

When she awoke, it was night. The boarding house was completely quiet, so it must have been relatively late. She was thirsty. She stepped into the hallway and noticed that only a few threads of light peeked through the boarders' doors. On her way to the kitchen for a glass of water, she looked at the boarding house clock and saw that it was midnight. She stepped out into the night. A few lights seeping through the windows indicated that not everyone was asleep. Yet everything was quiet. She walked through the deserted streets. She headed over to the stable where the haavls were kept. The placid animals were motionless, asleep, as still as rocks. She wondered what it felt like to be a cold-blooded creature, a 'reptile', as she had learned to call them from the books, dependant on external conditions for warmth, for coolness. She walked through the cave that lead outside the hill. Near the barrier, sentinels kept watch. One of them recognized her and stiffened. But she gave them a friendly wave. This evening, she wasn't going to escape.

She looked through the fence at the desert, the incredible expanse she had managed to cross. The slaves in the factory had said that the darztls were there before them and that they had enslaved the humans as a punishment for invading their territory. Some people didn't believe these stories, but she did. Human beings were poorly suited for this world and the planet wouldn't accept them. She slipped a hand under her coveralls and automatically rubbed her shoulder. The rough skin there still bore the mark of the sun, the cruel liirzt that had burned her. She wondered what it must feel like to be ever so happy under the burning warmth of the sun. To be large and strong and powerful enough to impose one's will....

She retreated along her route. She stopped in the central square and sat down on a stone bench. She looked around and decided that she could choose to live here. It was all in the word 'choose.' Not simply stay here, not simply put up with being here, not just getting used to the idea, but actually choose. Of course, it was not as if she had any better choices but, in any case, no one was going to force her to stay here.

She stood up and continued to wander through the village, pretending she didn't know where her feet were taking her. But once she arrived at Miekl's door, she hesitated, afraid he would scold her, that he would send her back to bed. Then she remembered that he didn't want to be her master. So she went in.

He was sleeping, lying on his belly on his bed of foam. His head was resting on his large, clawed paws and his tail reached to the ground. In one corner a radiator gave off a stifling heat. He breathed deeply, sleeping a trusting sleep. He did not hear her come in. She leaned over his bed and ran her hand over his scaly shoulder. Miekl awoke with a start and Marie also stiffened, out of reflex. Yet, even though the room was dark, she was willing to bet that the darztl's wattle turned a very gentle shade when he saw who it was.

"Marie?" he said in surprise. "But what are you doing here? It's been a long time since I've found you asleep at the foot of my bed."

"I didn't come for that, Master. Although, if you were to make me a little space near you..."

He sighed and shifted over to let her lie down next to him.

"Master, I need to know something."

"And you absolutely have to know it this night, eh?"

"Yes. Master, have you ever been a master?"

He sat up suddenly in the bed. He sighed again.

"It's important for you to know this, eh?"

"Yes, I think so. So, did you ever give orders to slaves? Did you ever beat them?"

"If I had been a master, what difference would that make to you?"

"I don't know. You're a darztl, of course. And as understanding as you are, your understanding does have its limits. You've never felt powerless before a master, never felt that you had to flagellate yourself to assuage the blood thirst of the darztl standing before you. Do you know what I mean?"

"And if I had been a master? You don't think masters can change as well?"

"If slaves can, then I guess masters can as well. But it would be more difficult for me, and possibly for you as well. I know that you don't judge me, that I feel as close to you as any human can with a darztl. But I would find it hard to see you as anything other than... a gentle master. And I think that you would find it hard to see me as anything other than a slave... a particularly gifted slave."

"And what if I weren't a darztl?"

She turned to Miekl, surprised. Then she considered the question seriously. "If you were a human rather than a darztl, things wouldn't have started between us as they did. You wouldn't have captured me and told me that it was for my own good. And then I'd have to know if you had experienced something similar to my experience. You know, I feel very distant from the other humans who have always lived free."

"Human beings aren't just enslaved by darztls. Men and women can do that quite well among themselves."

She looked at him, intrigued.

"The village has often taken in boys and girls, barely out of childhood, who had terrible tales to tell. Frequently, they wouldn't tell them right off, since terror had made them mute. These humans had escaped from bands of other humans. You do know that there are humans wandering about the desert?"

She nodded. The slaves had talked about free humans living in the desert, humans that even the darztls feared.

"Well, they may be human, but they're capable of inflicting terrible harm on other humans. Not all the bands are the same, of course, but some of them are very cruel. Particularly to weak and powerless people picked up in the desert when they were on the point of dying. The human boys and girls that come to us spent five, ten, fifteen years in these groups before they managed to escape and find refuge in the village. Five or ten or fifteen years of living with humans that only feed you enough when you follow orders. That have the power of life and death over you. Whose expectations are limitless, who make you work from dawn until dusk, like the masters made you do. Who also make you perform other services unknown between darztls and humans. It's a reign of terror, and I won't tell you what fate awaits those who refuse to cooperate. Life in the desert is difficult enough, particularly since the colony leaders abandoned the survivors, but the members of these groups of humans have turned it into hell."

All this time, she had lain on her back, listening. She thought for a moment, then sat up.

"If I understand you, you're trying to tell me that there are others with tales like mine?"

"What I'm trying to tell you is that our world is filled with horror stories. That even two similar creatures can make life difficult. And that even two completely different creatures can do what's right."

Marie thought for a moment again.

"Well," she said, "I imagine that people could say that you're a creature that has been good to me. So, I think that what I've come to tell you this evening is that I want to get to know you. No matter what you have been in the past, I just want to know it. After that, we'll see. I've told you a lot about myself since you captured me, but I've never asked you anything. You know, I'm not used to getting to know my masters, because the less I know the better things will go for me. But with you, since I've been here, it's not the same. What I've come here to ask is that you tell me about yourself."

"Marie, I have to show you something."

He stood up painfully. Darztls needed to sleep at night. Their metabolism slowed considerably and they weren't creatures of the night unless forced to be so. However, Marie had noticed that this didn't affect their reflexes, and they were as fearsome at night as during the day. When it was dark out, some were just more irritable than others....

Miekl pulled on some thermal coveralls and had a bite to eat.

"Do you want to come with me?"

She followed him without a word, intrigued. He took her to the municipal building located close to the northern portion of the rocky wall, but he didn't go in by the main door. He walked around the building and headed for a small entrance. He inserted keys in the heavy locks and pressed on signs drawn on white squares. Marie found this astonishing, since nothing in the village was ever locked. Then Miekl pushed the door open.

They entered a rock hallway that soon took them to a staircase, also made of rock. The walls were rough, as if natural and very old. They walked down the stairs and found a long irregular hallway at the bottom, pockmarked with doors, all closed.

"The underground passageway was already here," explained Miekl. "We simply arranged it to make it easier to use."

They walked along the sinuous hallway and Miekl stopped in front of a door.

"I'm warning you, Marie, what I'm about to show you is difficult to believe. It's also the best-kept secret in our community. If ever anyone outside were to learn about this, if the darztls ever learned about it, it would be much worse than if they were to get their hands on the objects you were carrying with you. It's not until we're totally convinced that the new arrivals have fit into our community that we tell them about our research."

"And you think I've fit in?"

She saw herself again, the day before, galloping away from the village.

"I know that I can trust you. There's something that has happened between us since yesterday. If I'm wrong... well... I will... we will all pay dearly."

He opened the door. The room was in deep darkness. He played with a button and a light pierced through it, weak, yet sufficient. Initially it looked like an office, equipped with a chair and a table on which files were stacked. But the shelving was special. Four humans were lying there, covered with a transparent material. They looked as if they were sleeping, and the series of machines connected to their bodies did not appear to interfere with their sleep. As she walked closer, Marie saw that there were three men and one woman.

"What happened to them?" she asked. "Are they dead or just sleeping?"

Marie looked into the four glass receptacles. The people sleeping there looked peaceful. They were all naked except for the equipment that covered a portion of their bodies. They were so still they looked dead. Yet their chests swelled slowly and regularly, in pace with the equipment located outside the glass shell and connected to each body by large pipes that crossed through the transparent surface and plunged into their throats.

"They're sleeping," said Miekl. "Sleeping very deeply. You could never wake them. Not without the help of someone who knows how to do that."

Marie walked from one body to the next, fascinated.

Miekl continued, "They're sleeping because they lack something very important. All of their thoughts. Their thoughts have been removed and stored elsewhere."

Marie was too dumbfounded to protest. Weakly, she said, "But how...?"

"By means of a special technique."

Miekl opened his coveralls partway and dug through the pocket in the leather and metal belt he always wore around his waist. He took out a tiny metal plate, from which a multitude of even tinier wires ran.

"We can put an individual's thoughts in this."

"Are there thoughts in this plate?"

"No, it can't be used. I keep it in my pocket simply to remind myself where I come from."

There was a long silence. Miekl motioned her to sit in the single chair in the room and he sat on the table. Marie slouched back into the chair like a sleepwalker.

"And why would anyone want to catch someone's thoughts in a plate?" she finally asked.

"In order to transfer them into someone else."

Another silence.

"But, why would someone want to do that?" she managed to say.

"Initially, the humans used this technology to save people. You know, sometimes someone has an accident that kills his brain completely, without damaging his body. And the opposite can happen as well: someone's body is completely destroyed, in an accident for example, but his brain remains intact. Our human forefathers thought it would be a good idea to transfer the active brain from the second individual into the still-functional body of the first."

"Humans are capable of doing that? They must be very powerful then! So how did they let the darztls capture them and reduce them to slaves?"

Marie thought about the humans she had known, living day by day, subjected to the will of their masters, incapable of making any decision on their own. Then she saw herself, fleeing into the dessert, using all of her cunning to escape the slave hunters.

"Because with talent comes pride, I suppose. I think they never once thought that the darztls were capable of attacking and defeating them."

Marie thought about what Miekl has just told her for a minute.

"So, the thoughts of these four people have been transferred into four other people?" she concluded.

Then she looked at the four bodies lying in the little room for a long time.

"But their bodies aren't damaged," she commented. "Why did anyone want to transfer their thoughts?"

"One day, the founder of the village had an idea. If thoughts could be transferred from one human to another, the same could be done from a human to a darztl as well. Think about it — there were a lot of advantages. This planet is very hard on human bodies. On the other hand, the darztls are perfectly suited to the climate. Living in a darztl body, a human would have a much easier life on Siexlth."

"And it worked?"

"Of course. Our founder was the first guinea pig. She was no scientist herself, but she gathered an entire team around her. At the end, she explored Remldarztl in a darztl body."

"And after that, Master? Did she try to free the slaves?"

"This was well before the darztls discovered the pleasures of mass slavery! At the time, they only had a small handful of slaves who were kept as hostages while they tried to convince the humans to leave. She saw them, of course, and found it disgusting, but she saw a lot of other things as well: a cultured society, fascinating individuals, an entire world that the humans were preparing to annihilate through terraforming."

"So she betrayed the humans rather than the darztls?"

"No. She decided that her experiment could be used to bring the two together."

Marie shook her head. She didn't see how darztls and humans could ever be brought together. There was too much disregard in the manner in which she had been treated the entire time she was a slave, and too much fear in the humans kept in slavery. Then, suddenly, she thought about the darztls she had met here, in the village. Mirntl, the female darztl who ran the boarding house, who had always been kind to her ever though, Marie, for her part had not always been receptive. And then Kthloold, who had taught her how to care for haavls. And Miekl, of course. And all the others she has encountered, even those who found her in the desert one day earlier — though that seemed so long ago now — and who had only left her there after negotiating with her for a long time.

"She was exiled in the desert for that," Miekl continued. "For that, and for other reasons it would take too
long to explain. She joined a small community that had
been formed following an earlier experiment — in which
scientists had tried to transform humans into darztls. She
was banished from the original human colony, although
she had previously been a person of influence. By negotiating, she managed to obtain equipment and, after five
years of theoretical research, her team moved here, into
this hill. That's when the practical part of the experiment
started. There were twenty darztl bodies in all, in a vegetative state — which means that their brains were dead,
or almost. One by one, as volunteers came forward, she
transferred capsules like this, each containing the
thoughts of one human."

"She wanted these fake darztls to infiltrate the enemy?"

"At the beginning, I don't really know what she intended. But if her plans were that belligerent, they
certainly changed over time. Particularly since, bit by bit,
dissident darztls joined the community. Especially after
the decisive battle between the humans and the native
population. You know, not all darztls support slavery."

Marie thought again. This was a lot to digest in one
night. Looking at Miekl, she saw how exhausted he was,
both from a lack of sleep and from the cold, which went
hand in hand in his case. For the past few minutes he
had been speaking slowly, as if his entire body was turning numb. She should pretend to understand and let him
go back to bed, but there were too many questions jostling
about in her mind.

"Do you mean that all the darztls I've met in the village
were once humans?"

Without quite knowing why, she was disappointed.
She felt astonishingly relieved, since she'd managed to
convince herself that not all the masters were monsters
as she had believed until that point.

"No! I told you that there were twenty darztl bodies,
and if you look around you in the village, you will see
many more darztls. Most of the hundred or so darztls

living here came to us because they do not agree with their kind. At the start, there were a few hybrids — individuals who were half human, half darztl — but they didn't live long. All of the darztls who have come through here, literally or figuratively, have been converted darztls, if I can call them that. As are many of the humans who live here, to a certain extent. You know, I've already seen what a band of humans can do to a defenseless darztl, and it's not a pretty sight. But here, in the protected enclave of the village, our founder's dream has gradually taken form. Her dream was to create a world where humans and darztls don't have to subjugate one another in order to survive. And in the event that this planet's sun eventually kills all humans despite these efforts, the dream is to allow their culture to survive somewhere in the minds of a handful of darztls.

"And what about you? Are you human or darztl? I mean originally."

Miekl headed to the body of the woman lying in her transparent sarcophagus.

"What do you think of her?"

The woman was older than Marie, but not much. Her face, framed by black hair, was rather pretty. Her motionless body was naked, like the others.

"Why do you want to know what I think of her?"

"Because she's me. Not quite as old as I would be under normal circumstances, but she is me."

Marie burst out laughing. Then her laughter died out as she digested the information.

"I wasn't always a darztl, Marie. Do you understand? That's what I've been trying to tell you. Becoming a darztl is a privilege that life has granted me. I wasn't always male either. That was just random chance, but I think things have worked out."

§ § §

During the second year, she tried to escape, but the mercenaries quickly captured her. Mr. Williams locked her up, beat her for a week, and deprived her of food for almost as long. Just enough to weaken her and prevent her from getting any other ideas.

The second time, she prepared her escape better. She didn't run off by day, but at night, and she had taken care to gather enough food to allow her to live for a while. It had been a long time since she had demonstrated much initiative, so no one seemed concerned about her. She allowed herself to be raped by Mr. Williams one last time and waited until she heard him snore. Then she slowly walked out of the shelter where he dwelt, picked up her bag and ran off as fast as she could, hiding from the mercenaries who stood guard. She didn't know where she was going, but she did know it would be better to die in the desert than spend another minute with that brutal band.

In any case, they might have eventually captured her. The desert may be large, but there weren't many hiding places. And the mercenaries were used to tracking small and larger beasts.... Fortunately, someone else found her first. She had been wandering the desert for a few days already and was starting to realize that she was going to die. She had food for two days and water for two more. But she had no idea what she would do after that. She was trying to avoid heading south, which she thought was patrolled by darztls. Instead she had headed east. She had been told that the people could reach the sea from the east. So she headed for the sea, hoping that she might find something to live on.

Then suddenly, a darztl, probably a female darztl judging from her size, jumped on her and shoved her in a bag.

She was afraid, even more afraid than when she had been with the mercenaries. She had wanted to escape from them and now here she was in the clutches of a slave hunter. As the mercenaries had eaten their portions of darztl meat, they had said that the enemy, for its part, ate humans as well. She was afraid the monstrous creature would devour her.

That evening, the darztl took her out of the bag and placed a chain around her neck. She was shivering all over, and started shaking even more when her jailer sat down to eat. But instead of chopping her into little pieces, the darztl handed her some food. Then before settling down

*to sleep, she threw a blanket over her, with a gesture that
was almost tender.*

*They galloped on the haavl for several days, the darztl
on the saddle, the human in the bag. Then they stopped
one last time, the bag was opened and she found herself
in the middle of a circle of curious onlookers.*

*She spent weeks unable to trust anyone. In five marsian
years, she had lost most of her social skills. She was used
to living like an animal, fighting for food, letting the strongest decide what he would do with her. Suddenly, she found
herself in a community where they told her everyone had
the same rights? That sounded highly doubtful to her. Plus
there were darztls here, plenty of darztls, who strolled about
the village freely. She had never seen darztls other than
threatening in the streets of the colony, weakened and
dragged behind a mercenary's truck, or worse yet, sliced
up on Mr. William's plate as he tried to force her to eat.
She had never met an actual representative of the indigenous species going about its chores, taking care of children,
taking pleasure with those of its kind — darztls and
humans. She was prostrate, overwhelmed, and refused all
contact.*

§ § §

They talked the rest of the night and into the next
morning. Miekl told Marie how the operation was performed, providing a mass of technical details that she didn't
understand but that seemed to postpone the moment when
the darztl would speak about himself. At one point a
human came in, but when he saw them both there his face
took on an understanding expression and he told them he
would leave them alone. The day was already well under
way when they finally left the underground facility. The
darztl, who hadn't eaten much since the previous evening
and had spent all that time in the coolness underground,
was very weak. Even though he was twice her size, Marie
supported him the best she could. She took him home and
helped him lie down in the blazing light that poured in
through the skylight. She prepared him something to eat,
then came back to check on him.

"Are you sure you are all right, Master?"

"Yes, yes. I am a darztl after all. I recuperate quickly."

"You should sleep now."

"Yes, but before I do, go over to my bookshelf and pick up the little green notebook to your right.... No, over a little more... that's it. You can read now. Try to get through it today if you can. And if you want, we'll talk about it this evening."

She waited for him to fall asleep, then left.

As she had done so often in recent weeks, she wandered aimlessly through the village. Now she responded when people greeted her, but today, more than ever, she didn't feel like talking to anyone. She needed to think. And to find a quiet place where she could read in peace. As if that were some kind of reprehensible activity. She held the notebook tightly.

She took refuge behind the village, near the rocky wall where succulent plants grew in the indirect light. Miekl had shown her this small, distinct place when he gave her his tour of the village in the early days. Here it was always relatively cool. She would be comfortable enough for what she had to do.

Trembling, Marie opened the notebook. *She was born when the colony was still a colony.* All those words made her afraid. She hadn't been reading for long and she had never read a text that was so long or so difficult. She didn't understand all the words, either. And then, every time she opened a book she recalled Master Hisstdl's whip, and believed she could still feel its bite. She closed the book. Then she opened it again. She could do this. She had gone to the end of the desert. She sounded out the syllables with difficulty but she persevered. She knew that this may be the first important book she had read in her entire life.

From time to time, Marie took a break from her reading. Some passages were too hard. They made her afraid, as if the words had the same power to hurt as a whip. The words danced before her eyes, like the Master's whip rippling before it struck. She shivered. The book talked about subjugation and she saw herself again, exposed to the masters' eyes, subjected to their every whim. Even when

she was with Master Hisstdl, she always had to be prepared to obey another master. Everyone had held power
over her. She had been an object, and they were free to
do what they wanted with her. Even disposing of her
when she no longer functioned. But when an object
doesn't work, there's no pleasure in shaking it to make
it get up and walk. Whereas certain masters, with her...
Of course, the story she was reading was of a different
order. Humans exercising power over other humans. And
when she thought about it, she couldn't decide which
situation was worse....

That entire day, slowly, laboriously, Marie deciphered
the text, decoded the story that brought her back to her
own experiences. *She didn't know it yet, but life had just given
her a second chance.* The words stopped there. Marie was
exhausted. And confused. It looked so much like her, and
so little like Miekl. How could he become what he was
after living what he had lived? How could she become
someone after being no one?

§ § §

Marie came back to see me only the next morning. She
told me that she had wanted to give me time to recover
and I was grateful to her for that. She had read my notebook and she had questions. I answered all her questions
to the very last one. She wanted to know everything, she
wanted me to confirm what she had understood as she
had painfully read the notebook. She also wanted me to
speak about my life before. After I had allowed myself
to be approached, after I had decided to make a life in
the village, after I had become a darztl.

"Who brought you here? Do I know that darztl? Is it
someone from the village? Is she still alive?"

"Yes, you know her. It's Mirnlt, the female in charge
of the boarding house. She's old now and no longer goes
out into the desert. But for a long time, she was our best
patroller. She brought me here and it was Mirnlt, as well,
who tamed me, who helped me tame the village."

"And when did you decide to become a darztl?"

"When I realized it was the only way to save other humans in the desert. And to make other darztls aware of the harm they cause humans. As soon as I knew the possibility existed."

"And Kthoold who works in the stable? Is he a real darztl?"

"As real as can be. One day, I'll tell you his story."

"And can I become a darztl if I want to?"

"No, I was the last one. There were no more bodies left."

"But, Master, all we have to do is catch some more!"

"No one here is prepared to annihilate another sentient being, a darztl, to replace him with a human. That goes against all our rules, against everything we're trying to build in the village. Now, we have to find other means. But not those they used in the early days of the colony, either. In the laboratory, we're working to adapt humans to life on this planet. Our experiments have been more successful since we're not trying to look like real darztls in order to try to trick the enemy...."

Marie came back often to see me and talk about all this afterwards. She needed to understand it, to understand herself. She often asked the same questions, but in a different way, to look at the matter from a different viewpoint. I knew what she wanted. She wanted me to describe the life that was opening up before her. Whenever I saw her getting agitated, demanding explanations, discussing, I once again saw the small, terrified human that I had captured, and I understood the distance she had traveled.

"Do you believe that the village will survive? That it will be able to resist the horror that surrounds it?"

"I don't know, Marie. One day, we might be attacked by a furious band. Humans or darztls, it's all the same. We can't predict what will happen."

I had no solution to offer her. I barely had a solution for myself. I had chosen my way thirty revolutions earlier and I continued to believe I had made the right choice. After everything I had lived through, I no longer wanted to belong to the world of humans. Not because I hated them. Well, at least, not after a certain amount of time had passed. It had not been easy, but I had set my bitterness aside. I was more useful this way. Once my initial anger had waned, I cast away my anger at the mercenaries. They lived in a hostile world and that was how they survived. Of course, they had chosen the wrong way, the way in which everyone loses, but it was their choice. One day, we might be able to convince them to live otherwise. Even though I had missed my parents for a long time, I no longer hated the humans on the mother ship who had abandoned us after encouraging us to settle here. Their solution was to give the group priority over the individual. Everyone won; no one got anything out of it.

However, I had decided not to be that kind of human any longer, because I was tired of a system in which the weakest is subjugated by the stronger, where those who are more numerous overwhelm those who are isolated. The humans in the colony had been defeated because they thought they were invincible, and yet the darztl attack had revealed just how weak they were. The mercenaries, on the other hand, weren't afraid of anything, but that was to the detriment of the weakest, the isolated darztls they came across and the humans in their community. They weren't safe from the darztls, either. I'd seen what darztls could do to a careless band of humans. And the darztls kept the humans enslaved because it was so easy to do.... I'd had enough of that battle for power. So my solution had been to take on the form of the strong and help the weaker. It wasn't the most courageous solution. With one swing of my paw, I could gut even the strongest human. And among darztls, I was invisible, which protected me. But it was the most effective means for me to help our little community, to help it grow and increase its influence.

Of course, I was a walking paradox. I lived in the body of a darztl from which the humans before me had removed the brain to learn how it worked. I was a living human in the body of a dead darztl, rescuing humans whom the darztls had tried to kill symbolically. But that was in keeping with the world we — Selm, the villagers and I — were trying to build. A world patched together from what we found on site. Mixing old and new, human and darztl, true and false, free and not free. Just like in real life.

EPILOGUE

I've lived too long. A life that wasn't my own, moreover. In a borrowed body that has become too old, that will never stop existing. I've seen too many tragedies. I've seen too many people tear themselves apart, too many alliances woven and then unraveled. I've seen too many horrors to ever hope to die in peace.

I, who am most appropriately called Selm, have lived two lives. Selm, the second of that name, divided, torn in two — I've always stayed on. First, there was my initial life, in the body of a little girl who had never overcome her birth in a fake new world, who had no existence apart from that which served to draw out her childhood dreams. Then a second life, larger than life, too large for me, a life that both filled me and submerged me, one that I never fully came to terms with because life is too long and vision too short....

I'm not a good person. I've only ever acted out of self-interest. I've always done everything possible to satisfy my fantasies. Fantasies of space, dreams of power, the illusion of being first one person, then someone else. I wanted to live first. Then I didn't want to live alone, and I dragged others behind me. They call me the founder, but I'd like to know what foundations I've laid. The mountain was there. We settled on it. The community came to us and we didn't close our doors to it. But that's all. Nothing terribly heroic, no reason to erect statues. In any case, any statues built here would soon be eroded by the wind. In a single generation they're whittled back down to stone. And that's fine with me.

I'm very old. I've seen legends burst into life and then die out. According to the most recent fables, an island of volcanic rock and salt is emerging from the middle of the ocean. Certain darztls, with better sea legs than others, have apparently landed there and discovered a luxurious land surrounding a castle of tortured metal. It's said that water flows in rivers on that island and that the plants are as tall as three darztls. I hope that's not true, I pray it's not true, or that some tide will quickly wash over the frail atoll. I may be old, but I have no wish to repeat history. I prefer to believe that our kind abandoned us, that they finally reached their destination five light years from here and that we are nothing but a rumor to them. As they will soon be a myth for us.

I've lived one hundred years, one hundred years too long, one hundred years too little. I've seen this planet take shape, fall apart, take shape again. I have witnessed its performance as a foreigner, looking for foreign solutions. I wanted to act, to change something, but I couldn't extricate myself from the contradiction, the double-edged sword where living means killing. I should have killed myself a long, long time ago, along with the little guinea pigs we had exterminated, before the premature death of the other subjects our experiment sent to the slaughterhouse. But the instinct to survive is strong, isn't it? And the little surviving darztl is now a grandfather.

I'm tired. I don't think I'll live many more years, many more revolutions. On this planet of sand and rock a year is a revolution. This body still holds mysteries for me, and I don't know how long it can continue to live and fight. I do know that if the little bit of conscience that resides in this body dies out, I could go along with the flow. So I practice death under the village where my remains do not lie. Unless the darztl sleeping in my body decides to wake up and take back what belongs to it...

TIMELINE

Mars Year 0000: Humans shipwrecked on Mars II. Birth of the first humans on marsian soil.

Mars Year 0023: Terraforming process starts.

Mars Year 0031: Hostilities between humans and darztls start.

Mars Year 0032: Alpha project launched.

Mars Year 0037: Alpha project interrupted. Beta project launched.

Mars Year 0039: Beta project fails.

Mars Year 0040: Gamma project launched.

Mars Year 0043: Founding of the experimental hybrid colony or "Village".

Mars Year 0048: Construction of a cybernetic-genetic laboratory within the experimental colony.

Mars Year 0055: Darztls attack the human colony; humans defeated.

Mars Year 0098: Darztl mariners note an island with unknown vegetation in the ocean.

Mars Year 0100: Disappearance of Chloé-Selm, village founder.

Our titles are available at major book stores
and local independent resellers who support
Science Fiction and Fantasy readers like you.

EDGE Science Fiction
and Fantasy Publishing

Tesseract Books

Dragon Moon Press

www.edgewebsite.com

Our titles are available at major book stores and local independent resellers who support Science Fiction and Fantasy readers like you.

Alien Deception by Tony Ruggiero -(tp) - ISBN: 978-1-896944-34-0
Alien Revelation by Tony Ruggiero (tp) - ISBN: 978-1-896944-34-8
Alphanauts by J. Brian Clarke (tp) - ISBN: 978-1-894063-14-2
Apparition Trail, The by Lisa Smedman (tp) - ISBN: 978-1-894063-22-7
As Fate Decrees by Denysé Bridger (tp) - ISBN: 978-1-894063-41-8

Black Chalice, The by Marie Jakober (hb) - ISBN: 978-1-894063-00-7
Blue Apes by Phyllis Gotlieb (pb) - ISBN: 978-1-895836-13-4
Blue Apes by Phyllis Gotlieb (hb) - ISBN: 978-1-895836-14-1

Case of the Pitcher's Pendant, The: A Billybub Baddings Mystery
    by Tee Morris (tp) - ISBN: 978-1-896944-77-7
Case of the Singing Sword, The: A Billybub Baddings Mystery
    by Tee Morris (tp) - ISBN: 978-1-896944-18-0
Chalice of Life, The by Anne Webb (tp) - ISBN: 978-1-896944-33-3
Chasing The Bard by Philippa Ballantine (tp) - ISBN: 978-1-896944-08-1
Children of Atwar, The by Heather Spears (pb) - ISBN: 978-0-88878-335-6
Cinkarion - The Heart of Fire (Part Two of The Chronicles of the Karionin)
    by J. A. Cullum - (tp) - ISBN: 978-1-894063-21-0
Clan of the Dung-Sniffers by Lee Danielle Hubbard (pb) - ISBN: 978-1-894063-05-0
Claus Effect, The by David Nickle & Karl Schroeder (pb) - ISBN: 978-1-895836-34-9
Claus Effect, The by David Nickle & Karl Schroeder (hb) - ISBN: 978-1-895836-35-6
Complete Guide to Writing Fantasy, The - Volume 1: Alchemy with Words
    - edited by Darin Park and Tom Dullemond (tp)
    - ISBN: 978-1-896944-09-8
Complete Guide to Writing Fantasy, The - Volume 2: Opus Magus
    - edited by Tee Morris and Valerie Griswold-Ford (tp)
    - ISBN: 978-1-896944-15-9
Complete Guide to Writing Fantasy, The - Volume 3: The Author's Grimoire
    - edited by Valerie Griswold-Ford & Lai Zhao (tp)
    - ISBN: 978-1-896944-38-8
Complete Guide to Writing Science Fiction, The - Volume 1: First Contact
    - edited by Dave A. Law & Darin Park (tp)
    - ISBN: 978-1-896944-39-5
Courtesan Prince, The (Part One of the Okal Rel Saga) by Lynda Williams (tp)
    - ISBN: 978-1-894063-28-9

Dark Earth Dreams by Candas Dorsey & Roger Deegan (comes with a CD)
    - ISBN: 978-1-895836-05-9
Darkling Band, The by Jason Henderson (tp) - ISBN: 978-1-896944-36-4
Darkness of the God (Children of the Panther Part Two)
    by Amber Hayward (tp) - ISBN: 978-1-894063-44-9
Darwin's Paradox by Nina Munteanu (tp) - ISBN: 978-1-896944-68-5
Daughter of Dragons by Kathleen Nelson - (tp) - ISBN: 978-1-896944-00-5
Digital Magic by Philippa Ballantine (tp) - ISBN: 978-1-896944-88-3
Distant Signals by Andrew Weiner (tp) - ISBN: 978-0-88878-284-7

Dominion by J. Y. T. Kennedy (tp) - ISBN: 978-1-896944-28-9
Dragon Reborn, The by Kathleen H. Nelson - (tp) - ISBN: 978-1-896944-05-0
Dragon's Fire, Wizard's Flame by Michael R. Mennenga (tp)
   - ISBN: 978-1-896944-13-5
Dreams of an Unseen Planet by Teresa Plowright (tp) - ISBN: 978-0-88878-282-3
Dreams of the Sea (Part 1 of Tyranaël) by Élisabeth Vonarburg (tp)
   - ISBN: 978-1-895836-96-7
Dreams of the Sea (Part 1 of Tyranaël) by Élisabeth Vonarburg (hb)
   - ISBN: 978-1-895836-98-1

Eclipse by K. A. Bedford (tp) - ISBN: 978-1-894063-30-2
Edgewise by Stephen L. Antczak (tp) - ISBN: 978-1-894063-27-2
Elements of Fantasy: Magic edited by Dave A. Law
   & Valerie Griswold-Ford (tp) - ISBN: 978-1-8964063-96-8
Even The Stones by Marie Jakober (tp) - ISBN: 978-1-894063-18-0

Far Arena (Part Five of the Okal Rel Saga) by Lynda Williams (tp)
   - ISBN: 978-1-894063-45-6
Fires of the Kindred by Robin Skelton (tp) - ISBN: 978-0-88878-271-7
Firestorm of Dragons edited by Michele Acker & Kirk Dougal (tp)
   - ISBN: 978-1-896944-80-7
Forbidden Cargo by Rebecca Rowe (tp) - ISBN: 978-1-894063-16-6

Game of Perfection, A (Part 2 of Tyranaël) by Élisabeth Vonarburg (tp)
   - ISBN: 978-1-894063-32-6
Gaslight Grimoire: Fantastic Tales of Sherlock Holmes
   edited by Jeff Campbell & Charles Prepolec (pb)
   - ISBN: 978-1-8964063-17-3
Green Music by Ursula Pflug (tp) - ISBN: 978-1-895836-75-2
Green Music by Ursula Pflug (hb) - ISBN: 978-1-895836-77-6
Gryphon Highlord, The by Connie Ward (tp) - ISBN: 978-1-896944-38-8

Healer, The (Children of the Panther Part One) by Amber Hayward (tp)
   - ISBN: 978-1-895836-89-9
Healer, The (Children of the Panther Part One) by Amber Hayward (hb)
   - ISBN: 978-1-895836-91-2
Hell Can Wait by Theodore Judson (tp) - ISBN: 978-1-978-1-894063-23-4
Hounds of Ash and other tales of Fool Wolf, The by Greg Keyes (pb)
   - ISBN: 978-1-894063-09-8
Human Thing, The by Kathleen H. Nelson - (hb) - ISBN: 978-1-896944-03-6
Hydrogen Steel by K. A. Bedford (tp) - ISBN: 978-1-894063-20-3

i-ROBOT Poetry by Jason Christie (tp) - ISBN: 978-1-894063-24-1

Jackal Bird by Michael Barley (pb) - ISBN: 978-1-895836-07-3
Jackal Bird by Michael Barley (hb) - ISBN: 978-1-895836-11-0
JEMMA7729 by Phoebe Wray (tp) - ISBN: 978-1-894063-40-1

Keaen by Till Noever (tp) - ISBN: 978-1-894063-08-1
Keeper's Child by Leslie Davis (tp) - ISBN: 978-1-894063-01-2

Lachlei by M. H. Bonham (tp) - ISBN: 978-1-896944-69-2

Land/Space edited by Candas Jane Dorsey and Judy McCrosky (tp)
- ISBN: 978-1-895836-90-5
Land/Space edited by Candas Jane Dorsey and Judy McCrosky (hb)
- ISBN: 978-1-895836-92-9
Legacy of Morevi by Tee Morris (tp) - ISBN: 978-1-896944-29-6
Legends of the Serai by J.C. Hall - (tp) - ISBN: 978-1-896944-04-3
Longevity Thesis by Jennifer Rahn (tp) - ISBN: 978-1-896944-37-1
Lyskarion: The Song of the Wind (Part One of The Chronicles of the Karionin)
by J.A. Cullum (tp) - ISBN: 978-1-894063-02-9

Machine Sex and other stories by Candas Jane Dorsey (tp)
- ISBN: 978-0-88878-278-6
Maërlande Chronicles, The by Élisabeth Vonarburg (pb)
- ISBN: 978-0-88878-294-6
Madman's Dance by Jana G.Oliver (pb) - ISBN: 978-1-896944-84-5
Magister's Mask, The by Deby Fredericks (tp) - ISBN: 978-1-896944-16-6
Moonfall by Heather Spears (pb) - ISBN: 978-0-88878-306-6
Morevi: The Chronicles of Rafe and Askana by Lisa Lee & Tee Morris
- (tp) - ISBN: 978-1-896944-07-4

Not Your Father's Horseman by Valorie Griswold-Ford (tp)
- ISBN: 978-1-896944-27-2

Of Wind and Sand by Sylvie Bérard (translated by Sheryl Curtis) (pb)
- ISBN: 978-1-894063-19-7
On Spec: The First Five Years edited by On Spec (pb)
- ISBN: 978-1-895836-08-0
On Spec: The First Five Years edited by On Spec (hb)
- ISBN: 978-1-895836-12-7
Operation: Immortal Servitude by Tony Ruggerio (tp)
- ISBN: 978-1-896944-56-2
Operation: Save the Innocent by Tony Ruggerio (tp)
- ISBN: 978-1-896944-60-9
Oracle Paradox, The by Stephen L. Antczak (tp) ISBN: 978-1-894063-43-2
Orbital Burn by K. A. Bedford (tp) - ISBN: 978-1-894063-10-4
Orbital Burn by K. A. Bedford (hb) - ISBN: 978-1-894063-12-8

Pallahaxi Tide by Michael Coney (pb) - ISBN: 978-0-88878-293-9
Passion Play by Sean Stewart (pb) - ISBN: 978-0-88878-314-1
Petrified World (Determine Your Destiny #1) by Piotr Brynczka (pb)
- ISBN: 978-1-894063-11-1
Plague Saint by Rita Donovan, The (tp) - ISBN: 978-1-895836-28-8
Plague Saint by Rita Donovan, The (hb) - ISBN: 978-1-895836-29-5
Pretenders (Part Three of the Okal Rel Saga) by Lynda Williams (pb)
- ISBN: 978-1-894063-13-5

Reluctant Voyagers by Élisabeth Vonarburg (pb) - ISBN: 978-1-895836-09-7
Reluctant Voyagers by Élisabeth Vonarburg (hb) - ISBN: 978-1-895836-15-8
Resisting Adonis by Timothy J. Anderson (tp) - ISBN: 978-1-895836-84-4
Resisting Adonis by Timothy J. Anderson (hb) - ISBN: 978-1-895836-83-7
Righteous Anger (Part Two of the Okal Rel Saga) by Lynda Williams (tp)
- ISBN: 897-1-894063-38-8

Shadebinder's Oath by Jeanette Cottrell - (tp) - ISBN: 978-1-896944-31-9
Silent City, The by Élisabeth Vonarburg (tp) - ISBN: 978-1-894063-07-4
Slow Engines of Time, The by Élisabeth Vonarburg (tp)
   - ISBN: 978-1-895836-30-1
Slow Engines of Time, The by Élisabeth Vonarburg (hb)
   - ISBN: 978-1-895836-31-8
Small Magics by Erik Buchanan (tp) - ISBN: 978-1-896944-38-8
Sojourn by Jana Oliver - (pb) - ISBN: 978-1-896944-30-2
Sorcerers of War by Kristan Proudman (pb) - ISBN: 978-1-896944-64-7
Stealing Magic by Tanya Huff (tp) - ISBN: 978-1-894063-34-0
Strange Attractors by Tom Henighan (pb) - ISBN: 978-0-88878-312-7
Sword Masters by Selina Rosen (tp) - ISBN: 978-1-896944-65-4

Taming, The by Heather Spears (pb) - ISBN: 978-1-895836-23-3
Taming, The by Heather Spears (hb) - ISBN: 978-1-895836-24-0
Teacher's Guide to Dragon's Fire, Wizard's Flame by Unwin & Mennenga - (pb)
   - ISBN: 978-1-896944-19-7
Ten Monkeys, Ten Minutes by Peter Watts (tp) - ISBN: 978-1-895836-74-5
Ten Monkeys, Ten Minutes by Peter Watts (hb) - ISBN: 978-1-895836-76-9
Tesseracts 1 edited by Judith Merril (pb) - ISBN: 978-0-88878-279-3
Tesseracts 2 edited by Phyllis Gotlieb & Douglas Barbour (pb)
   - ISBN: 978-0-88878-270-0
Tesseracts 3 edited by Candas Jane Dorsey & Gerry Truscott (pb)
   - ISBN: 978-0-88878-290-8
Tesseracts 4 edited by Lorna Toolis & Michael Skeet (pb)
   - ISBN: 978-0-88878-322-6
Tesseracts 5 edited by Robert Runté & Yves Maynard (pb)
   - ISBN: 978-1-895836-25-7
Tesseracts 5 edited by Robert Runté & Yves Maynard (hb)
   - ISBN: 978-1-895836-26-4
Tesseracts 6 edited by Robert J. Sawyer & Carolyn Clink (pb)
   - ISBN: 978-1-895836-32-5
Tesseracts 6 edited by Robert J. Sawyer & Carolyn Clink (hb)
   - ISBN: 978-1-895836-33-2
Tesseracts 7 edited by Paula Johanson & Jean-Louis Trudel (tp)
   - ISBN: 978-1-895836-58-5
Tesseracts 7 edited by Paula Johanson & Jean-Louis Trudel (hb)
   - ISBN: 978-1-895836-59-2
Tesseracts 8 edited by John Clute & Candas Jane Dorsey (tp)
   - ISBN: 978-1-895836-61-5
Tesseracts 8 edited by John Clute & Candas Jane Dorsey (hb)
   - ISBN: 978-1-895836-62-2
Tesseracts Nine edited by Nalo Hopkinson and Geoff Ryman (tp)
   - ISBN: 978-1-894063-26-5
Tesseracts Ten: A Celebration of New Canadian Specuative Fiction
   edited by Robert Charles Wilson and Edo van Belkom (tp)
   - ISBN: 978-1-894063-36-4
Tesseracts Eleven: Amazing Canadian Speulative Fiction
   edited by Cory Doctorow and Holly Phillips (tp)
   - ISBN: 978-1-894063-03-6
Tesseracts Twelve: New Novellas of Canadian Fantastic Fiction
   edited by Claude Lalumière (pb)
   - ISBN: 978-1-894063-15-9